THE TALENTS
OF
TAVEGNOR

By

Byron Cooper

Copyright
January 2012
ISBN-13: 978 1460908761
ISBN-10: 1460908767

Dedicated with great pride and greater love to my children

I wish to thank my wife Debbi who, with great patience and gentle prodding, made this book come to life. Without her encouragement this story would not have been written.

I would be less than gracious if I do not acknowledge the editor, Patrick. He has proven most definitively that an author should never try to proof his own work. If there are any errors left, it is because I failed to correct his red ticks…

I dislike the necessity of slaying another human being…

But in this world, the necessity exists.

Errol, Weapon master, Aide to the King of Tavegnor

Of all creatures known, man is the silliest…

He thinks he is superior to all the others.

Keven, Beast Master, Aide to the King of Tavegnor

If 'magic' were dependent on the reading of spells written in cumbersome tomes…I would choose to be a cobbler.

Karlyle, Master Magician, Aide to the King of Tavegnor

Words lie, thoughts cannot…I can learn more about a person from their silence than from their lips...

Ceikay, Master Mentalistener, Aide to the King of Tavegnor

I have, all my life, been a master at mediocrity…

It is time to become a student of success.

Beorn, Royal Witness to the Realm of Tavegnor

Tavegnor

Northern Sea

Sheir Island

Tampton Island

Spar Fortress

Regon

Break

Barron

Adar

Tampton

Jakor Island

Rachdol

Wolven Forest

Borster Island

Brentsad

Heston

Stanns

Fretara

Temora

Bracsdol

Arlindol

Minoline

Minoline
Plains

Carradol

Mahndol

Tynia

Gailent

Stelton

Wheisdol

Halster

Talavor

Rogan Pass

Tangier Pass

Arrendol

Bier

Raval

Kint

Darion Forest

Banstron Pass

Rameda Pass

Yannisdol

Orth Pass

Allujiun Islands

Pesha

Ludgen

Main

Javin

Talon Fortress

Halenester

Hirst

Dannon

Braccos Sea

Dellester

Orth

Tula Sea

Tynus

Osloman

Bourne

Callas Island

Tallas Island

Doran Channel

Doran

Esturin

Phalen

Lava Island

Youster

|———| 50 leagues

Hook Island

Wilter

✹ Region Capitols

Faeler Ruins

Claw Island

Prologue

It is time to put memories of great actions and heroism to printed word, for soon I will not be able to summon them from my tired and aged head. I must regretfully face the reality that I am at the beginning of my end. This is a reality that I now accept and acknowledge. Memories have begun to abandon me. The moments have so far been few, but there is no comfort in that. The process has begun, and my memories will lessen as my age increases.

My attempts to recall some past events are as lunging after wisps of smoke that dissolve away from desperately grasping fingers…

…I am a poor poet…I should just tell my story…

My name is Beorn. My latest profession has been, and still is; "Royal Witness to the King." I do not know how much further service I will be to the realm. The telling of this story is an admission that my usefulness will soon be at an end. I would not be putting this tale to parchment if I felt there was time to wait.

My good King and friends are not yet aware of my recent failings of memory. I assume no one is.

If you are familiar with the Realm of Tavegnor you will know what a "Royal Witness" is. If you come from distant lands, then it will become clear as you read further. The telling of this tale will reveal the reason why I am a Royal Witness. Also, as you read, be assured that what I write is accurate and not yet corrupted by the merciless hand of age. My distant memories are still intact. My talent has not yet suffered to the point that memories of long past have been taken away from me. Strangely, it is the most recently formed that I am losing.

Others have recorded events of the tale I will put to this paper. These scribes are for the most part accurate for what they know. My telling will merely add to the personal history of Tavegnor. I assure you there will be no contradiction to what is already commonly known and recorded in the official Parliamentary Archives.

This telling is about four young people who came into my life some decades ago. They are known as "Talents." I have been fortunate and honored to be a part of several of their adventures. What makes my tale different from the historical writings is the addition of my personal conversations and interactions with these four.

My tale begins on a special day...The night of the Mastiffs.

To most, the mastiff part of my story may seem a trifling event, but I remember it clearly because, rational or not, large dogs have always terrified me.

The story begins at the end of the ninety-fifth day of Second Summer in the year 2727 of our Agularion calendar.

...The day that changed my life

Boar's Hind Inn

I am a traveling Bard, or was, during an earlier part of my life. I earned my coins and keep by singing the telling of tales of heroes and their deeds. One night it so happened that I was paying for my bed at the Boar's Hind Inn when several men and their 'pets' came in for supper and drink. There were already seven other patrons in the big serving room and they had been politely enduring my narrations.

Accompanying the guards were dogs that looked like a cross between a wolf and a bear. I have since learned that they were a mastiff breed. These ten men and their beasts immediately took the best two long tables in the place. The tables had been conveniently vacated by their patrons when the mastiffs were allowed to sample their freshly served fare. Once seated, these newcomers took a dislike to my performance. Their mastiffs soon had me pressed into the corner near the stairs.

I will not report the particulars that put me up against the wall. For now, I write of the subjects of my story, Errol, Keven, Karlyle, and Ceikay. These four walked into the Inn that night and took the title of 'Bard' away from me.

1

As I stood pressed against the wall by the dogs, their masters howling and laughing at my discomfort, my eyes saw movement at the front door. The door of the Inn opened, and in walked a large man I soon would know as Karlyle.

Karlyle looked at no one, but his eyes swept around the big room as if absorbing the whole scene as a panorama. His left eyebrow arched high. He looked to be half a head taller than me, red head of hair, and had the look of a person who would not miss much in his examination. He wore a misty silver-green hooded cape that covered him from shoulder to boots. After several moments he stepped to the side as another of the same height came through the door.

Keven did not stop at the entrance as Karlyle had done, but walked into the room and calmly headed toward the three mastiffs. He did not glance at me, but rather looked at the dogs and nothing else. Now, to my great relief, the three monsters turned their attention from me and faced the stranger coming toward them. It was then that the merrymakers who had been having fun at my discomfort turned their attention to the newcomer. The room became quiet.

Keven stoped and looked down at the dogs. To everyone's wonder, the gigantic abeasts did nothing. Well, that is not entirely accurate; I mean to say they did nothing to Keven. What they did do is, after a moment, turn from him and silently return to their masters, who now sat quiet. The huge mastiffs laid down at the feet of the men at the end of their table.

Keven did not look at the guards. He calmly turned around and went to sit down at a table that Karlyle now occupied. He was dressed in an oak-brown traveling jacket with breaches not unlike the sort that Rangers wear in the Northern Forest of Wolven. On his feet were well-worn but well-kept boots from the Wheirsdol region.

Now, with the attention momentarily off of me, I decided to try for the stairs and up to my room for the night. As I made a discreet attempt to leave, one of the guards finally spoke up, or rather yelled to me, "Bard! Fetch water for our table!"

At that moment the front door opened again. In walked a big

man. I do not mean the tallest, or the widest man I've ever seen, but one of the most solid, most powerfully built individuals to ever cross a doorway. He was slightly taller than the other two, close to three hundred pounds as I estimate, and not an ounce of fat anywhere. His arms looked to be tree trunk size, and just as solid. His shoulders looked to be twice the width of mine.

This was Errol. He walked casually to the table occupied by Keven and Karlyle. His step was easygoing and controlled. Then, as he passed the guards' table Errol paused and turned to look directly into the eyes of the man who had ordered me to fetch drink.

"Friend," he said, "I suggest that you obtain your drink from the innkeeper. The Bard will not be able to honor your request. Beorn will be joining us at our table."

As he passed the guards' table, Errol reached down and patted the head of one of the mastiffs. He then turned and walked to the table where Karlyle and Keven were seated. No one moved. Not the guards, not the mastiffs, nor the innkeeper standing at the kitchen door.

While everyone else was trying to figure out why the mastiff had not bitten off the big man's hand, my mind focused on what had been said; I had been told to join the three newcomers. I had never set my eyes on these three before, but this stranger had just spoken my name, and announced that I would join them.

As I stood there, assuredly looking more confused than normal, Errol turned to me, "Well, Beorn, join us. You have not supped yet and neither have we, so please, do not keep us waiting."

It sounded like an order, but certainly no threat was in his voice. After only a moment's hesitation, I went over to their table. Before I had a chance to ask them how they knew me, and how they knew I had not eaten yet, the front door once again burst open and in walked the fourth, and as it turned out, the final member of this party, Ceikay.

Ceikay was a pretty young lady that I can now best describe as a volcano with a heart of gold. She could be your best ally and comforter, but when her temper exploded, even the gods ran for cover. Of course I saw none of her gentle side at first, just her

3

temper. She was about half a head shorter than me, brown hair and dark eyes, with lips set in a frown.

This young lady stepped through the threshold, strode straight up to Karlyle and launched a devastating kick to his shin that made his whole body jump a foot off the bench. The look on Karlyle's face told all…shock and absolute pain!

"OW!!...WHA…?"

"That is for leaving me to tend the horses," Ceikay calmly declared as she sat down next to Keven.

I saw that Keven was bent over the table trying unsuccessfully to hide his amusement. His shoulders shook with silent laughter. Errol had a large grin on his face but kept still and quiet. The gleam in his eye told me that he was not surprised at the attack.

"You did not have to break my leg," whined Karlyle as he vigorously rubbed the abused and, I assumed, rapidly bruising shin.

Errol chuckled, "Well, you should have known it was coming. You did promise her that you would stable the horses tonight."

"When did I promise that?"

"Last fortnight, when you were caught up gaming with your wizard partners. You asked Ciekay to take your turn feeding and bedding the animals. You promised her that you would handle the chore when we next stopped at an inn. Do you not remember?"

"Yes Errol, I remember now, but she should have reminded me outside!"

"Ah, but it would not have been as much fun for the rest of us!" Keven chimed in.

Whilst all of this was going on, I noticed that everyone else in the room was discreetly trying to concentrate on their own meals and tankards of ale. The massive dogs, on the other hand, appeared to be asleep on the floor and not at all concerned with Karlyle's short outburst.

Errol then turned to me. "If I may begin, Bard, you were invited to sit with us for serious purpose. I wish to ask of you…"

It was then that the innkeeper came over to our table, nervously twisting a cleaning rag in his hands. "A very hearty and sincere welcome to my establishment gentlemen and fine lady. How can I be of service to you? Would you care to sample my ale of unsurpassed taste and quality? Or try my boar stew? Can I interest you in my fresh baked round bread? If a meal is not what you desire, then how about my sheep's kidney pudding dessert served with aged port from the famous Safrigilly winery. Maybe you would be interested in…"

The innkeeper stopped mid-sentence when his eyes finally met Errol's. Whatever humor that was in Errol's eyes moments ago had disappeared.

Errol spoke curtly, "Thank you, Master Flind. We would sample a pitcher of your finest water, and please go to the trouble of fetching it fresh from the well and not from your barrels in the kitchen. We would also sample a loaf of your fresh baked round bread, not from your pantry, but fresh from your oven. You know the ones I speak of; the loaves that are still too warm for your wife's delicate hands, the loaves that are now cooling at the kitchen window."

Errol turned from the innkeeper but spoke once more to him, "Thank you, and we would appreciate your renowned speed when serving our table."

Confused and obviously intimidated, Flind nodded and quickly turned and rushed away to honor Errol's request.

I was startled back to attention as Keven now addressed me. "Good and glad meeting, Beorn. My name is Keven. Sitting to my right is Errol, that is Karlyle next to you, and now sitting next to Karlyle is the notorious shin-destroyer Ceikay the infamous mistress of mayhem."

After the polite nods, Errol spoke to me again. "Beorn, we would care to discuss your immediate future. Do you have a bit of your time to give us tonight?"

All four were looking at me intently. Because of the dogs I had wanted to leave this room, but now felt compelled to remain. After all, these four did save me from being taken apart and shared by the beasts. Also, good food had been ordered.

"Well, good sir," I answered, "you gave me deliverance from the dogs. I surely can give you my time."

Errol began immediately, "Good, sit please. We understand, Beorn, that you are a Bard with talent. Is that correct?"

I sat quickly and answered, "I suppose that is my profession at the moment. As for the talent, my singing is better judged by others rather than myself. May I ask how you know of me?"

Errol's eyes held mine as he spoke. "We are not here for your singing or tale-telling. We are interested in your real talent."

Not sure in what direction Errol was heading, I kept silent.

Seeing that I was not going to respond, Keven offered, "It has been told to us that you are gifted with outstanding recall for words and events."

After several moments' pause, I replied that I did indeed know some memorization tricks, "...tricks that anyone could learn if they took the time and effort."

"You see," I continued, "it helps me with my song writing and, as you say, tale-telling. That is what makes me a somewhat better Bard than others."

Karlyle answered with a grin, "So Bard, you do judge yourself then..."

Before I could answer, Keven spoke next. "No, Beorn, your memory is more than memorization tricks. Certain persons we have spoken with say you remember everything you see and everything you hear. It is effortless for you. Is that not the correct description of your talent?"

I looked at him and also shook my head. "Effortless is an incorrect word to use. May I ask who you have been speaking to concerning my skill at memory?"

Before I received an answer, the innkeeper rushed from the kitchen and came to our table with two large pitchers of cold, clear water and five clean-looking mugs. Close behind him was a rather small, delicate lady carrying a large tray loaded with steaming round bread, fresh-churned butter, and several flavors of fruit preserves, knives, and clean looking linen napkins.

"Sirs, and Lady, this is my sweet wife Clara; if there would be anything else you would be wanting, do not hesitate to call out. I pray you enjoy my humble offerings."

The innkeeper then nervously turned and ushered his wife back

6

into the kitchen.

After the water and bread were passed around, we started eating, all except Errol. He seemed to be studying me and finally spoke up, "Beorn, I would put you to a test of memory, please do not refuse. I would like you to agree to it."

Once again, his request was an order. Also, my ego was being pricked and I felt that I could, or should, show my skills if they so wanted a demonstration. I nodded my head in acceptance.

"Good, thank you. Now without turning your head, please describe to us the table behind you, just to the left of the fireplace; how many are sitting there and what are they wearing?"

My eyes met Errol's and I immediately responded, "There is no one at that table."

Errol looked past me for a moment, then looked back and calmly said, "You are incorrect. Are you deliberately giving me an incorrect answer or are you not as talented as we were led to believe?"

"He surely is not deceiving you, Errol." Ceikay looked right at me when she spoke to Errol. "He tells what he believes to be the truth. There is no deception in his thoughts."

Errol replied, "Then he is not what we want. He does not have the ability we are looking for. We may be wasting our time here."

I now closed my eyes and spoke again, "If you would put me to a test, then you should be more specific in your instructions. Your words were, '…Now, without turning around, please describe to us the table behind you, just to the left of the fireplace; how many are sitting there and what are they wearing…'"

As a bard I paused for dramatic effect. I opened my eyes, and then looked in turn to each of them.

I took a deep breath and continued. "The table just to the left of the fireplace is a serving table that is butted up against the hearth, and no one is sitting there. It is a round table two feet in diameter, used, I assume, for the placement of serving trays and soiled dishes during cleanup. No one is sitting there, so I was correct in my answer. Now, the next table to the left of the fireplace is the first table intended for patrons. It is approximately two spans long by four feet wide. This table is really two tables pushed together. There are ten men sitting at this table. They have the dark blue uniforms of the Duke Whorton's Guard. Four of them have full beards, two have mustaches and the rest are clean-shaven. The last time I looked, two of the bearded men had their post hats on. The two with mustaches were bareheaded, as were three of the clean shaven ones. The one shaven one with a hat looks to be about a hard forty years of age, has a scar that runs from his left ear to the corner of his mouth. He is also the leader according to his uniform insignia. He is a Company Leader with over twenty years in service according to his sleeve hashes. He is sitting at the far end of the table from us. To his left sits one of the bearded with no hat. He has the same number of years in the Duke's service as his comrade, but not the rank. By the tear on his uniform it looks as though a badge of Company Leader has been torn off recently. You can see the shape of the badge because the color in that area has not yet faded. The index finger is missing from his right hand. To the left of this man is a guard who is a castle gatekeeper. He still has the key fob attached to his belt that a man in his position carries. Naturally, the keys have been passed on to the current guard on duty at the Duke's castle. He is also bearded, and he has a two inch scar over his right eye. There is a..."

Karlyle cut in with a grin, "What did the man on the opposite end of the table from the leader do when Errol entered the Inn and patted one of the mastiffs?"

Without hesitation I answered, "He was sitting sideways at the table and started to reach for his dagger but stopped for the better of it. Of course weapons are not allowed in the Duke's realm by anyone except the Duke's men on duty. So tonight, being off duty, he had no weapon to draw..."

"Very well and done!" Keven grinned, holding up his hand to stop me.

The four said nothing but just looked at each other for several moments, then all turned to me.

Errol spoke, "We have a proposal for you."

I sat silent, waiting for one of them to speak

Karlyle leaned forward, "We would like you to consider..."

"Hold," Ceikay interrupted, nodding to a man crossing the room. "Keven, I do not think it would be wise for that man to leave the Inn right at this moment."

In an instant, one of the mastiffs was up and pouncing to the front door of the Inn. A rather ragged-looking traveler stopped in his tracks as the huge dog bared his teeth at him. The man froze reaching for the latch as the dog breathed menacingly on his hand. The guards at the table, startled by the sudden action of one of their dogs, were on their feet reaching for weapons that were not there. The other patrons of the Inn sat very still, also not knowing what was going on.

The guard leader, 'Scar Face' I'll call him, yelled out, "Hey Brucko, git yer scratchy arse back 'ere!"

The dog, not responding, kept the poor, shaken traveler at bay.

"Jake!" Scar Face bellowed, "Fetch Brucko back 'ere!"

As one of the guards stood up to obey, the other two massive dogs now jumped up to bar him from leaving the table. Their teeth bared, growls coming from deep within their bellies' low, and menacing. Except for the growling, there was absolute quiet in the room.

Only the innkeeper moaned, "Oh by the gods, 'tis bad witchcraft doin's in 'ere this night..." He then fled into the kitchen.

I heard Karlyle whisper to himself, "No witchcraft, no magic, not as yet anyway."

Keven now addressed the hapless patron. "Friend, it looks as though you are not meant to leave this inn right at this moment. May I offer a suggestion to you?"

The victim did not appear to hear Keven.

"I say again friend, may I offer a suggestion to you?"

Finally, the traveler slowly turned his head and nodded.

"Good," Keven continued in a soft, soothing voice, "Now, you might want to slowly back away from the door, turn around and come over and join us at our table...not too fast...no telling what those mischievous pups are up to tonight."

The traveler did as suggested, backing away from the door. The mastiff did not move. Then, as the traveler turned not to us, but toward the kitchen door, three fresh growls were heard that changed his mind. He quickly came over and sat down next to Errol.

As he settled into our table, the three monster dogs resumed their lazy vigil under their masters' table. This time the guards only stared at our group. They were clearly confused and baffled by what had occurred.

Finally, Scar Face gathered his courage and addressed our table, "Where ya all from, and what is yer bizness 'ere in the Duke's realm?" Are ya passin' through ur do ya hav biznes?"

Errol slowly turned toward the guard. "Are you addressing us sir?"

Scar Face looked around at his comrades as if to garner strength from them. "By the authority of Duke Whorton, I demand yer names an' purpose in 'is lands!"

Looking squarely at Scar Face, Errol replied, "Our names I will surely share with you, Errol, Ceikay, Karlyle, and Keven. Our purpose I will not share with you, as it is none of your concern."

"I will know now, or ya will know Duke Whorton's dungeon!" Scar face was now trying to save face by facing down Errol. He figured the numbers were in his favor…he did not seem to remember that the dogs were not quite on his side this night.

Errol responded by turning around and showing his back to the soldiers.

"Ya insult me with yer back, stranger?!"

It was Ceikay who answered, "Surely a man of your intelligence would know an insult if one were thrown at you, do you not agree sir?"

Scar Face turned to Ceikay with a puzzled look, obviously trying to figure out her meaning. Then he lifted an index finger into the air, his mouth opened…then shut…

Karlyle then yawned, "I feel it is time for more privacy."

At that moment, the sharp blast of an outpost horn blared across the pass!

"ALARM…ALARM!" Cried one of the guards.

"To the post, men!" Scar Face shouted as his men, as well as the dogs, jumped up from the table. They rushed to the door and out of the hostel. The strange thing to my eyes was the open door that no one had been close to a moment before. How was it that the entrance to the Inn was clear and open for the guards to run out so? I looked around at the others at my table. Their faces told me nothing.

The rest of the patrons now also decided it was time to hurriedly vacate the hostel. As our traveler rose to leave with the others, Errol placed a big hand on his shoulder to persuade him to stay in our company. The traveler slowly sat back down and was looking rather uncomfortable at that moment.

"Please, I do not know what you want of me, but I am just a poor traveler on my way to market to beg for a job. If you want money, I have only a few copper coins that I will gladly give you if you would let me be on my way."

"No, your words are not quite true," Ceikay said coolly. "You have deceit in you. To what purpose I cannot determine, but I know you are not what you say you are. You must not be allowed to venture any further tonight."

Errol then spoke. "Time is short. Those guards may come back when they discover the alarm was false. I am tired of their company; we do not want to be here if they do return. It would become tedious to have to deal with them again. Ceikay, will we get any information from this good man?"

"Not unless we really harm him. He is well-trained and will not succumb easily."

"Well-trained or no," Keven added, "he probably is trying to pass on information of our where-bouts to whomever he works for. I say he simply disappears…"

With that, the stranger turned very pale, but tightened his lower lip. It was not fear now, but defiance in his face…no…then it was fear again. I could clearly see that this man alternated between intimidation and resignation.

Errol turned to Karlyle. "Would you take care of this one this time?"

"I already have something good in mind." Karlyle muttered something, closed his eyes, started to moan, raised his hands and started to chant some strangely worded incantation directed at the stranger.

I looked back at the man…and he had frozen in fear.

"You gonna kill him slow?" Keven drawled.

Karlyle continued to chant.

Ceikay cringed: "That is his liquid fire chant! His worst! I have to turn my eyes away."

"Stop! Mercy of the gods! I am only a page for the Duke! My orders are to report to my lord any strangers that come through the pass! That is all I was leaving to do! Please don' set me afire!"

Then I saw the gleam in Errol's eyes and a hint of a grin on Keven's face. Ceikay turned her head to hide a smile.

"Hold, Karlyle." Errol turned to address the frightened informant, "Karlyle does not like to be interrupted when he is drawing forth an incantation. I suggest that you tell us the whole truth, or I will not be able to ask him to stop again once he restarts his chant."

"I tell the truth! Duke Whorton commanded me to stay around the Inn and tell of any strangers who pass through! Unusual travelers have been reported recently. I swear by all my ancestors' graves!"

"Ceikay?" Errol asked, not taking his eyes off the stranger.

"There is no lie in his words. He is being open and truthful with us now," she answered.

Errol spoke once more, "What sorts of travelers have Duke Whorton concerned?"

The man shook his head. "I do not know. I only act on his orders."

Errol looked at Ceikay. Her nod confirmed the man's answer.

Errol continued, "Thank you for being so candid with us. I suggest that you do as your Duke has commanded. We have nothing to hide from him, and he has nothing to fear from us. Tell him that we are only traveling east and then north to the city of Brentsad. We will be out of Whorton Realm very soon."

Keven then spoke, "Please give the Duke our best regards when you see him. You may go."

The messenger looked to Errol for confirmation. Errol only nodded. The shaken man quickly left us and the inn.

"Beorn," I looked at Errol as he addressed me, "time is

short. We would like you to go on a journey with us."

"What do you want of me?" I asked.

"We need your talent," Keven answered.

I looked around at all of them before I settled on Errol. "Then you are interested in my memory skills. What am I to chronicle, or is it something I already have in my head?"

"You are to observe, nothing more."

"What must I observe?"

"You are not to know that; otherwise, you might develop unwanted preconceptions."

"Where are we to be going then?"

"We cannot answer that as yet, for the same reason."

"Who will I report my observations to?"

"If your observations are ever to be revealed, they will be shared with the world. If not, no one will hear your report."

"Do I consider that a threat?" I asked guardedly.

"No, Beorn, it is not a threat. We would not have searched you out if we did not have absolute trust in your…discretion. You are highly recommended to us."

I grinned, "I am flattered. Am I to know who gave you my name?"

"We will not say, but you can probably guess, I am sure."

"It seems if I am guessing correctly, would my discretion be an asset to you then?"

Ciekay answered, "As mentioned before, if the rest of the world does not need to hear details, then we would like the details to be kept hidden."

I chose not to pursue the 'details' further, but in my self-interest I asked Errol about recompense if I agreed to help them.

"We can offer you nothing but food and shelter for this task. If it were known that you were compensated for what you saw, it might be argued that your impartiality had been compromised."

I sat there not really believing or understanding what I was hearing.

After a long pause I again spoke. "Let me reflect on this now. You are asking me to go along with four strangers as an observer, not knowing who you are, what your quest, or mission is, not knowing your personal histories, not knowing who you labor for, or even if you work for anyone at all, no payment for my time and sacrifices, whatever they may be..."

I shook my head at the prospect.

Finally I continued, "What do you think would induce me to say yes: my curiosity, my love of adventure, my desire to do good deeds? What if you mean to do bad deeds? I do not even know your motives. No, you have not shown me much, not enough to convince me to go blindly to who knows where, to do who knows what."

The 'Four' sat silently and let me ramble on.

Finally, Karlyle cocked his head and raised an eyebrow at me as if to ask, 'Are you quite finished?'

Keven leaned forward with a smile, "We did rescue you from the dogs."

I paused a moment, then spoke once more, "I have more questions. If I go with you, will I get any of them answered?"

Ceikay looked at me and grinned, "Some yes, some no."

The four waited in silence. Finally, I shrugged, "Yes, I will join the four of you. Why exactly, I do not know, but my trust and my fate are now in your hands."

Then I quickly added, "Could you at least give me an idea of any danger that might come our..."

Before I could get one more question out of my mouth, Errol was on his feet and tossing five copper Kopas onto the table, which paid for our supper three times over.

Darion Forest

The big man spoke as he turned toward the door. "Beorn, we do not know ourselves if danger will find us. All we can promise you is that we will protect you if danger appears. If you die on this journey, it only means that we have died before you. Karlyle, please gather the horses from the stables. Ceikay, the stable boy knows that we were leaving tonight?"

"Yes. I instructed him to feed and water them only, not to bed them down."

Karlyle suddenly turned to her with a frown and raised eyebrow, "The stable boy took care of our horses?"

Errol turned to Keven. "Keven, please go with Beorn and make sure he gets his possessions from his room, and see that he gets them quickly. I wish to be in Darion Forest before the moon travels much higher."

Karlyle reached over and tapped Ceikay's shoulder. "I got kicked…you did not tend the horses…the stable boy…and I got kicked?"

Errol looked at me "Please Beorn, we need speed from you."

I jumped up from the table and went for the steps. Errol could be quite polite while giving orders, but that did not lessen the

15

authority in his voice.

As I bounded up the stairs for my pack, I did not have a chance to hear the rest of Karlyle's conversation with Ceikay.

It did not take me long to gather my belongings; one leather shoulder bag and a bedroll was enough to carry all that I owned. Keven and I were outside and in front of the Inn before Karlyle came with the horses. Errol and Ceikay were in deep discussion when we came up to them.

"I see you travel light," Ceikay said, motioning to my bag. "Are you prepared to travel and sleep under the stars?"

"I am indeed. My needs are simple; you need not worry about my discomfort during travel."

She smiled and tapped my chest. "Ah, but we do, and we will, as long as you are with us."

Karlyle came up with five horses saddled and packed for travel. I had not given a thought to a horse of my own, but my new companions obviously had thought ahead. The reins of one of the horses were handed to me. He was a beautiful shiny black, well-muscled, and an obviously well-groomed animal that matched the other four almost identically. The main difference I could notice was that Errol's horse was a full hand taller than the rest. A good thing too, considering the load the animal was being asked to carry.

"You do know how to ride do you not?" Keven asked.

"Does that question mean that you may not know everything about me?" I challenged with a grin.

"Get on the horse," Errol growled at my attempt at humor. "If you cannot ride, we will tie you to the saddle."

Moments later my new companions were galloping east along Banstron Road with me following close behind.

Travel was not difficult since it was nearly a full moon night. Also, even though I had not ridden much before that night, it seemed that my horse adjusted for my comfort. He rode smooth and easy as we followed the others. I did not have to work at it at all. We quickly left the pass behind and approached the edge of Darion Forest.

The old Banstron Road is the main route that joins the traditional capitals of Talavor and Brentsad. We were heading east

16

toward Brentsad under bright moonlight so it was easy to follow the old road. We fell into a relaxed trot that allowed me to study my new companions further.

What startled me was the fact that they were all now well armed. When did they don weapons? They did not show any sign of arms at the Inn, and surely they could not have strapped everything on while riding on their horses. I would have seen all that.

I urged my horse up to Keven who was riding to the rear of the others. "When did you don the weapons?" I asked.

"Weapons are not allowed to be worn in Duke Whorton's realm."

"That was not my question."

Keven grinned and glanced my way, "We had them on all the while we were in the Inn. Karlyle just made sure that they were unseen. The effect is no longer necessary so Karlyle does not need to strain his energy any further in that regard."

I let my horse fall back a step and I continued to study each of the others. Keven had a short sword on either side of his waist. They each were about two feet long. Their sheaths looked to be made of a type of black leather that I was not familiar with. He also had strapped to his back a quiver of arrows and longbow of the type that huntsmen use, though this one was stouter than any that I had seen before. He also had tied to his saddle a formidable-looking crossbow. Karlyle had only one weapon showing, a sword known as a Katana. I had seen this type of sword once before, used with deadly precision by its owner. This type of famed weapon is said to have been made by a warrior class from an eastern continent that excelled in steel blades. It is said that no finer blade has ever been duplicated anywhere in Tavegnor. There are only a few known to exist in this realm, and this was only the second that I had seen.

Ceikay had a quiver of arrows and a short bow on her back. A short sword was on her left hip. She also had two daggers sticking out of her boots that could be seen as she rode. Errol had a weapon strapped to his back, a four-and-a-half-foot double-bladed broadsword that looked as though is could be used to chop down fully grown trees. The blade was three and a half feet long by itself. The hilt was another foot in length and simply decorated in rich, dark iron and leather. This was not a weapon that was built for show.

I thought of my little throwing daggers that I had stashed in my kit. I also had a stout stabbing dagger wrapped up in my bedroll. I was not sure what was expected of me, or what they expected to face when we got to where we were going. I only knew that if they were wearing weapons, I would also.

We rode on into the woods until the moon was fully overhead. After riding for several more leagues, Errol pulled up next to a well-hidden path to the left. I would not have seen it if he had not motioned to it. "This is our path to the cottage. Banator should be there waiting for us."

"He had better have fare ready, or I will introduce my boot to his shin." Ceikay muttered.

I noticed a slight grimace of remembrance on Karlyle's face.

Keven chuckled, "Now Ceikay is that any way to treat our good friend?"

"He promised to have a stew waiting for us next time we came by, that is all I am saying. You know how I feel about promises broken!"

Once again I looked at Karlyle.

He groaned and said, "Well let us get there, and may the gods help Banator if he did not keep his promise."

Errol led the way off the road, and after traveling about another league we came to an opening in the trees. In the middle of a circular clearing there stood a rustic-looking, but well-kept cottage. The roof was of thatch and the walls were of whitewashed clay bricks. Shining through the windows was the inviting yellow glow of a lit fireplace.

I was surprised. Most commoners' huts did not have full fireplaces with chimney chases. Generally, a fire pit was simply in the middle of the dirt floor, with the smoke escaping the room through an opening in the thatched roof.

The clearing around the house was neatly trimmed, possibly by goats, as was the custom with country folk.

We rode up to the cottage and Errol called out, "Hello the House!"

We waited and got no answer. Errol turned to Ceikay and asked in a low voice, "Where?"

Without pointing or turning around in her saddle she answered quietly. "Twenty paces to your left, hidden behind the pile of logs."

Without looking around Errol spoke again, "Karlyle, did you hear that?"

Karlyle nodded and closed his eyes.

After a moment of quiet I heard a shout of alarm. The large logs were rolling to one side, exposing a crouched figure with a look of shock on his face. He was well armed with two swords and had several daggers hanging on his belt, but was not brandishing them. He was not Keven and Karlyle's height but he looked to be just as muscular. He wore a forest green Ranger's outfit similar to Keven's. The man sported a short trimmed mustache.

He yelled out, "Hey! What if those logs went the other way?! They coulda'crushed me!"

Keven yelled back, "It is a good thing for us they did not. We would have been very inconvenienced if we had to bury you! Then again you would have deserved to be crushed for waiting in ambush!"

"Ya'll were so noisy coming through the woods that I figured ya needed a lesson taught to ya, so I figur'd I'd put a scare into ya!"

"Oh, but you forgot about me Banator!" Ceikay went on, "I would sense if there were others around. You know, other ambushers like you! By the way, is supper ready?"

"You eat like a bird, why do you inquire about supper lil' lady?" Banator asked, looking at Ceikay as he strode up to Errol.

Keven answered for her. "You said the promise word the last time we were together. You also know that the 'lil' lady' will hold you to it even if you had promised her you would bring a bottle of skunk oil."

Ceikay edged her horse closer to Keven. Keven wisely

maneuvered out of the way.

Errol dismounted from his horse. Banator strode toward him. With big grins they clasped arms in greeting.

Banator greeted each of the others in the same way. Ceikay was treated to a stifling big bear of a hug that lifted her off her feet.

"Where is your lady, Banator?" She asked.

"Hensha left me for a much uglier man."

"I know that to be an utter lie without even feeling your thoughts; for there is no uglier face in all of Tavegnor!"

Banator laughed heartily, then answered, "Welcome to my humble cottage. Hensha said you would be on your way to getting here. She regrets not being here to see all of you, but she has important errands for our king."

Banator smiled broadly and added to Ceikay, "And yes, supper is ready. But first, are ya stayin' fer' the night? If so, the barn has fresh water and clean hay for the horses."

A short time later the horses were comfortable in their stalls, each of us taking care of our own. We were soon all in the cottage enjoying a late supper.

Banator studied me a bit, glanced at Errol, then back to me, and spoke, "So Bard, I am told you are quite good at remembering things. Do you happen to remember how many weapons I had on my person by the logs?"

I answered promptly, "You had four daggers in the front of your belt and two on your back side, one in each of your boots, and one appeared to be hidden behind your neck under your shirt collar."

"Ah, but as you can see, I have only two daggers in the front of my belt, how do you explain that?"

"As we finished with the horses, you slipped two of the daggers from your belt and placed them into an empty water bucket hanging on the barn wall."

Banator laughed and slapped the table. "The reports are true. You do indeed have a talent, my friend!"

"Well, that was not so much memory on my part, but observation."

Errol grinned and chuckled, "He is right, my friend, you had

20

better think up a more demanding test for our companion."

Banator grinned and shook his head. "My new friend has convinced me; no more tests needed to win oer' this under-educated fool! So I will turn my attention to the feast before us, bein' it is about the best venison stew ever put together! An' do not ya'll insult me by leavin' any in the pot!"

Keven leaned into me and whispered with a grin, "Do not let his fake drawl and his disarming ways fool you. He is intolerably persistent and will try to test you again."

I grinned back, "Thank you for the warning."

As bowls were filled, emptied, and filled again, I listened to good-natured ribbing and banter around the table. No one was immune to cutting jabs or insults. But the banter was all in fun and no one went too far. It was obvious that these five genuinely cared for each other.

After supper was completed, Errol announced it was time to retire for the night. "Decisions are always made more wisely after a good night of sleep. We will talk of our plans in the morn."

"Who is Hensha?" I asked Karlyle as we began to get up from the table.

It was Banator who answered, "Another servant of the realm, my partner, my love."

It was clear that no other information was forthcoming as everyone turned to leave the table. I decided to follow Errol's suggestion and turn in for the night. There were two rooms for sleeping, Ceikay in one room, and the rest of us in the other. There were four cots in our room so I figured that I would be the one getting comfortable on the floor. As I turned out my bed roll Keven stopped me and announced that he would take the floor.

I resisted, saying that I was quite accustomed to sleeping on floors.

"You may be accustomed to it, but I prefer it," he countered.

"Thank you, but I am fine with…"

"Get into a bunk, Beorn," Errol cut in. "Keven never, ever sleeps in a bed. He prefers to keep his ear to the ground when he sleeps."

Keven looked at Errol, then at me. "He is exaggerating. I do know the soft side of a night's sleep. I just do not require it when we travel."

A short while later I was asleep in one of the upper bunks. I dreamt of giant dogs chewing on my backside.

I awoke to daylight, but not in my bunk. I was on my bed roll on the front landing outside of the cottage. I sat up confused and disoriented as to where I was. It took me several moments to absorb yesterday's events and assure myself it had not been a dream.

I turned at Ceikay's voice. "Good morning, sleepy Bard. We were wondering if we should throw a bucket of water over you."

"I usually get up at dawn, how past time is it?"

"Now is the time for breaking our fast," Keven answered as he approached from the barn. "Let us go in and discover what delights Banator has prepared."

I have to avow that Banator was indeed a superior cook. The smells coming from the hearth set my mouth to watering as soon as we entered the cottage. Errol and Karlyle were already sitting at the big table drinking charrol-bean tea.

Banator looked up from a steaming pot and waved the rest of us over to the table. "Get yur' selves a bowl before I give it all to these two!"

"Smells wonderful, whatever it is," I declared.

"It is my very own wild boar an' vegetable stew. Nothin' like it east of Talavor, or west for that matter! And donna' ask for particulars, the secrets I put in there will go to my grave!"

Ceikay spoke up as she sat down, "...and take us to our graves..."

Banator responded, "Jus fer that, lil' lady, you do not git ta kiss me when ya go!"

Ceikay rolled her eyes to the sky as if to thank the gods.

As we all dug into the delicious food, I asked anyone in general if they knew how I ended up outside on the front landing.

Without looking up from his bowl Banator answered calmly, "Ya snore."

I looked over at him, "I what?"

22

"You snore." He stated again.

"Now wait a mo…"

Ceikay suddenly held up her hand, "Someone approaches along the path. I sense haste, and it is a she…Hensha, and in earnest."

"She is here?! By the gods!" Declared Banator in alarm. "She was on her way to Brentsad. Why did she return so early? There must be trouble we are not aware of. Maybe she is hurt!"

I noticed that there was now no hint of a drawl or slang in Banator's speech.

"Settle yourself Banator, Ceikay said nothing of pain," Errol said quietly.

Banator did not seem to hear Errol's words. He rose from the table and rushed through the front door. The others looked at each other but said nothing. They looked absolutely calm, while I felt the start of a nervous tension. Why, I did not know. We waited inside as a horse came galloping from the woods and into the clearing. We could hear Banator and the newcomer converse in urgent tones. A moment later Banator returned, followed by a young woman who looked to be several years older than Ceikay. We all stood as they entered.

Without any preliminary greetings Banator spoke. "Hensha comes with dire news; Regional Ambassador Shelaylan has died in Brentsad. Her body was found outside the Duke's castle keep. It looks as though she fell to her death from the top of the keep. Accident or murder was not known at time of Hensha's riding."

"How can she accidentally fall from a keep?" Ceikay asked looking at Errol. "I question that, considering…"

Errol turned to Ceikay, "I agree. Events are getting more disturbing."

Karlyle turned to Hensha. "I am sorry you join us burdened with this information. You have ridden hard. Do you need to sit and break your fast?" He gestured to the table and the seat he stepped away from.

"Thank you for your concern and offer, Karlyle. Time is shorter than we desire. I must not rest here. I ride with speed to Talavor to inform King Ballistor."

Keven stood up and spoke as he went toward the door. "If you mean to ride to King Ballistor, ride from Banstron pass toward Raval. The King has left his palace in Talavor and is traveling to Hirst. He should be on the Telmar river road two days south of Raval. I will tend your horse while you eat."

I noticed Keven's subtle order had its effect. Hensha sat at the table.

"How do you know our Hing is there?" Hensha asked as she shook her head at the food.

Ceikay answered for Keven as he went out the door, "As we prepared to travel east on the King's order, he was preparing to depart south to attend the yearly trade meetings session with the Dukes of the Realm. Duke Rasher is to host the conference at his castle."

Errol walked up to Hensha and put his hand on her shoulder, "Hensha, it is important that you stay a bit longer. We all must consider the next steps that need to be taken, and it would be beneficial for you to eat something. Besides, Keven will tend your horse, and it will take a few moments for him to refresh the stallion for the ride ahead of you."

Hensha looked at him, paused, nodded, and reached for a bowl and bread.

Errol then turned to me. "Beorn, circumstances have changed. Your talents will no longer be needed. We thank you for your commitment to us, but we must part company now."

He then put a small pouch in front of me. "This is payment for your time and trouble. Maybe someday our journeys will allow us to meet with you again."

I looked down at the pouch but did not pick it up, "I know now that you are doing the bidding of our King Ballistor. Can you at least tell me why I was needed before this news?"

Errol did not speak for a moment, but looked at Ceikay and Karlyle. They looked at each other, then both turned back to Errol and nodded.

Errol answered, "Since our undertaking has changed, and your specific task is now impossible to complete, we can tell you: You were to hear Ambassador Shelaylan's account of an incident that she witnessed on Borster Island in Duke Hastid's Realm. What that incident was, we do not know. She sent a messenger to King Ballistor urgently requesting a Witness. We can only assume that she would not leave her post as Ambassador to Duke Hastid because she feared that suspicion would be aroused if she left unexpectedly. The message was disguised as routine information on trade issues, but encoded 'Highest Urgency.' Ambassador Shelaylan alluded to a major plot that, in her words, 'Direly threatened the kingdom's peace and that Duke Hastid may be involved.' More than that she did not divulge."

After a pause, he continued. "The King is concerned because Duke Hastid is the only Duke not attending the annual trade meeting. He has sent his regrets but not his reasons. It was important that Ambassador Shelaylan told what she knew. You were chosen to hear what she had to say and repeat it back to the Parliament verbatim, if that became necessary."

"Why did the Ambassador not get the complete coded message out by Royal Courier? And I still do not know why you needed me."

It was Keven who answered, "We do not know. Maybe she feared that her couriers were being watched, so she sent the short message via a personal servant."

Errol continued, "As for needing your services, you may know that the King's power is not absolute. He shares power with the other six Dukes of Tavegnor in what is called the Parliament. He rules by agreement of the majority. King Ballistor also holds the title of Duke of the Central Northern region, the Ballistor Realm. There are seven regions that make up the realm of Tavegnor, so there are seven Dukes that make up the Parliament. Each is lord of their own individual region. The King's responsibility is Tavegnor trade and security in regard to other kingdoms of the world. He also…"

"I know all that. I just thought…"

"Shush and listen!" Ceikay warned.

Errol continued, "Tavegnor is currently blessed with peace. But it is a fragile peace because of politics. Politics is the dirtiest habit man has ever practiced, and it rules our Parliament. The

Dukes do not trust the words of each other. Through much of our history, dishonest and self-serving leaders have cheapened the words spoken in our government. Now in our time, the Dukes demand absolute proof of honesty and accuracy of anyone who speaks in front of Parliament; including the King. So if there is currently a hidden threat to Tavegnor, then the King needs absolute proof before he can expect support and cooperation from the other six Dukes."

Errol paused for a moment so I prompted, "Go on."

Karlyle spoke up, "A written message, encoded or not, from Regional Ambassador Shelaylan would not be considered absolute proof to the Dukes. Written messages have been proven false before, so no written word is good enough, no matter how noble or truthful the messenger is. So, a system has been set up by Parliament to ascertain what is 'Truth' and what is 'False.' Each Duke has acquired a personal aide called a 'Truth Diviner.' These individuals have the talent to know when a person is telling the absolute truth. So when a person speaks…'Witnesses'… in front of Parliament, that person is judged by each of the seven Truth Diviners. If that person is lying, the Dukes are made aware of it immediately.

Because of your talent, you were to hear and remember everything that Ambassador Shelaylan reported to you. You were to be the King's 'Witness' in front of Parliament. You were to be the 'Written Message,' if you will."

"Why the secrecy? Why not tell me this at the Inn?"

Errol answered, "I believe we did explain why you were to know nothing. I will add this, though. It has been found that Witnesses make for more impartial reporting if they do not have prior knowledge or preconceived ideas of what they are to hear."

I still was not satisfied. "If this system is in place, the King must already have at his disposal a Witness that he has used before. Once again I ask, why me?"

For a moment no one spoke. Then Errol spoke as his eyes bored into mine. "The King's Royal Witness had a fatal fall from the castle keep in Talavor. Up until now, it was thought to be merely an unfortunate accident."

As I let that report sink into my understanding, Keven re-entered the cottage. "Your stallion is a beautiful animal Hensha, you take excellent care of him I see. He is ready for your ride through the pass and through to Raval. Do not try to go further than that tonight. He has heart to go to the ends of the earth for you, but his stamina does have limits."

Hensha took Keven's hand as she stood from the table. "Thank you, BeastMaster Keven. The gods have blessed your soul."

She then turned to Errol, "You mentioned plans to be discussed before I go…"

Errol nodded as he answered, "I was concerned with your stomach and horse. Both are ready for travel now. Your plan is still your own. Continue with what you set out to do from the beginning. Get to the King and alert him. Tell him we are continuing toward Brentsad to investigate Ambassador Shelaylan's death. Also tell him that…"

"You should also tell him that Beorn is still on his way to witness and record information for Parliament."

Everyone turned to me as I said those words.

Errol spoke in a quiet, but firm tone. "Beorn, we do not know what to expect from this moment on. When faced with the unknown, experience has proven it is wise to anticipate more, rather than less, danger. You are finished with our mission. We do not need your talents going forward. There is no point in you being put into possible danger."

I turned to face him. "I disagree. You chose me because the King's Witness died. I understand that now. I also have a notion of why you chose me over other 'Memory Talents.' I do not need to ask you who directed you to me. You said in the Inn that information was given to you that convinced you to seek me out. The only person close to the King who could possibly have known my potential is Duke Jaramas. I helped his family with a very sensitive problem. He is surely the one who gave my name to the King. You may not think that I usually follow Tavegnor's political intrigues, but I know that King Ballistor and Duke Jaramas are close allies in the Parliament. I do not know how much detail you know about my work with the Duke, but I can surmise that you

27

knew enough of my abilities to seek me out. You know that my integrity is unquestioned and that my discretion is absolute. Although I do not covet danger, you know that I did not run from it with Duke Jaramas."

I paused and looked at each one in turn. They waited silently for me to continue. "As I see the situation you now face, not much has changed because of Ambassador Shelaylan's death. There is still a crisis that needs to be uncovered and King Ballistor still needs a Witness to deliver that intelligence to Parliament. I say we will just have to find the murderer, or murderers. Then we can extract the information from the guilty...

"No, Beorn, our need for you is over." Errol said firmly, holding up his hand to me. "The King ordered that you were to listen to Ambassador Shelaylan and report her words to the other Dukes. With the death of the Ambassador, the King's mandate has ended. In any case, Parliament requires Witnesses to be impartial when they testify. You now know what was expected of you, therefore, it could, would, be claimed that your testimony was tainted from this point forward."

"On the contrary," I countered. "At this point, none of us knows why Ambassador Shelaylan and the Witness were murdered, as you seem to suspect. So, whatever I witness will be true, unclouded facts, and I will report them so."

"He has us there on reason, Errol." Keven grinned.

Errol was not convinced. "We now suspect with good cause that someone or something is willing to kill to cover up a dangerous plot. Two people close to the King have fallen to their deaths. One had information vital for Parliament to hear, and the other would have witnessed that information to Parliament. You are right, we do suspect foul deeds. Coincidences like this do not point to an accident; but rather to foul plans. Beorn, you were not sought out to unravel murders."

"Granted, but I may be useful in that regard also."

Errol looked at me and smiled. "If you mean by your 'Talent', I was not forgetting your past journeys and what you are capable of, but I am not prepared to make you a target. Anyone traveling with us further could possibly face grave danger."

"Hold there big man," Ceikay interrupted. "It is obvious we have started pursuing this mystery a couple of steps behind the unknown conspirators. For as little or as much as we know, Beorn might already be a target. If we discharge him from our protection now, he could be more vulnerable to an unfortunate fall or some other form of 'accident.'"

Ceikay then turned to Hensha. "When exactly did the Ambassador fall to her death?"

"Two days ago this past sunset. It happened before I was able to speak with her. I had just entered Brentsad when news of her death spread through town and to my ears. At the same time, word was being spread through the city that all of her personal staff was to be detained and confined to the Keep. Suspicion of loyalty was rising about the Ambassador herself. I had to change my plans. I decided not to announce to the Duke that I was seeking Ambassador Shelaylan. It would be wise if I did not reveal my presence in the town. You needed to be warned as soon as possible. I feared that I would have attracted unwanted attention to myself if I had turned around and left immediately. I waited until darkness fell, then rode east and south along the shore. Then I cut west through the forest and onto Banstron road, circled back twice to flush out anyone who may have been trailing me. I saw no one."

"You did well my love, I must be a good mentor." Banator grinned.

Ceikay started to speak, or rather reason, out loud. "The Ambassador died three days past. King Ballistor received the Ambassador's coded message seven days before that. Upon receiving the message, the King called us in and commanded that we find Beorn and escort him to Brentsad and to Ambassador Shelaylan. The King required Beorn because we all know that the King's Witness himself had 'fallen' just the day before the Ambassador's urgent message had arrived. Hensha was directed to report at speed to the Ambassador to inform her that a Witness was on the way. The two deaths cannot be merely innocent coincidences. It seems to me that someone knew that a vital, coded message was on the way to the King. That person also knew that the King would naturally send his Royal Witness. So the Witness was eliminated. But why did the Witness have to die? Why was it not enough to silence the Ambassador?"

Keven spoke up, "Coincidence is a possibility…but not to my betting…"

Karlyle added, "We also have to conclude that there is more than one murderer, and therefore, a conspiracy. Would, or could, one lone person, knowing that the Ambassador was sending an urgent message, rush ahead, kill the Witness and then, rethinking his wisdom, turn around and rush back to Brentsad and kill Ambassador Shelaylan? Or was a separate message sent to an associate in Talavor to kill the Witness? Then a separate conspirator, left in Brenstad, killed the Ambassador to keep…."

"Stop it, yar hurtin my head," moaned Banator.

Ceikay broke in, "He is right. We begin to speculate too much. If we continue, we will be tangled into inaction."

Keven continued, "No matter what the speculations are, we now should assume that a spy or spies have infiltrated the King's security. The Witness was behind the King's secured palace walls when he 'fell.' The Ambassador was assigned to, and lived at Duke Hastid's guarded castle. So, if spies have breached the King's security, then they surely know of the King's need for another Witness. They know of Beorn already."

Errol raised his hands to stop everyone. "Very well!"

He then turned to me. "Bard, it seems that you will be traveling with us to Brentsad. It would not be wise to leave you unprotected. We may be going into harm's way, but you are still safer than if you made your way alone. So it is decided. I am thankful that you are not afraid to continue."

"I did not say that I was not afraid."

With that said, Hensha declared, "I must leave now. All the gods' aid to your pursuit!"

Banator stepped to her and they embraced. They stood holding each other for a few moments.

Banator spoke softly into her ear, "Ride swiftly and safely my love."

Hensha smiled as she strode from the cottage and jumped into the saddle. Moments later horse and rider were gone.

Errol turned to Banator. "We must take our leave also. As always, you are a friend that can be counted on. Watch the road and all who pass. We will send word of our progress as we can."

Banator answered back, "No one passes along Banstron road that I am not aware of. I will be true to my chore!"

Soon after, the five of us were on our horses heading north to Brentsad. To my surprise, we did not increase our pace from last night. We now rode single file. Keven took the lead with Ceikay about ten paces behind him. Karlyle rode next about the same distance back. Errol directed that I ride a bit behind Karlyle. Errol kept ten paces behind me. Naturally, I had quite a few questions to ask, but this riding formation prevented me from asking them.

We traveled single-file through the beautiful oak forest known as Darion Woods. The oaks were of a rich black and all seemed to be healthy and strong, with huge spanning branches filled with leaves as large as your hand. The bright blue sky of the day filtered through numerous gaps in this canopy of leaves, lighting our way. We rode under this living canopy on a wide, well-traveled road. On either side of the road grew a rich, green carpet of shin-high grass that spread as far as one could see through the trees. There was no underbrush to speak of. There was abundant wildlife. The birds seemed to gather around the surrounding trees as we went by. Deer and other small animals did not scurry for cover either.

After a while, the shadows were starting to grow longer. Errol called a halt for rest and food. We stopped by one of the many streams running through and along the road. The horses took drink and Keven gave each of them several handfuls of grain. While Keven tended to the horses, Ceikay and Karlyle gathered up fallen twigs and bits of branches for a fire. Errol reached into a big satchel and brought out a large, round loaf of Sheppard's bread and a huge slab of dried beef. He also pulled out some ripe, red apples and two bunches of white grapes.

Trying to earn my way, I asked, "Should I gather up some stones to make a fire pit for your wood?"

"No, Beorn," Ceikay answered smiling, "we are not making a

31

fire here. The wood we are collecting is for tonight's camp. It is easier to gather twigs and sticks in the daylight. That is why we do it now."

"Then I will just help by picking up stones for the pit." I offered.

"Too heavy to carry." Keven grinned as he led the horses from the stream.

By this time I was feeling like the butt of a joke, with everyone grinning at me. "Sorry that I appear so dim-witted to you all."

Errol stood up and walked over to me. "If we thought that of you, you would not be riding with us to Brentsad. We have been together for such a long time now that we do things our way without really thinking about it. We forget that an outsider may not understand all our...interactions. We really do not mind your curiosity and questions. If it seems as though we are amused at your expense, please consider that as a sign you are liked. You will see in your journey that none of us will be immune to a bit of 'ridicule' from time to time. Here; if you still want to help for lunch, take this knife and slice up some of Banator's delicious smoked venison."

I put my feelings aside and took the knife.

Soon we were all sitting on collected logs and eating our meal. Errol spoke again, "Anything to report from your friends Keven?"

"Nothing out of the ordinary. The birds are calm, and the rest of the Forest is peaceful. If there is trouble ahead, it has not reached Darion forest."

"Do you have anything to add, Ceikay?"

"No Errol, no one has been close to us."

"Can you tell if someone is following us?" I asked her.

"I can tell if someone is close. But if someone were following us at distance, the birds would have alerted Keven by now."

We soon finished our meal and mounted our horses. Errol rode to my side. "I suggest you ride with Karlyle for a while, he might tell you more of his 'Talent.' The road is clear and nothing should be happening until nightfall."

Keven again took the lead, with Ceikay next and Errol behind us. As I brought my horse next to Karlyle, Errol called out, "Be warned though, once you get Karlyle started, it may take an age before you get him to stop. You may regret your curiosity yet!"

Karlyle retorted with his nose in the air, "At least when I speak, it is with supreme intelligence, unlike others of this assemblage."

Ceikay yelled over her shoulder, "Who ya callin' unlurnded?!"

"Must be me he's a refferin' to l'lady!" Keven laughed.

Karlyle turned to me, "Ignore the riffraff, what would you like to know?"

"So you are a magician...how much magic do you know?"

"I know as much as I have learned."

"...and what have you learned?"

"Quite a lot and not enough."

Now Ceikay yelled back, "I am going to come back there and break your shin if you do not answer him, Karlyle!"

Karlyle held up his hands in surrender, "Hold, I beg of you!" Then to me, "So you want to know about my 'Talent.' Well, the word 'magic' is often used to describe it. The word is misleading in the fact that people tend to simplify it down to a mystical 'snapping of the finger and the reading of incantations,' so to speak. As I prefer to describe it, 'Magic' is 'merely the science of the mind and earth not understood.'"

I nodded my head as if I understood, waiting for him to continue. "As I am sure you know, people have the ability to concentrate on development of certain, specific areas of their mind, to develop a specific 'Talent,' if you will. These talents that a person chooses to concentrate on are available to everyone. My area of training is what I like to call, 'Thought Focus,' or 'Thought Manipulation.'

"Each of us here, including you, has developed a part of our minds far above the average. Keven has chosen 'Primal Communication,' which is language communication with the other animals of this land. He is commonly known a 'Beast Master.' Errol chose 'Menta-Muscular development,' which means he has honed his body to be super-fast and strong. In other people's words, he is a 'Warrior Master.' Ceikay chose 'Sensa-Emotion delving.' She is able to know emotions and therefore motives of others before they speak. There are more names to describe these

33

talents, but you may be aware of them already. All of these are merely areas of the mind that can be trained and developed as one is so determined."

I kept quiet.

Karlyle paused a moment before continuing. "It is the same with your choice of memorization, Bard. Years ago, you made a conscious decision to strengthen your power of memory. Today you are at a level that seems supernatural and mysterious to most others. Remember what you said at the Inn: '...memorization tricks; tricks that anyone could learn if they took the time and effort.' Even though you may have been born with an advanced degree of your specific talent, it took years of practice for you to attain your level of expertise. It is the same for the four of us in our specialties."

Again he paused and I was quiet.

"To put it another way, it can be considered an art form. These are simply talents that we have developed into an art through mental and physical training. Everyone has the ability to become 'Masters of an Art.' As I like to describe it, one becomes a Talent Master."

Karlyle pointed ahead to Keven. "As I said, he is called a 'Beast Master.' He chose to study the common thread that connects us with the rest of the animal world. He can describe his knowledge better than I can, so I suggest that you speak to him for a clearer explanation of what he is capable of. As I understand it, words are not always exchanged between him and the animal. Thoughts are transferred and understood. Also the language of body gestures and scents is extremely important in the animal world. What I do know is that Keven has spent his life learning the origins, habits, communications and social dynamics of the major animal species. How that developed into the understanding of animal languages, I do not know, but it is certainly not mystical. It is through understanding and mental training. As I said, Keven can tell you more if you ask him."

Karlyle nodded toward Ceikay. "Ceikay's talent is a form of what our learned scholars call telepathy. Unlike Keven, she reaches out only to other human minds. And as such, her talent can be considered more difficult than the rest of ours. The human mind is the most deceitful creation ever created by the gods above. She also has developed better than the rest of us the ability to ascertain body mannerisms and movements.

Karlyle grinned as he turned to me. "Do not ever play one of those card games of chance with her if you want to keep your Kopas."

He then continued with his narrative. "You see, within their species, animals' habits stay very much the same, and are therefore predictable and learnable. Humans, on the other hand, are far more complicated and unpredictable. I study mainly the physical world, Keven studies the 'lower' animals, and Errol studies mainly the physical limits of the body. Ceikay studies the most complicated thing that the gods ever created: the human."

We rode in silence for about a league. My mind did not fully comprehend what Karlyle was explaining.

Then without warning, he spoke again. "So far, Ceikay has the ability to discern peoples' motives and emotions, but not their actual thoughts. She can also sense the presence of other people around her at a distance of about one hundred paces. Ceikay is younger than the rest of us; therefore, she has not developed her talent to the point we have developed ours. From what I have seen of her progress, though, I predict that she may surpass the three of us, relatively speaking and relatively soon. She is driven to excel and may someday extend her talent into genuine 'thought reading;' the ability to actually discern thoughts of an individual as he or she thinks them. To my knowledge, no one has succeeded to that level. We have also seen from her the beginnings of clairvoyance, but I will not go into that. Speak with her when you can, she will explain further."

Karlyle pointed toward Errol. "Errol has chosen the most common talent, and by its very nature, the most dangerous, Menta-Muscular Self-Defense, or, 'Art of the Warrior.' I do not call him a Warrior Master though; I call him a Weapons Master. He is also known as a 'Sword Master.' I use the word 'dangerous' because humans, due to their nature, have corrupted this talent into the art of killing for killing's sake. Because of this corruption there are two types of Sword Masters: Warriors and Killers. Warriors kill for justified causes; Killers kill for joy, or personal gain. Unfortunately, Killers far outnumber Warriors in this world. We are a violent species that excels like no other in the practice of murder. It is in fact the oldest 'Art' form, if you will. Our earliest and greatest heroes are warriors that developed their physical prowess to kill others. Remember also: the survivors tell the histories, and they always put themselves in the right, so they will never refer to their victories as being murderous."

We rode a while in silence. I sensed that Karlyle did not want my questions, so I asked none.

Finally he began again. "Now, Errol has studied the body's physical movements, limitations, and endurances. He has studied conscious and unconscious reactions to mental and physical stimuli. He has studied the histories of warfare, studied individual hand-to-hand combat, and learned everything there is to know about weapons of destruction. His weapon of choice, as you can see, is the greatsword, but in his hands, anything can be lethal. In deciding to hone his warrior talent, he has evolved into a consummate killing machine. The ironic thing is, he does not, and has never liked, the killing. That is why I do not call him a 'Warrior Master."

"Why does he pursue it then?" I asked.

"That is not part of my telling. In any case, he would be the one to answer that."

Karlyle then turned the subject away from Errol. "As for my Talent, for ease of this discussion, I will just use the term 'Magic.' Magic is considered by most to be mystical, forbidding, other-worldly and so on. In truth and fact, Magic is merely the mental capacity to manipulate the physical forces around you. It takes no 'hocus-pocus' chants or rhymes to create a 'spell.' So there is no such thing as a memorized 'spell' as is generally believed. If 'magic' was dependent on the memorizing of spells written in cumbersome tomes…I would choose to be a cobbler today.

"Also, contrary to general belief, there are no such things as 'curses' that could be placed on someone in order to harm or kill them. Most wizards, witches and warlocks are what I call

'Dramatics.' They use the fanciful costumes and pretty chants to impress the common folk who do not understand the art of the science of magic. When you see a wizard point his wand at an object to be manipulated, it is again misleading in that the stick has nothing to do with the 'magical effect.' It may serve for focusing concentration but certainly the real, only, power comes directly from the mental concentration of the mind."

Karlyle paused for a moment. "I see by your expression that I am overwhelming you. Let me think on this; how shall I explain it any clearer? Try to form a picture in your mind of a 'thought' as a continuous, solid stream of words or actions. Now consider that stream to be water shooting from your forehead outward. With enough understanding and training you can focus that stream of thought to manipulate a physical item."

He now pointed to the ground. "Take a simple rock on the ground at my feet. Imagine I now bend down and pick it up with my left hand and place it on top of a large boulder. My mental power caused that rock to be placed there. You look puzzled. Well, I desired it to be on the boulder, so I picked it up and placed it there. My mental thoughts ordered my physical muscles to direct my body to obey. Is that not correct?"

I nodded silently.

Karlyle continued, "My mental command was transferred from my mind throughout my body, and the parts that were required to move obeyed. Anyone can do this; pick up a rock. You do see that do you not? Good, now remember the thought as a stream of water. I next put the rock back on the ground. I will now try to pick it up using only my mental efforts and not my physical body. I direct my thoughts to the rock. They are streaming toward the rock and finally hit and now surround it. Remember the water comparison, only this 'stream of thought' does not splash away when it hits solid objects like real water would. Imagine that it surrounds and coats objects and stays connected to that object and also still stretches back to the sender's mind. That is what my thoughts are now doing with that rock. I am now in contact with that rock because of this mental stream. Information is coming back to me through this solid stream of thought. I can 'feel' the rock's shape and size; know the distance from where I am standing, and sense its temperature.

"But that is only part of what I am able to do. Believe it or not, I have just described the first, basic level of being a 'Wizard.' which is: Learning to 'find and touch' objects through thought!"

Karlyle paused to let me digest his words.

After a brief while he continued. "Now, for the second level, or I should say step: Grabbing and holding of an object. Now picture that stream of 'Thought' as an extension of my mind that I can manipulate as an extra arm. I have learned to gain physical control over that water stream and now 'grab' the rock and hold on to it. Where I now direct that 'stream', the rock will go also. Now my mental 'stream' can be redirected to the boulder with the rock in tow. I focus my thought 'stream' to shorten or lengthen just right and the rock is now hovering on top of the boulder. Now I redirect my 'stream' to lower the rock to rest on the boulder and now 'release' my mental hold. As you can envision, the rock is again on top of the boulder."

Again he paused, again I was silent.

Then he continued. "The third step is learning to control speed, direction, and duration of the 'stream,' the lifting, moving, and placing of an object is done only when the third step is mastered.

"The fourth step is learning to manipulate more than one object at a time.

"The fifth step is learning to control Water.

"The sixth is Air.

"The seventh step is Fire."

Karlyle turned to me. "Questions yet?"

I shook my head. Not because there were none, but because I knew not where to start.

Karlyle grinned and spoke again. "Many wizards believe there are more steps in the learning process. To my current knowledge, no one has mastered more than seven. What the eighth step will be is a matter of choice. I am working on my next step, but I will tell no one until I accomplish it. You see, there are no rules of order when it comes to learning to master nature. I should make it clear that the order of the first seven steps I gave you is my choice.

Other Masters may, and do, have a different order of steps they have taken. I feel that the route I took is the most logical route when you consider the stability quotient of the steps involved...."

Karlyle understood the silent expression on my face, "I see that I have lost your understanding. Well, I'll just say one more thing on this subject. Through years of mental training and discipline; I have developed a certain 'expertise.' But that in no way makes me superior to another, less 'educated' individual. It certainly does not make me invincible. I can be injured or killed just like anyone else. Magic does have its limits, believe my words on this."

His thumb pointed back toward his sword. "You see that I carry a sword. I rely on it more than magic when it comes to self-defense. The speed of the hand is still faster than mental manipulation, and I have the best to teach me, there is none better than Errol."

"You have given me a lot to think on." I said, "But at the Boar's Hind Inn you were about to set a man on fire with an incantation. Explain that to me."

Karlyle laughed. "We were deceiving him to scare the truth out of him. Ceikay knew that he was not a serious threat, or she would have alerted us in a different way. My 'show' was just that, a show, nothing more."

I was about to ask another question when Karlyle suddenly held up his hand to quiet me. Up ahead, Keven had stopped his horse. The rest of us did the same. He sat still and looked to the left of the road into the underbrush. Immediately I felt the others go tense and on the alert. It was only then that I noticed the woods all around were eerily quiet. I instinctively moved my hand closer to the knife now in my belt.

Keven then spoke quietly back to us, "The animals are in great fear here. They are hiding from something that does not belong."

He suddenly closed his mouth and held up his right arm. At that moment, a large, beautiful Redtail hawk came swiftly out of the forest canopy and landed on Keven's fore-arm!

Keven listened while the bird squawked and flapped its wings. Then, as suddenly as he had arrived, the hawk flew off, back up through the mighty oak branches and out of sight. I looked back at

Keven and saw that he had a loaded crossbow at the ready. Errol and Ceikay had swords drawn. I had not seen, nor heard, the three arm themselves. Karlyle had not drawn his blade. He sat on his horse motionless with his eyes closed, head tilted a bit up and to the left as if listening.

I slowly reached again for my long knife and this time pulled it from its sheath and held it out in a defensive posture.

Keven spoke again, nodding toward the underbrush. "There is a dead man and woman in the clearing about sixty paces yonder, they have been murdered."

"Ceikay?" Errol calmly called to her.

"Nobody in my range." She answered, back still looking into the woods.

"Karlyle?" Errol called out again as his eyes scanned the woods.

"I feel no unusual forces at work."

Errol then started his horse left off the road. "Beorn, stay close to Karlyle and Ceikay. Keven, let us take a look at the clearing."

Errol and Keven disappeared into the woods while the three of us stayed on the road. I noticed that Karlyle had now drawn his wicked-looking long blade and had it pointed down to the ground at his side. I also noticed that Ceikay had a short sword in each hand and had drawn her horse alongside mine. I was comforted that these two now flanked me. After a short time, there came a hoot of an owl from the woods to the left.

"Let us go." Karlyle quietly ordered as he started toward the clearing.

I stayed close behind Karlyle as Ceikay followed behind me. We went through a gap in the underbrush and soon came to a break in the trees. In front of us was a clearing about fifty paces around. The ground was covered in a golden layer of knee high wild grass. The sun was shining brightly through the gap in the canopy. Errol stood in the middle of the clearing. Keven and the horses were not in sight. Errol was looking down at two objects on the ground. Karlyle and Ceikay dismounted and walked toward Errol. I paused for a brief moment, and then decided to do the same. As I got closer to the center of the clearing I noticed that the objects were two bodies. I had seen dead bodies before so I did not flinch or turn away. What was unusual about these two victims was that they appeared to be asleep instead of dead.

Before us lay man and a woman of about middle age. By the look of their green leather clothing, they were woodland hunters. Each carried a hunting bow and a full quiver of arrows for small game. The two were on their backs, laid out as though they had merely fallen to the ground and had moved no further. The grass around them was not disturbed or matted down. I saw no wound on either of the bodies, no torn clothes. In fact, I saw no blood. That was the puzzling thing about the whole scene: Keven had announced that these two were murdered, but I saw no signs of violence.

"What have you found?" Ceikay asked as she bent over to study the bodies.

Errol bent down to join Ceikay. "Look to the nape of each neck just above the hairline and behind the right ear. There is a puncture wound. It looks like a wasp sting at first glance, but the fact that both of them have it in the same place on the side of the neck can not be coincidental. They were not expecting danger. Their deaths were quick. The stride of their tracks show that they were walking, not running. Their bows are still strapped to their backs and their knives are in their sheaths. By the peaceful look on their faces, it must be a painless poison that took them. It was not a killing for money; the man's pouch has twelve copper Kopas in it. Before we entered the clearing, the only tracks were their own. What struck them down I cannot tell. I have never seen killings such as these before now."

I could not resist a comment, "So it was a poison dart that killed them. How do you know that their deaths were quick?"

Errol answered as he continued to study the bodies, "I doubt that a dart killed these two. I have no knowledge of a dart making such a small puncture wound. Also, no dart is lying next to the bodies, and since the only tracks in this clearing were those of the victims, the murderer could not have retrieved the darts to hide the evidence. As for your question about the quick death, a slow-acting painless poison works by slowly drugging the victim into a

41

stupor and finally death. As I pointed out earlier, there is no sign of contortion in their faces or posture to indicate pain. Also, a person who is attacked by a slow, painless poison will begin to get drowsy or disoriented. If they were walking at the last stages, their strides would begin to wander and become uneven. These two walked in a straight and steady line right up to the point where they collapsed and died."

At this time Keven appeared on the far end of the clearing. "I found the couple's camp and equipment. Someone rifled through their gear. If they were looking for something it was not money, clothes, or food."

"How many were there?" Karlyle asked.

"Hawk told me there were three humans covered in elk skins." Keven answered. "I also found three distinct sets of human tracks heading west from the victims' camp. I almost missed them, this trio is very good at leaving no evidence behind. It seems they are careful not to break any twigs or kick over leaves when they travel. They are quite skilled at stealth. I lost their trail at a stream a short distance from here. They either went up, or down-stream a ways before crossing over."

"Can Hawk tell us where they went from the stream? Did he follow them?" Karlyle asked.

Keven paused before answering. "Two of Hawk's brothers tried to follow. They were killed by the three humans. They are not the only animals murdered though. I have found numerous small animals all around this clearing...all dead."

"How are you sure they were killed by the three men?" Ceikay asked.

"Hawk tells me that the men would look at an animal and breathe out. The animal would then drop to the ground."

Errol spoke, "Take us to one of the animals."

Keven led us to the far end of the clearing and through several lines of oaks. Lying on the ground around us were twelve dead animals; four birds, three tree squirrels, three opossum, and two chipmunks. Errol bent down to examine a squirrel.

Keven spoke, "The left eye is punctured."

"Would I be correct in saying that the rest died in a similar

42

way?" Errol asked.

"You would be correct," Keven answered.

For a few moments no one said a word. Ceikay stood with her eyes closed as if listening to the wind. Keven walked a bit back toward the glade, studying the ground. With an arched brow, Karlyle slowly scanned the forest canopy. Errol studied the dead squirrel.

"What happened?" I finally asked, not really expecting an answer.

Nobody answered.

Suddenly, with a quick flick of the index finger of his right hand, Errol plucked out the damaged eye of the squirrel! He had a knife in his left and proceeded to slice the orb in half.

"We do not have any answers as yet," Errol stated as he dissected. "Right now I am looking for some kind of tiny missile or dart, which I am not finding. There is only a puncture wound, which is promoting mystery rather than offering answers."

Keven returned from the clearing. "Let us find some answers then. We should go after the killers. Hawk will aid us in the tracking."

"I do not disagree," Karlyle offered, "but let us not forget our duty to the King and the mystery of Ambassador Shelaylan."

Errol stood up and thought for a moment. "We will split our party for a while. Keven, you are the one best suited in the tracking of the killers. I will go with you. Karlyle, Ceikay, and Beorn will continue on to Brentsad."

Errol turned to face us. "If we do not catch up to you soon, you three will stay at Bower's Inn in Brentsad and wait for us to rejoin you. When we are together again, we will visit Duke Hastid."

"Are you sure you two do not need us along?" Ceikay asked.

Errol answered, "No one is better than Keven in the forest. We will find what we are after. Also, you three may have an opportunity to garner some answers around town before we visit the Duke."

Keven now took his and Errol's horse in rein and motioned west, further into the forest. "Time does not favor those who stand

and talk…"

Errol turned to me. "Beorn, Karlyle and Ceikay will see that you are safe, but you must not be injured for lack of caution. They can only protect you so far. What we have gotten you into may be more than you might find comfortable. We cannot tell if these murders are isolated or will continue. We have to consider all possibilities. So as of this moment, all of us have to be on our guard. Do as Karlyle and Ceikay ask, and keep a low profile in Brentsad."

Errol then added, "If you are still of a mind to go with us."

I looked at each one of them in turn, "I made a commitment to you yesterday to come with you as a Witness. Today has not changed that commitment."

"The gods put a stout heart in you, Bard." Karlyle slapped me on the shoulder. "Let us hope that we do not come to regret your adventurous spirit."

"We must go now!" Keven insisted.

"Lead the way then," Errol said as he gathered his horse's reins, "Safe trip to Brentsad for you. You had all better be safe when we return, or I will be a bit annoyed. I do not want to be inconvenienced if you were made useless to our mission."

Ceikay chimed in, "We would not wish to make you angry, kind and compassionate sir. We promise to be safe until your glorious return to our humble presence."

Keven and Errol disappeared west into the forest.

"Karlyle watched them go and yelled after them, "We had better see you soon in Brentsad, we would hate to have to come looking for you!"

Then he turned to Ceikay and me. "Let us see what awaits us." He then mounted his horse as Ceikay did the same.

"Wait a moment!" I said without moving to my horse. "What about those two people in the glade? Should we not bury them?"

"We cannot do anything for them now. Their bodies will feed the forest just as well above ground as below. Besides, the clearing is a beautiful setting. I can think of worse places to lie dead."

I had to admit, his reasoning did make sense. "What about their gear then?" I asked.

This time Ceikay answered, "The dead do not need it, and we certainly will not take it."

Once again I pressed, "Shouldn't we try to find out who their family and friends are to tell them?"

Karlyle stopped and turned in his saddle to face me. "Beorn, we understand your concerns. We do not dismiss them out of hand. But this is an ugly world at times. We do not have the luxury of time to bury them, and certainly not the time to try to find kin to report their deaths. We have a directive from the King that must take precedence. If these killings are just a local matter, they cannot interfere with that directive. If somehow these deaths are related to the answers we seek at Brentsad, then we had better get there all the more quickly."

I still wanted to argue, but could not. But linking these unfortunate hunters to the Ambassador's death puzzled me, so I pressed. "How can you say that these murders are connected to our quest? Why should this not be just a coincidence?"

Ceikay answered, "The interesting thing about coincidences is that they are most often not."

Seeing that I was not convinced, Karlyle then added, "We were taught to consider everything and all possibilities. It reduces unwelcome surprises later on. You are right Beorn; right now there is absolutely no evidence of a connection. But our thoughts must still consider it."

With that said, we mounted our horses to continue our trek. Ceikay rode the front, I in the middle, and Karlyle trailing behind. We were quiet on the road. I had questions to ask but no desire to ask. I was keeping an eye on the surrounding forest and the underbrush as we went by. Ceikay was riding with her head slightly cocked to one side, obviously trying to sense any newcomers as they came into her range. I glanced back at Karlyle and saw him twisted in his saddle looking back along the road we had just passed. He then turned back around, making a complete circular scan. The mood of my two companions was calm but alert.

We rode like this until the shadows grew into the solid grey of dusk. Ceikay drew up her horse and pointed to a little rise off to the right.

"What say you, Karlyle?"

Karlyle rode past us and up the rise. "There is a little clearing up here. This will do us fine for tonight!"

Ceikay then motioned for me to join Karlyle, which I did, and she followed. The clearing was about ten paces across, covered in a pretty carpeting of wild grass. The last of the day's light lent a pleasant yellow-red glow to the glade. I would have considered it beautiful and comforting if it did not remind me of the earlier glade of the day.

"I know what you are thinking." Ceikay said, startling me back to the present, "You must not dwell on what cannot be changed."

"I thought you could not read minds," I said.

"I did not read your mind. I read the expression on your face and surmised your thoughts, which are mine also."

Karlye dismounted and led his horse to the edge of the clearing. Ceikay and I did the same.

Karlyle handed me his reins as I approached. "Beorn, please tend the horses while we set camp and prepare supper."

Soon, the horses were free of their packs and happily munching on rich green grass.

Suddenly the sound of muffled clapping started up all around us overhead. It seemed to come from the direction we had just traveled. I looked to the evening sky as the noise became alarmingly louder and closer. Then I knew what the sound was, it was the sound of birds. Hundreds of them! And then they came in, circled our clearing and began to settle into the trees surrounding us. They were crows, big ones. The sudden appearance startled me, but something else scared me: the lack their caws.

As they alit in the trees overhead and blackened the evening sky even further, I was shaken by their silence. Not a caw was sounded. It was not natural and I did not bear it well. I turned my head to Karlyle and Ceikay.

If they were as alarmed as I was, they did not show it. They just stood there and watched as the crows settled. It took only moments for all of the birds to circle and land. Then it was absolutely quiet and still.

Karlyle then held his hands out, palms up. "Thank you for your service! We are blessed with your protection and will sleep well tonight under your watch. May the wind always carry you safely!"

I then realized what had transpired. Keven had sent the crows to guard our camp for the night.

Ceikay looked over at me, "Yes, Keven has done this before. Crows are some of the most intelligent of animals. They are also equipped with a good alarm in that their cawing is loud and unmistakable. If anyone approaches us we will be made aware of it. Tonight we will be able to get some sleep."

It took little time for the three of us to settle in for the night. I brushed and tethered the horses. Karlyle started a fire, which did not seem to bother the crows overhead. Ceikay cleared away branches and stones to ready our blankets for sleep. When I sat down at the fire Karlyle had already laid out biscuits and venison stew. I was surprisingly hungry and wasted no time attacking my meal. Karlyle and Ceikay ate more slowly and said nothing. Both seemed to be lost in thought.

I, on the other hand needed to ask questions, but kept silent and waited for an opportunity to arise. After a while it became obvious that I would not get that opportunity. I sat before the waning fire and became aware of how tired I was. The night was fairly warm considering it was early fall. The leaves had not even started turning. The night air was fresh and still, and inviting me to sleep. Finally, I took that invitation and lay down on top of my bedroll. I did not bother to throw a blanket over me.

I had restless dreams that night, but as usual, the moment I woke up the next morning, my only recollection of them is that they occurred and that they kept me busy during the night. The details forever flew from my memories. As good as my memory is for the waking world; my memory for the dream world is dismal. As a result of those elusive, active dreams that could not be retrieved, I awoke tired and a bit on edge. I sat up to an empty canopy. The crows had all disappeared sometime earlier.

Ceikay called out, "A good morning to you this day! I will wager that you are ready for a little rest by now."

She was walking up to the camp from the direction of the road. She was smiling broadly as she spoke. "Morning tea is ready by the fire. The fire has long ago gone out, but Karlyle heated the water for us. Break your fast and prepare yourself for travel quickly, we will be on the road when you are ready."

I looked up at her and asked a bit testily, "What do you mean I should be ready for a rest?"

Ceikay laughed as she scattered the cold ashes and kicked the fire ring apart. "You fought and wrestled all night in your sleep. You mumbled and cursed and yelled, fretted and cried and…"

"I did not cry and fret!"

"Perhaps not, but you did curse." Ceikay laughed again and turned to me, "But you still have to work on it if you ever want to match Karlyle's talent."

Just then Karlyle came walking into the clearing. "I beg your pardon; I have never uttered any ungentlemanly vulgarities in my life."

"Oh Karlyle, you know where you go when you lie," Ceikay teased.

As these two bantered I got up and made myself some tea. It tasted delicious and went a long way to lighten my mood. By the time the tea was finished I had also devoured two biscuits and a large strip of venison jerky. I then gathered up my bedroll and headed toward my horse. Ceikay had already saddled him and had gone down to the road on hers.

Karlyle was on his horse strapping his sword to his back. "Let us not keep her waiting, or she will come back looking for a shin to kick."

"Do we have any word from Errol and Keven?" I asked as we left the clearing to join Ceikay.

"I do not expect to see or hear from them until Brentsad. We did not…"

Suddenly Karlyle stopped his horse and held up his hand to me for silence. His face was instantly stern and his whole body became tense and alert. We were about twenty paces from the road, still behind the undergrowth. I looked ahead toward the road. Ceikay was nowhere to be seen. The normal sounds of the forest were quieted and the air was still. I saw nothing amiss.

"Arm yourself," Karlyle whispered in a deadly tone. He slowly drew his sword and held it out and down to the side.

I pulled my stabbing dagger from my bed roll. As I did this, bushes in front of us were slowly rising to block my view of the road. I glanced at Karlyle for direction but he only stared at the road ahead. I then realized that he was elevating the branches to cover us from being seen!

For a brief time there was no sound or movement from the road. Then I heard a faint noise up ahead in the direction we were headed. At first I could not identify the sound. As I sat and nervously waited, the sound grew louder and turned into distinct noises; noises of several riders on horseback. I could hear the clop of horses' hooves and the jangle of riders' weapons and gear. They made no effort to quiet their progress. As they approached from up the road I could hear someone talking in a terse manner. I could not make out the words, but it was obvious by the tone that anger was salting the conversation. The group's clatter broke over the quiet as the riders and horses rounded a slight bend in the road ahead. As they came into our sight I could see about a dozen men cloaked in gray. They were covered in head-to-toe riding capes that effectively hid all features except their faces. Each man had a close-trimmed black beard and thin black mustache. They were all heavily armed. Each had a double-edged sword strapped to his side and a double-bolt crossbow on his back. From what I could see there was a knife on the side of each of their dark gray boots below the capes. Each horse was the color of; well, dirty brown-gray is the best I can describe.

As they neared I noticed a slight breeze coming from the direction of the road. I then smelled their horses; they were rank with sweat and foul of breath. It was obvious that these men were not caring for those poor creatures. I glanced at Karlyle and could see that he was finding it hard to sit there motionless. His face was hard as steel and his eyes blazed at the company before us.

We waited until the group filed past us and traveled down the road. Finally, their noise and stench dissipated. I had followed them with my eyes, so did not notice Ceikay until she was on the road in front of us staring in our direction.

"Dirty business there," she said to us in a low voice.

The branches before us receded and a path was again clear to the road. Karlyle nudged his horse forward and I followed. His sword was still at the ready, as was mine.

"What is going on? Who were those men?" I asked as soon as we joined Ceikay.

"Man Trackers," was all Karlyle said in answer.

"Man Trackers?"

"Man Hunters, Bounty Hunters, Dungeon Drivers, Horse killers, whatever you choose to call them." Ceikay answered. "How you name them does not matter, they are men to be avoided."

I had heard of these men but until now had never seen them. They were mercenaries hired by an authority to track and bring in fugitives. 'Fugitives' is a misleading word, though; Man Trackers will hunt anybody for a price. They have naught concern for politics or innocence. If they are commissioned to pick up an individual, then they will hunt that poor soul into hell if led there. Once they do get their man, or woman, they would just as soon kill the poor soul and then bring the body in rather than have to go to the trouble of feeding and guarding a prisoner.

"Let us get started to Brentsad," Karlyle directed as he took the lead and sheathed his sword.

As we headed north I rode next to Ceikay. "What can you tell me about those Bounty Hunters?" I asked.

"Those that passed us I cannot tell much about. I do not know their prey, nor if they even have one. They could be in between hunts for all we know."

"I take it you sensed them on the road before Karlyle and I left the clearing. Am I right?"

"Yes, I went up ahead to scout the road before us. I 'felt' a number of men coming toward me. As Karlyle has told you I cannot read minds, but I can sense intent. These men stink in more ways than thought. As I felt their presence getting closer, I also felt their character. Sometimes, rarely, a very intelligent person can mask his or her true intent or character if they practice at it. These men who we just sidestepped do not conceal their minds. They do not because they do not need to."

"How did you warn Karlyle? By mind signals, thought waves, what?"

"Whistle."

"What?"

"Whistle. I softly let out two short whistles like a red-throated finch. Did you not hear it?"

"No, I…"

"Well, Karlyle knew I was scouting ahead, so he was alert for a signal. He heard the whistle and stopped in time."

"Why did we hide from them? I'm not in the company of fugitives, am I?" I asked only half joking.

"We have nothing to hide, nor fear from those vultures. Unfortunately, they enjoy a type of diplomatic authority across the realm. If we had met with them, we would have been delayed unnecessarily."

"How do you mean?"

"Like it or not, these bounty hunters are part of a guild. A guild recognized by Parliament for their relentless and uncompromising 'professionalism.' By professionalism I mean that they care only for the hunt. They care not for the politics or reasons, nor for the people involved. Money is the only motivator. All of the Dukes use them from time to time to bring in the 'Wanted.' Also, the Dukes have bestowed on this guild the diplomatic freedom to cross any Dukedom at any point without needing to register with any border guard. The reasoning is because of the necessity of speed, the hunters are free to pursue their prey unfettered. Added to this power is the right given to them, once again by the Dukes in Parliament, to stop anyone on any road, at any time, for any reason. These Man Hunters can question those that are stopped. If we had run into them this morning, they would have attempted to stop us, and even though we are on the King's mission, they still have the right to delay us if they choose."

"How can that be? The King should not allow his emissaries to be subjected to that treatment."

"Remember, King Ballistor is also a Duke. His power is not absolute. His power comes from the collective agreement of all seven Dukes through Parliament. He agreed to the elevation of the 'Man Hunter Guild.' So his subjects, meaning us, are obliged to be stopped and 'inconvenienced' by them. Only if we meet with them of course."

"I do not understand why the Dukes allow these men to roam so freely. Do they not worry about spying and information being given to the other Dukes?"

"As I just said, politics, and business for that matter, do not concern the Man Hunters. The only honor they hold, if you can call it that, is the absolute self-rule that no information will be given that does not directly lead to the hunters' target. Their only concern is the hunt. Because of that, the Dukes do not fear any compromise in security. Therefore, the Guild has been given extraordinary powers to find and eliminate 'criminals of the land.' We may not like it, but as of now it is the law of the realm."

"So we do not have any idea who those men were working for?"

"My guess is that they were not on a hunt right now. They were not making any attempt at speed or stealth. They probably finished whatever quest they were hired for and were now returning home. Their horses were spent and they were arguing with each other. You see, when they are on a hunt they work very efficiently and coherently. In other words, like deadly hyenas; focused, relentless, and terribly ugly!"

"I have heard of bounty hunters before, but I guess I never paid much attention to the stories."

"I am really surprised, considering you being a Bard and all."

"What do you mean by that?" I asked, a bit on the defensive again.

"You make your living telling stories. You should be better at paying attention to everything and everyone around you. If you are careless enough to be lazy, then your tales can be incomplete, or worse, inaccurate."

I looked at Ceikay and realized that I could not argue the point.

I rode a while in silence thinking about what I should be paying attention to.

We rode the rest of the day with nothing else of interest happening. I did not feel like talking to my companions as we made our way along the old Banstron Road so I studied the woods as we went. I noticed the gradual change in the trees and undergrowth. The variety of trees was increasing as we traveled north. I saw cedars, ash, and several more types of trees I did not know the names of. More undergrowth was creeping toward the road and closing us in. The only sky to be seen was directly over our heads, but I did not feel confined or boxed in. Rather, I marveled at the beauty of the colors and smells enveloping me. Since it was late in the warm season and early in the cooling season, I was surprised to see the colors of the leaves were starting to change the further we went north. I had heard of the colors of the Darion Forest, but until now had never passed through to experience the peaceful beauty of this region.

Then without warning, we were out of the forest. We emerged onto a large plateau that stretched for leagues in front and to the left of us. The plateau was covered in a blanket of rich green grass that continued to the mountains west and north of us, and, I assumed, beyond a rise several leagues away. Even though I had not before traveled this way, I knew this to be the great Brentsad plains. Some of the finest horses and milking cattle came from this region. The road continued north with the woods to our right.

I still did not speak to the other two as we rode, my mind focused only on the surrounding scenery. We eventually crested a little hill and I now had a panoramic view of the plains. In front of us, about a half day's ride, was a ribbon of river. From this distance I surely could not see the direction of the water flow, but knowing that the mountains were to the west, and the ocean to our east, the flow went from west to east.

"We will stop here for the night; set camp in the woods. Maybe Errol and Keven will still join us before we enter Brentsad."

I looked at Karlyle in surprise as he spoke. It had been hours since any of us had spoken. I had forgotten how late in the day it was getting, and I had forgotten about Keven and Errol. Karlyle had brought me back to the present.

I now noticed that Ceikay had already left the road and had entered the forest. Karlyle did not follow but swept his eyes back and forth along the road. I sat quietly on my horse and waited for instructions.

"Did we bruise your feelings earlier, Beorn?" Karlyle turned to look at me, waiting for my answer.

"At first you did offend me, but how long can one long be offended by the truth?"

"Are you saying that you are changing your lazy ways?"

I knew that I was being baited, but I answered anyway, "Acknowledging truth does not necessarily promote change."

"It sounds as if I am still talking to a lazy man."

I turned to face Karlyle directly. "Why are you so concerned about my habits?"

Before Karlyle could answer, Ceikay returned to the road. "There is a small clearing a short distance from here. We can set camp and wait for the others there."

By nightfall the horses were fed, we were fed, and the crows were again in the trees watching over us.

As we sat near the small fire Ceikay broke the silence. "It is strange that we have not seen travelers on the road. Only the Man Hunters have come south from Brentsad. Normally we would see merchants of all types journeying along Banstron Road. Something is stopping normal travel from the north."

Ceikay looked at both of us through narrowed eyes. "The questions are many; are the answers connected I wonder? Any suggestions, Beorn?"

"Why ask me? I am too lazy to figure anything out."

Karlyle suddenly roared with laughter. "You still sting from my words? By the gods, Beorn, I will not give up on you yet! You shall rise to the challenge or I shall break my sword!"

Seeing my black look directed at Karlyle, Ceikay tried to disarm me with a compliment. "Do not seethe, Beorn; he does like you or he would not tease you so."

"It is not that he teases me, it is just that his words are too close

54

to the truth."

I suppose nothing more needed to be said, since we all just decided to lay our heads down on our bed rolls and fall off to sleep.

I awoke to whispering and knew that it was not near to sunrise. I sat up and looked across the still bright campfire. Errol and Keven were sitting on a log talking to the others. I saw no smiles.

Errol turned to me as I sat up, "Greetings, I am sorry to have disturbed you, but then again it is good that you woke this soon, we have not yet told of what we have found. You are party to this adventure so you are welcome to hear everything."

I waved off the apology but nodded to hear the news of what they found.

Errol began his telling. "We tracked the three killers through several streams and out the west end of the forest. There we came upon the foothills. Tracks soon led us to a cave opening at the base of the mountains. The tracks entered but got lost among the hard stone floor. I will not describe now the odd and wonderful rooms we entered; that will be saved for a later day. Our hunt soon became a futile endeavor in endless labyrinths."

Keven nodded silently.

Errol continued. "After exiting the caves we returned to Banator's cottage. We told him the story of the three killers and the cave. He had no knowledge of any travelers coming south along the road and had seen no one in the woods to the west of the cottage. Two merchant wagons passed his place on the road traveling north; whether they were on their way to Brentsad or Gailent he did not know. At length we decided that Banator would travel to the King and give the alert on this new mystery. Keven and I rushed to catch up to you and continue with our original plan."

"No merchant wagons have passed us on the road to Brentsad, so those merchant wagons Banator saw must have been going to Gailent," Ceikay surmised.

Karlyle continued, "I should plan to visit those caves in the future. They sound too interesting not to explore in detail."

"Let us finish the night with a bit of sleep." Ceikay said as she moved to her bedroll: "I foretell that our days are going to get busier from here into the future."

Brentsad

Just after first light we left our clearing and started on Banstron Road. We came back to the hill with the panoramic view and for the first time saw Brentsad as a dot to the north. It was on the far side of the river that I had seen the day before. The river is called Adar. This river separates the Dukedoms of Hastid to the north and Whorton to the south. As we traveled further I saw the road that connects Brentsad with the town of Pretara. This road is called Estwist. Karlyle also told me that the origin of the name is not known, but it is generally assumed that it had simply devolved from 'East/West' road.

As we rode nearer to Brentsad I began to make out its appearance. The first structures I recognized were the enormous, twenty-span-tall guard towers. Every major city in Tavegnor has these giant sentinels watching over them. They are either cylindrical or eight-sided, depending on the town. All are built of granite. The base is five spans across and the walls are at least one span in thickness. Each tower tapers to a width of three spans across at the top. At the top of each tower is a two-level, wood-covered structure that can house up to twenty archers. This wooden structure overhangs the stone tower all around by three hands. The

57

cupola that covers this structure is usually made of sheets of copper to ward against fire missiles. There are no exterior doors to these towers. They are entered through underground tunnels that connect from the castle which is generally at the center of each town.

The reasons for their construction are well known. After the last Great War for territory and dominance, the seven Dukes hammered out quite a number of pacts and treaties with the purpose of putting a permanent end to feudal warfare. One of the agreements was that no town was to have walls built around it. This would insure the goodwill of each kingdom by not allowing 'total' defenses, thereby discouraging any one Duke to build up for war. But, it was also agreed that watch towers could be built surrounding the Dukes' castles. The stated purpose of these towers was protection from marauding wildlife and roving bands of rogue mercenaries and brigands that plagued the land after the war. It was agreed that these towers would not be enough to ward off a full army, but rather deter any smaller threat to the population. The exact dimensions I stated above for the towers are the ones hammered out and finally agreed to in the Great War treaties.

No Duke is allowed to build a tower exceeding those dimensions, but all have been creative in defending their towns and castles in other ways.

Nonetheless, as I said about Brentsad, as we approached the town I could first see the towers. They were the cylindrical type. They looked to be surrounding the town about two hundred paces from each other as they circled around to the far end. Before Brentsad, the Estwist road joins Banstron Road from the west. The River Adar crosses Banstron Road just past Estwist and before Brentsad. As we approached the joining of the roads Ceikay noted out loud that no travelers were coming from Brentsad and turning onto Estwist. "No one travels the roads. The Duke seems to have closed Brentsad. Both travel ways were empty except for us."

Errol, leading our party, spoke up without turning around, "We will go directly to Duke Hastid and not to an inn. Time is critical and with no one on the road we will be the focus of the guards in the towers. It is clear that the Duke has shut down travel from

Brentsad and will be promptly told of travelers coming north. We can be sure that his personal guard would seek us out if we do not report to him directly."

We soon passed over the River Bridge. That was, and still is, the only name used for the bridge over the Adar River. Soon we neared the first towers. I looked up to see guards staring down at us from above.

Ceikay spoke in a low voice as we approached the first two towers. "It seems we will be greeted by a dozen guards."

At that moment from behind the two towers, twelve mounted soldiers moved to block our progress into the town.

The lead soldier held his arm up in a gesture to stop us, "Hold and state your business in Brentsad!"

We all halted our horses, except for Errol. He continued to ride up to, and stop directly in front of the soldier who spoke. "Since when does the town of Brentsad treat its visitors so inhospitably?"

I heard Karlyle softly let out a groan of complaint.

The soldier did not flinch nor move back, but his companions instantly raised their weapons and aimed them directly at Errol. The weapons in hand were all crossbows, charged and bolt-ready! My companions sat still on their mounts. The silence was only broken by the snorts of a couple of the horses. It seemed that time and movement stopped. Errol did not seem to take notice of the weapons focused on his chest. I turned from him and looked to the other three. Keven was not looking at anyone, but scanning across the field beyond the towers. His hands were folded on the pommel of his saddle. Karlyle was looking up. My eyes followed upward and saw for the first time a large number of arrows pointing at us from the tops of the two guard towers we were stopped under. These arrows were strung to longbows that were being aimed by steady looking arms. I then turned to face Ceikay only to find her looking at me.

"Steady, Beorn.," She said, smiling at my panicked expression.

Errol spoke again, "Did you not hear my query, or are the Duke's Personal Guards instructed to be rude?"

The soldier answered back, "Why you are trying to provoke us I do not know, nor do I care. I do not banter with fools who try to intimidate me or bluff their way into my Duke's city."

He paused and looked around to the rest of us, then spoke again. "Your question is reasonable, though. We do not normally close our city to travelers, but recent days are rife with unease and distrust. My Duke Hastid has been warned of travelers that would come to do harm in his realm. At this time we do not know much more than that, so we are forced to treat everyone with suspicion until we can discern true motives."

The officer paused, looked back to Errol and then continued. "Although I do not have to explain, nor apologize to you, I do so now to show you that conflict is not our desire. Please excuse me for my rudeness in stopping you, but my orders are specific and I am to use all force necessary if pressed. Be assured though, if conflict is your objective, I will make sure that your traveling ends here under these towers."

If the threat disturbed Errol, he did not show a response. However, he did acknowledge the apology. "Thank you for your answer to my question. It also answers my second question and I shall let it pass from us"

Errol now sat up a little straighter and called out. "We are emissaries of King Ballistor wishing to have an audience with Duke Hastid. We are also seeking to visit our Ambassador Shelaylan and give her the King's warmest regards."

The officer responded just as officially, "I am Captain Elexele of the Duke's Superior Guard. What are your names, and may I see your Seal?"

Errol reached into his tunic and pulled out a rolled and sealed parchment and handed it to Elexele. "You will notice the King's Royal Seal. I am Errol of the Northern Realm. My companions are Keven, Karlyle, Ceikay; also from the Northern Realm. We escort Beorn of Minoline. Beorn is to be the new Aide-de-Camp to Ambassador Shelaylan and will stay in Brentsad; with the Duke's consent of course."

I stared past Errol in stoic confusion, my eyes not daring to meet others. Elexele took the parchment and examined the wax seal that was the King's. He paused and seemed to be debating within himself on what to say. Finally he waved his left hand down to his knee. The guards behind him lowered their crossbows, but did not disarm, nor put them away.

"As I said before Errol, these are times of unease. It is not my position to tell you of recent events. The Duke, I am sure, will inform you of all important happenings here in Brentsad. Please allow me to escort you and your companions to the Keep. There you will be able to rest and freshen from your journey while you await the Duke's summons."

Elexele now pulled his horse back to the side and waved us through. His guards split to both sides and fell into a close 'escort' around us. Elexele then took the lead as Errol followed close behind. The rest of us followed. My horse automatically moved with the party as my mind was trying to comprehend the 'Aide-de-Camp' title that Errol had attached to me.

Also; what did he mean that I was to stay here in Brentsad?

...and the Ambassador falling to her death...did we not know that?

As we passed under the towers I dared not look up to see if arrows were still pointed at us. I did soon become aware of the present again though; now there were another twelve guards riding with us as we made our way into the town. When they joined our little band, I do not know.

The road branched off at different points and directions to become surrounded by various shops and houses mixed together. People were out in numbers doing what people do in towns and villages; walking, talking, shopping, visiting, and whatever other business made up their day. I cannot say that people were alarmed as we went by, but they did stare at us as we passed. It was clear that they were not at ease seeing our group ride through, closely guarded by a company of the Duke's Royal Guards. The town got denser as we rode further. Then we came upon a huge clearing that I suspected, and soon found to be true, was the center of the town of Brentsad. In the center of this clearing was the castle of Duke Hastid of the Realm of the Hastid Clan that rules the northeast part of Tavegnor.

I recalled reading in the archives that the family Hastid built this castle four hundred years ago. Although I had never before been to this realm, I knew the castle because of the drawings in the King's Royal Library at Talavor. Walls were not allowed by treaty to be built around towns, but castles…well…castles are a series of buildings connected by walls. Or else by definition they would not be castles?

So, Hastid Castle has walls a third as high as the ring of guard towers around the town. There are no openings in the walls. The road leading up to the castle travels under the wall. The road dips down sharply, and then rises sharply back up on the inner side of the wall into the castle courtyard. The portcullis, under the wall at the center point of the lowest part of the road, is cranked up into the wall by a ratchet and pulley system. It can be raised quickly, and lowered instantly in time of peril simply by releasing the ratchet. The portcullis is made up of thick oak and heavy vertical iron bars a full hand thick.

I easily saw the defensive advantages of this entrance. I would not want to be the one trying to breach it!

We entered through this depression and went straight to the Keep. Elexele held up his hand and the company quickly broke ranks and formed a gauntlet around us with horses and riders facing inward. We were channeled to, and stopped at, the double oak doors of the Keep.

Elexele dismounted and walked up to Errol. "Please leave your mounts with our pages and proceed into the Keep. I will report to the Duke of your arrival and you should be summoned to his presence shortly. My guards will accompany you to insure that nothing is lacking in our hospitality. I would not want you to think me…rude."

Captain Elexele bowed, then turned and disappeared around a corner.

"Quite a fall, or a push…"

I turned to Keven as he muttered under his breath and saw him looking up to the top of the Keep. It took me a moment to get what he meant: Ambassador Shelaylan.

I then followed my companions into the Keep. "Errol…" I tried to get his attention as soon as we entered.

Ceikay put a firm hand on my arm. "No questions now. Let us

quench our thirst on the fine wine that I am sure will be provided to us."

She then directed my attention to a serving table at the far end of the entrance near the huge stone fireplace. As I quickly walked over to the table to find a goblet and fill it, I noticed that Errol, Keven, and Karlyle had not moved to the fare. They were scanning the surroundings thoroughly…and silently. I decided that I should remain quiet for now. Soon though, my companions came to the table. All of us were sampling the wine, breads, and cheeses available on the table.

Nothing was said by the four after their scanning of the hall. Our escorts stood at attention near the entrance. They were fully armed, but no weapons were drawn or at the ready. I should say that the wine was surprisingly good, and the cheeses were aged and smoked deliciously. The breads were a little hard for my pleasure, but extremely flavorful. Savoring the meal eased my tension and I began to relax.

Then Errol spoke for the first time since the guard towers, "Ceikay, do you have thoughts on this fine hall and fare offered to us?"

"I am enjoying this fine table set for us. The wine I believe is from the southern Mariom region and quite lovely."

Keven held his goblet up as he spoke, "No, Ceikay, a red wine such as this can only come from a Halster vineyard. The coloring is the key…"

Karlyle then added his opinion, "I believe that it is a local wine, and if so, then we have indeed found a new source for the King's table."

Errol nodded, "Karlyle is on the mark. We should ask the Duke if this fine wine is available from his vineyards. I notice that Beorn likes the taste since he is enjoying his third goblet. Tell us your opinion if you would, sir."

Third goblet or not, I was still sharp enough to realize that we were now engaging in a conversation meant to go nowhere except to misdirect any ears that were possibly listening in. I also supposed that I knew why Errol started the conversation with the question directed at Ceikay. She did indeed sense hidden ears pointed our way.

So I joined in: "Thank you for asking. I do believe that…"

…and so our conversations went until early afternoon.

Eventually, Captain Elexele entered and conversation ended. "The Duke is ready to receive you now, if you would follow me."

He led us through a side entrance to the right of a large fireplace. We entered a long hallway that curved to the left. There were doors to the left and right as we walked, but none were open. Hallways branched off in both directions. Soon we came to a large set of double oak doors. Two burly armed guards stood in front of them.

At this point Elexele stopped, turned to us and spoke. "I would ask you to leave your weapons here before going in to have an audience with the Duke."

Errol looked at Elexele calmly and then responded, "We are emissaries of King Ballistor. Since when does a Duke disarm the King's representatives before granting an audience?"

"It is not my position to explain, only my duty to enforce my Lord's orders."

Ceikay spoke next, with a light grin. "If we do not honor your request, what will you do, Captain?"

"It is what I will not do, my lady."

Ceikay arched an eyebrow to encourage Elexele to continue. "I will not allow you see the Duke."

I stole a look at Keven and Karlyle. Karlyle's eyes were burning and directed toward the guards at the door. Keven seemed to have an amused grin while looking and picking at his fingernails.

After a long pause, Errol nodded at Elexele and began to disarm. The rest of us followed his lead. Once our swords, assorted daggers and a mix of other weapons were covering a table to our right, Captain Elexele smiled and nodded his head to Errol in a sort of silent 'Thank you.'

Elexele then raised his right hand and the two guards snapped to attention and immediately opened their half of the huge wooden doors. Our group passed through and into the Duke's Great Hall. The huge hall was over fifty paces long and about thirty paces wide. The wooden arched roof reached at least that high. The huge trusses that spanned the walls were covered in scroll-like carvings. The floor was polished stone, and a large walk-in stone fireplace stood at the center of each of the four walls. Each wall was covered in old tapestries that showed past notable events of the Hastid line, as is custom in each of the other Dukes' halls.

Toward the far end of the hall stood Duke Hastid. He stood alone, away from his entourage of advisors and attendants. He was of average height, and looked to be in firm condition. It was well known for him to be about fifty years of age, but he looked not yet forty. His brown hair and beard showed no sign of grey. He wore plain aqua-colored leggings and black riding boots. His tunic was the same aqua color and richly ordained with gold lace scrolls and designs. He wore an aqua colored band around his forehead. His hair was cut short, as was typical of a common soldier of the realm. He held in his hand the King's letter that Errol had given to Elexele earlier.

As we approached I could see his dark eyes studying each of us in turn. Guards from both sides of the room stepped forward to form another gauntlet. We passed through and were stopped about ten paces from the Duke by two pike-armed guards bringing their weapons around toward us.

Elexele continued past the pikes, turned to the left, and stood three paces from the Duke. He said nothing as he turned to face us, only gesturing to the guards to lower their pikes to the floor.

Errol ignored the two guards standing at our faces and spoke in an official tone, "King Ballistor bids me to thank you for your indulgence in seeing us today. He sends his warmest greetings and hopes that you and your family are well this day. He also prays that all is right and peaceful in your realm. He wishes for me to…"

Duke Hastid held up his hand to silence the standard, ritualized greeting, "I am fully aware of the King's well-wishing and concern. What is your purpose for this visit?"

If Errol was shaken or offended by the Duke's interruption, his face did not show it. "Your Lordship has the King's letter of introduction and purpose in your hand. Did you not read it?"

The guards all started at Errol's words. Elexele took a step forward.

Duke Hastid held his hand out and down to stop him, then spoke, "I see the good King sends me rudeness."

"I only respond in kind, your Lordship." Errol stood firm and tall. "The rudeness was yours; I speak for the King."

Duke Hastid's eyes bored into Errol's. "Distrust breeds rudeness, young man. You need to explain your reasons for being here. I need to explain nothing to you."

The Duke paused before continuing. "I choose to explain, though. Strange, unfortunate happenings have put me on guard and on edge. I like order and security in my realm, and when that is threatened, I will be...rude...if you will. It is my right and, more importantly, in my power to treat you as I see fit. The King be damned."

For the first time I felt the awful tension that I would eventually become familiar with, the tension of my four companions in real anger, and real danger.

The anger was in my companions. It was fear that washed through me. None of the 'Four' moved or said a word. Their eyes betrayed neither emotion nor action, but I sensed an almost overwhelming unifying force of frightening power run through our group.

I slowly looked around at the guards; they were visibly nervous...tense...

Finally Errol calmly spoke, "Is this the message you wish me to take back to my King?"

"You are not merely rude, you are impertinent. Are you also foolish?"

Errol answered the Duke's question with another question, "Do you feel safe enough to threaten the unarmed Emissaries of your King in your hall?"

The Duke growled threateningly, "I can guarantee you will not survive to leave this hall if you press my patience any further. What can you guarantee me, my young emissary?"

"One thing only..." Errol said calmly, yet firmly, "If you give the order to harm us, you will not live to see your order carried out.

66

That is my guarantee."

Elexele now drew his sword and stepped toward Errol.

"Stop! Hold your sword!" Duke Hastid yelled with a raised hand.

Aching silence now hung in the hall. No one moved nor breathed. I had never before felt physical tension to such a degree. Beads of sweat were forming on my brow, but I dared not wipe them away. Errol's body appeared calm and relaxed, but his eyes held a deadly stare at Duke Hastid. My other three companions slowly scanned the hall in all directions with their eyes. I saw no grins…only deadly determination.

Finally, slowly, the Duke spoke again to Errol. "No one has ever threatened me in my own hall before today. Be assured that I am not afraid of you or your threats. I surround myself with the best warriors in Tavegnor, and Elexele is among the greatest. If you were to attack, you would be dead before your first footfall toward me. It is clear that you want in diplomatic skills, so I will allow a bit of tolerance."

Errol stood in silence.

The Duke continued, "My reasons for rudeness are mine to reveal at my discretion, not at your demand. I now ask again, why are you here?"

Errol answered with no hint of timidity or apology in his tone, "We are here to deliver a message of well-being from King Ballistor and to introduce Ambassador Shelaylan to her new Aide-de-Camp, Beorn of Minoline."

Errol paused and looked from the left to the right, then spoke again, "Why is it that our Ambassador Shelaylan is not in this hall? It is customary for her to attend an Emissary's introductory visit, is it not?"

With no hesitation Duke Hastid answered flatly, "Ambassador Shelaylan is dead."

For the first time I saw surprise and alarm on Errol's face. I quickly looked around at the other three. They had stopped scanning the hall and were now all looking at the Duke with similar expressions.

I was now so confused that I must have had the same look.

Duke Hastid calmly looked at all of us in turn. I then realized that he was gauging our reactions to his announcement.

Errol, visibly shaken, held out a hand, palm up. "My Lord, may I ask for details?"

In response to Errol's sudden change of demeanor and sign of humility, Duke Hastid turned to a man standing back by the Duke's Throne Chair.

"Bring me the letter." Hastid ordered.

The man stepped forward and handed a piece of parchment to the Duke.

Hastid then turned back to address Errol. "This is my advisor Westal. He found this letter in Shelaylan's quarters after her death. It is in her handwriting and on her personal parchment.

"The words read, 'Because of my treachery I have compromised my King and Tavegnor. I am not fit to face ordered justice so must end my life in shame. It is the only way. Please forgive me'."

Hastid paused, and then looked up at Errol. "Ambassador Shelaylan jumped from the top of my Keep. The treachery she wrote of I do not have knowledge of, but I will discover the truth ere long. Advisor Westal has also uncovered word that Shelaylan secretly sent for four of her cohorts before she had a change of...heart. I have shut down travel from my city in order to more easily track new arrivals. The four of you plus the new 'Aide-de-Camp' are my only new arrivals."

The Duke looked at each of us in turn before continuing, "Do you now see why I am so wary of you?"

Errol responded, "The King's Seal shows that we come at his orders, not at Ambassador Shelaylan's request."

"And that is why you are not at this moment down in my cellars being questioned, my young warrior captain. The King's Seal is your only protection at the moment."

More words were traded between the two, but I cannot tell you what they were, because I happened to glance for the first time at the Duke's Advisor and was jolted to attention. I had seen him before.

My mind raced trying to untangle the thoughts rushing through me. Could this be a twin? How could this man be one and the same? How could he get here ahead of us? He cannot be the same man.

"Beorn of Minoline...!"

I started at my name and looked up to see Duke Hastid glaring at me. Everyone seemed now to be staring at me in expectation.

"I beg humble pardon, your Lordship, I did not hear you address me."

"If you are an Aide-de-Camp, then your inattention is a dire flaw. I asked if you knew the Ambassador."

"No, m'Lord."

The Duke continued to look into my eyes as he spoke, "Short answer you give. Can you elaborate by giving me details of your personal history?"

"What specifically would you like to know, m'Lord?"

With a big sigh, Duke Hastid shook his head. "Your personal history if you will..."

Without thinking of the consequences I asked a question of my own. "How long has your Advisor Westal been in your service?"

Now I again saw surprise on my companion's faces.

The Duke showed surprise at first, then his face turned red with anger. He now spoke softly to no one in particular as he looked up, "Is this whole party trying to goad me into losing my patience altogether?!"

I stole a glance at Westal. Our eyes locked. He was looking at me with a new and alarming glare.

Duke Hastid spoke to me again, "Why, Beorn of Minoline, do you ask that of my Advisor?"

I dared not look at my companions. I took a deep breath, and then answered the Duke. "When my King Ballistor commanded me to serve under Ambassador Shelaylan, I took it upon myself to become familiar with your realm. I went to the Grand Library at Talavor to get facts, historic and personal. Your staff is listed in full, as are all the Dukes of Tavegnor. Advisor Westal is not listed."

I did speak the truth about the Grand Library, but my true reason for speaking out about Advisor Westal I kept to myself.

The Duke paused before speaking. "I no longer know what to

do with all of you. I tire of this game. It is certain that if I begin to ask questions of the other three, I will meet with the same frustration..."

After another long spell of silence the Duke spoke again. "I will draft a letter to King Ballistor. You will take it to him and also deliver the ashes of your Ambassador back to Talavor. At tomorrow's sunrise you will leave Brentsad. In addition to her ashes you will carry Ambassador Shelaylan's personal possessions. We have quarters in my castle for you. If you accept them, know that you will be heavily guarded during your night's stay. If you wish to find your own lodgings at one of the Inns, then know that you will be heavily guarded there also."

"Is it possible for us to see the Ambassador's quarters and belongings before we are assigned to our lodgings?" Errol asked.

"Her quarters have been cleared of everything and her belongings are already packed on a wagon for travel back to Talavor."

"Then may we question her staff and servants?"

"Two of her staff committed suicide upon hearing of her treachery. The rest have vanished. A search is being conducted as we speak. Now, once more I ask, have you made your choice of lodgings?"

To my surprise Errol accepted the offer of the Castle's quarters.

Soon we were being led by Elexele and his guards out of the hall. As I glanced back over my shoulder I saw Duke Hastid looking at us as we walked away. Advisor Westal was whispering into the Duke's ear. It seemed to me that Westal was still glaring at me. We were allowed to retrieve our weapons outside the Duke's hall. No one spoke as we were led through the passages to our quarters for the night.

Elexele broke the silence as we entered our rooms. "Everything you need for the night will be made available for you. Lady Ceikay, your bed is in a separate room behind the tapestry on the west wall. Linens and chamber pots are to the left of the fireplace. Food and drink will be sent shortly. You will have no need to leave these quarters until the Duke sends for you tomorrow morn. Guards will be outside your door for your protection."

"Your guard for our protection is it?" Keven asked with a slight grin.

Elexele glanced sideways at Keven, but did not respond with words.

Once again I was nervous. I noticed that Karlyle was watching the guards standing back at the door; their swords were half drawn. I looked to see Errol facing Elexele. Then with a sigh and a formal nod to Errol, Elexele turned and walked out of our rooms. The guards followed and shut the double doors as they left.

We were alone for the first time since coming to Brentsad. I remained silent, waiting for someone to speak first. Ceikay began to circle the large room. I surmised that she was scanning for listeners behind walls. After a couple of circuits she stopped in front of us and looked at the door where we knew the guards were on the other side.

Then, with her head tilted down to the floor, she stepped in front of Errol. After a long pause she looked directly at Errol. Suddenly her foot shot out and smashed hard into his shin.

"OWWW," Errol winced, "What was THAT for!?"

"You put us in danger back there! Do you know what the word tact is? Have you ever heard of the word? Did you not bring your mind with you today? Are you..."

"Hold there, gentle lady!" Keven laughed, "let us hear what Errol has to say before you pummel him with any more words and kicks!"

Errol sat down at the large wooden table in the middle of the room, rubbing his shin. He motioned to Karlyle who stepped to the table. Keven and Ceikay did the same. I followed. Karlyle closed his eyes held his breath.

Suddenly, we were swallowed in a vortex of air! It spun around us and the table. It was like a wind devil that you see on a blistery hot day, dusty, loud, and gyrating out of control. It remained steady but did not suck up any debris and carry it along. I can only describe it as a wind tunnel...and we were inside its quiet center!

Errol now spoke in a normal tone. "You might think that I may have gone too far with my words, but I did not come to Brentsad to

71

be talked down to by anyone; and it should be obvious why I had to talk to the Duke in an offensive manner."

Keven sat down at the table next to Errol and chuckled, "Well, my leader, good that it was obvious to you. And did you only say, offensive manner? I wish to toss in the word dangerous."

Errol frowned. "Perhaps next time you can be the messenger Keven. You seem to have found amusement in the meeting."

"More of a show than a meeting," drawled Karlyle.

Ceikay added her agreement, "You are right in that regard. It was a show, and everyone was watching us!"

"I know I was right," Errol sighed. "Think about how we have been treated since we entered Brentsad: The welcoming escort we received at the towers; the long wait with the guards before seeing the Duke; being disarmed before entering the Duke's hall, and Duke Hastid interrupting me when I began to speak."

Errol looked at each of us in turn before continuing. "This was a not too subtle 'show' to test who we were and what our intentions were. Duke Hastid wished to see our reactions to all this discourtesy. If I had responded with sugary diplomacy, he would decide that we were either stupid or lying. I responded by confronting and threatening him in his own hall. Now, he may still think we are dim-witted, but he cannot guess if we are lying. Confrontation was the last thing he expected, because it obviously was not to our benefit. Spies usually act to their best interests by avoiding conflict…."

Karlyle sat down next and spoke, "So you are saying that you were under absolute, control at all times in the Duke's hall?"

Errol answered simply, "You have never seen me otherwise."

Keven spoke again, "I am not sure I agree with your reasoning, Errol, but it will not serve us to argue this matter any further. We should speak of developments. We received a grim surprise concerning Ambassador Shelaylan's letter of confession. That letter is obviously a fabrication. We are unable to get information from any of her staff; and her quarters and belongings were evidently searched by the Duke before we ever got here. What is our next step?"

Errol answered, "I fear we are at a slow and unfruitful end here

72

in Brentsad. Whoever is behind this has made sure that their plans are well designed and well under way. Our Ambassador was murdered to quiet her tongue. Evidence was laid out to convict and discredit her. Shelaylan's staff and personal servants have conveniently disappeared. Word was put out that fellow conspirators were on their way to Brentsad. It appears by plan that we are the 'conspirators.' Our words and motives are now suspect.

"Now that we have been compromised, Duke Hastid will not listen to us. Nor will he allow us to roam freely about his castle or city to gather information. Our mission as ordered by the King was to meet with Ambassador Shelaylan to learn of her discoveries and concerns. That is no longer possible. As I see it, our next step is to escort the Ambassador's remains back to Talavor as Duke Hastid has directed. When we return to Talavor we will report to King Ballistor on our findings, or rather, Beorn will report for us."

I quickly corrected Errol, "King Ballistor is in Hirst at this moment, not Talavor…"

With that, Keven turned to me. "You, sir, did well in front of the Duke. I was impressed by the way you sidestepped his question. Your memory serves you well regarding Advisor Westal."

"When did you review Hastid's realm?" Karlyle asked.

I paused a moment before answering, "Remember my participation in helping Duke Jaramas with a very sensitive matter?"

They all nodded. "Well, my timing of research was a bit misleading. Two seasons ago I began to write down some of the history of it. Not to publish or reveal it, though. I had Duke Jaramas' permission to record it for his access only. I went to Talavor's Library of Official Persons and Notables to insure accuracy. While there, I glanced through all of the realms, just to satisfy my curiosity."

"Good fortune that you did that," Keven smiled, "and quick-witted to set Duke Hastid off balance."

I looked at them in turn, "Well, yes, sort of, well…no…not in truth…"

They looked at me with expressions that invited me to continue. "My question to the Duke was not a clever diversion. I blurted it out from shock really. You see, Advisor Westal was one of the guards at the Boar's Hind Inn."

Errol sat forward with a sudden hard look on his face. I saw the others' looks. They were not different from Errol's.

I continued, "Westal was the bearded guard to the left of the leader at the Inn."

"Tell us how you can be so sure. " Errol pressed.

Karlyle leaned forward, "Westal has no beard, but you say at the Inn this man did."

I continued again, "Westal is clearly one of the guards. The beard is gone but not the pale skin where the beard used to be. The index finger on the right hand is cut exactly at the same first knuckle on both men. The shape of the head is exactly the same. Every persons' earlobes are unique in appearance and the earlobes on Westal and the guard match."

I closed my eyes to better study the 'picture' of the two men in my head.

"Both men have the same sneer with the left side of the upper lip curling up. Both men have a lazy eye; the right eye is slow to follow when the head turns. I was sure the two are the same, but the final proof was when I broke out with my question. Westal's glare was full of hate; exactly as was the guard's at Boar's Hind Inn. Their expressions are identical."

The silence after I stopped was long. No one moved nor spoke.

Finally, Errol got up and looked in the direction of the hall, "Beorn has given us our first direction in solving this mystery. We now can plan our…"

Ceikay suddenly held up her hand, and Errol stopped talking. She nodded to the door. Errol nodded to Karlyle and the vortex around us abruptly stopped. A knock at the doors broke the momentary silence.

Keven walked over to the doors and chimed, "Who may we ask is calling on us?"

Without answer the doors were suddenly opened and trays of hot food and cold ale were brought in by four servants. A man followed immediately behind. By the way he walked and was dressed I could see that he was a royal cook to the Duke.

"Who is it? Who is it you ask!? I am Dailus, Duke Hastid's personal cook. I stand in no hallway begging to be let in. If you would not want to go hungry, then you will treat me with the respect that all great artists should command! Do you want this feast or not?"

Keven backed away from the door and held up his hands in mock surrender. "Please, I will not toy with you Sir Dailus. Your food will be gratefully appreciated by all of us tonight. Even in Talavor your name is legend in the kitchens of the King!"

I could see that this had a great affect on Dailus. He puffed out his chest and proceeded to direct the servants in the placing of the trays on our table. After Dailus was satisfied that everything was in order, he ushered his servants out as fast as they had first come through the door.

Our guards shut the doors behind them once again. This time I looked at Ceikay waiting for her report. I was beginning to learn their routine, so I kept silent.

"Dailus is genuine and there is no guile in his thoughts. He would not sabotage his food to harm us."

Then Karlyle spoke, "I sense no manipulations in the food, or the ale..."

Then to my further surprise, Keven spoke. "There are no poisons in the food and wine. The smells are consistent with what is served."

Errol sat down and waved for us to join him. "At least the Duke has not decided to do away with us through his cook."

Nothing more was said while we ate our supper. I had not realized how empty my stomach had become, and I certainly ate my share. At the end of the meal, Errol called for another talk in the vortex. We discussed, or rather they discussed, while I listened, the problem of Westal and what to do about him. It was agreed that he would need to be talked to somehow. Different options and ideas were deliberated, but I was tiring at this point, so did not pay much heed to what was being said.

Finally, Errol suggested that we bed down for the night and let sleep take over to develop ideas for the morn. I chose the cot in the corner and headed for it. I think I was asleep before I realized I was lying down. No ideas came to me that night.

I awoke in the room behind the tapestry. Once again I sat up confused and disoriented.

Then Ceikay called from the other side of the tapestry, "Welcome to the morning, Beorn! Come join us for some charrol-bean tea, fresh hen's eggs, and delicious scones. Good Dailus has sent us food to break our fast!"

As I got up and lifted the tapestry I suspected why I was in the separate room, but I had to ask. I walked over to the table to join my four companions who were already dressed and washed for the day. "How did I get into the other room?"

"You were put there." Ceikay answered.

"Why?" I asked.

"Because you snore," Keven said without looking up.

My frown was obvious to the others.

"Please," Ceikay said, "we are not teasing you. We are simply telling truth."

Inside I knew that to be true, but some morns I do get short-edged. I left the others to wash up in the water closet. After my traveling bath, soldiers call it a spit-bath or short-bath, I returned to the table still in illtemper.

Childishly, I wanted to put any or all of them on the defense, "Has anyone thought to look to our horses and their care?"

Karlyle looked at me with a raised eyebrow. Errol smiled but did not answer.

Ceikay looked at Keven and addressed him, "Whose turn is it to care for the horses?"

"Why, Beorn's of course," he answered.

I just shook my head and gritted my teeth.

Keven now turned to me with a smile, "Beorn, our horses are in fine care in the Duke's stables. One thing about Duke Hastid; He is renowned for his love of horses. No matter what he may think of us, he will not let our horses be neglected under his charge.

Moreover, lest you forget my talent, Bard, I would immediately know if our steeds were in danger or neglected in any way. What I say to you now, do not forget: I will never allow anyone to harm or neglect our steeds."

Keven's smile vanished as he continued, "I have the capability to instantly respond as necessary to protect them. Besides, it was not us who forgot about our horses; it was you until this moment. So do not try to put me on the defensive again."

As I looked back at Keven, I realized for the first time that under the relaxed and jesting attitude, the Beast-master was a deadly serious advocate for his charges. I also realized that people tended to underestimate Keven, and that he probably liked it that way.

Errol brought me back from my meditations. "Eat if you can Beorn. Once we begin the day's journey our time for meals may be scarce indeed."

My mood was much improved after tea and scones. No one said anything of importance as we gathered our packs and made ready to leave.

"When does the Duke send for us?" I asked.

"Now, I believe." Errol answered as he stepped to the doors and swung them open. What happened next was all a blur to me at the time. Later, when I had time to recall the events in my head, did I see the details. The guards in the hall jumped in surprise and leveled their weapons directly at Errol. "Hold!" One of the guards yelled as they each prodded a six foot pike at Errol's chest. In a blink of an eye I saw the two guards thrown past Errol and into our room! Errol spun back around to face them as they flew through the air. He had the two pikes in his hands. It was all so fast that I had not seen Errol grab the two hapless guards!

As they flew into the room, Keven and Karlyle both sprung forward to meet the hapless men. Before I could see how it happened, both guards were face-down on the floor with their arms pinned behind their backs! A knee was pressed into each of their necks.

Ceikay hadn't moved. She was looking beyond Errol and into the passageway. I knew that she was 'listening' for more guards. Suddenly she turned around and pointed to one of the tapestries, "There, the shield of the mounted knight!"

Instantly the left arm of Errol launched a pike into the shield on the tapestry! It stuck through on what sounded like wood. A sharp cry, more like a yelp, rang out. Then the muffled sound of running feet behind the wall.

Ceikay yelled out again, "They will be coming now!"

Errol turned to Keven and Karlyle, "Let them rise."

The two guards were released but they did not move from the floor.

"You two are free to go," Errol said to them. "Tell Elexele we are ready for the Duke's release to return to Talavor. We wish to depart now."

Karlyle and Keven picked the two guards up and led them to the doors. To our surprise the two guards turned around at the doors and drew their swords!

One of them spoke, "You have proven that you are able to kill us if you so desire, but our orders are to keep you in these rooms. Our Captain has given us charge to stop you if we can. We stand here ready for you if you attempt to leave."

"You are willing to die then?" Errol asked.

The second guard answered, "One must never be willing to die. One must be willing to do one's duty unto death."

Silence met the man's words.

Finally, Errol dropped the pike in his hand. "Well spoken. We will not go through you. Our watcher in the tapestry has assured that Elexele is on his way. Our point has already been made."

At that moment, footfalls were heard coming swiftly down the passageway. The two guards at the door snapped to attention and swung to the side. Elexele strode into our room. His sword was still sheathed. Behind him a dozen guards took up space blocking the entrance. Errol and Elexele stood opposite each other, neither moved.

Finally Elexele folded his arms and spoke, "What is it you are trying to accomplish?"

Errol crossed his arms in the same manner before answering, "We are weary of your confinement, and we are weary of your spying. Tell your Duke that we wish to be on our way to Talavor…his hospitality is lacking."

"My guards have never been asked to spy. You slight them as

well as me. Should I draw my sword or will you explain to me your words of insult?"

Errol gestured back toward the tapestry. "Do you see the pike in the wall behind me?" Elexele looked up at the tapestry. For a brief moment I thought I saw a look of surprise cross his face. He said nothing as he turned back to Errol.

Errol continued, "That pike frightened away a listener in the wall. Someone who had a keen interest in what we might be saying in the privacy of our quarters."

With his eyes still on Errol, Elexele called over his shoulder, "Take that pike and tapestry down! I would look at that wall!"

Four of his guards stepped forward as ordered. Moments later Elexele was at the wall inspecting a boarded-up window that was, until now, concealed by the tapestry. The pike thrown by Errol had penetrated about a foot's length below what was obviously a listening hole!

Elexele turned to one of his officers blocking the door. "Break this open and follow it to its end. I want its source. Officer Bonnic, you will direct this task and report everything to me...to me alone. Do you understand?"

The junior officer quickly stepped forward, "Understood Sir!" He then ushered several guards into action.

Elexele now walked up to Errol. "On my honor, this was not known to me. I will do all in my power to find the listener."

Errol did not seem to be appeased by Elexele's words. "If you were not responsible for the listener, then how is it that you knew to come running with your guards?"

To my surprise, Elexele smiled. "A good and wise Captain-of-the-Guard always places extra guards at the end of each passageway. The moment you opened the door, one of those guards was running to me. Trust me when I say this, I was never at any time far from your quarters."

Errol looked directly into Elexele's eyes. "If not you then, shall I suspect Duke Hastid?"

"My honor is rooted in Duke Hastid's honor. I would not serve a dishonorable man. I swear to you that he did not order this."

Errol glanced back at Ceikay. She nodded once.

Errol then turned back to the Captain. "My companions and I have been treated with suspicion by your Duke. I am not easily convinced by your declaration of his truthfulness and honor."

Elexele answered firmly, "Duke Hastid is dealing with treachery in his city. He has a responsibility to his subjects, not to you. He has a right to treat you as suspects if evidence warrants it."

Errol took one step toward Elexele. "We have the right to leave Brentsad, or does your Duke choose to hold us?"

Standing firm, Captain Elexele calmly began to answer, "I can request audience with Duke Hastid to ask him on your behalf. I will return with an…"

"No!" Errol interrupted, "That is not good enough." The guards at the wall stopped and faced Errol. The rest at the door tensed and held swords out.

Errol sighed and continued in a softened tone, "Elexele, I pledge you my word and my honor that we mean no harm to your Duke or your realm. Please permit us to go to our horses and prepare for travel to Talavor. We will deliver Duke Hastid's sealed letter and Ambassador Shelaylan's remains as the Duke desires."

The room was still after Errol's unexpected plea… Finally, Elexele turned to address his guards. "Escort these travelers to the stables and have the pages assist them for their journey."

He turned back to Errol. "I am sure that Duke Hastid has finished the letter to King Ballistor. The next time you see me will be in the courtyard. I will have your release to go."

With that, Elexele turned and left the room. Half of the guards went with him. The rest separated and made a path for us.

An officer stepped forward and addressed us, "If you are ready, we will escort you to the stables."

Soon we were on saddled horses waiting for Elexele. We did not have to wait long. He came with a sealed letter and orders for our return to Talavor. The wagon containing Ambassador Shelaylans's property and ashes was brought to us. Two wagoneers were to travel with us. They were to be responsible for the wagon and the two horses pulling it. After delivering the property to Talavor, they were to return to Brentsad.

Ceikay discreetly probed them, and found them to be simple servants of the Duke who would complete their orders faithfully.

Elexele approached Errol and handed him the Duke's letter. "Duke Hastid bids me to release you to Talavor. Give this letter to King Ballistor. It explains what has happened here in Brentsad."

Then Elexele addressed the rest of us. "I regret that your brief stay in Brentsad was not…pleasant. God grant you speed and safety. If we meet again, may it be on better terms."

Elexele turned and bowed directly to Ceikay. He then turned from us and left the courtyard. A full company of The Duke's personal guard escorted us and the wagon to the river bridge.

My first visit to Brentsad was over, and I had not the opportunity to see the city.

Once across the bridge our escort turned their horses, and without farewell, galloped back to Brentsad.

Errol then announced that we would separate from the wagon. He pointed out that speed was not possible with a wagon as traveling companion. The wagoneers were ordered to continue to Talavor and report to the King's Steward.

Errol also directed that we were to ride in haste to Hirst, Duke Rasher's Castle city. The Annual Trade Meeting traditionally spans twelve days, so we knew that King Ballistor would still be found there.

I will not tell the whole tale of that ride to Hirst. For this telling, the first night will be described. It was during this night that I began getting at ease with my four companions.

After we left the wagon behind, the travel was swift but not hurried. We kept a pace for the horses that would not wear them out. We did not stop for a mid-meal, but ate jerky as we rode. It was not until well after the daylight was gone and the stars blanketed the sky that we stopped for sleep. We each rubbed our own horse down before laying out our bedrolls. Karlyle made a warm fire that lit up our little clearing. It was then I saw the crows again sitting in the trees, watching over us.

I was just lying down next to the fire when Ceikay addressed me, "Do you not have questions for us?"

"Why do you think that I have questions?"

"You usually do."

"You make getting the answers tiring. I am already tired tonight."

For several moments no one spoke. Finally, Karlyle offered, "You feel like you were left in the dark back there in Duke Hastid's hall, do you not?"

I was surprised enough to lean up on my elbow. "Yes…yes I was, as you say, 'left in the dark.' It was obvious that you 'Four' had prepared for the meeting. You deliberately misled Duke Hastid about your knowledge of Ambassador Shelaylan's death, and you had this story ready that I was to be the Ambassador's Aide-de-Camp. I would have certainly felt better had I been let in on the subterfuge."

Keven just shook his head and grinned.

Errol then spoke, "We are sorry for deceiving you. Yes, we deliberately left you out of our plans concerning the meeting with the Duke. Let me explain why, It is obvious that you do not forget details and events, but you may not always remember arrangements."

I silently waited for him to continue.

"By arrangements, I mean specifically the arrangement and makeup of the people in the hall. Remember that each Duke has a Truth Diviner at his service. We knew that Duke Hastid would surely have this advisor in the hall when we were brought to him. The Duke was ready to test all of us, including you.

What I tell you now, only the King knows; we four can fool a Truth Diviner. Ceikay has developed her talent to a point that she can mask her motives and emotions from any Mind Listener or Truth Diviner. Her close relationship with us is such that she can shield us also.

Because of Ambassador Shelaylan's letter to the King this last fortnight, Duke Hastid is suspect in some plot or scheme we have yet to uncover. We had to mislead the Duke; hence the lies.

You, though, do not have a trained mind that can shield you from a Truth Diviner, and Ceikay is not yet able to shield you. Therefore, you had to remain uninformed. You see, the Truth Diviner would only read you as a low-level servant that was confused and disturbed at what was going on around you. You were not to be in on our lies. Therefore, you would not give up lying thoughts to the Diviner."

Ceikay spoke up, "Believe that we are truly concerned for your safety and welfare, Beorn. Please remember, we have vowed to protect you."

Then she smiled and continued, "…And I promise that I will teach you mind shields that will protect you in the future!"

Thinking on their words I saw the logic. Finally I smiled, "Very well then, I am satisfied with that account. Now, since you have encouraged me to ask questions tonight, explain the commotion with the tapestry, and why you chose a conflict with the guards, and why you decided not to make an issue of Duke Hastid's Advisor/Guard that I recognized, and why you made no attempt to find and question any of the Ambassador's staff, and why you left the wagon to go on its way without even looking through the Ambassador's belongings for any clues or anything that might have helped us in…"

"Oh by the gods! Stop now!" Errol put his two hands out as to halt me. "Beorn, I hereby swear to you that we will keep you advised of our strategies from this time onward! You are the most detailistic person I have ever known!"

Keven chimed in with his usual grin, "I do not think 'detailistic' is a word, Errol."

Errol ignored Keven and continued with me. "I will answer your questions one at a time, starting with your last one. The personal effects of the Ambassador would not tell us anything. Her letter of confession was found in her rooms by Advisor Westal. So that letter, which was obviously forged to frame her, was placed in her rooms by someone who would surely search her belongings to take away anything that might have helped clear her, let alone reveal a sinister plot.

As for questioning the Ambassador's staff, you remember of course, the Duke saying that they were nowhere to be found and that he was searching for them himself. We had no chance of searching for them since we ourselves were being watched. They have either been killed, fled the city, or have gone into deep hiding somewhere in the city. It was pointless to try to find them. Hopefully, some of the staff or servants of Ambassador Shelaylan will make it to Talavor soon and reveal themselves when they feel it is safe.

As for the confrontation with the guards; it was imperative that we get out of Brentsad as soon as possible. By breaching the door we got the attention of someone who had the authority to send us on our way, Captain Elexele."

"Why Elexele and not Duke Hastid?" I asked.

Errol now turned to Keven, "Keven, do you want to answer Beorn on this?"

Keven nodded, and then responded, "I learned that Duke Hastid left the castle before light this morning. Advisor Westal was with him. Where they were set to travel is unknown to me."

Keven quickly held his hand up to halt my next question. "Before you open your mouth to ask, I will explain: I have the capability to see through my horse's eyes. We have a bond in which he trusts me to use his sight. That is part of my talent with the animal world. I cannot enter all animal minds, only those who trust me absolutely allow it. That is because the animal is essentially blind once I enter its mind and take over.

"Early this morn I asked Hell'sfire, my horse's human name, for access. He allowed me to scan the stables. We wanted to be alert for anyone who would prepare to leave the city. Through Hell'sfire's eyes I saw Duke Hastid, his Advisor Westal, and a number of others mount horses prepared by their pages. They were packed for extended travel. Sound is not yet one of my capabilities, so I cannot hear conversations. Where they are traveling to, we do not know, but my hawks will hopefully soon tell me."

Errol stepped in. "So you see, we knew that Duke Hastid had left the castle earlier this morning. We waited for several hours for word of our release. We knew that Elexele had direct orders of some sort concerning us, so when we decided that we had waited long enough, we threw some guards around for the purpose of summoning Elexele."

I cut in at this point, "So Elexele lied to us about seeing the

Duke for the letter…"

Karlyle now spoke, "Do you remember Elexele's words? He did not lie to us."

At Karlyle's urging I thought back. I recalled Elexele's words: 'I am sure that Duke Hastid has finished the letter to King Ballistor. The next time you see me will be in the courtyard. I will have your release to go.'

Karlyle finished his point, "Captain Elexele never said anything about seeing the Duke or that the Duke was near or gone."

Errol then began again, "As for your first question, the tapestry. Ceikay felt a presence move in. When this person crept behind the tapestry through some hidden passageway, Ceikay was able to sense the intrusion of a trained listener. It soon became clear to Ceikay that whoever was listening in on us did not have kind intentions toward us. Ceikay then hand-signaled to the rest of us to be careful and alert. And through our hand signals we agreed it was finally time to create a commotion and leave the castle."

I held my hand up, but before I could speak Keven stopped me, "Yes, Beorn, before you ask, I promise that I will take it upon myself to teach you our hand signals."

I lay by the fire for several moments absorbing what they all were telling me.

Finally I turned to Karlyle, "Well, good magician, everyone else promised me something. What about you?"

Without hesitation Karlyle answered without looking at me, "I promise, if you ask one more question tonight, I will make a needle appear out of thin air to pull a thick thread of hemp through your lips and permanently seal your mouth off for all eternity…"

That night I had a good night's sleep, and from the next morning on, my relationship with the 'Four' was much improved. They were true to their words; each day as we traveled they took turns teaching me some of their secret signals.

Hirst

I will not dwell on the City of Kint. It is a typical town just east of the Tellis mountain range. We did not stop at an Inn for the night. We traveled through without even a nod from the city guards.

We soon came to Talavor Road, which parallels Telmar River.

At first sight of the road I thought of its name: Talavor was the name of the first great King who conquered and united the whole continent of Tavegnor. His wife was named Telmar. Talavor was also the one who first separated the land into seven territories, or realms as they are called now. Seven realms, because he had six generals that he wished to reward. King Talavor deemed that he should rule one realm, and his six trusted generals would rule their own.

We traveled with purpose to the city of Hirst. I had been to Hirst several times before this journey, and remembered it to be a busy trading hub for all of Tavegnor. The road we now traveled south on was well traveled and well-populated. Merchants of all kinds were to be seen.

We stopped at one Inn while in route, Wheatbasket Inn. It was a dirty, ugly hostel that had no proper bedding, no fine foodstuff, and no ale of any decent quality to offer a weary traveler.

Even a traveling Bard looked to better lodgings…

As we approached Hirst from the north we could see towers circling the city. These towers were similar to the towers of Brentsad. In truth, they looked to have been constructed by the same masons. The only difference was the rope bridges that connected each one. Some call them catwalks; parallel ropes strung across to each tower with wooden planks tied off below as a path to walk on.

Even before we reached the towers we began to pass various encampments of all sorts and sizes on each side of the road. Our road led us past these campsites, under the towers, and into the streets. Besides the camps, the major difference that we first noticed from Brentsad was the number of people on the road in and out of the city. Unlike Brentsad, travel in the city of Hirst was not restricted. Also, during the time of the yearly trade gathering, the host city is always crowded with thousands of visiting merchants, tradesmen, and patrons from every realm. Along with these extra citizens are the Dukes' Personal Guards and assorted entourages. I had been to several other trade gatherings before this year and the crowds were the same as the one we were walking into this day, loud and seemingly alive as one mammoth undulating creature!

Once in the city, the road turned to the right and began to spiral inward between houses and shops. Only one road served the whole city of Hirst, this one we were traveling on. The buildings we passed were all built of the same granite of the towers. The structures were joined together to form blocks of ten units. Between these groups of buildings were narrow alleyways barely wide enough for a person to walk through. After every four sets of block buildings the alleyways widened enough to allow a wagon to pass through to the next inner spiral.

Eventually we found ourselves facing the castle at the center of the city. Duke Rasher's castle was a double-walled fortress that dwarfed everything else in Hirst. Normally Duke Rasher's own flag flew atop the keep. This day the flag of King Ballistor flew; as was custom when the king was visiting.

Standing at the open entrance of the castle stood a tall soldier.

He wore the uniform of the King's Honor Guard. By his insignia and ribbons, I could see that he was high in rank. Behind him, standing at attention, stood four junior officers. Like their superior's, the four soldier's uniforms were well tailored and looked to be new. Obviously, the King's Guard was at their best for this trip.

As we approached and stopped, Errol held up his arm in greeting. "Hail good Officer, you look like a pigeon dressed up for supper. Or should I say trussed up?"

The recipient of those words spoke in a stern and threatening tone, "Change your insolent tongue or I will have it cut out of your mouth and handed back to you!"

Ceikay then stepped directly up to the officer, "Men who dress up as pretty as you do surely cannot be warriors. Are you part of the Royal Dance Group? Are you here to put forth entertainment for us?"

The officer looked down at Ceikay for a moment before saying anything, then shook his head and responded, "My lovely Ceikay, I can handle those other three wretches that you travel with, but you always disarm me with your sweet and flattering words. I surrender to you. Please spare me and my men."

Then Keven spoke up, "You surrender not because of her words; you realized that you allowed her to get close enough to your unprotected shin…"

Suddenly the officer laughed and nimbly jumped back out of range from a possible kick.

Karlyle then called out, "Your reflexes are still impressive, old man!"

The officer answered Karlyle's remark with a raised eyebrow and a friendly grin.

He then turned to me, "You must be Beorn. I am Commander Velstor in command of the King's Personal Guard. I truly regret your fate; to have to be in company with these three excuses for men. You must have greatly angered the gods to suffer this indignity! Your only boon is the beautiful young lady who dains to ride with the rest!"

"Beware Commander Velstor…" Errol spoke in dire tones,

"We have begun to train him in our habits."

Velstor then threw up his arms in obvious desperation. "Then this man is truly lost to any chance of redemption!"

Then Errol spoke again, changing the tone and the subject of our conversation. "Velstor, it is good to see you are well. We wish to see King Ballistor and beg you for an early audience. We have dire news of Ambassador Shelaylan."

"You must not say another word, Errol," Commander Velstor responded in hushed tones. "We know of her fate, but we will not speak of it here. You were seen from the towers as you entered the city. Our King sent me to meet you. He is impatient to hear of your visit to Duke Hastid. I will escort you to your chambers where you can freshen and change out of traveling clothes. Please, not another word of this before you report to the King."

He then turned and led us into the castle.

Duke Rasher's castle is a concentric, circular double-walled edifice. The outer wall is as high as Duke Hastid's castle wall. The inner wall is another five spans higher. Between the two walls is a grassy bailey twenty paces wide. Coming in from the outer gate the roadway turns left between these two walls and ends at the gate of the inner wall twenty strides distant. Once past this gate we entered the inner ward. It was awash with tents and banners of each of the Dukes' traveling entourage.

I noticed that Duke Hastid's banner was not displayed.

A number of people in the square called out greetings to my companions as we headed for the castle Keep. The four waved in acknowledgement but did not stop to exchange words. Once inside we were each taken to separate chambers. In mine a warm bath was waiting for me. I was sure my companions were met with the same.

After my rare and long soak, a servant arrived with a new set of clothes. She informed me that the others were in the adjoining room awaiting my company. I quickly dressed and pulled my now clean hair back, then went to join my companions.

As I left my room and entered the passageway, three monks clothed in hooded tan robes walked past me. They all silently nodded in my direction and smiled. They continued down the hall and around the corner. I assumed that they were visitors from the Bristin Monastery nearby. Several other castle citizens also passed as I was led through the halls, all smiled warm greetings.

The servant girl had told me the door to my companions was to the left. I entered and was met by an appetizing aroma that woke my hunger. My four companions were standing by the serving tables examining the food. They were dressed in clean and simple outfits decorated in the King's colors.

Commander Velstor was with them and talking in low tones to Errol. Errol was saying nothing, but nodding his head in response to what the officer was offering.

At my entrance, everyone greeted me. Then Velstor declared that the time for eating had begun. During our meal I said little. I listened to the others and surmised that the Commander and the 'Four' knew each other quite well, and that a long friendship connected them. Velstor asked about their home village and asked after the welfare of various individuals.

As I sat amongst my companions I was disturbed to realize that in these last days, I had not even considered asking my companions any sorts of personal questions.

This night I found out that Errol, Keven, Karlyle, and Ceikay were all from Bresk in the northern realm of Ballistor. Bresk is a village hidden in the northern part of the Great Wolven Forest. I had never been to this village, but that night resolved to visit it in future travels.

The day was losing its sun when Commander Velstor announced that King Ballistor would like to have our company in the great chamber. Velstor then turned to me and stated that Duke Jaramas requested that I pay him attendance when my business with the King was ended.

As we made our way through the passageways we passed several more monks dressed in the same robes. Each smiled and nodded, but did not speak. I mentioned out loud that I thought monks were allowed to speak. Velstor then told me that during each Trade Gathering all the monks of the Jovet Monastery on Callas Island made the trip to the host city to give blessings on the coming year. During this time they are not allowed to speak to others not of the Priesthood.

Presently we turned a corner and came to a large double oak door guarded by four of the King's Royal Guard. They snapped to attention as Commander Velstor approached.

He then called out, "At rest now, and let us enter on the King's orders!" Immediately they separated and one rapped three times on the door. It was opened by two armed soldiers from the inside. Velstor walked in as the rest of us followed.

This room turned out to be the waiting room for the King's inner chambers. Two older men in the traditional dress of Royal Advisors stood facing us as we entered. The Commander stood before them and spoke simply, "The King's emissaries have brought Beorn the Witness as our lord has ordered."

The taller of the two advisors then responded in formal speech, "The King will see all of them now, including you, Commander Velstor. He waits in his Meeting Room. If you will follow me please..."

The meeting room was off to the right and through another set of double doors. The Advisor rapped on the stout oak with his staff.

"Enter!" Came the response from within.

Inside, as we entered, I saw for the first time in my life, the King of Tavegnor, King Ballistor.

He was standing at the far end of the room next to a large eight-sided table. He looked to be about the same height as Keven and Karlyle, and about as heavy as Errol, though his mass was not as solid looking. The King was dressed in a royal green hunting shirt and breaches. His green riding boots were the finest I had ever looked upon. A green floor-length cape was tied in the front by golden chains at the neck. He wore no crown or other jewelry. The king looked to be my age. A thick black beard dusted with gray covered his face. His eyes were dark and piercing.

Surrounding him stood five men. By their dress I guessed that four were Advisors. The fifth was Banator.

King Ballistor beckoned us to come near. We approached and all bowed formally. I stayed in the back trying to be unnoticed.

King Ballistor spoke first. "It is good to see you all safe and returned. As you can see, Banator is with me and has told me news. I await yours, but first…"

He turned to his Advisors. "See to it that the couriers get their orders and that they are on their way before the moon rises. Use the Royal Seal to authenticate their papers."

The advisors bowed and left the room.

Banator now addressed the King. "With your permission, Sire, I would also like to leave as soon as possible. I will stay if you so desire, but if I am not needed now…"

"You have my leave to go. Take six of my personal guard with you. You have my Seal of Authorization. The Master-at-Arms has your horse readied and supplied. God speed to you and I will have a search begun in Talavor."

Banator then bowed to King Ballistor and turned to us, "My friends, I regret that I cannot stay in your good company. I hope to see you soon and in good health." And with a quick nod to each of us, Banator rushed from the room.

Velstor answered our unspoken question. "Hensha has not been seen since she left Banator's cottage. Banator is leaving to search for her."

Errol turned to the King as Banator left. "Is there anything we can do to help in the search Sire?"

"No Errol, I've already given Banator broad authority and resources. It sounds cold and hard, but we have other priorities and concerns at this time."

King Ballistor then turned to me, "You are the Bard-turned-Witness then. You know why you are here Beorn. I will now listen to your statement of your visit to Hastid."

The King then went to the table and sat down. Velstor and the 'Four' followed and sat down also. I stood there not knowing what say or when to begin…

My first thought was confusion at the others sitting down; No one sits in a King's presence.

King Ballistor saw my inaction and laughed. "It seems your companions have not prepared you for me. I am abrupt and to the point. I waste little time on greetings and formalities, especially now. Sit down and begin telling me everything that has happened in your presence since these four young folks abducted you."

I walked over to the table but hesitated before sitting...

"Beorn, another thing they clearly failed to tell you, When I have private meetings with my closest confidants, I require that all sit. It is favorable to straightforward and level talk. I find that patronization is eliminated when talk is amongst men and ladies when all are equal. So take that chair, sit, and begin your telling."

I promptly sat and began my narrative.

The moon was almost midnight high when I finally finished. No one spoke. Occasionally King Ballistor got up and paced the room, obviously absorbing my tale.

Finally he spoke. "The King be damned eh...? Duke Hastid said that. And...he did not come to this annual meeting."

After a long pause along with the slow pacing, Ballistor continued, "Something ill-boding is starting to drift into Tavegnor like a fog. We must try to cut that fog and find its source."

King Ballistor walked slowly and silently around the large table. Then he stopped at one end and commanded, "Velstor, tell our friends what they do not yet know."

"Yes, Sire." Commander Velstor then turned to us and began, "Yesterday a messenger arrived from King Ballistor's daughter Hellista. As you know, she is steward of the Capitol City while the King is here. Her message tells us that four days ago one of Shelaylan's personal staff rode into Talavor with the news of the ambassador's death. This servant could not report much except that Ambassador Shelaylan had no reason to commit suicide.

In truth, she was to be betrothed to a traveler from the southern continent. He is a royal guest of our Duke Hastid. This guest's name is Prince Valon of the country of Cornella. This is the first that we have heard of this Prince Valon. It is unfortunate that Duke Hastid did not feel it necessary to inform the King that foreign Royalty was visiting Tavegnor.

Shelaylan's servant also reported that two days before her fall from the Keep, the Ambassador was greatly shaken by a fierce argument she had had with this Prince Valon. On what was argued, the servant did not know.

The Ambassador then gathered all of her staff into her private chambers. She was visibly tense while she spoke. Ambassador Shelaylan told everyone to prepare for a secret departure from Hastid. No one was to leave yet, but in the event of an accident to the Ambassador, all were to leave in secrecy and with speed. The staff was also told that a message had already been sent to King Ballistor warning of possible intrigue. Unfortunately, she did not share any further details."

Captain Velstor took a deep breath and continued. "This messenger who arrived in Talavor did not know the fates or locations of any other of Shelaylan's servants. When news of the Ambassador's fall from the Keep spread through the city of Hastid, this servant was at the market square. Immediately, the servant went to a friend's house rather than back to Duke Hastid's castle. It was not until much later that this servant was able to be smuggled out of the city hidden in a quarry wagon headed to Rogan Pass. From there the northern route was taken back to Talavor."

King Ballistor now spoke. "As of last night, I have ordered that riders be outfitted and set in place on all main roads of Tavegnor. If it happens that Ambassador Shelaylan's concerns were justified, I want information headed for me as it happens. These outriders are also instructed to look for any of the ambassador's servants who might be trying to make it back from Hastid. I have sent messages to the Admirals of my northern and southern fleets to be on the alert for anything unusual along our coast. If this Prince Valon is in any way connected, then a threat from outside Tavegnor is possible. Our fleets will be alerted to patrol our coastline."

Then King Ballistor turned to address me. "Beorn of Minoline, not sooner than three days I will call for a Counsel of the Dukes. I wish you to be my Royal Witness at the gathering. I want you to re-tell everything you have reported today. I expect Duke Hastid will not attend since he apparently has his own agenda...One I hope soon to uncover.

The reason for the three day delay is twofold. First, I will try to get answers from my outriders on Duke Hastid's travels and motives. Second, Duchess Mariom has not arrived for our gathering. Messengers report that due to a sudden serious illness of Duchess Mariom's husband, Lord Harold, she has reversed her travel to return to him in Arlingdol. A rider has been sent to find her in route and ask that her Senior Advisor attend the Counsel in her name."

King Ballistor then turned and addressed Ciekay. "Tell me of your thoughts and readings on Duke Hastid and everyone around him."

Ciekay promptly began, "Well Sire, Duke Hastid was on guard and hostile to us. As you yourself know, being a Duke, he has been trained enough to shield most feelings and motive thoughts from Mind Listeners. However, I was able probe into him somewhat and could sense that he had anger and distrust against us...and you. He was also confused at our, or I should say, Errol's defiant manner toward him."

The King glanced at Errol and shook his head.

Ciekay went on, "The Duke was without doubt holding something from us. I could not determine if he at any time lied to us, but I did know that he was not telling us everything he knew."

"What did you draw from the Duke's Captain of the Guard, Elexele?" The King asked.

"His mind is also trained to shield, but to a lesser degree. He is fiercely loyal to the Duke and will follow orders without question. He was truly surprised that we were spied upon by someone behind the tapestry. It was surely not by his orders that it was done. He was also suspicious of us. Although he did not lie concerning the Duke's departure in the early morn, he did not share that information with us. He is very efficient and would be a formidable opponent in a battle because of his discipline and intelligence. I was very much impressed by him."

"As for the rest of the characters in the Duke's presence; anything you think may help us?" The King asked.

Once again Ciekay quickly answered, "The Advisors were all quite ignorant of any intrigue as I could sense, with the exception of one, the one that Beorn recognized from Boar's Hind Inn: Westfal. He was trained in masking his emotions but I was successful nonetheless. The advisor was full of guile and hate.

He was not revealed at the inn because I failed to deeply probe the soldiers. I underestimated that level of threat, so therefore missed him. He is one who is dangerous and has to be dealt with if we can find him again."

"Was he the one behind the tapestry?"

"No. This person had no feelings that I could ferret out. This person was probably a Mind Listener like me."

King Ballistor sat down and kept silent for several moments. We too sat silent and waited.

Finally he spoke again, turning to Keven. "Can you call your eagle from here?"

"Not directly, Sire. We have to be within fifty leagues of each other to communicate. His aerie is atop Delshar Mountain, just west of Minoline Plains. I can relay crows to find him if you wish."

"Yes, I wish. We will need your eyes to fly for us; to help find answers from the sky."

The King next turned to Karlyle. "How many of your Guild will be able to gather here in the next three days? We may have great need of them."

Karlyle raised his eyebrow before answering, "I can alert all thirty of them this day. How many are close enough is unknown, Sire. I do know that two are presently in the city of Halenester."

King Ballistor smiled and nodded, "Please do call on them and relay my warmest regards…and invite them to my presence."

Abruptly, King Ballistor stood up. "It is late! This meeting is ended. Errol, Commander Velstor, I will have you two stay a while longer. We must discuss military matters should we need to take such action. Let us set the maps of Tavegnor to the table."

To the rest of us he nodded his head to the door as he spoke. "Thank you for your presence and information. Karlyle, Keven, you two can begin as I asked. Ceikay, you are responsible for Beorn. See to it that he is prepared for attending the Counsel of the Dukes."

As we went to the door King Ballistor called out to me, "Beorn…"

I turned immediately to face him, "Yes, sire?"

"As my Royal Witness, you are required to recall anything and everything at any time while you are here. That is your post and responsibility. Stay alert."

I bowed formally, and quite nervously, "Yes, sire."

No one spoke until we got to the passageway outside our rooms. Keven was the first to break our silence. "I suppose I will ride out beyond the towers to summon the crows. Also, I am concerned about Hensha. The crows can help with Banator's search."

Ceikay then spoke. "Tomorrow Beorn and I will tour the city's markets and squares. If Hensha is in Hirst I may have a chance to find her."

Nothing else was said. Karlyle nodded at the rest of us without saying a word. He seemed to be lost in concentration. I entered my room and gladly headed to my bed. I laid there thinking about the disappearance of Hensha, but soon sleep overtook me.

I knew nothing until a persistent rapping on my door woke me. Remembering where I was I jumped up to answer the summons.

A page dressed in gray stood at the opening. "Good morning sir, Duke Jaramas requests your company at morning repast if you are free of appointments with the King."

"Duke Jaramas! Of course, yes! Tell him I will be at his chambers shortly after I freshen and dress....or are you to take me to him?"

"I am to wait as you ready for the day. My Lord fears that you may get lost or distracted on the way. I am to personally escort you to his rooms. Please hurry, sir."

Shortly thereafter I was being led into Duke Jaramas' great chamber.

The Duke was already sitting down enjoying his meal. "Beorn, it is a joy to see you this morn! You have an outstanding memory when it comes to faces and events, but it is clear that you have trouble remembering when a Duke requests a meeting!"

"I am regretful your lordship, I was busy with our King last night and it was late when we finished and I..."

Duke Jaramas held up his hand to stop me, "Do not explain

further. I am sure you know it was I who gave your name to the King. Something is amiss in the realm. With the death of his Witness, you were the best replacement. He needs your attention and talent more than I."

The Duke waved me closer as he spoke. "My reason for summoning you is merely to thank you once again for your service and, more importantly, for your discretion. Please sit and enjoy this fine fare with me."

We talked well into the morn. Duke Jaramas did not ask details about my work for the King. He knew that I would not tell him if he did ask. He asked after my health and travels since I left his service.

I in turn asked about his family's health and how his various crops were doing this season. Duke Jaramas' realm grows the richest grains and vegetables in Tavegnor. His territory is mostly flat and very fertile for growth. The richest land for wine grapes is also in the Jaramas realm. It is said that the soft rolling hills along the western coast were specially made by the gods for the crafting of wine.

Duke Jaramas spoke of the King's problems only once: when I was leaving his chambers. "Beorn, The King has chosen not to share with the rest of the Dukes what is going on. We are sure that he will do so soon if and when he needs our assistance. I do know one thing though and share it; one of my personal couriers arrived this morning from Hastid."

My eyebrows raised at the news.

After a brief pause he continued. "News has arrived that Ambassador Shelaylan has died from a fall. I do not know much more than that. Also, Duke Hastid did not find it necessary to send his personal envoy to inform the King and the rest of the Dukes. That troubles us. Right after you leave here, the Lords and I will meet in Rasher's hall for discussions. I am sure that we will request to have an audience with King Ballistor shortly after. As for myself, I have already placed my personal guard on alert."

Duke Jaramas now pointed his finger at me. "As for you; stay alert and close to your four companions. Remember what happened to the King's previous Witness."

I nodded but still said nothing; finally I smiled my thanks, turned and left Duke Jaramas' chambers.

I needed no escort to return to my room. When I returned to my chambers, Ceikay was waiting inside. "Good morning dear sir." She said cheerfully, "Did you enjoy your repast with Duke Jaramas?"

"Good morning to you dear lady. Yes I did. We spent the morn talking. He wanted to thank me for past services. We also dis..."

"No need to explain. I am not surprised that he wanted to see you. Are you ready for a day in the markets? Or do you have other appointments with any of the rest of the royalty? Should I wait until the day lengthens more?"

I smiled at her teasing. "No, I am very disappointed that the others have not called for me yet. I guess that I have nothing better than to go with you today."

"Thank you for your generous company!" Then her smile disappeared. "Now, in seriousness, I will be probing for Hensha. I know her well, and therefore will be able to easily recognize her thoughts. If she is close by I will know it."

"Do you believe she is in Hirst?" I asked.

She paused and then turned away, "No...no I do not. In truth, I have been busy in my search while you were with Duke Jaramas. I have twice walked the town since sunlight touched the towers."

Soon we were walking along the spiral road outside of the castle. The markets were crowded with merchants hawking their wares and customers buying them. We did not talk for a long while. Ceikay was probing with her mind in a slim chance of finding Hensha. I was preoccupied with my own thoughts.

"We cannot stay out here too long today," Ceikay said to me after a while, "We should return to the castle soon to prepare for Duke Rasher's ball."

"Is it this night?"

"Yes, tonight. Every year the host Duke, or Duchess, puts on a ball for the visiting Royalty."

"We are not royalty, why would we be going?" I countered.

"You are now a member of the Official Court of King Ballistor. As his Royal Witness, you are invited."

"But my position is a temporary posting. I am a Bard by trade."

"You are the King's Royal Witness at this moment, so you will attend the ball."

I saw the wisdom in not arguing further, so I changed the subject. "Are you 'Four' on his Official Staff, or Court; and if so, what are your official titles?"

Ceikay laughed and walked ahead. She did not answer my question. Abruptly she turned in the direction of the castle and increased her pace. I guessed it was time to return to our quarters. As we entered the castle gate and walked through the courtyard we saw Keven standing by the stables. We walked over to him.

He smiled as we approached, "Ah, I see that you two have been about the city today. Did you see anything of interest that I may have missed?"

Ceikay answered for both of us. "There were some pretty girls asking for you Keven. Beorn told them he was your father and that you were not allowed to come out of the Keep."

Keven laughed and shook his head. "Beorn, do you have any straight and honest words for me, or are you going to be as difficult as Ceikay?"

"If we are telling truth, I *am* quite a bit older than you."

Before Keven could respond, Ceikay broke in, "Where are Karlyle and Errol?"

Keven promptly answered, "I do not know as of this moment. Errol and Velstor went out early this morning to the King's encampment. One hundred of the King's guards are bivouacked just outside the towers. Velstor was to organize troop placement and send more messengers off to try to get information on Duke Hastid's movements. Karlyle left last night to go to Halenester just north of here. Two of his guild live there and he plans to bring them back in time for King Ballistor's Counsel three days from now."

"Where are you bound for?" I asked, nodding toward his saddled horse standing next to a stall.

"I have just returned" he answered. "I have been beyond the city listening to my winged friends. They have contacted Hawk.

He is now on his way to Eagle on Belshar Mountain. Eagle should be here two days hence."

Keven paused briefly, then continued, "The crows have no news of Hensha. I am fearful that foul play has visited Hensha on her way here. I also suspect that her disappearance is connected to Ambassador Shelaylan."

"Keven that is an easy misgiving to come to," Ceikay said quietly. "But I do hope that you are wrong, and that Banator's love will show up soon."

"But for the while..." she continued on a different subject, "I will see to it that Beorn stays out of trouble until the ball tonight. I am taking him back to his quarters where he will be locked in, and therefore, out of mischief until I come to get him. Will you be in attendance, Keven?"

"Yes, I must be there in order not to disappoint the ladies." He grinned and winked at me as he turned to stable his horse.

Ceikay and I entered the double oak doors to the castle.

The soft down-filled bedding caught my attention as I entered my rooms. For the first time in many years, I was able to take a mid-day nap.

When I awoke, the sun's rays were weak. The room was dim with the failing day. It was time to get ready for the ball. A clean green outfit was waiting for me in my dressing closet. Official Witness garb, I assumed; long-legged hose that stretched to the heels, long-sleeved rich linen shirt that fell to the thighs. An open-front tunic made from the finest silk also lay before me. Once dressed... I felt truly uncomfortable.

On the table was placed a gold medallion attached to a long gold chain. It had King Ballistor's family coat of arms on it. Only two objects were imprinted on the shield, an eye, and an ear; the official symbols of Witnesses before Parliament.

I dressed out my hair and washed my face before putting the medallion around my neck. A knock then sounded on my door.

Ceikay called out from the other side, "Are you prepared, Beorn? It is time for us to fulfill our royal obligations!"

I chuckled and called back, "I am just now putting on my fancy lamb-leather boots that I am sure the King personally had made for

101

me!"

Once dressed, I quickly opened the door. There stood a beautiful young lady! Ceikay was a naturally pretty girl normally, but this night she was stunning in her green silken gown. Her long brown hair was put up and pulled back in the style of the fairest ladies in court. Her fingernails had been painted. I had never seen that before. It was a good effect on the hands.

I stood there knowing that all the young men at the ball were going to be vying for her attention this night.

She smiled at my scrutiny. "Do you suppose I have a chance to snare a man tonight?"

"No other lady will have a chance with you there. May I now escort you to the ball, m'lady?"

"Why thank you handsome sir. I would be honored."

We both laughed and were on our way.

Soon after, we were standing in the Grand Ballroom along with at least five hundred other royally dressed citizens. King Ballistor was at the back of the large hall standing on the elevated stage. He was surrounded by numerous people I did not recognize.

I spied Errol at the foot of the stage talking to Velstor. The Commander was dressed as he was at the castle gate yesterday. His ceremonial sword was shining at his side. Errol was dressed in green Ranger type clothing, only this was new, crisp looking, and creased. He had two matching ceremonial swords at his hips. His boots were clean and polished.

Keven was near the center of the room and was dressed nearly identical to Errol, including the two swords. I knew Karlyle was not to be in attendance since he was in Halenester.

The rest of the Dukes were scattered around. I could tell where they were by the color groupings of the gathered crowd, The greens were near the stage, since green is the color worn by King Ballistor and his entourage. The reds told me that Duke Rasher was near the fireplace on the south wall. The grays were Duke Jaramas and his entourage by the entrance. Duke Castus wore brown. His party was in the center of the room. Dark blue was predominating near the fireplace on the north wall; hence, Duke Whorton was there.

102

Standing at attention with their backs to the wall, about ten feet apart, circling the room, were guards in ceremonial uniforms and weapons. By their colors I could tell that there was an equal number of guards from each of the five attending Dukes. These guards were separated so that no two dressed in the same color were next to each other.

As Ceikay and I strode across the floor toward Errol, I noticed that a large number of young men, older men also, stole glances at Ceikay.

Suddenly a royal horn was sounded that stilled everyone.

Duke Rasher's Master-at-Arms stepped to the middle of the floor. He held up The Duke's ceremonial scepter and spoke, "Attention Royal attendees, It is Duke Rasher's pleasure and privilege to welcome you to his realm and to tonight's ball! Our good King Ballistor will first address this gathering! Then Duke Rasher will speak. But as for tradition that begins each royal ball; please step from the center of the room to make way for the Jovet Monks of Callas Island. They will give the gods' blessings for the new trade year!"

The floor cleared as directed. From the great double doors came the monks. Hoods were now covering their heads and shadowing their faces. I estimated that there were about fifty in number. They walked in silent formation to the center of the room and formed a square, facing out to the quests. Once in place they stood silent and still.

After several moments of quiet, one monk stepped inward to the middle of the square. He began to chant in the old tongue
                    ...then Hell took over.

Suddenly, Ceikay lurched foward and screamed, "ERROL...!" At this precise moment I heard and saw Errol jumping into King Ballistor, knocking him sideways!

Errol yelled out as he jumped, "ASSASINS...!"

Suddenly I was slammed to the floor. Ceikay yelled in my face, "STAY DOWN!"

The look in her eyes froze me. I was paralyzed with sudden and terror and confusion. She was suddenly up and gone.

In an instant my world was in utter chaos. My ears were now filled with screams, yells, grunts, and clanging of metal.

At first, my eyes only saw feet and legs stepping on and around me. I was being kicked from all sides.

Then people started to fall to the floor next to me. Some were tripping over each other in a panic to get up. Some were falling and not moving.

The sounds blended into the loudest howling storm I had ever suffered.

The color red was becoming more dominant in my panicked eyes.

Then to my horror, I realized that the red was the blood pouring out of wounds of people all around me.

Fear now had command. I did not want to regain my feet, but I also did not want to stay on the floor watching and feeling the blood that was now splashing on and over me.

I got to my knees only to be knocked down several times. The more I tried to get up, the less I was felled by the panicked mob…it was the blood I was slipping on that kept taking me to the floor.

A sudden roar within my head came with a new pain to my forehead. My senses started to dim. I tried to wipe the sweat from my eyes. My hand came away from my face covered in red. The red filtered my vision.

The roar of the melee around me turned into the roar of a monstrous wave pounding down as if onto a drowning swimmer.

I slipped one more time in the red gore and landed on my back. I looked to the ceiling to see a monk stepping over me. He raised his hand. A knife was clenched in that hand! The hand sped down to my chest. My arms sprang up. My hands met his. I desperately grabbed hold. The knife stopped right at my shirt.

The monk and I struggled and squirmed on the bloody floor. He put his free hand over the knife and bore down with all his weight. I swore and prayed to the gods to take this mad monk from atop me.

The weight was too much. I was weakening. I glared into the monk's eyes and prayed for strength. I gritted my teeth and vowed he would not thrust that dagger further.

The next moment I heard a piercing, then gurgling scream that roared over all the other noise. My eyes looked up and saw Keven pull a sword from the monk's neck.

Without a word, Keven then reached down and grabbed my shirt and tunic front. He easily pulled me to my feet, then suddenly yanked me behind him as his sword pierced the stomach of another monk who was jumping at us.

Even as Keven was pulling the sword out of the falling monk, he was dragging me to a side door of the ballroom.

That is the last of my memory of the struggle…

Throbbing in my head brought me up from darkness. I opened my eyes in confusion. I wondered how I got this terrible headache. I tried to raise my hand to rub my eyes, but it would not move. The other hand responded in the same manner.

I was weak. My arms would not respond to my demands, so I decided to move my legs; the same result, no movement.

Fear and confusion came to me again. I groaned with my efforts.

Then I saw Ceikay. It appeared she was sitting nearby while I was sleeping. Hearing my groans and efforts, she stepped over me and peered down into my eyes.

I groaned once more, and then spoke, "What…?"

…I was unable to finish.

Ceikay did not smile, "You received a blow to your head. You were unconscious for a time."

I did not comprehend her answer. "How did I get this pain in my head?"

"No more questions until you recover more. Do not try to move or get up. The more still and quiet you are, the sooner you will feel better for it. I promise you, I will not leave you until you recover further. Now close your eyes and rest your mind."

I gratefully followed her orders and lowered my eyelids.

Ages later I awoke in a panic. "NO…!" I bolted upright. Ceikay was instantly at my side holding me firm from jumping to the floor.

I had remembered everything, and it came back in a flood that brought my fear to a pitch once again.

"BEORN…! It is over! It is over…!"

I stilled my thrashing and looked at her. She then released me and backed away one step. I looked around and saw that I was in my own room. My head throbbed greatly still. I raised my hand to my head and felt cloth.

Ceikay saw the puzzlement on my face and answered, "You struck your head on a table as Keven threw you through a doorway. You were cut by the impact but by the gods, did not suffer a fracture. Our physician has tended you and I have cleaned you. Your recovery my friend, will be complete."

Suddenly the door to my room opened and Keven walked in.

Before I could speak a word he held up his hand to stop me, "Please, do not ask questions now. I am truly sorry that I tossed you into a table. It was important that you were out of the Ballroom as soon as possible. I had no time to be…gentle. I come to you because the King greatly needs your talent now. Can you walk on your own or shall I summon servants to carry you?"

"I will walk. What am I to do?"

"The King will answer your questions when you report to him."

I began to rise to my feet. "Then the King is alive?"

Ceikay now spoke up, "Of course he is. As long as Errol is near him, no one will be successful in killing our King."

I found that I needed the assistance of Keven to steady me as we walked to the ballroom. The passageways were filled with men and women running in both directions. Some bumped into me and ran on. If Keven had not been holding on to me I would have easily been knocked down.

Soon we turned a last corner and approached the double doors of the big room. They were wide open and men were bringing out bodies.

We walked through the doors and into absolute carnage.

I had never before seen such slaughter. Several scores of bodies were still on the floor.

I turned to Ceikay, "How long was I unconscious?"

"Only a little more than two turns of the hourglass." She answered.

"How long was I asleep after the first time I awoke?"

"A moment...or two."

"That cannot be," I said. "It seems like days!"

Keven spoke, "Head wounds affect a person's recollections and sense of time. The truth of it is, we have not yet even seen the first of the sun since this atrocity happened."

"Are you saying that this really is the same night...?"

Before Keven could answer, my name flew across the room, "Beorn!"

I turned to the sound and met eyes with King Ballistor. He was standing over a long row of robes and red linen. I then realized that he was standing over bodies...monks.

"Beorn, has your wound left you dumb? Do not stand there looking at me, step over here now!"

"Yes, Sire!" I uneasily stepped over bodies still lying on the floor.

When I got to the line of monks in front of me, King Ballistor grabbed hold of my arm. "Are you steady enough to look at all the faces of the monks? Some are gruesome to look at, but I must know if you recognize any of them, as in Duke Hastid's Advisor Westal..."

Quickly I proceeded to study the line of dead faces. Some looked to be asleep while others were not all intact. I recognized no one, but then again, something was missing...

King Ballistor saw my uncertainty. "What is it that you have found Beorn? Do you recall a face?"

"No, sire. I do not recall a face that is here. Although I do recall three faces that should be here but are not."

"Explain."

"When we first arrived here we were shown to our rooms. When I left my room to meet the others, three monks passed me in the passageway. They are not among the dead lying here."

"Are you sure of what you say?"

I raised my eyes up from the dead and looked directly at the King. "Sire, at this moment that is the only reality I am sure of."

King Ballistor now raised his voice to fill the great room. "I want Duke Castus and all the remaining Captains of the Guards to meet me in the War Room now! Beorn, I wish I could release you to rest, but you are needed there also. You have just enough time to find a meal for nourishment. Duke Rasher's kitchen staff has been setting up field meals in the greeting hall. See that you get there and fill your stomach."

"As you order Sire."

"Ceikay, stay with him and make sure that he gets to the War Room. You will take your fill also I assume."

Ceikay nodded her reply.

We both left the blood-soaked room. I was suddenly very hungry, though I was unsure if I could keep anything down if I ate.

We said nothing as we made our way through the throngs of people in the passageway. Ceikay kept her hand on my arm the entire way.

I did eat, and it stayed in my stomach.

During our repast I finally had the courage to ask, "Was Errol wounded?"

"No, and to answer your next question: He is with Commander Velstor down in the courtyard. Rest assured, he will be in the War Room when we arrive there."

"Who survived?"

"You mean of the Dukes, yes?"

I merely nodded.

"Beyond King Ballistor, Castus is the only one who survived the massacre."

I was stunned in disbelief. Dukes Jaramas, Whorton, and Rasher, all murdered as swiftly as that.

"How many others in that room?

"Half of the Royalty of Tavegnor were slaughtered."

Softly I spoke to no one. "We are at war then…"

Ceikay answered plainly, "Yes, we are at war. But with whom is not yet known."

Ciekay then stood up. "It is time for us to gather with the others. Maybe our questions can be answered in the War Room."

Shortly thereafter we were in the top floor of Duke Rasher's

Keep. It can hold one hundred when filled. This morn it was nearly so. A large round table stood in the center. A map of Tavegnor covered the table. On the stone walls hung large rugs with depictions of great histories throughout the Rasher realm

At the opposite side of the doorway, King Ballistor stood over the table and was studying something I could not clearly see.

The room was quiet. Everyone was waiting for the King to speak first. Several more men came in behind me as we waited. I had time to study some of the gathering. Errol and Keven were to the right of the King. Both now had their own ranger outfits on. Errol had his huge sword strapped to his back.

Commander Velstor stood to the left of the King; his right hand was bandaged. He was well armed as well.

The rest were officers of various rank in the five colors of the Dukes that had been in attendance at the now forgotten Trade Meeting. Some were wounded, all were grim, and all were well armed.

Karlyle apparently was still not returned from Halenester.

Suddenly a man marched quickly into the room. I recognized him to be Duke Castus. His tunic was torn and bloodied, but I could see no wounds.

"Ah, Duke Castus has returned," The King said. We shall get started. Errol, before we begin theories and strategies, tell everyone what you have found."

Errol nodded and stepped to the table. He laid a folded napkin down on the map for all to see. "I have found these on most of the monks' bodies."

He opened the cloth and revealed several flat, smooth stones about the size of a hen's egg. The shape was similar to an egg except that it was flattened to the thickness of a man's little finger. Next to the rocks were a number of needle-like sticks just a little shorter than the egg shaped rocks. These needles were very fine and tapered to a sharp point on both ends.

Duke Castus walked over to the items. "Errol, what are these?"

"These are the assassination weapons of the monks my Lord. These were successful in killing the three Dukes and several

109

others."

"How did the monks use them?"

Errol gestured to the table, "Pick up one of the stones, but do not touch the needles; they are poisonous."

The Duke picked up a stone and turned it over in his hand. He studied it for a moment and then held it closer to his eyes, "There is a hole through one end and through the other end. It looks to be grooved inside..."

He looked at Errol. "I presume that this holds one of those needles, but I saw no monk throw a stone. They only had knives and their warrior-trained hands. How does this object work?"

Errol picked up a second stone from the napkin and held it up, "We found these in several of the monks' mouths. I have studied them and know how it was accomplished. They blew the needles at their victims. One of the monks facing our King had this one in his mouth."

Silence from the rest of us prompted Errol to continue. "As you are can see, the stones are smooth and shaped in an oval. This is so that they are able to be placed and held undetected in the closed mouth with the lips barely parted. A needle is placed in the hole. On one end of the stone, just inside the hole there are two tiny prongs that form a notch; a notch to hold one end of the needle so it would not fall back into the mouth.

"Duke Castus mentioned the grooves in the hole, or tube as I will call it. There are grooves, but he did not notice that they are spiraled. Since these needles do not have feathered fins as a regular dart would have, the needle will not fly true. The spiraled grooves spin the needle as it is blown out of the mouth. As a result, the needle flies straight because of the spin."

Errol turned to King Ballistor. "Shall I tell the whole story m'Lord?"

The King nodded assent. "Several days ago, in the Darion Forest, two people were found dead in a clearing. No signs of wounds were found on their bodies except one. On each of their necks was a small puncture wound that looked to be no more than a wasp sting. A number of dead birds and animals were nearby. I cut one animal open to examine the wound but could find no dart or any stinger. We suspected poison darts, but did not know the weapon. We now have the weapon lying before us.

"The Dukes who were assassinated in the ballroom had the same marks on their necks and faces. No needles were found in their bodies though."

"How can that be? What happened to the needles, then?"

Errol turned back to answer Duke Castus. "I assume now that they dissolved. I will give these needles to Karlyle to examine later, but for now, we have to guess that they are made up of a quickly dissolving compound that absorbs into the body tissues. My guess would be a mixture of sugar and poison."

Again Duke Castus had a question. "What is the connection to the deaths in Darion Forest and the attacks here?"

King Ballistor answered, "We do not know, but that is one mystery we will strive to uncover."

One of the officers spoke up. "Why did these monks attack? Who directed them to ambush us?"

King Ballistor answered once more, "Again, we do not know. What we do know is that we cannot wait here for another attack from our enemy. We do not even know who our enemy is…and that makes us easy prey.

"So, we will go on the offensive as of now. I am taking charge of the loyal armies of Tavegnor. Duke Castus has already ceded control of his forces to me. The forces of Jaramas, Rasher, and Whorton are now under my command. Are there any objections to this?"

No one spoke. "Good and done. Right after this counsel Duke Castus will return to his realm in the south. His ships will be escorted by my personal flagship. He will see to it that his realm is efficiently defended. Then, if possible, he will send all troops he can spare for the defense of the mainland of Tavegnor where ever that be."

King Ballistor continued, "Outriders were sent north to my realm earlier. The rest of you will prepare and get your riders out as soon as possible. At this moment we are blind. We need information from every corner of Tavegnor. Riders must race to every city in Tavegnor to prepare and defend for war. Our armies are scattered at the moment and are vulnerable. Let us hope that they are well trained and will perform as needed if attacked."

King Ballistor turned to face an officer in gray. "Captain Bocxer, you are the senior officer left here in Jaramas' Command. You are responsible for finding Duchess Mariom. She should still be traveling in your realm. Take one company of your Royal Guard. Find her. Inform her of what has happened. Tell her that three monks have not been accounted for. She must keep her bodyguard close at all times. Also tell her that a state of war exists and that I am exercising my authority over her troops as per Parliamentary contract.

"Her first duty is to strengthen her forces at Yannisdol. That port city must not be taken. In addition, she will place five thousand of her troops at my disposal. They are to report to the city of Talavor and wait for further deployment. I have a suspicion that we may be attacked from the northwest. The rest of her forces she will use as she sees fit to protect her realm."

Captain Bocxer stepped forward. "Sire, what of the territory of Jaramas? When can I muster my forces to defend my Lord's realm?"

"I understand your desire to first secure your realm, Captain, but you must act as I have ordered. Before you depart, send me your two most senior officers and I will coordinate the rest of your forces for protection. By the time you have completed your task with Duchess Mariom I will have moved from this castle. My riders will let you know where I am located. You will report back to me for further instructions. Go now and warn Duchess Mariom."

Bocxer snapped to attention, slapped his right hand to his heart in salute, spun on his heels and swiftly left the room.

King Ballistor dictated until the pre-dawn light started to break through the windows. One by one the officers left with their orders.

Duke Castus had only a few more words to say before he left the war room. He nodded to Ceikay and then to Keven. "I want to thank you both for saving my life in the Ballroom. I truly wish that I could reward you as you deserve, but this day we see only fighting and death. Rewards must come later. May the gods grant that we live through this...treachery...so that I may honor you in my realm."

With those words, Duke Castus turned and marched out of the room. The next to get orders and leave was Commander Velstor. He was to rush north to Talavor and coordinate the defense of the King's realm. Only a few officers were now left now. King Ballistor was precise and direct. Orders were given and soon the soldiers had all departed.

The King was quickly and efficiently mobilizing all of Tavegnor for war.

Finally, the only ones left in the War room with the King were Errol, Keven, Ceikay, and myself.

It was my turn to be addressed by the King. "Beorn, you were originally asked to witness before Parliament. Now there will be no Parliamentary Council as we face war. Your talent is needed still, though. I wish to be very clear, you must continue to be of service to your King, and therefore to Tavegnor. I do not release you to go. Do you accept that?"

"My King, I fear war, and wish that it was not upon us now, but I am part of Tavegnor and I will not turn from this that threatens us all. I can be of use to you, so you have my services and my loyalty."

"Well said!" Errol slapped me on the shoulder as he spoke. "I pray you do not regret your gallant words later on."

I then noticed Keven and Ceikay smiling broadly. I suddenly became a bit self-conscious about my little speech.

King Ballistor did not smile, but his words flattered me. "To the gods I pray that we have enough souls like you in this land to beat back our enemies. Now Beorn, you have declared that there are three monks not counted among the dead. I have no doubt in your talent, and I believe they are still meaning and able to do harm. We must find those three before they kill, and just as importantly, before they are killed."

King Ballistor paused to see that we understood his meaning.

He then continued, "As I said before to Captain Bocxer, I believe that they are on their way to kill Duchess Mariom.

Whoever planned this mass assassination counted on all of the Dukes to be present at the ball. It is indeed fortunate that Duchess Mariom was absent, or she might have been a victim of one of those needles. The unfortunate thing is that she is unaware of her danger at this moment. First, Errol, Ceikay, and Beorn are to go to Duchess Mariom to help protect her...if we are not too late already. Second, Beorn and Ceikay will use their talents to ferret out those three monks.

"I must stress that these monks are not to be killed. They are to be captured so that we may get information from them. We need to know who is behind this attack as soon as possible."

I could not help but ask, "Please excuse my interruption, Sire, I mean no disrespect, but you ordered Captain Bocxer to ride to Duchess Mariom to tell her of the..."

King Ballistor held up his hand to stop me. "I take no offense at your interruption. You are confused about my orders, and rightly so. Captain Bocxer is to leave Hirst with a full company of heavily armed cavalry. He will be traveling on main roads, which means that his ride will hold no secrecy. If there are spies here in Hirst, they will surely know that he is traveling to locate Duchess Mariom. The enemy will be paying attention to him. I want no one to know your mission. You will leave quickly and quietly. Once outside Hirst you will avoid the roads. Go due west to the port. Duke Castus is preparing to leave for his realm as we speak. One of his escort ships will have one of my personal banners mounted at the gangplank. You will go to that ship and request to board. I assure you that you and your horses will be accepted. This vessel will immediately leave port and take you past the delta and to the other side of the Telmar River. Talk to no one. The crew will have orders not to speak to you, nor ask questions.

"From there the ship will head northwest. That whole flood plain is crowded with farms, so try to travel the fields that are along the way. You will head to Tymia Road, to a point fifty leagues outside Halenester. I have sent word to find Banator and have him meet you on the road. His search for Hensha must wait, considering the new state of affairs we are in. Your small number will be able to travel faster than Bocxer's company. Hopefully you will be ahead of any unwanted spying. The plan is to have you in place and ready for the assassins if they are indeed in route to Duchess Mariom."

The King now nodded toward Keven. "Keven is to race to Halenester and locate Karlyle and his two other guild members. Keven, you will direct the two other wizards to report to me. Then you and Karlyle will race west to meet the others. Once you are all together, you will be responsible for the Duchess' safety."

King Ballistor paused, and then asked, "Questions anyone?"

No one spoke. King Ballistor continued, "Then you will leave when you are ready. And may the gods shield your party from Evil's arrows."

We all bowed and turned to leave.

King Ballistor spoke once more, "Errol, in the outer chamber there is another group of officers including my Third-in-Command. Send them in to me as you pass."

Errol bowed slightly as he answered the King, "As ordered, Sire."

Talon Fortress

Soon we were horsed and out of the castle. Keven left us with a wave and rode openly through the streets and out the main roadway of Hirst. The mood in the streets was fear, but the crowds were surprisingly calm, considering events in the ballroom were well known throughout the city. The markets were still closed this early in the morning. They showed no signs of opening. No merchants were laying out their goods for display. Everyone was either scurrying about or talking in small groups. Soldiers were rushing to and from the castle in numbers. As we slowly rode through the streets I began to see wagons being loaded for travel. It seemed that half of the populace was preparing to leave Hirst, while the other half was standing around considering it.

Ceikay was leading the way, I followed, and Errol rode last. With Ceikay's mind probing, she was able to scan the area to insure that no one was paying undue attention to us. At various spots in the spiraling road were paths that were either empty, or had only a few people in them.

We went through Hirst this way until Ceikay finally led us out of the mass of buildings. Before us were the many military camps of the visiting Dukes. We could see that soldiers in these camps were mobilizing for departure. As we passed between the towers I felt sharp eyes watching us from above.

We immediately headed west to the port of Hirst. The short trip was uneventful.

We soon saw Duke Castus' vessels. The activity onboard showed that they would be on their way shortly. To the left of the dock we saw King Ballistor's colors next to a large schooner. We dismounted and led our horses to its gangplank. Errol hailed the boatswain to come aboard. We were waved on deck without a word being said. Within moments the ropes were cast off and we were leaving Hirst behind.

The sun had barely shown itself when we left the dock. The vessel ran true and smooth. None spoke during the brief voyage. I noticed that Errol's eyes stayed closed. I wondered how anyone could sleep. I envied his calm.

Before the sun had reached mid-morn we landed just west of the great delta. We disembarked and mounted our horses. The captain of the schooner nodded his farewell, then turned back to his crew. With a few curt commands the vessel was soon sailing south.

The area we now began traveling through is known as the floodplains of the River Telmas. This area is rich in soil and many crops are produced in abundance. The area south and west of Halenester is mainly corn producing. We rode swiftly through these cornfields while Ceikay stayed alert probing for any kind of suspicious activities. We saw no panic on the back roads in farmers or other travelers. News of the massacre had not yet reached the outlying areas.

We kept our horses at a constant gallop where we were able. In some areas we could only trot at a slower pace. By noon we were on Tymia Road. I marveled at the stamina and strength of our fine horses.

On arrival at Tymia Road we stopped for food. The horses were let free to drink from a stream at the side of the road. We sat down and ate some jerky and hardened biscuits.

While there was a pause I decided to ask a few questions. "Are monks trained to shield their minds?"

Errol smiled, which surprised me.

I struggled to clarify my question. "In the ballroom, how did they surprise us?"

Ceikay answered, "I believe I know what you are trying to ask. First: Why did I not sense that the monks had murderous thoughts the moment they entered the ballroom? Second: If they indeed have their minds shielded from probe, then what made me cry out in alarm just before they attacked? Is that what you are puzzling over?"

"Yes, if you can read my mind, then why not those of the Monks?"

"I cannot read thoughts, but it is an easy thing for me to reason that you would not understand what happened in the ballroom. Curiosity would push you to eventually ask; and this is the first opportunity for you to question us."

I nodded at her reasoning.

She continued, "Monks are trained somewhat to shield their minds. It is a mandatory part of their training from the moment of their initiation into the monastery. They believe that it promotes mental discipline, and that it also shields them from the influence of the evil gods. Unfortunately I was not able to uncover their intent as they marched into the ballroom. Would that I had; less people might have died. But I swear by all the gods, I will eventually be able to break through even their strongest mental shields."

Errol then cut in with a harsh tone. "Ceikay, you will not start faulting yourself. You are forgetting that a collective shield was in place."

He turned to address me. "You see Beorn, the monks combine their powers to cover their numbers; the greater the number of like minds, the more effective the shield. Ceikay did well considering she was against over forty well-trained monks working as one. Now Ceikay, continue your explanation."

With a sigh Ceikay continued, "So, as I was explaining, they came into the ballroom shielded. Their point of failure was in the signal to attack. Obviously, one of the monks was in charge of setting off the rest. A certain signal was prearranged to trigger the onslaught. What that specific signal was, I do not know. We do know though that it was not a physical signal, since the monks were facing in four different directions. It could have been a mental "scream" by the leader, a sudden mental stab that each monk was waiting for. It could have been simply a certain verse in the chant that the assassins were waiting for. But, like I said, the specific signal to attack was not discovered. What I sensed was the sudden change in the mental wave that exploded from one of the monks standing near me in their square. Whether this was the leader, or a monk that mentally "jumped" ahead of the rest is again unknown to me. I picked up this mental explosion and instantly knew it for what it was, that is when I screamed and threw you to the floor."

"What do you mean that you recognized it?" I asked.

"There are certain patterns of thought, or I should say emotion. Certain patterns of emotion that are universal in humans. This particular wave that broke from this monk was unmistakably the initiation of violence. At the moment a person decides to 'erupt' into a violent act, his thoughts betray him. The emotion of violence is impossible to mask or to shield. This one individual either was the leader, or merely acted before the rest, but in any event, the moment he sprang, the other monks reacted.

"So when you screamed, Errol knew to protect the King, so he jumped…"

"No," Ceikay shook her head, "Errol was jumping before I screamed."

I looked at Errol. He said nothing as he picked at some bread.

"Go on Errol," Ceikay chided, "You wanted me to tell my story; explain your talent for a change."

"There is nothing to explain."

Ceikay got up from where she was sitting and began to walk toward Errol who was sitting on an old cistern.

He quickly yanked his legs to the side, "All right! I will talk."

Ceikay stopped her advance.

Errol began, "I watch people; I study people. I have studied people all of my life. It is part of my training. There are what I call tics, or nuances that are universal when it comes to human

119

behavior and actions. Most people are unaware that their bodies give off these physical hints. It is to my great advantage that I am aware of them. The monks in the room gave off hints that I picked up on. To be sure, these physical hints are very similar to the mental hint that Ceikay picked up to alert her to the surprise attack."

Errol paused; it was obvious that he was reluctant to explain further.

"Go on, Errol," Ceikay urged, "this is Beorn. He deserves your enlightenment."

Errol looked at me, nodded, and then continued. "Whenever a person begins to prepare for a sudden violent move or attack, that person reveals certain physical signs, such as a deeper than normal intake of breath. He may hold for a moment or two, or explode in an instant. Another sign is the black of the eyes, the iris as 'Healers' call them. These irises will contract just before the body springs. The cheeks also flush at the moment before action. A muscle twitch may give it away. The eyelids stop their normal rate of blinking and may stay open longer than usual. The eyes may squint ever so slightly. The weapons hand may move a fraction of an inch. The body may crouch just a hair. The jaw may suddenly twitch. There are many more signs, but these are enough to give you an idea of what I am trying to explain."

I nodded once and he continued. "Now these clues taken separately do not signal imminent attack, but taken collectively give me a picture of a person ready to jump. As I watched the monks enter the room I saw no signs of violent intent. When they all formed their square and faced the watching crowds, I did notice that the stance they took was not really normal for standing and chanting. Their legs were slightly separated in a posture convenient for jumping forward. Each one of the monks had one foot slightly turned and slightly behind their body."

I closed my eyes to see the scene again. I nodded again to Errol.

"When the monks began to chant, did you notice that not all chanted? There were four in the row facing me who kept their mouths slightly opened with their lips stilled. Just as I noticed this curiosity, these four monks all turned their heads to face the King. It was at this precise moment that I remembered the deaths in Darion Woods and realized what was happening. My eyes took in the rest of the clues these assassins were showing me. The moment the four monks took a big breath at the same time, I jumped at King Ballistor to knock him away from the darts that were about to fly out of their mouths! In truth, I did not hear Ceikay scream."

I had more questions. "How did Keven and Ceikay have time to save Duke Castus? When the attack came, Ceikay first knocked me down, so she surely did not have time to knock the Duke down. So Keven must have been the one to get to the Duke first. If so, what alerted him to act so fast?"

Errol answered, "Keven has his own ways. We will let him fully explain his talents to you later, but I will tell you how he knew the Monks' evil intent."

It was Ceikay who now smiled. Why, I did not know.

Errol continued, "Keven's senses surely detected that violence was about to explode. In truth, he gave us a secret sign to be on alert even before the monks finished entering the room."

"So he saw the same signs as you with the monks facing him and jumped when they moved!" I smiled at my guess.

"No," Ceikay corrected me, "He jumped when I screamed. He is not as astute as Errol in minute body twitches. He cannot interpret the instant mental waves as I can. On the other hand, Keven's talent does enable him to sense certain dangers before us, but even though his senses alert him to impending danger, they cannot pinpoint the precise instant the action is about to happen. He relied on us to spring."

"How did he know then?" I asked.

Errol shook his head as he answered, "We will let him explain that to you."

"All right, then tell me why he chose to save Duke Castus and not any of the other Dukes?"

Now it was Ceikay's turn to shake her head, "It was simply because Keven was close to Duke Castus when the attack started. So it was a matter of blind luck of positioning that Duke Castus is alive and the others are dead."

I decided that I should stop the questions for the moment.

In the pause Errol got up and looked down both directions of Tymia Road. He rubbed his chin and frowned,

"It is strange that we see no one on this road. We have had our rest and our lunch, and no one has passed us going either way."

Ceikay got up and joined Errol. "It reminds me of the road to Brentsad. Normal road travel should show a lot of activity. I can understand normal travel being cut off from the east, considering war preparations. But military outriders should already be on their way west."

Errol continued her thoughts out loud. "Yes, and travel coming from the west should be normal merchant travel. What is stopping the merchants?"

"War."

Both Errol and Ceikay turned to me as I said it.

Errol was about to say something when a screech from above turned our eyes skyward. A large golden eagle swooped down on us and I crouched low and covered my head with my arms as the huge bird of prey passed low over our heads. I looked over at my two companions, and saw them smiling and waving at the creature.

The eagle then circled several times over our heads and turned east toward Halenester. Our gaze left the eagle and fixed on the road. In the distance we could now see riders on horseback coming toward us. We also saw the eagle swoop down on them, but the bird did not rise back up into the sky. It looked as though it alit on the shoulder of one of the riders.

Errol finally spoke. "It looks like they quickly found Banator. They ride at speed. We should ready for travel."

We then gathered our horses. They were rested and appeared ready to carry us for another fifty leagues. I truly admired those animals.

As we rode to meet the figures coming our way, the eagle rose to the sky and flew over us toward the west. As the riders came close we now saw their expressions, all very serious.

As we met, Keven spoke to us without greeting. "Dire news! A force has attacked the capitol city of Bourne in the Whorton

Realm. Duke Whorton's steward has abandoned the city and is retreating to Orth Pass."

Karlyle cut in, "We must rest our horses. We can use that time to tell you of the events. Then we must race to find Duchess Mariom."

Moments later we were all afoot while the horses grazed nearby.

"Let us hear your news, Keven. But first, how did you find Eagle so fast?" Errol had assumed his authoritative voice.

Keven answered simply, "Eagle was already looking for me."

No one asked for explanation so Keven continued, "Riders are coming in to King Ballistor with news of war. Right after we left Hirst a messenger from Bourne rode in with word that two days ago a force surprised the city with siege machines and assault troops. Steward Rastus could not hold the city. He evacuated the citizens while a holding company was left in the castle in a suicide delaying action. Riders have been sent northward to Dannon to warn and prepare that city for invasion."

"What do we know of the enemy?" Ceikay asked.

"Not much," Keven answered. "What information the messenger gave us, was that the war flags of the invading force were not of any realm of Tavegnor. Numbers and types of troops are not known; except for the heavy mounted cavalry and the assault infantry that swept through the city."

Banator then spoke for the first time. "Worse news we have to tell. Riders from Talavor have arrived to report an invasion of the northern city of Stannis…and the war standards were recognized. Duke Hastid's war flags are the ones invading Ballistor's realm!"

No one spoke as the impact of this news was absorbed.

Errol muttered in a low voice, "Invasion from within and without…"

Ceikay then surprised me by her question, "What is the news concerning Hensha, Banator?"

"No word or sight of her from anyone. She has completely disappeared. I am gravely worried."

Errol now spoke to our three new arrivals. "I assume that King Ballistor sent outriders to you with orders, as well as this news of war."

Keven nodded. "The King did send orders. We are to continue on to find and warn Duchess Mariom as ordered."

"Where was King Ballistor planning to go?" Ceikay asked.

"I do not know the answer to that," Keven responded. "I am sure when the King sent the messenger to us, even he did not know at that moment, but I am…"

Suddenly Keven stopped, held up his hand, and closed his eyes.

Everyone stood silent and looked at Keven. I started to open my mouth but Karlyle held his finger up to his closed lips. I understood and kept silent. This quiet stillness went on for several long moments.

Finally, Keven opened his eyes and spoke. "Eagle has shown me where Duchess Mariom is. Her personal banner is leading a regiment of her army south of Ludgen toward Talon Fortress. They march at speed just to the west of Talon Road."

He closed his eyes again. This time he remained motionless much longer, as did the rest of us waiting for him. No one said a word or moved lest they disturb him. I surmised what was going on while we waited. As in the case of his horse, Keven can 'place' his eyes into the eagle and see what the eagle sees! Right now Keven was soaring above the earth taking in information. The rest of my company had understood this from the start and were patiently waiting for him to report.

Then he opened his eyes and spoke. "I tried to get to Talon Fortress to see what was happening there. It was too far for my range with Eagle. But I do confirm that Duchess Mariom is on her way to the fortress in haste and in force."

Errol looked at all of us in turn. "It may be that Talon Fortress is under siege also, and that Duchess Mariom has gotten word of it. Since she is on her way there, we will travel to the fortress and meet her there. We should be able to assist her in its defense. We will leave this road and head southwest."

Errol then addressed Keven. "Keven, how far from Talon is Duchess Mariom?"

"One day's ride as a regiment travels."

Errol thought for a moment before speaking again. "I estimate that we are right now about one hundred leagues from Talon. Rest will have to wait, as we will ride through the night to get there to aid the Duchess. Since she is mobilized for war, then we can rest assured that her Personal Guard is on full alert for any sabotage or assassination attempts, but we still must attempt to find the three monks if we can. The information they hold is much needed."

Keven retrieved his horse as he spoke, "As we travel closer to Talon I will soon be in range with Eagle. Then we will see the action there."

We all followed Keven's lead and mounted our horses. We left Tymia Road and headed southwest. Since secrecy was no longer an issue, we rode openly and quickly over back roads and through the farmlands. We rode past farmers along the way but did not stop to warn them of war. Time would not allow us to warn everyone we passed, so we warned no one. I prayed to the gods that harm would not visit this peaceful area.

As the shadows stretched longer, we alternated between galloping and trotting to pace our horses. After a long while, Keven maneuvered close to Karlyle and handed his reins over. Without a word, Karlyle took Keven's reins and led his horse.

I watched as I rode behind them. Keven then lowered his head and I guessed what he was doing, shutting his eyes and flying.

After a while, Keven raised his head and took back his reins. Ceikay was riding to the front of him but still knew she could now speak to him. "What news do you have to share Keven?"

"There are siege engines and catapults facing the fortress on the seaward side. The banners over the besieging armies are unfamiliar to me. They have not begun attacking as yet. They seem to be setting up the war machines as we travel."

"Good," Errol called out from behind me. Duchess Mariom will not be too late and neither shall we."

Banator then added, "I pray to the gods that a battle takes place and that I may release my anger on these invaders. If they are a part of my Hensha's disappearance, then I pray that I may kill them all."

I looked over at Banator who was riding next to me. There was

125

no humor on his face, only a dark and deadly glare.

We rode on in silence again until the shadows of our horses stretched behind us to the horizon. We passed farms whose bare windows began to show the lights of evening candles. Still we did not stop. It seemed that our horses could go on forever…while my backside would soon fail.

Several times Keven took 'flight' and reported on Duchess Mariom and Talon Fortress. Duchess Mariom had stopped to bivouac for the night. Her troops were on Talon Road and a half a day's march from the fortress. The besieging armies at Talon were lighting campfires and appeared to be settling in for the night.

Finally, long after last light, and traveling with the moonlight, Errol called a halt to our ride. To our left was an old mill house that appeared to have been abandoned seasons ago. Ceikay now led our party off the small road and to the mill. The door had long ago fallen to the side, but the roof was intact.

"We will be no good to anyone at Talon Fortress if we arrive with no rest. Since night has fallen and the invaders are not in a hurry to attack, we will rest ourselves and our good horses here. But before first light we must be up and riding again."

Happily I dismounted and began to massage my backside.

Banator and Keven took the horses and began to unsaddle them. Karlyle and I gathered sticks and small logs to fuel a fire. After a full day on horse I was ready for a hot supper. Errol and Ceikay entered the mill and began to clear spots for sleeping. They took our bedrolls inside and laid them out on the earthen floor.

I did not say a word to anyone; I was too tired to talk. Once the fire was started by Karlyle's 'magic' I went inside the mill and fell onto my bedding. I did not stay there long. The smell of fresh plucked hens being roasted over the fire quickly woke me and my stomach. Once outside again, I saw that everyone was sitting around the fire in anticipation. Plates were in hand, already loaded with warm biscuits and red potatoes. A fully loaded plate was handed to me as I sat down next to Banator. For the first time today I saw him smile.

"…Knew ya'd be out here soon…" he drawled.

The rest smiled also.

Sensing my question, Ceikay answered me, "From Karlyle's little bag of goods we get the biscuits and potatoes. The hens were taken from the farm past the overgrown field behind you. Do not fret; we left two copper Kopas as payment."

We did not talk much during the meal. Errol soon announced that everyone should turn in for the night. I heard no objections.

It seemed only a moment after I put my head down on my bedroll that Karlyle was nudging me to get up,

"Beorn, it is time. We must be on our way."

I got up without complaint and rolled my bedding. It was still dark, but I knew the night was nearly over and I had gotten some sleep. I found that I was terribly sore, but I determined not to show it to the others. I gamely went outside and found that my horse had already been saddled and was awaiting me. I carefully climbed into the saddle. I stiffened my back and prepared to travel.

Just then Keven came around the corner of the mill and approached his horse. He spoke before he mounted,

"I do not know about anyone else, but yesterday's ride surely put a sore on my rump!"

To my amused surprise, everyone else nodded and grumbled in agreement.

Soon we left the mill behind and were on our way to Talon. The horses were fit and fresh. They showed no signs of being ridden hard the day before. As the first light of the sun began to push aside the night, Keven handed his reins once more to Karlyle. His eyes stayed closed for a long while as we rode. No one spoke as we waited for him to return. In time Keven opened his eyes and reported as we rode on,

"The invaders still do not attack. Their war machines are in place. In numbers they seem to have enough to assault the fortress. They have ladders at the ready to mount the outer walls. Why they are waiting I can only surmise."

Errol called to him, "Then surmise for us, Keven."

"As you so demand, my large leader." Keven grinned and

127

continued: "Heavily armored infantry troops are in formation on the beach. I see horses but no mounted knights or archers. They might be waiting for reinforcements from off shore. We are too far away at this time for Eagle to travel out to sea, so I do not know the size or type of fleet of the enemy. In truth, I do not even have proof that a fleet is out there. We have to get closer."

"Where is Duchess Mariom?" Errol pressed.

"Her regiment is on the road and will arrive at Talon just after the height of the day's sun. We will be at Talon not long before her."

Nothing more was said for a time. We ate in saddle. The jerky and biscuits were enough to keep us going. We passed around a bladder-bag of water as we rode.

Eventually the land began a gradual rise in elevation. We were entering what is called the Talon Plateau. This is a high point at the very mouth of the great Doas Estuary. This high point elevates the promontory that Talon Fortress is built upon. Talon Fortress was built to protect and supply the King's fleet that patrols the entrance of the Inlet. The fortress overlooks the small sheltered cove that serves the fleet. To ward off attacking ships, fire catapults face the water side.

This is a vital defensive fort for the country of Tavegnor. Therefore, it is heavily fortified by an equal number of each of the seven realms. Each contingent is made up of five companies of one hundred and twenty officers and soldiers. This massive fortress can hold over four thousand fully armed soldiers.

Not long after we gained the plateau we saw Talon Fortress. Even from the extreme distance, I could see that it was massive. By the telling, it was larger than any castle or citadel in Tavegnor. We could not see the besieging armies from where we were. Keven told us that they were on the far side of the fortress, on the seaward side. From the fortress the road led away north, to the right of us. There was no sign of Duchess Mariom's army.

Ceikay turned to Keven, "Where is Mariom?"

"Wait just a moment; you will see the vanguard coming down the road."

As Keven predicted, the tops of about a dozen war standards

appeared at the far ridge of the plateau. Soon we saw the horsemen carrying those standards rise over the horizon. They stopped about a third of a league from Talon Fortress. Duchess Mariom's personal coat-of-arms could be seen at the head of the banners. Even from our distance we could hear the cheers of the soldiers inside the fortress.

Banator rode up next to Errol. "Which direction do we go; to the fortress or to Duchess Mariom?"

Errol did not answer right away; a frown crossed his face as he sat silently on his horse.

Finally he did answer, "We were ordered to report to Duchess Mariom, so that is what we will do. But we will not go to her at this time. We will wait."

What is it that you are thinking, Errol?" Ceikay asked.

Errol just shook his head and muttered under his breath. "I do not know yet. I am not sure. I want to see all of the Duchess' guide-ons before I know. We should not near the fortress just yet."

It seemed that we had not been noticed by the fortress and now Errol announced that we would retreat back below the plateau and await the main party of the Duchess. Only then would we advance in the open field to meet her.

The others of my party did not seem to find this strange. We dismounted and let our horses feed on the fine grasses that covered the ground around us. We ate a little jerky and biscuits.

Presently, Keven announced that it was time to mount. Duchess Mariom was gaining the plateau.

We rode again up to the plateau and saw the main body of soldiers. It was marching smartly toward the stationary vanguard. Then we saw the whole group disengage from formation and begin to spread out over the plain. Groups of infantry were following their guide-ons away from the road. As we watched, it became apparent that a field encampment was being set up.

While this was going on I wondered why Errol did not have us go in to the rapidly forming camp. He merely looked out onto the plateau and waited. For what, I did not know.

Shortly, a tent larger than the rest went up in the middle of the new camp. Instantly, The vanguard standard bearers turned their

horses around and trotted back to the main body. Duchess
Mariom's personal banner could be seen headed to the large tent.
At that moment, a horn sounded atop one of the towers of the
fortress. We could see that the portcullis of the main gate was
being raised. One of the huge gates behind the portcullis now
swung open and out rode a group of riders. They headed for the
encampment.

Now Errol spoke as he spurred his horse forward, "That is the
fortress commander riding out to greet the Duchess. We must
hurry! Ride in close and formal formation. Banator, unfurl the
King's banner so that we may be recognized. We do not want any
skittish soldier tossing a javelin or two at us as we approach."

Then he called out to me with orders I found confusing at the
time, "Beorn, stay close between Karlyle and Keven. Be alert for
our signs, and do not hesitate to draw your sword if we tell you.
Remember the signs!"

The signs he was referring to were some simple hand signals
that they had been showing me since leaving Brentsad.

We rode in tight formation as Errol ordered. King Ballistor's
coat-of-arms was flying on a lance that Banator was holding
upright. I did not think it strange that a lance had suddenly
appeared in our group. I merely wondered at how Karlyle did it.

Our speed and direction was bringing us to a point of intersect
with the fortress commander just before he was to enter Duchess
Mariom's camp. I could see that Errol was deliberately intending
to meet up with the Commander before reporting to the Duchess. I
could also see that we were now being noticed. Riders were
mounting horses in the camp, and they were beginning to form a
line between us and the camp's perimeter. I could see that the
riders from the fortress saw us also, and were slowing down. Soon
they were at a complete stop and were obviously waiting for us.

We slowed as we neared the commander's group. There were
seven riders. It appeared to be six escorts and a senior officer.

"Hail and well met!" The leader called out to us as we pulled
up to his group. "There is no mistaking your large silhouette in the
saddle, Errol! I recognized you and your poor horse right off!"

"It is well to see you, Commander Vandor!" Errol saluted the

Commander as he spoke. "And doubly well that we intercepted you before you entered this camp!"

Vandor saw that Errol's manner was all seriousness; his smile disappeared as he spoke again. "It is good to see the rest of you, but I see that there will be no good tidings to share at this reunion. What news do you bring me?"

"There is a lot to tell. For now, I caution that you be on your guard in this camp. This is not the place or time to explain my concerns. As the King's agents we respectfully ask permission that you allow us to join you in greeting Duchess Mariom to Talon Fortress."

Vandor formally responded, "Permission is not given because permission is not required. As the King's Representatives, you have the right to enter the camp with us. Please, let us continue in."

As Errol rode up to join Vandor, the six escorts backed their horses to allow the rest of us to fall in formation just behind the two lead riders.

At this time a full company of light cavalry rode out from the camp toward us. Errol quickly leaned over to Vandor and I heard him speak, "As I said, be very careful in this camp. If you value your life and the lives of your men, you will not allow our group to be separated."

Vandor looked at Errol but kept quiet. The next moment we were surrounded by the Duchess' cavalry and being led into camp.

We were soon stopped in front of Duchess Mariom's tent. Four of her personal guards were at attention at the front flaps. Standing in front of them was an officer in full leather armor. He was strongly built and was about Errol's height. A large bastard sword was strapped to his back, and he carried two daggers in his leather belt. He had the insignia of Regiment Commander; equal in rank to Commander Vandor, who now dismounted and faced the officer.

Vandor saluted and spoke formally. "I am Commander Vandor of Talavor. Talon Fortress is under my command and I officially welcome Duchess Mariom. I wish to be granted an audience with the Duchess as soon as possible."

The officer returned Vandor's salute. "I am Commander

Baltoron of the realm of Mariom. I am responsible for the personal safety of Duchess Mariom. The Duchess is Royal Commander and is presently inside waiting for you to report to her. You may proceed inside."

With that said Commander Baltoron stepped aside and waved the four guards away from the tent. Commander Vandor stepped forward and the rest of us began to follow.

Suddenly the spears of the four guards shot out in front of the rest of us! Eight more guards stepped from around the tent and leveled their spears at us.

We stopped still. Commander Vandor looked back and to the pointed spears. He now stepped close to face Commander Baltoron.

"What is the meaning of this? Let my party through!"

Commander Baltoron stood his ground. "This is not your party that came from the fortress. They have not yet identified themselves to me."

"They clearly show the King's banner! They met me outside of your encampment and formally requested to join my party in welcoming Duchess Mariom. I know them and vouch for them. Let all of us through!"

"The Duchess does not permit it. They will stay outside."

Now Errol took one step forward and addressed Baltoron. "Your being here in force proves to me that you and Duchess Mariom are aware that a state of war exists in Tavegnor. If you know protocol, you know that in time of war the King's Representatives cannot be denied access to a Duke or Duchess. The King is the supreme Commander of military forces, and this is a military encampment. Duchess Mariom must see us, as this is law. We have news that is vital to her safety."

Once again I felt that irresistible influence that Errol's words and tone could project. Commander Baltoron hesitated for a moment, and then announced that he would confer with Duchess Mariom. He entered the tent and left us to face the spears a bit longer.

Several moments later, Baltoron exited the tent. "Duchess Mariom has graciously granted permission to see all of you."

He stepped aside and waved the spears off. We all entered the tent. The tension was high.

Duchess Mariom was standing to the rear of the tent as we entered. She was facing us and waiting for our approach. I did not look at her. The moment we walked into the tent I saw the monks...

...only, they were not monks this time. They were officers in Duchess Mariom's Personal Guard! And this time I was not taken with surprise and confusion. I immediately signaled to my companions. The signal was simply the scratching of my right ear. Keven had earlier instructed me to scratch my right ear the moment I recognized anyone or any threat. So, as I stood there scratching, Commander Vandor began to speak.

"Hail and good long life to you, Duchess Mariom. Thank you for coming to assist Talon Fortress in breaking of the siege. The enemy is at our seaward walls but fortunately has not yet attacked. Your arrival should discourage them from further action."

Duchess Mariom turned her back on Vandor.

This sudden, insulting move quieted the Commander. He stood there looking at her back, not knowing what to say.

Duchess Mariom now spoke, still with her back to us. "Do not come into my tent and begin to tell me what to do with my armies Commander."

She then turned around and continued, "I will tell you what is to be done, and if you or your friends of the King object, so be it. I will report to the King when I see him next and tell him of your concern."

None of us moved. Memories of Duke Hastid's welcome came back to me. I did not feel calm as my companions appeared to be.

The Duchess now grinned as she spoke. "What I will do first is to send four companies of my Personal Guard into your fortress to inspect and ensure its security. As they are proceeding in, you will stay here, giving me a complete report of your preparations for defense. After that I will remove the siege engines from your walls."

Vandor began to protest. Duchess Mariom retorted back...

While this exchange was going on, the rest of my companions

were communicating with each other with subtle signals.

I admit now that I was actually being seduced by the intrigue that I was a part of in that tent. My blood quickened in anticipation.

In the tent I was also busy giving signals to my partners. These signals were pointing out the three so-called monks. Errol signaled that he understood and slowly maneuvered around to stand directly in front of the three. His moves were so subtle that even I at first did not realize his change of position in the tent. I was signaling the others and receiving signals back. I was told by Karlyle to take a step back.

Suddenly my attention was brought back to the Duchess and Commander Vandor. The Duchess' hand and voice raised at the same time.

She raised her hand as to strike the Commander. "You dare to insult me by continuing to question my orders?"

Now Errol surprised and stopped the Duchess with a sudden question. "Where is your heavy cavalry Duchess Mariom?"

The question momentarily quieted the room. I glanced at Errol and he was smiling benignly at the Duchess.

Duchess Mariom turned to Errol and looked at him coldly. "Why do you ask that, and who are you to address me so with that disrespectful grin?"

"I only ask because normal military dictum would have you with at least a regiment of heavy mounted knights to lift a siege. I see only one company of the light cavalry of your Personal Guard, the one that surrounded us as we entered your camp."

Duchess Mariom hesitated before answering. Then one of the officer/monks answered for her. "You are right; your eyes serve you well. We have eight full companies of Heavy Horse to the rear of our encampment. That is why you do not see them now. They will march forward when Duchess Mariom gives the order."

I saw Keven's subtle sign of falsehood in that claim.

Errol responded to the monk, "Thank you for clarifying that for us. By the way sir, what is your name?"

The monk/officer squared his shoulders and answered him, "I am Captain Nellustus, Second Commander of Duchess Mariom's

Personal Escort."

Errol spoke again, now ignoring the officer and addressing the Duchess. "Duchess Mariom, as King Ballistor's representative, I was given the order to tell and warn you of the outbreak of war. Also, of a possible threat of assassination by three arrant monks."

Errol's pause was met by tense silence.

He then continued, "But we see that you were under full armed march before King Ballistor knew of any attack on the land of Tavegnor. Why is that, Madam? And why is it that three monks are in your tent dressed in officer's uniforms?"

Duchess Mariom did not answer. Her guards stiffened and reached for their weapons. The Duchess held up her hand to halt further action. She stared at Errol with her mouth slightly open, obviously angry and taken by surprise at his words.

She slowly pointed a finger at Errol. "I will not stand here and be insulted by you any longer. You will..."

Ceikay suddenly stepped forward and directly into Duchess Mariom's face. The dozen guards around the room drew their swords.

Ceikay grinned, and then spoke, "Why is it that your hair is dyed? Can it be that you are hiding your age?"

Duchess Mariom's eyes became as big as saucers. She began to stutter, and then reached for her sword. Immediately Ceikay grabbed the Duchess' sword hand and slammed her forehead into the Duchess' nose! As Duchess Mariom's head shot back, Ceikay wrenched the sword out of the sheath and swung it at a guard who was springing at her. The tip of the sword sliced through the guard's throat and the guard went down.

The rest was a blur while it happened. Only later, when I was given time, was I able to recall every memory.

The moment that Ceikay hit the Duchess, Errol launched his body at the three monk/officers. In his hands were daggers that now stabbed at the throats of the two at the side. As the daggers were entering flesh, Errol was already past the two hapless monks and crashing into the third.

Keven's eyes were closed and immediately I heard the scream of horses outside the tent. Two guards now rushed to him, swords held high for attack. Karlyle stepped to these guards and swung his long thin sword in a figure eight motion and suddenly I saw the arms of the two guards fly away in different directions. Then Karlyle's swift sword decapitated two more guards charging from the other direction.

Banator rushed to the tent opening and quickly slew two guards rushing in. Commander Vandor jumped at three more and quickly sliced them down with his curved sword. He then swung at the tent itself and sliced a big hole in the side.

As for my actions; it is strange that my memory blurs at this point. I know that I must have killed for the first time. How many guards came at me I do not remember. Why my memory fails here I cannot explain, but I clearly remember my short sword swinging and covered in blood.

I also remember being pulled out of the tent by Keven and being thrown onto a horse.

"Ride to the fortress!" Keven yelled.

I did not know which direction the fortress was in, so I spun around several times in panicked confusion. Somehow horsed, Ceikay rode up and grabbed my reins. She pulled me from the chaos surrounding the tent. The noise was deafening.

I now realized that we were riding at full gallop. I spun my head back and saw flames leap up from Duchess Mariom's tent to stab at the sky. Arrows were falling toward my back, but they mysteriously veered away at the last second. The rest of my companions rode fast behind me. As we got closer to the fortress I saw arrows fly from the walls. They were flying over our heads and into our pursuers.

I then looked past Ceikay and saw the huge portcullis being raised, allowing us to ride through the walls and into Talon Fortress. Once inside the walls, Ceikay swung her horse around and jumped from her saddle. She ran up and roughly pulled me from my horse. What then stunned me was the sight of Duchess Mariom straddled face down on Vandor's saddle. Monk/Captain Nellustus was thrown to the ground by Keven from the back of his horse!

The rest of our company followed through the gates. I was

surprised that our whole group, including the six escorts, made it back from the camp. As the last rider of our group raced under the wall, Commander Vandor yelled out orders to shut and bar the gates. Arrows were now flying from the walls of the fortress in great numbers.

Talon Fortress was now under attack, and by Duchess Mariom's forces.

Bugles from the encampment started to sound. Suddenly, shouts were now coming from the west wall of the fortress. Looking toward the noise I saw soldiers on the parapets fighting each other. Soldiers inside the fort were attacking other soldiers right next to them. The metallic clang of sword on sword joined the growing noise of men yelling and screaming. The clang of metal on metal grew to surround us in the quadrangle.

I stood and watched the violence around me in the fortress. I wondered how Duchess Mariom's troops got inside in such great numbers. The gates had been closing as we rode in. None had time to follow us through.

Then I heard Commander Vandor's voice yelling out, "Mariom's garrison in the fortress has turned on us! We must crush them before our walls can be breached!"

He ran to the fighting on the west wall, calling out orders to his officers as he ran.

At this moment a loud whistling could be heard growing over our walls. Ceikay screamed out, "Arrows!"

Standing next to me Karlyle suddenly threw up his hands to the sky. I saw the arrows arch over the walls and come toward our courtyard. Then Karlyle wrenched one arm over his head and the arrows above instantly veered upward and shot over and past us!

I now looked to Errol. He had the officer/monk by the scruff of the neck. Nellustus was staggering and unable to stand without Errol holding him up. He then threw Nellustus to the ground and yelled to one of the six escorts that rushed from the camp with us,

"Get this man in chains and guard him with your life! He must not escape, and he must certainly not die!"

Duchess Mariom was now sprawled in the dirt at our feet. She had a dagger in her right hand and tried to rise up. Errol stepped over and backhanded a fist into her jaw! Her head snapped back and she flew back into the wall. I thought surely that she was dead!

But Errol then yelled at a guard, "Place her in irons and see that she stays alive also!"

Errol now turned to the rest of us. "Talon Fortress must not fall! Get to the parapets!"

We all ran up the wide ramp that led us to the west wall. I saw Vandor off to my right: he was surrounded by soldiers in gold uniforms…Mariom's soldiers. Errol lowered his left shoulder and plowed his way to Vandor. His great sword swung like a toy in his big hands; a deadly, swift toy that drew blood wherever it struck!

Soon he had reached Vandor and freed him from the circle of attackers. Together Errol and Commander Vandor now fought to the edge of the wall.

Keven grabbed my arm and yelled in my ear, "We must protect Karlyle! He is vulnerable!"

I turned to see Karlyle standing at the wall over the great portcullis. His eyes were closed. His sword in his right hand pointed down to the ground. He seemed to be in a trance. I saw and realized that he was diverting the arrows coming in from the archers outside the fortress! Ceikay and Banator were on either side of Karlyle. As Duchess Mariom's soldiers tried to hack at Karlyle, they themselves were hacked down by his two protectors. I found myself swinging my sword at gold uniforms. How effective I was, I do not know, but I do remember that when I got into trouble, Keven was there at my side to dispatch my opponent.

The fight seemed to go on for ages. I was wringing wet with sweat and blood. It seemed that the whole world was exploding in war! As I fought, I could still see the tops of siege ladders swinging to the walls. Some were being thrown back, most stayed, and soon men were jumping up onto the walls from these ladders, adding to the slaughter around me. Men were yelling and snarling like animals as they clashed. The wounded screamed and cried as they fell. The lucky ones died quickly. Those who fell and still lived were trampled by those of us still fighting.

Suddenly I was grabbed and spun around. I swung my sword

at my attacker. It was easily brushed aside…and I found myself facing Errol!

"Beorn!" Even though he yelled right in my face, I could barely hear him, "Follow me!"

He turned and ran down the ramp. I followed, along with a dozen other soldiers. I noticed that none were wearing gold. They were the loyal men from the other six realms of Tavegnor.

Down in the courtyard I saw Commander Vandor run up to Errol. They stopped and Vandor yelled in Errol's ear. He was pointing to the eastern part of the fortress as he yelled. Twice they were interrupted by the fighting. The other dozen soldiers and I surrounded the two and fought off the attacking enemy.

Suddenly Commander Vandor slapped Errol on the back in farewell, and then turned and ran back to the battlements and disappeared into the melee on the wall.

Errol grabbed me by the shoulder and yelled, "Stay close to me! Run, and do not stop to fight!"

We ran to the east wall of the fortress. There was no fighting at the top of this area. Everyone was at the west wall repelling the besiegers and fighting the traitors inside.

Errol did not run up the ramp to the east wall. Instead, he led me and the dozen soldiers toward the base of the wall and to a large wooden door. Standing at the door was an officer, by his insignia, I recognized the symbol of Master-of-Arms. At this part of the courtyard the din of the battle was lessened by the distance, so Errol did not have to yell.

A raised voice was enough to be heard. Errol stopped in front of the Master-of-Arms, "Are you Collis?"

"Yes sir! Commander Vandor sent me here to meet you. I am to lead you down to the grotto. The passageways down there are deliberately misleading. It is a maze that only a few know. Follow me!"

He turned to open the huge oaken door; Errol grabbed me by the shoulder and pulled me close. "Mariom's contingent that was stationed here at the Fortress has attacked their Talon comrades. The traitors are trying to take the fortress from within. Some of them were seen entering this doorway. Vandor fears they may be intending to open a sealed entrance to the grotto. Invaders must be waiting there to rush into the fortress from below. Vandor has directed us to stop them from succeeding!"

I nodded as Errol continued, "Beorn, from this entrance on, it is vitally important that you pay attention to the route! We are going down to an abandoned entry to the docks, and as you heard the Master-at-Arms, it is a maze! If the rest of us fail or need more men down there, I will need you to run back up to alert Commander Vandor! Is that clear?"

I gave one quick nod.

He added, "You are to stay back and not fight! You are only to find your way back if needed! Understand?"

I nodded twice.

Errol now turned and we all entered the passageway to follow Collis. Collis had a flaming torch in his left hand and held a short sword in his right. His was the only light. No torches were hung along the way. I was third behind Errol and struggled to find guide markings on the walls. They were all smooth finished and no help to me at all! I soon realized that I had to remember the route by the turns, and the distances between the turns. With the tension and the fear dominating my emotions, I prayed that my memory would prove true. Now doubting myself as we ran deeper into the earth, I prayed that I would not have to find my way back up alone!

Some parts of the passageway were only wide enough to walk two abreast; other parts were wide enough for eight men side-by-side. Numbers of other passageways branched off in random intervals and directions. Four times we passed through a junction with four or more openings. As we hurried past these black openings, I feared that someone or something was going to jump out at us.

Eventually Collis slowed and held up his hand to signal stop. The silence was complete. Then I began to hear faint pounding in front of us.

Collis whispered softly, but urgently, "We are close, and they are breaking through the iron gate that separates the catacombs and the grotto. We must stop them now!"

He turned and ran toward the noise. We were right behind him. As we ran I noticed that instead of the huge bastard sword, Errol now had two short swords. They looked like large daggers in his hands.

We rounded a corner and immediately ran into a dimly lit room. Errol jumped to the right and suddenly the Master-of-Arms collided back against me, knocking me back into the narrow passageway. Immediately the deafening noise of battle filled my ears, the manic yelling and screaming, the now familiar clanging of swords. I pushed Collis away from me toward the room. He did not jump back into the fray. Instead, he slumped down to the ground as the rest of the soldiers in our group rushed to join Errol. Collis had two short spears stuck through his heavy leather armor and into his chest! I stood stunned looking down at his open eyes. He was looking up at me…then he sighed and his eyes slowly closed.

At that instant, a soldier ran out of the room and toward me! I saw no weapon, but I did see his gold uniform. Desperately, I lurched forward and drove my sword into his stomach. The soldier screamed and rushed past me. He kept on running down the passageway. I looked to my hand and my sword was gone! I bent down and grabbed Collis's sword from his limp hand. Before I could turn and enter the room though, Errol came crashing out and pinned me to the side wall.

He yelled out, "Do not move!"

Five of the dozen soldiers in our group now ran past us, they stopped, turned around and pressed against the side of the passage. It was then that I first heard, and then saw the arrows whizzing out from the room and past our heads. The noises from the room were at a loud roar. Men were yelling, the arrows were whizzing, but no one came around the corner after us. Then I heard a deafening crash.

I looked at Errol standing next to me.

He gave me the answer: "We quickly killed all of Duchess Mariom's men, but they had already opened the iron gates. An iron portcullis is still barring the entrance, but the invaders on the outside are now ramming it with a large timber! Their archers are

141

at the bars firing through to keep us away!"

I yelled back at him, "All we can do is wait for them to break through then?!"

"I wait, you run!"

Before my mouth was completely open, Errol held up his finger to my face. "You must get back to Vandor and tell him that the grotto has been breached! We will hold this passageway. Vandor feared rightly that this was going to happen. You were not brought here to fight, but to return and tell him if it became necessary. And it is now necessary for you to go!"

I looked to the other soldiers waiting next to us. They looked calm and steady. I felt weak in the knees, but I knew that Errol was right.

The flight of the arrows had now stopped, but the banging in the room was louder and rhythmic. The enemy was determined to get through.

I yelled back at Errol, "I will go, and help I will bring back, I promise you!"

He nodded and briefly smiled. Errol then turned and faced the room. We said nothing further. I headed back the way we had come. It was then I realized that I had no torch. The passageway now disappeared into the blackness. The only light was coming from the room behind me. I knew that I was not going to retrieve our torch; not with the archers waiting back there! I had no choice but to step into the darkness and trust to memory. I had not gone far when I decided to close my eyes. They were useless at this point. Closing them seemed to help me 'picture' my way through the halls. Soon, the sounds behind me grew dimmer, but the sound never really stopped. I could feel the rhythmic pounding of the ramming on the iron barrier. As I went further, my confidence returned. I knew where to turn at the appropriate times; I kept one hand on the walls as I progressed. I anticipated the distance between the other passageways and rejoiced whenever the wall suddenly fell away at the predicted times, proof to me that I was headed in the right direction! I began to quicken my pace...

Suddenly I tripped over an unfamiliar object and fell forward onto my face.

I was lost! Nothing was on the floor along any of the route when we first passed. Where had I erred?

I scrambled to my knees, and my fumbling in the dark caused me to hit the unknown object again. It was not hard. I felt with my hands and pressed a finger into an open mouth. I yelled and jumped back, hitting the wall. I dared not breathe, and heard no other breathing either. Suddenly, I knew what was there in the dark. It was the body of the soldier that ran past me earlier. I crawled forward and probed for the body. I ran my hand down until I felt what I was looking for; my sword.

Regaining some degree of calm I stood up and repositioned myself in the dark. Soon I was rushing along at cautious speed, but it seemed as though this black hole I was in would go on forever. Soon I started to hear and feel deep thuds in the walls around me. I wondered what that was as I kept running.

There was no pattern or rhythm to the thuds so I knew that it was not coming from the grotto. I did not really concentrate on the sound, since my concentration was on my flight back to the courtyard.

Then I saw a dim light ahead of me. I picked up my pace and recognized the slits in the wooden door that Master-at-Arms Collis had first led us through. Along with the increase in light came an increase in noise. The noise was telling me that fighting was still going on in the fortress. As I now neared the door, I marveled at the continuing fighting. It had not stopped while we were down in the grotto. It felt as though I had been inside these forsaken passageways for days. But the sights and sounds that met me when I broke through the upper doorway jarred me back into the reality of the fight. It took several moments for my eyes to adjust to the light of the day, and only an instant to remember Errol. I ran to find help as my eyes were adjusting. The fighting around me was a blur and seemed to be at a great distance. My thoughts were only on finding my companions and Vandor.

The huge fortress gate was surrounded by fighting! I ran past and onto the ramp of the west wall. I ran to where I last saw people I knew. They were not there. The fighting was raging at the top of the wall, but I ignored that and frantically looked around.

Then I saw Karlyle. He was walking through the enemy. I could see that they were trying to cut him down, but he was a windmill. He was holding his slim sword by both hands and swinging it in a circular arch alternating from left to right.

I momentarily stood watching the speed of that sword. It was a blur, and it chopped up anyone who was foolish enough to get in its way. He was headed to one of the battle towers on the west wall. I saw arrows raining down from the top of the tower he was nearing. The arrows were hitting the loyal Tavegnor warriors. The second tower was ablaze. The flames reached high into the sky. Smoke from inside poured out onto the walls and surrounded the battle. Men ignored the black smoke that enveloped them.

The fighting went on...

As I tried to get to Karlyle, Commander Vandor and Ceikay stepped before me. Vandor was yelling but I could not hear him.

They pulled me to the edge of the wall away from the thickest fighting. He yelled again in my ear,

"What news of the grotto?!"

"They are breaking through the bars! Collis is dead. Errol and a few others are waiting in the passageway. They need help! We have to get there as..."

Vandor cut me short, "No! We are being overrun here! We need everyone to close the breach in the wall! You and Ceikay must help Karlyle to clear that tower of Mariom's troops! They are slaughtering our men on the wall! We cannot repel the ladders!"

I yelled back, "Errol needs us! They are coming through the grotto! Send him help now!"

I looked to Ceikay to tell Vandor. She shook her head vigorously at me, "Beorn, Vandor is right! Everything is lost if the wall fails! Errol will hold until we can break away from here!"

"No! I promised Errol!"

Vandor backed away from me, "I waste too much time here! Ceikay, he is yours!"

The Commander turned and raced to the tower, gathering his soldiers to him as he ran.

Ceikay now grabbed my face and turned it to hers, "Beorn, look around you! We must fight here! If anyone can hold the

144

grotto, it is Errol! We will get to him when we can!"

At that moment my mind calmed a bit. In that narrow passageway, no one was going to get past Errol. Not any time soon at least!

I nodded and ran after Vandor.

Then the wall behind me was rocked by an explosion that tore out a large chunk and sent shards of broken stone flying through loyal soldiers as well as the enemy. The trebuchets and catapults on the beach were throwing barrel-sized boulders at the fortress. I suddenly realized that was the thudding I felt as I ran in the dark passages earlier!

After that I fought in a daze. I fought not to save the fortress; I fought to end the fighting on the wall and get help to Errol as soon as possible. I lost sight of Ceikay. I lost sight of Karlyle. I lost sight of Vandor, and I never did see Keven.

Eventually we retook the tower on the wall. Our archers were now on the top shooting at the enemy. The other tower was burned out and no one was left in it. The defenders gradually cleared the wall. Most of Duchess Mariom's fortress garrison troops were now dead. The rest were either surrendering or jumping over the walls…and dying. I saw Karlyle at the top of the remaining tower with the archers. He was facing the huge siege machines on the beach. Karlyle looked exhausted, but I could see that he was being successful in diverting the missiles away from the walls.

I swung at one last attacker. My sword grazed his arm as he turned and ran to a ladder on the wall. As he jumped up to swing down the far side, an arrow from the tower pierced his neck and he fell from my view. I slumped to the ground exhausted. I was next to the inner edge of the wall and looked down to the courtyard. I saw Keven leading a group of men from out of one of the barracks. Vandor ran up to him and the men. I saw them talking and gesturing toward the eastern wall. Keven then looked up and scanned the wall, and then his eyes locked on me. He pointed to me and then waved his arm to summon me to join the group. I was spent, but I knew what they intended to do. I jumped up and ran down the ramp.

With torches in hand we ran through the passageways. I led

the way. I listened as we ran. No sound could be heard in front of me. We came across the body of the soldier I had slain. We ran on, but still no sound. Finally we turned the last corner and saw the entrance to the grotto room. The bodies of two of the loyal soldiers were lying on the floor. We stepped over those and entered the room. It was knee deep in bodies. Every spot on that floor ran with blood. At the far end of the room we saw the broken portcullis. They had been successful at gaining entrance to the passageway. Several of our soldiers rushed over to the opening and stepped through. The rest looked for wounded. Keven and I looked for Errol. We did not find him among the dead. He had disappeared.

Keven finally spoke, "Praise the Gods he held."

"Where is he?" I asked to no one in particular. "Did they take him? Is he a prisoner?"

"He is probably hunting," Keven offered, "No one would be able to knock him down and take him out of here. If they had killed him, then his body would be lying amongst the others. If he were dead, the invaders would have climbed over his body and we would be fighting in the courtyard right now."

"What is he hunting?" I asked.

"Not what: Who."

"Well, what or who, we are going after him...yes?"

Keven did not answer right away. He walked over bodies and looked through the broken and twisted bars of the portcullis. He then studied the large iron double doors.

Finally he answered me, "You must remember that Errol is a Sword Master; which means that not only has he had a lifetime of weapons training, he also has an unmatched knowledge of tactical military movements. He chose to leave this room to enter the depths of the grotto, which tells us that he felt that this entrance was now secure from the invaders. He also knew that we would be down here eventually, but he did not leave a message for us to follow, which tells me that he did not want us to follow."

After a silent pause, Keven continued, "No, we will not follow Errol this time. He is hunting. Hunting, I am sure, for information to bring back."

"What then will we do?"

"We start by throwing the bodies of the invaders and traitors outside. Then we will close and secure the iron gates. Guards will be left here in case the invaders try this again. Our dead soldiers will be taken up to the courtyard."

Just then, the soldiers who had gone through to the grotto earlier came back. They reported seeing nothing and no one, the grotto was clear.

Soon after, Keven and I climbed out of the passageway and back into the courtyard. I blinked around in surprise. The sun was completely below horizon and the moon was shining above. We had been fighting all day! Suddenly my body broke down. I simply sat down on the dirt and hung my head to my chest. I wanted to sleep forever right at that spot. I started to shake. Fear was taking over again. At that moment I did not care what Keven or anyone else thought of my weakness.

Keven then sat down next to me.

"By my soul, Beorn, That is the best idea of the day. We will sit here for a few moments to gather our strength."

I did not know if Keven was truly exhausted, or that he was helping me save face. Either way, I was grateful for the brief rest.

Shortly thereafter, we were walking again, back across the courtyard.

The scene around us was changed from the violent, deafening confusion of battle. Hundreds of men lay on the ground; in every grotesque position a dead body can fall. Wounded were calling out; some for help, some for the release of death. Scores of others besides the dead and wounded lay on the ground also. These were too exhausted to move, let alone help the wounded who cried out.

Then there were the ones who were still on their feet: cooks, pages, stable hands, chamber maids. Everyone in the fortress who could stand, was running to aid the tired and fallen.

I looked to the walls and saw the same scene. I also saw that along the walls stood soldiers on guard against another assault.

Talon Fortress had not been overrun.

I saw Commander Vandor by the front gate. He was walking with a squad of guards and several junior officers. They were assessing the aftermath of battle. I could not hear his words, but I could tell by the gestures and responses of those around him that Vandor was giving orders to clear away the dead and to tend the wounded. Wooden planks were being brought for the wounded, and carts brought for the dead.

Commander Vandor then saw Keven and me as we approached. He turned to greet us.

"I understand that the grotto entrance is secured and guarded, where is Errol?"

Keven answered, "He is not to be found, so I believe that he is gathering information."

The Commander frowned: "Why did he go by himself? Why did he leave the grotto before we got there?"

Keven again spoke, "Commander Vandor, You know Errol well. His reasons we may not understand, but we know we must trust him in this. We will see him again and then everything will be explained."

"True words you speak, Keven. I will not worry about him. I will worry about preparing Talon for another assault. First light might bring quiet, or it might bring battle back to the walls."

Vandor looked around and then continued, "Before then I will want to meet with my officers and your companions. As for now, my kitchen is at full strength and food is abundant. Get something to fill your stomachs and try to rest. I will send for you before first light."

Keven nodded and asked, "Where do we find the kitchen?"

"Straight behind you in the Keep, the ground floor is where the cooks have set up the kettles."

"Thank you, Commander Vandor. You will find us with Karlyle and Ceikay on the west tower."

A messenger ran up and saluted. Commander Vandor turned his attention from us and we turned our attention to get food.

Once again, I suddenly felt a sharp pang of hunger and thirst.

I practically ran to the Keep. I found that there were hundreds of soldiers already there. Some men were eating; most were waiting in lines to be served. The manner of the men waiting surprised me; no one pushed or hollered. Everyone was calm and waited their turn. Keven caught up with me and we both stepped into one of the lines. Praise to the cooks and their hard work, we did not wait long and soon we were taking food shares up to Ceikay and Karlyle.

Climbing up to the west tower, we saw more bodies being taken away. The wounded had already been taken below to the barracks. At the top were a dozen guards standing alert and watching the invaders' camp on the beach. On the floor just below us, guards who were not on watch were asleep. Karlyle and Ceikay were on the top of the tower in one of the corners. I was surprised to see that they were sleeping. I had fully expected to see them planning our next moves. I also wondered about something else...

"Where is Banator?" I asked Keven, looking around.

"He went over the wall. He is looking for Errol."

Keven put the pots of food down beside the two and sat down next to the wall. He motioned to me to join him.

I soon found that I could not shut my eyes for sleep. My mind was too filled with the day's slaughter. I sat with my back to the wall and stared up into the night sky.

Keven startled me back from the stars. "You will need that sleep Beorn. Close your eyes and rest."

I looked over at him. "If I close my eyes, my dreams will only take me back to the battle."

Keven smiled and nodded: "You are right. I am afraid that I too will be battling again in my sleep. But...we must try, lest exhaustion slows us too much in the next battle."

This time I nodded, but did not smile.

Moments later, sleep came to me...The dreams did not.

I was awakened by one of Vandor's pages, "Sir...sir, please, I ask your pardon; Commander Vandor requires your presence."

Sleep had not brought dreams, but it did not bring renewal either. I opened my tired eyes and nodded. Slowly my body answered my commands and I got to my feet. Ceikay and Keven were standing at the stairwell waiting for me. Karlyle still lay on the tower floor, asleep.

Ceikay saw my question, "Karlyle must rest as much as he can. He must be ready to battle the siege engines in the morn. He must do nothing else but sleep and 'deflect' while the fortress is under siege."

The page pressed, "Please, the Commander waits."

We followed the page down the stairs and entered the huge courtyard. By this time it had been cleared of the dead and wounded. The speed in which it was done amazed me. As we passed the keep I saw that the kitchen was still fully staffed. The cooks and their servants were preparing ahead.

Then my eyes saw Commander Vandor and his officers standing outside the east barracks. A large oak table had been set out and a map of the fortress and surrounding area lay open. He smiled as we approached,

"Let us hope that you have rested. We have a full day."

Keven grinned, "We would like one more day of relaxation…"

"Shall I send you chambermaids also?" Vandor also grinned but the grin disappeared quickly, "Now, let us get started. Captain Gallus, report on the condition of the walls."

An officer stepped forward, "Sir, the walls are in good order and stout. The trebuchets and catapults of the attackers did little damage thanks to the wizard Karlyle. The front gates and portcullis were not attacked yesterday so they have no damage. The northwest tower is burned out and therefore not suitable for archers. We will be weakened slightly if the enemy attacks from that direction. The remaining perimeter of the fortress has not been assailed and therefore has no damage."

Commander Vandor nodded and turned to another officer,

"Captain Forsun, report on our losses."

Another officer snapped forward,

"Sir! Our original compliment of soldiers before yesterday was four thousand two hundred. We now have fewer than two thousand nine hundred able to defend Talon. Of the six hundred troops of Mariom's contingent, five hundred and sixty-seven were killed. The rest are being held in our dungeon. Of the loyal casualties, three hundred and ten were killed and two hundred and ninety-eight injured. Of the injured, our healers expect fifty at least to die before this day is over. Another twenty will live, but never fight again. The rest are not wounded seriously and will be able to man the defenses soon."

The Commander turned to a third officer. "Company Commander Hanic, what are our communications with the fleet?"

The officer stepped forward. "There is a sea battle under way at the mouth of the Inlet. Fleet Commodore Disellis last sent his signal ship close to shore just before last light yesterday. He did not give us much information on the battle. His signal pennants only told us that a foreign armada was attempting to enter the Inlet. He did want to know our situation. We signaled him of the attack by Duchess Mariom and asked for assistance to clear the beaches. He signaled back that he was unable to get any of his vessels free at that time.

"My men are currently on the signal platform awaiting first light and the signal ship. I am sorry, Commander: that is all that I can report to you at this time."

Commander Vandor nodded, and then asked a question of the officer, "Have there been ship's lanterns sighted at all during the night?"

"No Commander, the battle must still rage far off shore, else our ships would be back to assist us. Or, if we are defeated on the sea, then the enemy's ships would be closing in to destroy our docks."

As Officer Hanic finished speaking several women approached. I saw that they were kitchen maids. One of them spoke nervously as they placed the baskets on the table,

"Please pardon our intrusion Sirs, but Master Pelora insists that you eat....and...oh please Sirs, these are his words, not mine...but he ordered me to say them to you, 'Tell Commander Vandor that if he an' his men donna' eat their fill, then I will come over an' hold all them down and force the food inside em'!'"

Saying that, the three nervous servants ran back to the keep.

We looked at the baskets and could now smell fresh hot bread.

Commander Vandor watched the kitchen servants rush away, then spoke with a slight grin, "I can only speak for myself on this, but Master Cook Pelora is closer to four hundred than three hundred pounds. I 'donna' want to be sat on by him and force-fed, so I am taking some of this bread!"

The rest of us quickly joined him.

Some moments later, Commander Vandor spoke again. "It is the gods' blessings that we have Cook Pelora here. Soldiers need good food, and plenty of it to sustain strength and morale. "

He then turned to Ceikay. "What of Karlyle?"

Ceikay smiled. "He is resting as we speak. The efforts of yesterday took a toll on him, but he will be ready for the day's onslaught."

"Will you stay with him today?" Vandor asked.

"I will protect him."

The Commander turned to Keven, "My friend, what can you tell us about the strength of our enemies?"

"Duchess Mariom's forces are at our gates in force. Her battle standards we saw on the field indicate two separate regiments. One regiment consists totally of archers, long bow, short bow, and crossbow. The second regiment consists of mostly soldiers of foot, lightly armored pike and short sword. Despite what was told us in Mariom's field tent, there are only two companies of light cavalry. The total on the field is approximately eight thousand troops."

"A heavy force against us..." One of the officers muttered out loud.

"Surprisingly, no," Kevin continued. "The force Duchess Mariom brought against us is a strange mix of strength. The more I flew over the troops, the more I started to..."

Another officer cut in, "Flew over? I do not understand your meaning."

Commander Vandor held up his hand for silence. "Our friend and benefactor is a Beast Master. If you need more explanation you will get it at a later time. Just believe that what he reports is true. Please continue Keven."

"Before we rode to meet you on the plateau yesterday, I flew over the troops and began to wonder why her forces were made up as they were. I discussed this with Errol before making ourselves known to you. He agreed that something was not correct.

"On analysis we decided that her forces were not suited to

break a siege of Fortress Talon. She would need heavy cavalry and heavy foot to push the entrenched invaders into the sea.

"Also, the Duchess was not equipped to fight another force in open field. She would have brought Heavy Lance Cavalry and certainly more Light Cavalry. Her foot soldiers would have included several companies of Halbred to repel a cavalry charge."

It was Vandor's turn, "So you decided that she was here to help the enemy to lay siege to the fortress…"

Keven smiled and shook his head, "Just the opposite. Her force was not fit to lay siege either. Once again, we had to think about what she did not bring to the field: no siege engines, no siege towers, and more importantly and telling…no battering ram.

"If Duchess Mariom was planning an attack on the fortress, the lack of siege engines and towers could be explained away easily, First, speed and secrecy to get from her realm to here; and second, the fact that the enemy at the beach had them made them unnecessary to bring along. As for the battering ram, It could have been transported in parts hidden in several wagons that were made to look like supply carriers, but in my flight over her troops I saw few wagons.

"That was another mystery, too few wagons were there to even supply her two regiments for any amount of field travel, let alone hide a battering ram or two!

"As for the siege forces already on the beach; siege towers are too big to be transported by vessel, so it is no surprise that there are none aligned against us. We all know that the bigger supply ships of fleets can offload trebuchets and catapults, but they are not there in numbers sufficient enough to take down the walls of a fortress of this size.

"Taking all this into consideration, Errol and I began to reason that Duchess Mariom did not plan to aid Commander Vandor and lift the siege by attacking the enemy. As I declared earlier, she did not have the right forces."

"So what was she planning then?" asked an officer.

Keven continued, "So what did she intend to do? A couple of factors started to disturb us. First, the fortunate timing of the sudden illness of her husband that forced her to leave Hirst before the Trade Ball and the assassination of the rest of the Dukes. Second, the timing of her march to the Talon Plateau. It was obvious that her forces were already in route from the opposite direction, and that she had met them by design."

Now I spoke. "By design, maybe she could have been on her way back to her husband and maybe one of her outriders intercepted her on the road, told her of the siege and she then diverted to Talon…"

Keven responded, "That is one consideration that kept us in doubt. We knew that we could not confront her outright at first. But there was another factor that pushed our suspicions further, and finally decided our actions. We wondered what would be the most effective purpose of Duchess Mariom's forces? She had large numbers of archers, light footmen armed with short swords, no heavy cavalry that mattered, and no siege machines.

"Then we surmised it; forces in that strength are best suited to defend a fortress such as this one!"

One of the officers leaned forward. "Yes, but if, as you say, Duchess Mariom did not bring forces to take Talon, and the enemy on the beach did not have enough forces, then how could she have hoped to defeat us? And then in turn, defend the fortress, and from who?"

Commander Vandor answered, "They almost succeeded in taking Talon. If it had not been for our friends riding up and meeting me before I entered Mariom's camp, Mariom would have walked right in the open gates. I would have been the one duped into leading her in. As it was, her plan was foiled by our friends here."

My eyebrows raised in understanding as the Commander continued. "Unfortunately for us, her forces inside were prepared for a fight. The moment they saw us act and that their Duchess was not going to walk in, they started attacking us from the inside. Yesterday we came close to losing Talon Fortress. It was fortunate that Mariom did not have forces to tear at our walls and break open our gate with a battering ram. That kept us free to turn to the traitors inside."

Keven now spoke, "Another factor helped in our defense; the

siege engines on the beach did not start casting projectiles at us until half the day was fought away…why? They had not planned to use them on the walls. They most probably had planned to use them from inside the walls once Duchess Mariom secured the fortress!

"That being the plan, and the plan being broken, it took them a while to set up, align and load. That delay gave us time to fight off Duchess Mariom's soldiers already in the fortress."

Now Commander Vandor finished for Keven. "Duchess Mariom had planned to take Talon Fortress by surprise and not by force. This fortress is vital to the defense of Tavegnor, and Duchess Mariom was to hold it in strength against a counter-attack by King Ballistor's forces. Then she had planned to sit here and wait for Tavegnor's fleet to come in for resupply. Her plan then was to seize the fleet by surprise, or destroy it if necessary. That would open the way for the enemy to sail into the Inlet and all the way to Hirst."

Ceikay spoke up for the first time. "Speaking of the traitors, what of our guests, Duchess Mariom and Captain Nellustus? Have they been made comfortable?"

Commander Vandor turned to her and grinned. "Are you aware that you broke her nose? And Errol apparently broke her jaw! Is that any way to treat a Duchess of the Realm?"

Ceikay turned her eyes to the side in mock embarrassment. Everyone grinned as she answered to the charge, "Should I go and apologize…?"

Then Vandor went on, "We have Mariom and Nellustus confined in a lower dungeon, safe from rescuers and tormenters alike."

Have you tried to question them yet?" Ceikay asked.

"We have, but they are stubborn and quite well trained. They have not told us what we need to know; mainly, who is the outside invader, and what is his strength."

"How do we get that information?" I asked.

Everyone looked at me but said nothing.

Finally, Vandor answered, "This morn at first light we will look for Fleet Commodore Disellis's signal ship. Commodore Disellis has a specialist on board his flagship…a certain advisor that has a certain skill that enables him to extract information from prisoners. We will request the use of this man. If Commodore Disellis can loan him to us, then we will make arrangements to get him ashore as soon as possible."

Once again I had more questions, but decided to hold them until later.

Seeing that I would not press further on the subject, Vandor continued, "If there is nothing else then, let us talk about what must be done to prepare for the next attack. Keven, I assume that Eagle will be joining you this morn?"

Keven nodded.

"Good, we can keep an eye on our enemy from the sky. Ceikay, you are going to stay with Karlyle?"

Ceikay nodded, and then added, "Yes, but if you would allow, I would like to try something on the wounded first. I am not a healer, but I would like to try something new I have been working on."

Commander Vandor smiled. "Obviously I will give you access to our wounded. What is it you will try?"

"I will try to mentally mask their pains. I cannot take away the causes of the pains, but I may be able to change the sensations."

Commander Vandor looked as though he wanted her to explain further, but then gave his consent by simply nodding.

Vandor turned to me. "As for you, Beorn, I would like you to stay out of the fighting today."

The look on my face made Vandor hold up his hand and smile. Shaking his head he continued, "Please, do not argue. You have proven that you are brave and willing to fight. But this day will not be so desperate as to force non-warriors to wield a sword. I would rest easier if you stayed with Ceikay and Karlyle up on the tower, away from the walls. You are more valuable to us as a witness at this time."

Keven now grinned at me, "Vandor just does not want to take the time to explain your death to King Ballistor…"

Commander Vandor moaned in mock complaint.

He then looked at me directly. "Do you understand my

request?"

I nodded and answered, "I need no convincing to stay out of battle today, but if you need me, do not hesitate to..."

Vandor cut me off. "You do not have to convince me any further. I trust you as I trust your friends here."

He then turned to his officers. "Each of you knows your duty already, defend your sections, but be wary and prepare for any and all surprises. Instruct your men to look for Errol and Banator, if they should happen to be running around outside our walls asking to be let in, then yet the arrant louts in!"

The officers saluted and departed.

Keven, Ceikay, and I were now left alone with Vandor. I could not help but ask another question: "Commander, you said that this day the fighting would be less, why do you say that?"

"I said it would be less desperate, not less fighting. You see, yesterday we were taken by surprise from the inside. This fortress came close to falling. We all fought like savages just to stay alive. Today the threat only comes from the outside. And since we have Duchess Mariom and one of their captains, and also the fact that their ploy did not work, they have to now rethink their options. They did not bring a siege force strong enough to take Talon Fortress by direct assault.

"A prudent leader would wait for reinforcements, but since time is now on our side, they have to still attempt to take us."

"How is time on our side?" I asked.

This time Keven spoke. "From a strategic standpoint, they have to take the port. In order to take the port, they must first take the fortress. While Talon holds, their invading fleet cannot sail to Hirst and establish a foothold in our heartland. Our fleet can still come in for repairs and rearmament while this port is still in our hands. The longer we can hold out, the less chance the enemy has of accomplishing its strategic goal. So you see, time is on our side as long as they cannot take Talon!"

Ceikay stopped my questions. "I see that the sun will be showing itself shortly. I am going to the barracks to see to the wounded. I will see you later on the tower, Beorn. Go there now."

She left quickly. Then Keven nodded to me to join him. We

saluted Commander Vandor and went to the tower.

By the time we reached the top, only a few stars still competed with the coming sun. Karlyle was awake and eating from a large basket. I again smelled hot bread. I also saw hen's eggs and slices of boiled ham. There was also a wine jug.

Keven walked over to Karlyle and pointed at the jug, "Well, what is this? Does this increase the power of your spells?"

Karlyle did not look up. He was rummaging around in the basket as he answered, "I do not do spells…and no, you cannot have any."

Keven looked hurt, but took hold of the jug anyway.

Without looking up, Karlyle stated, "I spit in it."

Keven looked at me; I grinned and said, "Yes, I will be happy to share Karlyle's wine with you."

Keven smiled broadly, "I think you have promise, Beorn."

He took a big swig, and then handed the jug to me. I did the same and handed it back to Karlyle.

"You are welcome," was all Karlyle said.

Keven tapped Karlyle's shoulder. "How do you feel this morn? Did you rest your head enough for today's battle?"

"I feel fit and ready. I am thinking of starting some commotion soon."

"How so?" Keven asked.

Karlyle looked up at us. "I am thinking of setting a trebuchet afire."

Keven looked over the tower toward the siege engines on the beach. "I know you can form fire, but at this distance?"

"Yes."

"Why is it that you did not use your fire yesterday?" I asked.

Karlyle answered promptly, "Calling up great fire at such a distance is difficult. The mental manipulation of the physical must include the generation of massive heat energy. That takes a lot of hard and determined concentration. Yesterday I was either fighting with my sword, or deflecting the incoming missiles. Even though the deflections of the boulders took quite a bit of mental manipulation, it only consisted of movement; not heat generation. Therefore, the taxing of my energies was less."

Karlyle looked back down at his food. "Today, I must take advantage of the stillness before battle to gather my concentration for an explosion of fire. It takes time and brooks no distractions."

"What the wizard is saying," Keven said, "is that we are to leave him alone and stop pestering him."

I nodded and kept silent. I wanted to see the fire explosions on the enemy.

Karlyle looked past us, "Where is Ceikay?"

"She is helping with the injured," Keven answered. "She hopes to comfort them from their pain...or take their minds off their pain...or soothe their pain waves...or something to that effect."

Karlyle did not smile as he commented, "I see you jest at her attempt. Let us hope that she is successful in any case."

Keven looked down at Karlyle for a moment before replying, "You know, humor in times of stress ofttimes helps to relieve that stress. You should really work at developing some."

Karlyle stood up, "Which do you mean? Develop some humor, or develop some stress?"

"See! I knew you could!" Keven exclaimed.

I ceased trying to understand their barbs and stared out at the beach.

Karlyle burst out, "Step back before I set you afire!"

Grinning, Keven stood back next to me.

Karlyle walked over to the side of the tower and leaned against the stonework. He faced the siege engines down on the beach. He closed his eyes and stood rigidly still. His chin slowly lowered to his chest. He stopped breathing.

Suddenly one of the soldiers yelled, "By the gods! Fire! The wizard did it! Look! The catapult is on fire! See?"

Everyone on the tower leaned over the edge and stared at the beach. As the guard had yelled out, one of the catapults was ablaze in yellow and orange flames! Soon the whole machine was engulfed. The guards cheered and shook their weapons. Keven looked at Karlyle and smiled broadly. I stood there with my mouth open, too amazed to speak.

Karlyle then shook his head and turned from the scene. He sat down with his back to the wall. He frowned but said nothing.

Keven sat down next to him and slapped his thigh. "Well done Master Wizard! I will not tease you again. You did well!"

Karlyle did not answer. He stared straight ahead.

I spoke up, "You ought not speak to him just now, Keven, he looks to be trying to recover."

Keven nodded, "I was not thinking. Let us sit down and take one more sip from the jug."

We sat down next to Karlyle. We were careful not to distract him. We did not talk at all.

Finally, Karlyle spoke, but in a whisper. "I did not set that catapult ablaze."

We both looked at him. Keven leaned over to him and whispered back, "What did you say?"

"I did not start that fire."

Keven asked, "Then how did it start? By magic?"

Karlyle did not seem to be amused. "I did not set that fire. Something else did."

I spoke up, "But we saw you. The fire started. What do you mean it was not you? How do you know?"

Karlyle looked at me and shook his head. "I know what it takes, the process is very precise and timely. I had not yet summoned the energy reserves to travel that distance."

He paused a moment, and then continued, "I will explain: Think of an archer drawing his crossbow. He pulls the string back until he notches the string on the pin. He then picks up his dart and places it into the notch and backs it onto the string. He then lifts the crossbow to his shoulder and points the weapon at his target. It is only after those several steps that he is ready to release the missile."

Karlyle shook his head and continued, "I was only at the mental point of notching the string onto the pin. I was not ready to release my arrow of fire. Something or someone else started that blaze."

I could say nothing. For once, Keven had nothing to say. He just stood up and looked over the wall to the beach.

Finally, he muttered, "Well, it sure is a good looking fire..."

Karlyle got up and stood next to Keven. I walked over also. We studied the enemy's camp for a while.

Keven leaned onto the parapet, "I wonder then, how…"

Ceikay's voice joined us, "What were you wondering?"

We turned around as she walked up.

Keven answered her, "Oh, our friends down on the beach are trying to extinguish a fire. Since Karlyle refuses the credit, we were wondering the cause. How did your visit with the wounded fare?"

"I had little results that I could see. I still do not know how to take away the pain for them. Just holding their hand gave them more comfort."

"Bless you for trying, Ceikay." Keven said. "Maybe the gods will not allow you to take the pain away. If it were that easy, then war would be less avoided."

Ceikay shook her head. "I will still try to develop that talent, by the help of the gods."

Then Keven looked into the sky. I followed his gaze and saw Eagle. He was circling over our heads.

"Well, it is time for me to see what is out there for us." Keven then sat down, leaned against the wall and closed his eyes.

Suddenly, Eagle flew straight away toward the beach.

Karlyle then announced that he would try the fire again. Ceikay and I stayed quiet. Karlyle stared down at the siege engines. Moments passed, and then I began to see beads of sweat on his forehead. We still kept quiet. More time passed. Still he stared at the beach.

I stood silently watching Karlyle. Ceikay must have seen a puzzled look on my face. She reached over and tapped my shoulder.

Startled, I looked her way.

"What are you thinking?" She asked.

I paused, and then answered, "In Karlyle's first attempt, he had his eyes closed and his head down. Now his eyes are open and he is staring at his target. I thought he just told us that the process is very precise and that there are certain steps that had to be taken."

Ceikay stopped me by hitting my arm. "This is still new to you so I will try to explain for him. It is not body motions or body positions he describes. It is the mental processes and steps that he must perform. By the gods, Beorn, If Karlyle wanted to stand on his head, the mental processes, if done correctly, will still deliver the desired results!"

I wanted to ask one more question when the explosion happened! I spun to face the sound.

I saw a great burst of flames shoot out of one of the trebuchets. Flames were leaping out in all directions. The machine soon disappeared behind yellow flames and black smoke. Once again the guards on the tower cheered. I turned back to Karlyle to see his expression. He now had his eyes closed and head down.

"Was that you?" I asked.

He nodded, "Yes, this time I did succeed."

"Good!" I smiled broadly, "Can you destroy all of them today?"

"Only if I can rest between each attempt. But if our enemies begin to use those things, then I will be busy deflecting their missiles. I must sit down now."

Karlyle sat next to Keven.

Ceikay had picked up the wine jug and now handed it to Karlyle, who drank deeply.

Suddenly, the guards on our tower jumped to attention. I heard commotion and turned around. Commander Vandor was walking toward us. Behind him were four pages carrying water casks.

The Commander spoke loud enough for all on the tower to hear, "Make sure that our bellies are full of water today! Fighting steals your body's water as fast as a sword will steal your blood!"

Vandor lowered his voice, "I should not disturb Karlyle. How long has Keven been gone?"

I answered, "Not long as the eagle flies. He just went out to sea."

Commander Vandor stood and looked to the sea.

After a long pause he said, "I am going to my quarters. I have not rested since yesterday morn. I have assured myself that everything is secure and my men are in place. Beorn, I would like you to deliver Keven's report to me when he returns. Ask one of the pages in the barracks and he will take you to my quarters."

He then turned to Ceikay, "Thank you. My healers were quite impressed with what you did."

Commander Vandor turned to leave. He paused at the ramp and turned back, "Thinking on it...I should remain long enough to hear Keven's report from seaward."

He then walked back to the wall's edge and looked to the distant fires.

Suddenly I thought of our missing companions. Without addressing anyone specifically, I asked, "Where are Errol and Banator? Are they still alive?"

"I know Errol is." Ceikay answered, "I am not as close to Banator, so I cannot know for sure if he still lives. As for Errol, he will be back soon. Whatever task he went out for, he will succeed."

"I do hope and pray he gets back here soon."

Just then Keven sat straight up. "He will be back Beorn. In truth, he is going to need our assistance right about now!"

He jumped up and kicked Karlyle, "Awake! Stand ready Karlyle! Everyone! Look to the beach! Vandor, get men to the gate! Have them horsed and ready it for a quick opening!"

The Commander was off the tower in an instant.

Enemy Camp

Keven then leaned over the inner ramp and yelled down to the soldiers below us, "Look to the beach, men! Get ready your arrows! Protect the riders coming in!"

He turned back to the beach and pointed. For long moments we waited and watched. Commander Vandor could be heard down in the Quadrangle barking orders.

I peered toward the beach. I saw no one or any commotion in the beach encampment other than the fires.

Then an explosion! Where Keven was pointing I saw two large tents fly into the air engulfed in a ball of expanding fire. As the tents still hung in the air I saw men running toward the fire and smoke. Suddenly, two horses jumped out of another large tent. This tent was about one hundred paces from the conflagration. The horses leaped over the low parapet of the camp's perimeter, and on the horses were two men. The steeds now raced toward the fortress at full gallop.

I saw needles fly toward the horses from the camp. Arrows! They looked so small from here, but I knew they would be deadly to the riders.

Keven called out, "Karlyle!"

164

Instantly Karlyle held up his right arm and pointed to the far encampment. The arrows suddenly veered from their course and stabbed into the earth to each side of the running steeds.

Now I saw another dozen horses break from the camp. They were heading after the first two. The two in front were clearly slower. I could now see that the first horse carried a rider too big for its back, and the second horse's rider was lying down, straddling the saddle! The second rider was bouncing around and forcing the slowing of the horse's gait. This was allowing the other riders to catch up to the first two. These dozen riders had bows and javelins at the ready and were about to get into range. Then about twenty more horse and riders broke from the opposite side of the camp, the side nearest our walls. We could see that these new horses were trying to head the first two off before they could reach the safety of our archers on our walls. As they raced toward us, Karlyle kept deflecting the missiles soaring through the air.

One of the horses in the group of twenty ran faster than the others. He began to close in on the two. The rider was armed with a javelin and readied to throw. Just then even from this distance we heard a screech from the sky. Eagle was diving from the east and heading straight at the charging rider! Just as the man raised his arm to launch his missile, Eagle swooped down and hit the hapless man in the neck. The claws must have raked deep; the rider's head was thrown back, the javelin was thrown at the ground, and the rider's legs were thrown up into the air! The rider rolled off the back of his horse and tumbled to the ground. His horse, now free of his master, immediately slowed and veered away from the chase.

Then I heard the sound of battle horns to my right. I looked to the Fortress gate and saw it opening. The portcullis was being raised and I saw Ceikay along with Commander Vandor and a full squad of mounted cavalry! I marveled at how calmly they sat on their horses as they waited for the gate to rise. It looked to me like they were ready for a simple drill on the parade grounds

I turned back to the beach. I now saw another rider. This lone rider was racing behind the larger group of horses. The horse was a big looking animal, strong of muscle and long of legs. I could see that the rider was an expert. He did not hold reins. He held swords in both hands. He was quickly catching up to the others.

Karlyle was still deflecting arrows, but I could see that he had to switch from one group of chasers to the other. This was allowing a few arrows to fly true to the two fleeing ahead. One arrow suddenly pierced the rider on the second horse of the two being chased.

I looked to Keven; his eyes were closed and I knew where he was. I turned to look for Eagle. I saw him swoop down again and hit another rider. This victim threw up his hands and fell to the ground.

At that same instant, the last rider came up to the rear of the large group of horses. His swords now came down onto the backs of two of the rear riders. The unsuspecting riders fell from their mounts.

A moment later the fortress horns sounded again. I looked to see Vandor, Ceikay, and the other horsemen break from the fortress and race to their left. Their horses now had to leap over the dead still lying on the ground from yesterday's failed assault. I saw that it did not slow their speed. They flew toward the two riders.

As I stood there and watched this chase unfold, I wondered what I could do to help. I desperately wanted to join in, but did not know what to do. I realized that the only thing I could do is witness. At the time, it did not seem enough.

Before I could get lost in my own thought, another horn sounded from the top of the gate. Turning back to the sound, I now saw commotion at the perimeter of Duchess Mariom's field camp. I had forgotten about them! A line of horses were being readied. These were the light cavalry that I had seen when we first entered their camp yesterday. I could see pages holding the reins while soldiers were beginning to mount. They would be ready to charge shortly!

I yelled at Karlyle, "Mariom's cavalry is coming!"

He did not answer; he was straining to protect the two riders from the javelins and arrows. I yelled again at him.

Finally he nodded briskly and waved his left hand to me as if to yell 'Silence!'

Shouting was heard down in the courtyard. I now saw more of our cavalry mounting!

The sudden sound of metal clanging made me turn back to the field. Four horsemen had turned on the lone rider and had now engaged him in a running sword duel! The lone rider was swinging his swords desperately to fend off the other four. By the bodies I could see on the ground, he had dispatched another three before they had turned on him. The rest of the enemy was still closing the gap between them and the first two. The first twelve were now just about on top of the two. They had their swords drawn and readied for attack.

I quickly looked to Mariom's camp. The horsemen were lined up, all mounted and in line to charge.

Then an explosion of noise spun my eyes around back to the beach side. Vandor had intercepted the large group of attackers and smashed into them with swords swinging! I could see Ceikay and a group of eight riders run past the two riders racing this way. Ceikay's group now crashed into the surprised twelve. An instant later, six of the enemies were down and the other six were veering back to the beach.

Vandor's charge had had the same effect, only five were left of the enemy, and they were running also. I saw that Commander Vandor had not stopped to engage the lead riders. He had ridden past and smashed into the four who were attacking that one lone rider! A moment later, those four were dead.

I now saw that the two lead riders who started all this were nearing the gate of the fortress. Ceikay and her riders had turned around and raced behind them.

Commander Vandor and his men surrounded the lone rider and they too were racing back to the gate.

I was sure they did not see the threat from Duchess Mariom's camp. I yelled at Karlyle to do something. He turned to face the light cavalry lined up and at the ready.

I followed his gaze. The cavalry at Mariom's camp had not moved.

I watched as the gates opened to allow our riders in. At the same time I watched for the attack of Mariom's cavalry. I saw all of our riders enter. I saw the portcullis lowered. I saw the gates close, but the attack never began.

Looking over the edge of the tower ramp I now saw who the riders were: Errol was on one of the two lead horses. He was the big rider I saw out front. The second rider, the one who was lying down across the saddle was not someone I had seen before. The third rider, the lone rider, was Banator.

Karlyle grabbed me as I looked down at the courtyard, "Come Beorn!"

We raced down the steps of the tower. I could not keep up with Karlyle. I was thinking that he should be spent from his efforts. When we reached the courtyard I could see Ceikay standing in front of Errol. I could also see that he was bent over rubbing his shin! His look toward Ceikay had a menace to it that made me slow my run. Karlyle stepped up to Errol and smiled.

Karlyle looked at Ceikay and then back at Errol. "You just do not learn, do you?"

Errol frowned at Karlyle, "You have something clever to say to me?"

Karlyle held up his hands in mock surrender. "Eh...welcome back?"

"Looks to me like Banator had to save your rump again!"

I turned around to find Keven at my side. I had not seen him come from the tower with us.

Commander Vandor stepped up. "Errol, Banator, you will both report to the war room when I call for you! I want a full and account of your escapades, and a full explanation of why you placed my cavalry in peril! By the way," he added, grinning, "you are in wrong uniform."

I then realized that both Errol and Banator had on brown uniforms with foreign looking insignia.

Banator now walked up to our group and prodded at Vandor, "Ah, it is good to see you too my friend! Errol has brought you a visitor."

As he said this, Banator reached for the rider who rode face down behind Errol. The rider was still on the horse; his hands and feet were bound by hemp. His mouth was gagged by a length of heavy burlap. Banator yanked the rider down from the saddle and threw him, not kindly to the ground.

Banator smiled and swung his arm down toward the now prostrate rider. "Let us welcome back to Talon Fortress, A Captain of Duchess Mariom's regiment: Captain Bretis."

Commander Vandor now walked over to stand over the officer. "I assumed you were amongst the dead Bretis. It would have been better for you if you were. As for me, it is surely a pleasure to see you alive."

Vandor then turned to one of his officers. "Take our friend Bretis to join Mariom and Nellustus. Make his stay comfortable until the arrival of our Interrogator. I also see that he has an arrow sticking out his side."

Vandor studied the wound more closely, "It is a good thing that the leather armor stopped you from dying too soon"

Vandor turned to Errol, "I am glad to see you two back, but I must see to the defense of Talon before I can speak with you. You and Banator will get washed and don a change of clothes. Do not fail to get a full belly before we will speak. I will be in the War Room when you are ready."

Commander Vandor turned and hurried away.

Ceikay now spoke, "Welcome back, brother."

Errol smiled down at Ceikay, "Nice welcome, you probably broke my shin bone."

"Next time let us know when you decide to go and fight a war all on your own."

"As for you, Banator," Ceikay began...

Banator immediately stepped back.

Ceikay continued, "You went to aid this idiot. I thank you."

Banator then bowed to Ceikay. "I do not know why. He sure put me through some rough moments back there on the beach."

A short time later we were sitting outside the fortress keep. The kitchen staff had laid out a sumptuous meal for us. While they ate, Errol and Banator did not speak of their visit to the enemy camp. They were keeping their story for the war room.

Presently, a page approached, "if you please, Commander

Vandor would like to see you now."

Shortly thereafter, we were facing Commander Vandor.

We had walked into the war room and waited while runners and messengers were taking their turns with Vandor. He listened to everyone and then dispatched orders. Finally, our group was alone with him.

We waited for Vandor to speak first. "We have heard from the Fleet Commodore's signal ship. We have exchanged messages. The Specialist we require will be delivered as soon as they are able to get him from the Commodore's command ship. They are also sending a Witness to give a full accounting of the rest of the war that we know of so far. "

Vandor then gestured to the east wall. "Interestingly, I received word that Duchess Mariom's forces outside our gates are requesting an audience. They can wait. I will hear from Errol and Banator before I speak to our enemies outside the walls. Errol, please report what you have found."

Errol stepped up and nodded, "I will begin with the night before, in the grotto passageway."

Commander Vandor nodded, "Please; and forgive me if messengers interrupt you. I have given orders that any news from Commodore Disellis be reported at once."

The following is Errol's account of his foray into the enemy's camp. These are his words in total:

"As you know, in the grotto I sent Beorn back to report and to get reinforcements. I will begin from that point.

After Beorn ran into the darkness I waited with the other soldiers just to the side of the arrows' paths. I could hear the bashing of the ramrod against the iron portcullis. It was only a matter of time before they would break through. We waited in silence. Then, we heard the sound of a sudden crashing. A moment later a yell rang through the catacombs...the portcullis was down! The invaders swarmed in as we rushed back into the gate room! The battle was fierce. We fought and clawed and stabbed.

The noise was deafening. Slowly, one by one, my men began to tire and fall. The room was small, and became smaller as it filled with the dead and dying. My men were desperately holding the entrance, but it was only a matter of time before we would fail.

Though my men were dying, the enemy was dying at a far greater rate. The fighting began to turn; the invaders seemed to slow and falter. Amazingly, they began to back away from the grotto entrance. I now had time to get a good look at our attackers. It was then that I recognized one man. It was Captain Bretis! I had met him the year before in Talavor. It was at that time that King Ballistor had commissioned him to head the Mariom contingent at the fortress. As I looked in his direction, our eyes met. He knew that I recognized him. He then turned and ran from the grotto entrance. I fought on and eventually the enemy was turned. We pushed the surviving attackers out of the portcullis entrance and they ran also. There were three of us left and we gave chase. It was a short distance to the grotto and we killed any invaders that failed to outrun us. We came to the grotto by the docks. It was clear of the enemy.

We proceeded to the shoreline and began to follow the fleeing invaders along the beach. I did not fear someone getting behind us and getting through to the catacombs and into the fortress. This was the only path to be taken and we had flushed the enemy out before us. Any new invasion would have to get by us.

We soon had no one else to kill. We carefully searched in all crevasses as we went forward. We found no one. Apparently the enemy had thought that we were guarding the passageways in force. They had abandoned this route of entry.

Eventually we came to a wide opening onto a beach. One of the guards with me recognized the landing and reported that the enemy camp would be about five hundred paces ahead to the west. We now slowed and became cautious lest someone find us. We hung close to the sandy hillock to our right. We could see the light and hear the noise of the camp ahead of us. It was clear that a battle was still raging on the plateau above us. The creak of the catapults would be heard as they released their missiles. We stopped just outside of the perimeter of the camp. We waited until we were sure the attention of the invaders was to the landward side and away from us. I motioned to crawl in closer.

Suddenly torches were thrown down in front of us. We were discovered!

Shouts rose above and arrows started to hit the sand around us. We spun around and found that arrows were being loosed behind us to prevent our escape! The only direction for us was the water. We ran straight to the breakers and jumped in. I dived deep and stayed under as long as my breath would allow me. I swam straight out from shore while arrows broke the water around me. Finally I had to breathe. I sprung to the surface and stretched to the night sky and gasped. While taking in huge gulps of air I looked toward the shore. Two long boats were being pushed into the water. I saw about twenty men jumping into them. I twisted around in the water to look for my companions. They were nowhere to be seen.

The boats left the shore and were rapidly coming my way. I dived under the water again and began swimming further from the shore. When my body demanded more air, I raised my head and drank in the night sky. I turned to see the two boats still coming out. At the bow of each one stood a man holding a bright torch high. I swam further away from them. I realized I was getting quite tired, and realized why, My two short swords were still at my side. I sorely did not want to discard my weapons, but I knew that I had to rid myself of weight. I finally unlashed my belt and the two swords fell to the deep. I consoled myself that I still had two daggers.

172

I finally succeeded in eluding my pursuers by treading further from shore. Darkness was fresh settled, and the moon had not yet risen. The two boats swept to and fro with their men looking in earnest. I floated in the darkness, watching their maneuvers. I did not see them capture or attack my two companions. I can only assume that they had been hit by arrows as they entered the water.

Before the moon had fully shown itself, the two boats turned back to shore. I saw guards were now posted along the beach in the chance anyone would try to come back to land.

I swam parallel to land until I could not see the lights of their camp. I slowly floated toward the beach. I could see dark shapes forming in front of me as I neared. Soon I could see that they were boulders jutting from the shallows. I used them to shield me from the shore and bluffs as I slowly moved in. Off in the distance I could see the lights of the enemy camp. I prayed that I had gone far enough not to be spotted.

Finally I crawled up on the beach and collapsed. I tried to breathe softly, but my body gasped for air. Slowly I gained control and strength and crawled up to grass-covered dunes. I lay there until the moon was high overhead. Soon I was fully recovered in strength. I made my way cautiously toward the enemy's encampment.

As I crept closer I could see soldiers and servants running everywhere. I also saw, and was grateful, that no one was guarding the perimeters on this side of the camp. They had not considered an attack from this quarter.

Several large tents were now directly in front of me. These were either supply tents, or personnel tents. I decided to crawl to these and find a haven to get my bearings. The noise of the day's battle was over, but the remnants of it were still covering any little noise that I was making. Men were busy repairing and damaged siege machines and other equipment throughout the camp so I was not worried about being heard. I did fear though that I would be spotted if I stayed in the open. Once I got to the first tent I listened for noise within. Hearing nothing, I lifted up a bottom edge. I cautiously looked in…and saw no one. I quickly crawled in and lay behind some large crates. I rested a bit more and listened for movement. Soon I got up and looked around. This was a weapons supply tent, loaded with spears, arrows, and javelins. I saw no swords.

I now decided that I needed to get a uniform. I knew that in order to get around camp, I had to disguise myself as one of these invaders. I rummaged around in this one tent a bit more. I found only more of the same weapons. Because of the noise outside, I decided to wait awhile before venturing any further. At the back of the tent behind several large crates I lay down and waited. Several times voices came louder toward the entrance of the tent, but the entrance flap never opened.

Eventually the voices in the camp grew fewer and quieter. I slowly lifted up the bottom edge of the canvas. It was time to make some sort of progress. I crawled out and made my way to the next tent. This time I found uniforms, but not the brown ones that these invaders were wearing. These were gold. These were the uniforms of Duchess Mariom's realm! They were not folded in any order; rather, they were all strewn around and trampled into the sand. I then saw in one corner of the tent a little pile of brown. There were about half a dozen brown uniforms, the type that the invaders were wearing. Upon inspection, these uniforms were new and clean. They had not been worn as yet.

The gods were with me, as I discovered that one of the uniforms was big enough to fit and quickly I donned it. When I looked further, I discovered that all the brown uniforms were either really large, or really small. None of them could fit an average man. I thought that strange as I donned my uniform…

Then the answer came to me. This was a changing

tent! Guards who were originally wearing gold, changed into the brown uniforms! The gold uniforms were dirty and had the smell of a long march. The brown uniforms left in the corner were of sizes not common amongst an average soldier. That was why they were not used.

I wondered at the change of uniforms. Footsteps were nearing. I quickly fell down and crawled under the large pile of dirty uniforms. Just as I completely covered myself I heard the sound of the tent flap being folded back. I heard rustling for a brief couple of moments, the sound of the flap once again...and silence after that. I determined that I was alone again. I quickly crawled out from the bottom of the smelly pile of discarded uniforms. The pile of brown uniforms had disappeared.

Not wanting to waste any more time, I now peeked out from the tent flap. I saw no one. I then stepped boldly outside. Walking toward the center of the camp I began to hear more conversations. It was strange that the language and even the accents of this invading army were familiar to me...but not so strange considering my suspicions by now.

In front of me were a number of small fires; around some of these fires sat soldiers talking in low tones. No one gave me any notice nor questioned me. Around other fires, men slept. I decided to lie down next to one of the prone men and feign sleep. I knew that soldiers off duty are free with their tongues. I would get information by keeping my eyes closed and my ears open.

The conversations around the fires confirmed our own conclusions. In truth, more information that I did not expect!

First, as my suspicions were leading me, this so-called invading army on the beach is really Duchess Mariom's. The men and siege engines were not secretly deposited from ships traveling from the southern continent. They had traveled south along the beach from the Mariom city of Yannisdol. The barrenness of the

Western Dunes insured that they would not be spotted by routine travelers. They traveled by night so as not to be seen by trading vessels sailing along the coast. The trip took twelve days.

Second, they were to set up a siege encampment on the beach within sight of the fortress and wait for Duchess Mariom's land forces to appear on the plateau. The Fortress commander was then supposed to believe that Duchess Mariom was its savior and therefore welcome her through open gates. Duchess Mariom's forces would then take the fortress from within!

Third, since the plan did not work, these men sitting around the fires were not in a heartened mood. They had fully expected to be resting inside Talon Fortress this very night. They are none too cheerful at Duchess Mariom's failure. Because of this failure, they were now forced to fight!

Fourth, these rank and file soldiers are not convicted to the cause of their leader, Duchess Mariom. In truth, they do not understand the orders for attacking Tavegnor's fortress. They are openly questioning the wisdom of this battle.

After a long while, I was hearing complaints being repeated and I decided that I would not hear anything new. These soldiers had not been told the whole strategic plan. I decided to move on to gather more information.

I rolled over as if just awaking up. I scratched myself and lazily walked off. No one seemed to take notice of me. I now moved toward a busier part of the camp. It turned out to be the field kitchens. I saw the cooks and their mess boys hard at work. Large pig-iron pots were being cleaned; pewter dishes were being stacked, and so on. Over to the side of one of the mess wagons stood a large open water barrel. I walked over to it and ladled out several mouthfuls. I sloppily wiped my lips on my sleeve.

It was then that I saw the first officers since gaining

the camp, Two of them walked briskly by me as I leaned against the wagon. By their insignia I could see that they were Squad Commanders. One of them saw me wiping the water from my mouth with my sleeve. He suddenly stopped and faced me. He looked at me from head to foot. Then he must have decided that I was not worth the effort. He turned from me and shook his head at his companion. They both walked off. My gaze followed them as they left the clearing. I noticed a large tent to the front of them. The two were heading toward its entrance. In a moment, they had disappeared through the tent opening. I now casually turned and walked away from the kitchen clearing and headed away from the officers' tent.

Shortly though, I circled back through a row of smaller tents. These small shelters are the four-man field tents that the common soldiers use. I quickly came to the large tent that now housed the two officers I mentioned. By this time most of the camp was asleep. The only troops I saw outside now were the guards on station at the perimeter, and they were facing outward.

Inside the large tent I could now hear words. I quietly stepped to the tent and listened. By their tone and words I soon discovered that these officers also were none too happy with the day's developments.

A sudden light caught my eye to the right of me. Instantly I crouched down, prepared to either run or fight. The light came from the brief opening of a tent flap. A large tent was to my right about twenty paces away. Someone had just opened the flap and thrown out a bit of food scraps onto the sand. I now saw the guide-ons at the entrance; this was the field commander's tent!

Surprisingly there were no guards. I crept around to the back side of the commander's tent. It was then that the guards came. Two of them marched to the entrance and posted themselves at attention. Because of the location the two guards placed themselves, I was now penned in. If I had attempted to move from the rear to either side of the tent; these two guards would have instantly spotted me.

Since it was still dark I was not in danger of being found…so I listened.

I soon heard heated words from inside the tent…that turned to arguing…that turned to yelling! For a brief moment I thought that fighting would break out. Then the yelling stopped. The arguing did not. By the voices that I identified, there were four men inside the tent.

Then the name was spoken; or "cursed forth" is a better description, '…the fault is with *you,* Bretis! If you had acted sooner, my men would have been successful at taking the catacombs!'

Then a man spat back. "Do not attempt to pin the blame with me, Captain Alluj! You failed to send men in adequate numbers to push their way through!"

A third voice now rose between the two others, "Both of you will have to answer to our Duchess when this is over! For now, we must stop this bickering and get messengers over to Mariom for further orders!"

Now a fourth cut in, "Why should we send riders to her? She is our leader and should send her riders to us. So far her camp has not sent word to us at all!"

Suddenly, I felt something small strike the nape of my neck. It did not hurt. Whatever it was fell at my feet. I stayed crouched with my head still pointed at the tent. My hand slowly went to my belt. I pulled a dagger slowly out of its sheath, ready to spin. Another something struck my neck. My eyes followed my legs down to the ground. Next to my left foot lay an olive. A third attack on my neck; a new olive fell next to the first. Slowly I turned my head around, my body slowly followed. Behind me stood two rows of small tents. In the small pathway between these tents a black shadow stood. Then the shadow stepped forward and a face came into the moonlight: Banator.

I saw his grin and then saw his hands. He started to signal me with gestures.

With the night surrounding us, and with no word spoken, we devised our plan.

Our plan was to grab Captain Bretis and bring him back to Talon Fortress for interrogation. Banator was to create a diversion as I gathered up our prize and make a break for the fortress gate.

Once we were done signing, Banator slowly backed away from me. Soon his shadow disappeared and I turned back around to listen again. The words inside the tent had toned down to normal conversation. As I listened, I got a clearer understanding of our besiegers.

Captain Alluj was the Commander of this camp. From the way they used their familiar names with each other, I knew that Alluj and Bretis were equals in rank. The other two officers were also Captains, but junior to Alluj and Bretis. They were in command of the two companies that made up the troops on the beach. Alluj and Bretis were blaming each other for the day's failures.

Then I heard the tent flap open at the front. I heard Captain Alluj speak to the guards, 'Go to the kitchens and get bread, meat, and wine.'

'Yes Sir!' I heard the sound of footfalls rushing from the tent.

I now had an opportunity to back away from the tent. One of my goals was to find a horse. I remembered a row of horses staked out for the night back in the direction of the first tents. I made my way back and was glad to see that they were not guarded. The two horses on the end of the tether looked like good prospects. I soon found saddles piled in a heap. I took two and carried them into the tent with the discarded gold uniforms. The saddles were soon covered by the heap.

I made my way to the line of horses to untie the two that I had picked out. I saw a shadow moving along the same line; Banator was picking out his horse for the ride back.

We met and stood casually by the horses. Banator leaned on the rump of one while I picked at another's tail. We talked in low tones developing our plan. Twice soldiers passed us without a greeting or even a glance. We kept our talk quiet. I was to 'persuade' either Bretis or Alluj to accompany us to the fortress. It was decided that if the two were still together when I came looking for one of them, I would kill one and grab the other. Banator was to create a diversion at the other side of the camp to allow me to get my captive on a horse and break from camp. Soon the rising sun would be raising the sleeping soldiers. We knew that our waiting was over. Action was to begin.

I found my targets together...Banator started fires...and here we are..."

This was the sudden end of Errol's report.

We sat facing Errol for a few moments before all realized that he had finished his telling.

Finally, I spoke up, "You are not finished, are you?"

Errol looked at me. "The fact that we are here tells the rest of the story. Does it not?"

I was not satisfied. "You said that you found your targets. Bretis is now in the fortress. What about Alluj?"

Errol answered with a sigh.

After a moment, Banator answered for him. "Of course, if Bretis is here, then Alluj is dead. Were you not listening to Errol's report?"

I turned to Banator, "Yes, I was listening, but maybe I just do not understand why Alluj had to be killed. Why not tie him up and gag his mouth?"

Now Commander Vandor stepped up, "You do not understand, Beorn. Please, I mean no criticism. You are not trained as we are. I will explain, we are now at war. Errol needed to bring back a prisoner for interrogation. The two best candidates in the camp

180

were Bretis and Alluj. They were the Senior Officers, and therefore the ones with the most tactical and strategic information in that camp. Errol and Banator rightly reasoned that two prisoners would be too much of a risk to try to spirit away. Also, these two senior officers would have basically the same information and therefore be redundant.

So, one officer was to be brought back. It did not matter who in this case. This meant that the other officer, if he were witnessing the abduction must be quieted so as not to rally for help. Yes, he could have been rendered unconscious, or bound and gagged. That would have solved the alerting of the rest of the camp."

My silent stare prompted the Vandor to continue. "But there was another reason Errol did what he did. This is where your inexperience in warfare causes your questioning. Since Bretis and Alluj were the two senior officers in camp, the killing of the one left behind took away the leadership of the camp. It would not guarantee that the siege from the beach would end, but anytime that an army's top leadership is eliminated, that army is weakened."

I nodded and said nothing more.

Keven now spoke, "So Banator, we can assume that you started the fire that burned the siege engine."

Banator nodded, then spoke excitedly. "But then, shortly after, just as I was about to set fire to a trebuchet, the forsaken thing erupted into an inferno! That monster exploded right in my face and threw me back ten paces! I sat there stunned and confused while flames spread and soldiers came running! One of them pulled me to my feet and yelled at me to clear the horses from the area."

Banator grinned and continued. "Naturally I had to obey, as his uniform outranked mine! The horses were now panicking so we had trouble herding them. Finally, I saw one with a saddle and reins. I went after that one! By the time I gained control of it, I saw Errol and his hostage racing away. I then saw others jumping upon their horses and rush to follow. I grabbed two swords from men too busy running for horses to notice. I then jumped onto my horse and commenced to scatter the rest. Before anyone could fully understand my actions, I spurred my horse from the camp to aid Errol's retreat!"

Banator paused as his grin widened, "...and as Errol would say...and here we are...!"

I had more questions. "You have not explained..."

A messenger stepped into the war room. "Commander Vandor Sir! I bring messages from Commodore Disellis!"

"Report." Commander Vandor ordered briskly.

The messenger quickly stepped forward. "His personal sloop is sending your requested specialist. He has also sent a Witness to report to you as promised. The sloop will be rounding the jetty momentarily."

Vandor smiled, and then turned to one of his officers. "Make arrangements to meet our guests and get them in here as soon as possible."

Before the officer could respond, the messenger stepped forward once again. "Beg pardon Sir, But the Captain-of-the-Watch was on the keep as we received the pennant signals. He has already sent a squad down to the docks for escort."

Commander Vandor once again smiled. "Thank the gods that I have better officers than Duchess Mariom! With that settled then, while we wait for our guests to arrive, let us find out what Duchess Mariom's people want!"

He dismissed the messenger with a nod. The other officers were sent off in different directions with different orders.

Commander Vandor now turned to the rest of us. "So, if Errol and Banator are through telling tales, let us proceed to the gate."

As we followed Vandor, I fell in step with Ceikay. She had not spoken in the meeting. I asked if she were troubled by something.

"Yes. Why do you ask?"

"Because you are so quiet, but your eyes still tell a lot."

She glanced at me but did not answer. I pressed her some more, "Ceikay, why is your silence loud enough to get my attention?"

We walked along behind everyone for awhile. I prodded her shoulder with my finger.

Finally, she spoke, "If you must press, I will tell you. I was deathly afraid for Errol and Banator. They may be two of the best single warriors in Tavegnor, but they took too big of a risk. It took more than their skills to get them out of that camp and back here. It took luck. …and luck is a fickle ally to rely on in war."

She glanced at me briefly. I then saw for the first time the beginning of tears; but she did not cry. Her face hardened, and I decided to not press further.

Soon we were on top of the breastworks of the gate. We were looking out over the plateau at five horsemen. They were on the road about fifty paces from the fortress. One was leading while the other four were two abreast behind him. The one out front was holding a staff with a white truce banner. He had the uniform of a Captain. These five were motionless and obviously waiting to be acknowledged.

After a few moments of silence on both sides of the wall, Commander Vandor shouted down to the horsemen,

"I am Commander Vandor of Talon Fortress. I assume you are here to talk terms of surrender."

I kept my head facing the plateau, but turned my eyes to watch Vandor. I noticed that he spoke with no humor, and had no humor in his eyes. I could see that no one else moved. Everyone still was looking down at the riders.

The officer on the field yelled back, "You assume correctly!"

"Then I accept your surrender!"

The officer paused a moment before responding, "You misunderstand, sir!"

Commander Vandor smiled and vigorously shook his head, "You misunderstand sir! I am ready to except your surrender!"

I could see the other four horsemen trade glances with each other.

Vandor called out again, "…and who is it that rides to me with a flag of surrender and does not identify himself?!"

Now I could see that the officer was getting a bit impatient. He fidgeted in his saddle before answering formally, "I am Captain Piercon of the Realm of Mariom. I am the Senior Officer in Command of Duchess Mariom's field army on the plains of Talon.

And this is not a banner of surrender! You know well that it is the universal signal of truce and parlay!"

Commander Vandor yelled back, "If you are the Senior Officer on the field; then where is your Commander Baltoron?"

The officer sat straighter in his saddle as he answered, "You must know that he was cut down by your treachery in the Duchess's Royal pavilion!"

On hearing this, Commander Vandor turned to Errol with a questioning look.

Without taking his eyes off the plateau, Errol answered simply and calmly, "It was the King's Royal witness."

I spun my head as Commander Vandor's eyes met mine. His eyebrows rose as he cocked his head, urging me to speak.

I could only shake my head in mute confusion.

Keven then quietly spoke for me. "Yes Commander, it is true; our warrior Beorn was whirling around not knowing what to do when action started inside the tent. As I was dispatching a guard, I saw Commander Baltoron rush directly at Karlyle's back. His sword rose for a killing blow. Beorn stepped between the two. For a split instant, Baltoron was thrown off balance at the surprise in his way. He tried to correct his swing that was already headed at Karlyle's head. Karlyle suddenly moved to the right to engage two more guards. Beorn saw Baltoron's sword swing down between himself and Karlyle. That is when Beorn stabbed upward through the stomach and into the heart of Commander Baltoron. At that instant a dying guard was thrown across the tent, colliding with Beorn, separating him from the Commander. Beorn was instantly stabbing at the dead soldier…"

Vandor held up his hand to stop Keven.

Vandor looked back at me, "Do you not remember any of this?"

My silence was my answer.

Commander Vandor walked over and stood directly before me. "They did not tell me that you were such a fierce warrior."

Vandor's grin was broad. I was not sure if I was being teased.

He continued, "Remember our earlier discussion about Errol's killing of Captain Alluj. If you cut off the head of the Senior

184

Officer of an army, then that army is weakened. You, my friend, have succeeded in that result yourself."

I looked at Commander Vandor, not knowing how to respond. I then looked at the others. Errol stood facing out, not trying to hide a big grin. Karlyle and Keven each glanced at me and grinned. Ceikay stood looking forward. She was not grinning.

I did not see the humor either.

Finally, Vandor turned back to the plateau and addressed the waiting horsemen. "I will hear you out, but do not waste my time if you are going to ask me to open Talon to you!"

Captain Piercon urged his horse forward a step. "I demand, no...request information on our Duchess Mariom's condition! Is she being cared for as befitting her station?"

Commander Vandor answered without hesitation, "She has experienced several wounds. They are not life threatening. She has been tended to by our best healers. As for her station; it is in our dungeons that she is stationed at this time."

Captain Piercon was not visibly shaken by that news. "I am not surprised that she sits in your dungeon. I would do the same if I were in command of Talon Fortress. I ask permission to have her personal healers attend her!"

"My permission is not given!"

The officer yelled back up, "Our healer knows Duchess Mariom and can better care for her! Please, I must repeat my request!"

Commander Vandor yelled again, "I must repeat my answer. There will not be any contact between Duchess Mariom and any of her minions! Our healers are second to no one in Tavegnor. They will assure her full recovery."

The horseman called up, "Do they assure her safety also?"

Commander Vandor now leaned over the wall. "They do not have control, and therefore, assurance of her safety. I am the one responsible for her now! And rest assured, Captain Piercon; as I live, so will Duchess Mariom!"

Vandor then straightened back up, "Are there other requests you wish me to consider sir?"

"None, Commander, but hear me now. I do not pretend to be a

185

Senior Commander with unlimited resources! I am but a junior officer suddenly in command of an army! I am determined by my oath and my honor to do my best for my troops and for the Realm of Mariom!"

The office sat forward on his horse. "I commit to you that I will not authorize further assault on talon Fortress! But I will not lift the siege either. I know that my forces cannot take your position. You must also know that you do not have the forces to break out from my encirclement! No outriders can come by land from King Ballistor. His forces cannot come to relieve you since they are themselves under attack from a number of fronts. I know that you can signal to ships offshore, but you dare not escape by that route, because we both know you must stay and hold Talon Fortress for the fleet's resupply."

Captain Piercon paused and looked back to his companions as if for support.

He then continued, "I will tell you that I have sent riders out to contact First Commander Borcke. Are you familiar with that name Sir?"

Commander Vandor nodded and yelled back, "I do know that name. He is second only to Duchess Mariom in military command of your realm. Where is he, by the way? Will he be coming here to visit with me also?"

"You must know that I will not reveal where he is, or what his plans might be. I will say that he heads a strong force that already has surprised your King. Since Duchess Mariom cannot now lead us, Field Commander Borcke will decide your fate at Talon. I will not insult you by asking for your surrender, but if you choose to reconsider and offer it to me before Commander Borcke turns his full attention and forces this way, I will be generous!"

Commander Vandor motioned to the camp on the beach. "Do you speak for the siege engines, Captain Piercon?!"

"I do, since you have made me the Senior Officer there as well."

Having said that, Captain Piercon turned his horse around and trotted back to his camp. His four escorts followed.

Commander Vandor stood and watched as the horsemen rode

away. He then shook his head and spoke to no one in particular,

"For a junior officer, this Captain Piercon has a good grasp of what is going on. I am impressed with his skill already. Too bad he will be hung for treason in the end."

Errol walked up and stood next to Commander Vandor. He nodded after the receding riders. "If he had been in command when Duchess Mariom's army arrived at the plateau, this fortress might already be in Mariom's hands."

Vandor smiled, "It was your arrival that made the difference. But I do like his brashness."

"Ceikay!"

Ceikay stepped up to Commander Vandor, "What would you like to know, Commander?"

"How did you read this man? Was he in your range?"

She thought a moment before answering, "He is an honest man. I felt no deceit, and surprisingly no hatred. He has the rare ability and balance to feel humble about his experiences, but proud of his abilities. He is not intimidated by the leadership with which he has been entrusted. He is not happy in the role as Commander on the field, but he also does not fear it."

Vandor glanced at me. "Maybe we would be better off having Commander Baltoron still facing us."

Ceikay shook her head, "No. In Baltoron there was evil guile. In Piercon there is at least honor. You should feel confident he will not attack as he has promised."

Vandor answered, "Ah, but honor can still justify cunning. So I will beware his cunning but not his guile."

Ceikay smiled her agreement.

"What do we do now then?" I asked.

Commander Vandor turned to me. "Our redoubtable Captain Piercon is correct. We are cut off by land. My riders have been turned back from the east. So for now, we must hold this fortress for our fleet. We stay in place for a while. The good in this, is that our wounded will have time to rest and recover."

As he spoke, a messenger ran up to us. "Commander Vandor, Captain-of-the-watch sends word that our visitors have been retrieved and are now coming through the catacombs. They will be in the War room directly."

Vandor nodded, but before dismissing the messenger he asked, "Who is the Captain-of-the-watch this morn?"

The messenger snapped out his answer, "First Company Leader Sedroy, Sir."

"Thank you. Return to Officer Sedroy and tell him we are on our way."

Soon we were back in the war room of the keep. While we waited for the newcomers, Errol, Banator and Commander Vandor were in a deep and earnest discussion. I was not close to them so I could not hear all of the conversation, but what I could hear was enough to tell me that Banator was arguing his case to leave Talon Fortress to further look for Hensha.

As I leaned over, about to ask a question to Karlyle, the heavy oak doors of the war room opened. In walked an officer followed by two others. One was a woman dressed in the dark blue colored uniform of the Whorton realm. The insignia on her uniform showed that she was an Official Witness. She was about the height of Ceikay; brown eyes and hair. She carried herself very straight and had a formal air about her.

The man following her was dressed in a long hooded robe of the sort a wizard would wear. This man was the tallest individual I had ever seen...absurdly tall. He was at least two hands taller than Errol. He was very thin and his skin was pale. He looked as though he would break if someone were careless enough to bump into him. The color of his robe was a deep, burnt red. The trim was black around his collar and hem. He wore no jewelry other than a gold pendant on his forehead. The shape of the pendant was that of a healer's knife.

The officer that first entered now spoke. "Commander Vandor, I present to you Witness Dorian of the Realm of Whorton, and the Royal Interrogator Davaas."

The two newcomers bowed in a formal greeting.

Commander Vandor nodded his head in return, and then addressed the officer. "Thank you Captain Sedroy, you may return to your post."

"Sir, as you order, but forgive my correction sir; I am not a

Captain, I am a Company Leader Sir."

Commander Vandor quickly answered, "One of my Regimental Captains went down in yesterday's battle. I need a replacement. I am impressed with the way you take initiative. You are to complete your shift as Captain-of-the-Watch today, then seek me out tonight for further instructions. Any questions or objections, Captain?"

The new Senior Officer snapped to attention and saluted, "No, Commander!"

"Thank you, you are dismissed."

The new captain spun on his heels and quickly left the room.

Commander Vandor now turned his attention to the other two. "Welcome to Talon Fortress. I do not know how much you know, or what you expect while you are here, so I will tell you what I want from you. If you have a different set of instructions, then we will discuss those afterward.

"First I would address Interrogator Davaas...."

Interrogator Davaas held up his hand to stop Vandor, "Please Commander, I only answer to my simple name, Davaas."

When he opened his mouth and spoke, I felt shivers climb up my back and raise the hairs on my neck. His voice sounded normal to my ears, but I could not help getting an eerie and disquieting feeling.

I looked at Vandor to see his reaction. He hesitated before answering. "I will call you as you so wish, but I do not appreciate your interrupting me for such a trifling correction."

"Sir, I apologize for correcting you as I have done. I must tell you though that it is not my personal whim to be addressed so simply. King Ballistor has ordered it so."

Commander Vandor looked over at Karlyle as if to ask him why.

Karlyle simply shrugged his shoulders and shook his head.

"Can you tell me why our King has deemed you to be addressed so simply...without a title?" Vandor asked Davaas.

"I cannot, because he has not explained it to me."

Vandor rolled his eyes, and then continued, "All right Davaas, I forgive your interruption. Now, as to why you are here; we have

189

three prisoners that need to give us straight and honest answers to questions we will be putting to them. I understand that you are the best for getting straight and honest answers. Is that true?"

"I will not say that I am the best. I can say Commander Vandor that I have yet to fail in an interrogation. My subjects have always given me whatever I have asked for."

Vandor nodded, "I expect no deviation from those results then. You will begin as soon as possible if you please."

Vandor now turned to an officer and ordered, "Take Davaas to the dungeons so that he may begin his work."

Davaas held up his hand again. "Commander, as per King Ballistor's directive, I am to always make sure that my methods are understood by all involved. Do you know my methods, Sir?"

Commander Vandor looked at Davaas and nodded. "Your methods are well known to me Davaas. Let us just say that I am thankful I am not one of your assignments."

With that said Davaas bowed once more and left with his escort.

Attention was now directed toward the Witness. Vandor addressed her, "Now, is there a specific title that you must answer to?"

"Sir, I am known as Witness Dorian."

"Excellent. Thank you, Witness Dorian. You have been directed to witness the war's accounts as told to you, is that correct?"

"Yes, that is one of my assignments, Commander."

"Before you begin, Witness Dorian, I have ordered food and drink to be brought for us. It will be here shortly and you can refresh yourself as you speak. Now please, since you reveal that you have more than one assignment, begin with the first."

Witness Dorian stepped forward and began, "My first directive is from our King Ballistor. He has ordered that if his six representatives are currently in Talon Fortress, they are to board, without delay, Fleet Commodore Disellis' flag ship to be transported to Hirst immediately and to report to the King. The names of his representatives are as follows: Sword Master Errol of Bresk, Beast Master Keven of Bresk, Wizard Master Karlyle of

190

Bresk, Mind Listener Ceikay of Bresk, Ranger Banator of Heston, and Royal Witness to the King, Beorn of Minoline."

She stopped to let her words be fully absorbed and understood.

There was silence from all of us. Finally, Commander Vandor spoke, "I need clarification..."

Witness Dorian answered promply, "As I complete the announcing of that order, they are to make ready for travel. Commodore Disellis' small boat is waiting just off the shore for them as I speak."

Vandor frowned, "Do you mean now?"

"Yes, Commander, King Ballistor made it clear that time was critical and they must not delay."

She then added, "I was also directed not to give further witness until they acknowledge the order and are on their way to the boat."

I looked around at the others and then to Commander Vandor. The look on his face told all that he was not happy.

After several moments of silence in the room, Vandor again spoke, "What of the prisoners' information? Does the King want news brought back along with his representatives?'

"No, Commander, the King anticipated you would ask that question. He ordered me to tell you that he would not wait on Davaas' results. Send the representatives now, and send news of Duchess Mariom's cooperation later on the next available vessel."

Commander Vandor turned to the rest of us. "You heard King Ballistor's orders. I desperately want that you would stay, but needs take you elsewhere. Banator, our discussion earlier is now moot. You must continue your pleas with our King now. Gods bless and aid your search."

The Commander now addressed me. "As for you Witness Beorn, tell King Ballistor everything that has happened here."

He smiled and tapped the sword at my side. "Including your contributions."

Commander Vandor now turned to each of the other four. He did not speak. He went to each one and shook their hands. He hugged Ceikay.

Vandor walked over to the large table. "Witness Dorian, the King's Representatives are now on their way. Would you please come to the table and finish your report."

I stood watching the Commander. A tug on my tunic turned me to the door. I followed the rest out. Before the sun's shadows could lengthen one full pace, we were all on a small boat headed out to open waters.

Hirst and Beyond

Leaving Talon Fortress so swiftly, I did not have time to consider what we may have left behind. As we were sitting in the boat, I now had the time.

I suddenly sat up and looked back toward the shore. "Horses! What about our horses?"

Keven sat up and looked back also. "I have already arranged for them to leave the fortress this night. They will go through the grotto and make their way east. Eventually, they will meet us in Hirst."

By now I knew enough to know that Keven could communicate a plan to them. I wondered how they would manage to get past the ring of enemy forces on the plateau.

"Are you not worried Piercon's men may capture the horses on the plateau?"

Keven smiled. "Not with Eagle flying over to help guide and distract."

Nothing more was said until our boat came within sight of Commodore Disellis' Flagship. I was not impressed with the size of the vessel as we approached.

As if reading my mind, Ceikay spoke to me, "This launch will take us to Commodore Disellis' ship."

I smiled and nodded. I was not surprised she had answered my unspoken concern.

"Then Ceikay, you have been on the flagship before..."

"No, but I have seen it moored outside of Spar Fortress. Two seasons ago we were preparing for a journey to the Northern continent. Commodore Disellis was returning King Ballistor from the Southern city of Esturin in the realm of Castus."

"What does the flagship look like?" I asked.

"It is truly a wonder to look upon!"

I turned to Errol's voice as he stepped over to us. He continued with the description. "It is the first of its kind: a new, larger, three-masted sailing ship. It is the only one in the fleet at this time, but the shipyards at Hirst are building more."

I tried to imagine the look of a three-masted ship. "I have seen two-masted vessels before. Where did they put a third mast?"

Errol pointed to the vessel we were approaching. "Take a look at the ketch as we approach. See the two masts and where they are positioned. The foremast is larger than the aft mast, is it not?"

I nodded, and he continued, "The sails on the two masts are boomed to one side. There are two triangular masts from the bowsprit to the foremast...do you see that?"

I nodded again, not really understanding.

He continued, "Now on the flagship, the foremast is brought forward while the aft mast is relocated further to the stern. The third mast is put amidship. This new mast is called the mainmast, and is the largest. The aft mast is now called the mizzenmast; this is the smallest of the three. The foremast and the mainmast now are rigged with square sails while the mizzenmast is rigged with tri-shaped fore-and-aft sails as before. The triangular sails at the fore of the foremast are called jibs, and the different jibs are called..."

As I struggled to listen I noticed both Keven and Karlyle shaking their heads.

Suddenly Errol's narration was cut short by a jarring bump on our skiff. We had reached the transport vessel.

The pilot of our boat yelled out, "Climb the ladder if ya will,

Lady 'n Lords! I hev' ta get myself back ta the docks!"

We all scrambled up the rope ladder as directed. Last came the silent Banator, who I had almost forgotten was with us.

As we stepped aboard we were greeted by an officer. "Welcome aboard the Silverfish. I am ship's Captain Relenemis. I am to deliver you directly to Hirst. Commodore Disellis sends his regrets that you will not join him on the flagship. He must pursue the enemy on the seas as he finds them…and right now…they are finding him!"

He pointed aft. "You are welcome to go below or stay on deck. I have ordered the ship's cook to prepare meals for you. As the King's Representatives you have free run of my ship, so relax and I shall get you to Hirst ere sun sets this day. With your leave I will have Ship's Mate Tackart take you in hand."

The Captain called another sailor over. "Mr. Tackart, you will show our guests the ship and be at their service until we set them off at Hirst."

The First Mate crisply nodded, "Aye Captain!"

Captain Relenemis tipped his hat to us and went forward.

Mr. Tackart turned to us, "If you would follow me, I will deliver you to the galley. Our cook already has food and ship's drink laid out for you."

I smelled the fare as we got closer to the galley. It smelled delicious!

After a big meal of fresh boiled pork, fresh baked bread, bread pudding, fresh baked vegetable pie, and excellent ale, I settled back to loosen my belt.

It was then I first noticed that Errol was not at the table with us.

"Where is our leader?" I asked as I yawned.

"If you mean Errol…" Karlyle pointed his finger upwards, "He prefers topside and the fresh air, rather than below decks with the fresh food."

I glanced at the others, "He is not hungry? Why would he miss all this food?"

Ceikay held a finger to her lips, "Shush. He might hear you."

Still not understanding, I offered a solution. "If he does not like to be confined down here, why do I not I put a plate together and take it up to him?"

Karlyle answered, "It is not the confinement that prevents him from eating. It is the rocking back and forth."

Then understanding came to me, "Are you saying that Errol is seasick?"

Keven nodded. "Every time he travels on the ocean he is worthless. He could never be a sailor, even though the ocean is his first love."

At first I did not notice that last statement. I was too intent on asking more questions.

How come he was not sick on the small boat? Why did he get sick now? Is this boat not bigger, making the rocking less harsh? Most of all, if he does not like the ocean, why does he have so much interest and knowledge in sailing vessels?"

Ceikay again held up her finger to stop me. "We cannot explain his reactions, or why he does not get sick in a small boat and waves. He has studied seagoing vessels because he is fascinated by them. The only answer we can fathom is that his mind convinces him to be sick only when he boards an ocean-going vessel."

"Yes, but Errol is in control of everything else. Why then can he not control this?"

Keven rose from the table and placed his hand on my shoulder, "It is best that you drop this questioning. Errol is aware of his failure in this regard. He is a very sensitive individual."

I grinned but my companions only stared solemnly at me.

"Then the offering of food would be a mistake," I concluded aloud.

Keven turned to the others, "That is a good decision." He turned back to me, "Beorn, please heed my warning, Errol can be prodded and teased only so far. In this matter, do not offer humor at his expense. At least not so that he may hear."

Even Banator could grin at that. "Well, I am going topside to see my good friend. The poor soul might not feel up to our company, but he might like our sympathy and understanding."

Karlyle spoke as he got up to join Banator. "Even you do not believe that, but if you insist on tempting fate, I must come along to pull you from harm's way."

Now Keven spoke as he followed Karlyle, "Who is going to protect you then?"

Soon, we were all on the after-deck watching Errol. He was sitting on the deck with his back pressing the foremast. His eyes were closed and he did not move. Captain Relenemis stood off to the side, also watching him. No one dared to approach Errol as he sat. Finally, Ceikay called out gently,

"Errol? Errol, how are you doing?"

Errol opened his eyes and stared ahead, then whispered, "I am fine. Just you leave me to myself."

"Errol," Ceikay continued softly, "the Captain needs his deck back. You are in the way. The crew must trim sails, and you are sitting in their path. Could you at least roll to the side?"

Errol shook his head, "They can work over me. I will not take offense."

We took turns trying to convince Errol to move away from the mast.

The rest of our brief voyage to Hirst, deck hands gingerly stepped over and around Errol to get their jobs done, but the good Relenemis did not once appear angry or put out. He gave the strictest orders to his men to tread lightly around our seasick companion.

The next time Errol moved was when we were let off the ship onto the dock at Hirst. I was amazed at how quickly he recovered. He was on his feet and looking over the side as dock hands threw lines to secure the vessel.

As we were put off from the Silverfish, Captain Relenemis called down to us, "Gods' speed to you all!"

With that sentiment, Relenemis turned and yelled out orders to his crew. His attention was already bound for the open sea.

We were back in Hirst. It had been only three days since we had left to warn Duchess Mariom. The sun was down, the sky was dark, and so was the city. We saw no lights in windows. The usual noise of a city at night was not heard either. The towers surrounding Hirst were not empty, though. We saw the light of torches and the silhouettes of soldiers. I knew that they were watching us closely as we stood on the docks. I felt the aim of a thousand arrows on us.

The dock that we were standing on was surrounded by merchant and fishing craft of all shapes and sizes. At anchor a short distance off the docks were hundreds of vessels. Moments before, as we were threading our way through these boats, Captain Relenemis had told us that just about every non-military vessel had run into port for protection. As of now, merchant trade was effectively shut down in all of southern Tavegnor.

A squad of soldiers on horseback rode up to us. The lead rider saluted and spoke: "Welcome back to Hirst. I am Geltus, First Officer of the Third Light Horse Regiment of the Realm of Rasher. I am to escort you to King Ballistor's field tent. I have provided horses for you, so if you would not delay..."

We quickly mounted the horses and began our short trip to the King. Our escort led us not through the city and to the castle, but rather around the towers to the right and into the fields beyond. I now saw thousands of torches and camp fires in front of us. Tents by the hundreds blossomed out of the dark ground. The quiet of the city was replaced with the commotion of the military camp before us. As our group rode into the camp I began to distinguish the different colors of uniforms on the soldiers and officers. I could not tell where one realm's boundaries ended and another one began. It seemed to me that war had forced a melding of the different armies.

Soon I saw guide-on flags ahead. The banners told me that the King would be in the large tent in the center of a larger clearing. There was not another tent within thirty paces of the King's. Twenty Halberd-armed guards stood at attention surrounding the clearing. One heavily armed guard stood at each of the four corners of the huge tent. They faced out toward the ring of guards at the perimeter.

We entered the clearing and rode up to the tent's entrance. Officer Geltus and his men did not dismount. Suddenly the flap to the tent opened and out stepped King Ballistor. I saw that he was in full battle armor.

The King nodded briskly, "Well met, my friends. Come inside, without delay."

He then turned around and disappeared back into the tent. We quickly dismounted and followed. We did not bid farewell to our escort since they had already ridden off.

Inside the tent was a number of Senior Officers of the five realms still loyal to Tavegnor. They were surrounding a large table that held a large map of our country.

The moment we entered King Ballistor spoke again, this time addressing his officers. "Gentlemen, these are my special Envoys from Talon Fortress. They have news of the fighting there, and also of Duchess Mariom. My Royal Witness Beorn will give report presently. But first I must speak to them alone. I will send a runner for you when I want you again."

One by one the officers left the tent. Some of them knew my companions and nodded greetings as they walked past us and through the flap.

Once my companions and I stood alone, the king spoke. "Banator, I have news to report to you. Before I speak though, I ask if you want your friends with you now."

At once my chest felt like Jakor leadstone. My eyes darted to Banator. I saw no reaction except his jaw muscles twitching.

No one moved. We waited for Banator to speak.

Finally he inhaled deeply and spoke, "I wish my friends to be here, Sire."

"I did not think you would have answered otherwise." King Ballistor stepped close to Banator. "My friend, Hensha is dead. Her body was found yesterday morn. I am sorry…"

Before the words were out of the King's mouth, Ceikay let out a sorrowful moan and put her face in her hands. I saw Errol lower his chin to his chest. Karlyle and Keven both stood in place with hardened stares.

Banator fell to his knees and lowered his head to his chest. He did not utter a sound, nor did he cry. He just froze in that position.

King Ballistor put his hand on Banator's head and again spoke, "We are grieved beyond all words son, I will not give you flowery epitaphs."

199

Banator spoke softly with his head still down, "Can you tell me where she was found…and how she died?"

The King paused before answering. "I know that you must hear, so I will tell you everything we know. She must have arrived at Hirst days ago. Her body was found by a merchant who was gathering supplies to flee the city. At the outer perimeter, near the towers he has an old warehouse that was used for storage of old and broken wagons. Hensha was lying in a grain wagon. She had been bound. My healers examined the body and determined that she had lived for several days while suffering burns and knife cuts."

Banator's head rose. His now glazed-looking eyes stared straight ahead. "Was she…"

King Ballistor anticipated the question and quickly answered, "No, she was not violated, Banator. It seems that whoever did this wanted information only. The wounds she suffered were ones that an expert torturer would inflict."

Banator rose to his feet and faced the King. "It had to be someone who she knew…a citizen of Tavegnor."

Errol added in agreement, "He is right, Sire; Hensha was too skilled to be ambushed by strangers. She was on her guard in route to report to you and would not have let a stranger get that close to her. She met someone who she felt safe with; someone who betrayed her."

King Ballistor nodded. "This 'someone' has betrayed all of Tavegnor. May the gods grant us the boon of finding this traitor."

The King addressed Banator, "If you desire to see Hensha, we have cleansed her and have prepared her for a burial of the highest honor. You have my leave to go to her now if you wish. Your friends will represent you at the war meeting."

Without hesitation, Banator stood up and faced the King. "No, Sire. My duty is to defend Tavegnor with my life. I will mourn my Hensha when our enemies have been driven into the oceans!"

King Ballistor looked hard into Banator's eyes: "Then you will stay and listen. We are at great peril and I do need your strength beside me. Thank you, loyal son of Tavegnor. We shall avenge Hensha on the battlefield."

The King now turned to the rest of us. "You are to refresh and eat if you can. Take Banator with you and do not let him refuse food. It is important that you all eat well as you are able. I will send for you when I am ready for Beorn's report. As you leave the tent, you will see one of my pages waiting outside. He will take you to our field kitchens."

Ceikay stepped forward. "A moment Sire, before we go?"

King Ballistor understood her request. "Yes, a moment would be good. I will step outside and check with my sentries."

He then stepped out of the tent and left us alone.

I spoke, "I think I should leave also."

Banator turned at once and replied, "Stay. We are comrades together in this war. I want...I would ask you to stay...please."

Then Ceikay stepped over to Banator and hugged him. Her tears smudged his tunic. They both embraced for a few moments in quiet. Ceikay then stepped back. Keven and Karlyle each in turn embraced Banator. Errol was next. His big powerful arms held tight for a moment, and then he backed away.

After a long pause and silence, Banator looked over at me. "My friend, I need your energy also."

Feeling a little awkward I stepped over and put my arm out and we shook hands. For a strange, brief moment, I felt as if energy truly passed between us. After our hands parted I was surprised that the gesture I was giving to comfort Banator had in fact, comforted me also.

Ceikay somehow knew my thoughts. "That is how the gods designed it, Beorn: friends are needed in life."

No other words were spoken. We now stepped outside the tent and saw a page standing ten paces away. Seeing us emerge, the page hurried up to us and quickly spoke, "Please, I am commanded to make sure that you eat."

He then turned and began to leave the clearing. We followed close behind.

The field kitchen was not far away. Soldiers and officers were still eating at the long tables. We were served large portions, but Errol was the only one who emptied his plate. He then finished a second one. None of us spoke.

Presently, a messenger ran up to us and broke the silence, "Pardon, but the King requests your presence as soon as possible. He also says that you may bring your meal if you have yet to finish."

A few moments later we were back in the tent. No one brought food.

King Ballistor was standing at the table flanked by his senior officers. He looked up as we entered. There was no sign of softness or sympathy on his face as before.

His countenance was once again formal and curt as he spoke, "Now we can begin. Beorn, we would hear your witnessing of the siege of Talon Fortress."

Taking the King's cue and remembering Witness Dorian's formal presentation, I stepped forward and began. I started from three days ago when we first left Hirst. I left no detail out. No one asked questions of me. I spoke uninterrupted until well after midnight. No one sat while I reported. Several times my companions nodded in agreement or support, but they too never uttered a sound.

One item I deliberately did not relate: Errol's condition while at sea.

Eventually my report was complete, and I announced it so.

King Ballistor wasted no time. "Thank you for that thorough accounting. There will be no questioning from me or my officers. There is no time. I want everyone over to the map. We must all of us understand what we are facing."

The map of Tavegnor filled the large table. It spanned about three paces by two paces. King Ballistor turned to one of his officers, "Captain, tell us your report of the invasion."

"Yes, Sire." The Captain began his formal dialogue, pointing to the landmarks on the map as he described them.

"As you can see by the pieces I have placed on the map, Tavegnor has been invaded at least in one area by a foreign army. We have confirmed that Bourne in the southeast has been overrun by at least thirty thousand of the enemy. What is left of Duke Whorton's army at Bourne has retreated to the Orth Pass and is under attack as we speak. At first invasion of Bourne, outriders

202

were sent from there to report to Hirst. We were told also that outriders were dispatched north from Bourne to alert regiments at Dannon and Pesha. No word has reached us yet on how these regiments of Whorton are faring.

"We are under attack from the north area of the Ballistor Realm. None of our outriders have returned with information on who exactly is up there. The only outrider to return was injured in an ambush. He told little before he died. What he did tell us was that Hellista of Ballistor rode north with two regiments of heavy cavalry, and has not been heard from since.

"We also know that the traitorous Duke Hastid had marched north in force several days before the massacre at the Trade Meeting. If he has been joined by a foreign army, we do not as yet have confirmation.

"As we have just heard from the witness, Talon Fortress is under siege by one of Duchess Mariom's armies. Where the rest of her traitors are, we again have not yet received intelligence.

"We have no word on the Southern Island of Tavegnor. As you know, Duke Castus left Hastid in his flagship. We pray that he made it back to his realm to ready his forces for a counter-attack. That is all that we know at this time."

The Captain stepped back as he completed his report.

King Ballistor now spoke again to all of us, "As you can see, we do not yet know much in this war on our land. We have been taken completely by surprise. Tavegnor has enjoyed peace far too long. We have grown lazy in our defense. As your King I am responsible for that. I apologize to each and every one of you. Saying that does not excuse my failings, nor does it remove my responsibilities from this point on."

King Ballistor paused briefly, but no one spoke. He then continued, "I have put in motion the best defense as far as we can plan. Captain Lunus will report on our troop strength and mobility."

Another officer stepped forward and began his report, pointing to the map as did the first officer. "We have confirmed only seventeen thousand troops under our control and still in communication with the King: Five Thousand here at Hirst, one thousand at Javin to the north of us…two thousand at Halenester, two thousand at Dellester, one thousand each at the cities of Tynus and Orth, and four thousand troops at Osloman. We have no word from anyone else."

Captain Lunus nodded formally and stepped back from the table. I was shocked at how brief his report was.

King Ballistor spoke again: "As you can all see, we are in a perilous position. It was a very well planned surprise attack that left us blind and cut off from each other. Two Realms have turned on Tavegnor and are now squeezing us in the middle. Their foreign ally is on our shore in at least one place that we know of. Time is not on our side. Let us pray that the gods are.

"Now, look to the map. This is what I plan to do: first, we know for certain that Orth Pass is where the enemy is. We will meet him there with what we can spare of the seventeen thousand. We must stop him from going any further. I am forced to leave a certain number of troops behind in case of attack elsewhere. Each city with troops under our control will keep half strength and send the other half to meet in the city of Tynus. That will give us eight thousand five hundred strong to march to Orth Pass. Right now Whorton's troops hold the pass with just three thousand. Outriders report an estimated force of the enemy facing them is around twelve thousand. The pass is narrow and can slow down the invaders for a while, but not indefinitely. We must get to them at speed. Already I have ordered our forces to travel. They should start to arrive from the nearest cities by tomorrow noon. I will lead the two regiments from Hirst. I intend to leave by sunrise this morn."

The King paused and looked around at each of his men. Then he continued, "Each of you officers in this tent already have your orders. You must carry them out with all your efforts and your resolve. Are there any questions before I end this council?"

One officer stepped forward. "Sire, what of the relief of Talon Fortress? Will we send troops there?"

The King shook his head, "I regret that we cannot spare troops. Commander Vandor is one of our most capable officers. He must hold on his own strength, and I am confident that he will."

The king looked around. No more questions were voiced.

He spoke once more, "I must speak with my envoys and give them orders, so I dismiss the rest of you to your duties. Good luck and the gods' speed to you."

Once again we were left with the King, and once again, he was direct: "I do not know what is going on in the north. I want you to get up there as far as you can. I want to know why my outriders are not returning. I want to know where my daughter Hellista is. You are my best hope of finding her and keeping her safe."

King Ballistor turned to Banator. "Banator, I now put you in charge of my outriders. From this time forward, you will be responsible for the clearing and securing of Talavor road. I give you four full companies and the rank of Captain. You are to escort your five companions north. On the way, you will re-establish the relay stations for the riders. Banator, you are a Ranger with skills of the roads. No one knows them as completely as you. Ferret out the ambushers and kill them. Tavegnor needs its roads back. Do not fail me in this."

Banator did not visibly react.

King Ballistor raised his voice slightly and pressed him, "Banator, do you understand what I want from you?"

Banator looked at his King and answered stoically, "Sire, I understand. I will not fail you."

The King now turned to me, "Beorn, you have proven yourself valuable to me. I cannot release you now. You must continue to be in my service. You will go with your four companions and observe for witnessing. It is vital that I have your accurate account of all events."

King Ballistor then added, "I am impressed by your actions to this point, but I am concerned on one account: Do try to stay away from the close fighting. You are more valuable to me as a live observer rather than as a dead hero."

To my surprise, I answered back, "Sire, I am finding that lately, I cannot always plan my day ahead."

Everyone turned their heads in my direction.

King Ballistor stared at me, and then turned to the others. "Humor at the King's expense? It strikes me that you four are already corrupting this man."

He smiled and turned back to me. "Duke Jaramas was very fond of you. I can see why. So, think of it as a personal favor to your King; try to plan your days around staying alive."

I stood there, embarrassed to answer again.

He then addressed all of us together: "My duties keep me down south. I must break this army at Orth Pass. You will have my Seal to act with all authority to take command as you see fit. If you find that we still have a fighting force in the north, then help it push our enemies into the sea, no matter who they are. If we are already routed, then I fear that Tavegnor will fade from history. Are there questions to be asked?"

Errol stepped forward. "Our horses are making their way from Talon. We hope to see them arrive by first light. Do you wish us to be on the road before then?"

The King shook his head, "I wish you to get sleep before you leave this camp. Your horses will be tended for you as they arrive. They should be fresh also when you go. If they do not get here before noon of this new day, they will not have had time to rest before you go forth. You must then leave on horses we provide. You horses will just have to get to you later."

The King addressed Banator: "Waiting outside is your Second in Command. He is a good officer and will take you immediately to your tent. There you will clean, rest, and then put on the uniform provided you.

"The rest of you will be escorted to your tents also. After suitable sleep you all will be reunited and released north."

The King looked at each of us in turn. "I will not see you again this day. I will be traveling to Tynus to take charge of our gathering army."

King Ballistor stood at attention, saluted, and then walked out of the tent.

For a moment, we all stood looking at each other. We then followed the King out. Our escorts were waiting for us. We each had our own escort and tent. A few moments later I stepped inside mine and was alone. I saw the bedding on the floor and did not even bother undressing. I lay down and sleep quickly took over.

Once again, nudging and urging broke my slumber. I awoke to the sound of a page speaking over me, "Sir...Sir, it is time. You must rise and prepare to leave."

I opened my eyes and saw the full light of day through the canvas of my tent. I groaned as I sat up. I looked over at a small table and saw more food and drink. I also saw fresh clothes laid out for me.

Green of course, but not Ballistor green. Before me were the clothes of a Ranger, showing no rank or insignia. The food was welcome. I was surprised that I enjoyed the taste of the ale so. Soon, I was dressed and stepping through the tent flap.

To my great surprise, I found the camp deserted. During my sleep, most of the tents and their soldiers had left. Now there were only a dozen or so tents standing. My page had been waiting for me outside, and now led me to my four companions. They had all donned new outfits.

I nodded greetings and they did the same. No words were spoken. I noted that the general mood was still grim.

Banator now rode up to us on a beautiful white horse. I stared at him as he approached. He was splendid in a crisp green uniform of the King's Royal Guard. He sat tall and straight. He showed elegance I had never seen in him before.

"I bring new horses for you." His words were formal. "Your own will not be leaving with you this day. They have had a rough escape from Talon. Please mount so that we may be on our way."

We did as he directed. Errol was given a beautiful golden-brown stallion a full two hands taller than the rest. The rest of us were given black stallions, similar to the ones we had ridden before.

Banator spoke again, "Errol is to ride with me. Ceikay, please ride with Beorn at your side. Keven and Karlyle, I would like you to follow behind."

No one said a word. We rode as directed.

Presently, the camp, the towers, and the city of Hirst fell behind us. For the first time I fully realized the numbers in the four companies that King Ballistor had given to Banator. Close to five

207

hundred mounted warriors were riding north with us. Two companies of one hundred and twenty each were ahead of us...and two more were following.

We rode north along the Talavor road a long while before I felt like speaking. Naturally the first words out of my mouth were questions. "Ceikay, was Banator an officer in Ballistor's army before this?"

She glanced my way, "Yes, yes he was. I am not surprised that you guessed that."

"Is that the reason why Ballistor gave Banator the commission?"

Ceikay again glanced my way as we rode. "The question you asked, is not the one you want answered, I believe. I think you are asking if our King had any ulterior motives in placing Banator in charge of such a force."

I nodded, but said nothing. Ceikay had guessed my meaning, "Yes Beorn, King Ballistor is a wise man. He gave Banator great responsibility in order to keep him focused on winning the war, and not grasping for blind vengeance. But that is not truly the wise part. The wisdom in the King's decision is that Banator is indeed the best choice for securing the roads of Tavegnor."

We rode awhile longer before I asked another question, "When was he in the King's military?"

Ceikay thought a few moments before answering, "Ten full years ago if my memory is correct. He was a tracker at first, then an officer of the Royal Guard. He petitioned the King to leave official service."

"Why?" I asked.

"To this day I do not know. I have tried to get answers from him, but Banator keeps silent about his past."

I decided to stop the questions for a while. We rode north along the Talavor road. The road is named after the river that flows next to it. Talavor River is a wide, old river that songs have been sung about for ages. Its source is in the northern regions of the great Tellis Mountains. The river south of Alsoner Lake is not fit for merchant commerce. The sand bars and narrows prohibit large vessels from navigating north or south.

I rode alongside Ceikay until the light of the sun began to fail. We had seen no travelers coming south, which means that no outriders had passed us either. During this time I had not noticed the riders ahead of us. Now I heard a screech from the sky and knew that it was Eagle. He had come back! I looked up and spotted him circling over us. I then looked to Keven. He was shaking his head. Errol and Banator had twisted back in their saddles to watch Keven. Once Keven shook his head, the other two turned forward and continued to ride.

I guessed that Keven had seen nothing ahead of us to this point.

As we rode further, I now studied my companions. Keven's eyes were closed. I knew that he was flying with Eagle. Karlyle was turning his head from side to side, scanning the horizons for any movement. Errol and Banator still rode side by side. They talked together and sometimes pointed off in the distance as if searching for our enemy. Ceikay stayed quiet and rode facing straight ahead.

We rode this way until the sun was completely below the horizon. When I could spot the sixth star in the sky, Banator called a halt to our march.

He yelled out, "We will camp here for the night! Squad leaders organize your watch groups and set up a perimeter guard!"

I tried to help set up our camp, but the soldiers knew what they were doing and politely nudged me out of their way. Presently, I was being led to my very own tent. My horse had been taken from me by a steward.

Captain Banator marched around camp as it was being set up. He gave directions and orders as if he had been an officer in the regular army all his life. He did not show any of his relaxed drawl or humor. He was a Senior Officer in speech as well as actions.

Soon the cooks had a fire going. The aroma of the food reminded me that I had been in the saddle for a full day. When a plate was handed to me, I happily emptied it. Unlike the late nights of the camp at Hirst, Captain Banator soon ordered fires out.

Once again, sleep came to me quickly.

Once again, sleep was pushed away too soon. The next

209

morn's sun was shining through my tent flap. A soldier poked his head in and yelled at me to ready for travel. My eyes opened in protest.

Before my mind could accept it, I was on my horse and traveling north again. Ceikay was at my side. She seemed to have rested quite well. Her hair was neatly brushed back and her face looked fresh washed. Her clothes did not look as mine did, wrinkled with sleep. She did have the same expression on her face as mine though. So I knew that she had no humor this morn. Our other companions' faces held the same look. We rode in silence.

The morn turned to noon, which turned to past noon. We rode in silence. We made good distance at our pace. Then, Eagle swooped down and screeched. Errol and Banator turned around and looked at Keven. Keven's closed eyes now opened.

He twisted in his saddle as if trying to get his bearings before he spoke, "I see twenty leagues ahead that the road is blockaded. Two hundred afoot of halberd entrenched. On either side, about one hundred paces away from the road are one hundred horsemen of light cavalry. The color gold tells me that Duchess Mariom's forces are the ones intercepting our outriders at this point."

Captain Banator rode back to Keven. "Did you see archers?"

Keven shook his head, "No archers, but a rear guard of ten light horse cavalry…probably to run and give alert if the blockade is threatened."

Errol joined them and asked, "Any more forces that may come to reinforce their position?"

Once again, Keven shook his head: "Out of my range if they are there."

Banator now called to his officers, "Center on me men! We will clear this road!"

The four Company Commanders joined us. Banator now gave orders. He pointed at one of them, "First Officer Blatilis, you will take your troop east two leagues from the road, go north fifty leagues. Wait for lightning in the sky for your signal to ride at speed back to Talavor road."

Captain Banator turned to another officer: "You will take your company and cross Talavor River to the west. At this point, the river is shallow and slow so you will be able to cross. You will then travel fifty leagues north and wait for lightning in the sky. When you see it, rush east in full battle charge. Cross the river and attack the enemy as you meet him."

Then Banator told us what he was planning: "The rest of us will ride ahead on the road. The enemy will spot us. They might fall back or they might put up a fight, either way..."

Keven held up his hand for silence. His eyes were closed again.

Ceikay now coughed and pulled casually on her braided ponytail.

Instantly I felt my four companions stiffen at her signal.

Errol slowly maneuvered his horse next to Ceikay's and softly spoke, "Tell me."

"Three men hiding in the tall grass on the bank of the river; they are watching us. They are enemy...they are holding weapons...possibly crossbows."

As she was reporting that, I saw her hands fold on the pommel of her saddle. Her left hand covered her right hand. The forefinger of her right hand now pointed to a spot by the bank. She was telling us exactly where the three men were.

Banator now came near. "Did they see my men ride off to flank?"

"Yes."

Now Karlyle whispered, "Would you like me to flush them out so that you may have a conversation, Banator?"

Banator kept looking at Ceikay but answered Karlyle, Why yes, that would please me if you could arrange it my friend."

Karlyle turned his horse to face north. He began to scan the road ahead, as if trying to see something in the distance. Suddenly, to our right and about one hundred paces away, flames leaped up from the grass! The unexpected fire quickly spread to the left and right. I could see that it was rapidly coming toward the road...toward us!

Strange, the smoke billowed away from the road. I realized that Karlyle was making the fire come against the wind, directly at the hidden men!

We waited several moments. The fire widened and rushed closer. I could hear the roar now. Then we heard screams above the noise of the fire. Three men jumped up just as the fire was engulfing their position. The only place they had to run was right at us. Banator's men saw the three and instantly drew their swords. The hapless men came meekly toward us with their arms raised.

Captain Banator now shouted orders over the roar of the fire. "First Officer Trent, Secure these men, I will question them in a moment!"

Suddenly the roar of the fire stopped. I looked to the bank. The fire was gone! What startled me along with the rest of my companions was the lack of any trace of a fire being there! No charring...no smell...no smoke...just grass as it was before!

Errol turned to Karlyle, "You faked a fire?"

Karlyle nodded slowly. "It was something I had been working on for some time now. I reasoned that a real fire might be seen in the distance. I did not want to alert any other eyes. I manipulated the air over the grass to simulate fire. The grass never even felt heat."

Karlyle grinned and continued, "Did you like how the smoke billowed away from us? Even though the wind was coming our way, the men in the field were too panicked to notice the difference!"

"Why did you make the smoke go opposite the wind?" I asked.

Errol answered for Karlyle, "The main purpose was the direction of the smoke, and not its relation to the wind. You see, since Karlyle was making an illusion of fire, the smoke was also not real. Therefore, if the smoke would have billowed into the hiding men, they would have felt no heat, nor would their lungs have been choked by the smoke. The effect would have failed."

Karlyle nodded in agreement.

"What about the noise, the roar of the flames?"

Karlyle answered this time, "That is relatively easy. The wind was already blowing our way. I just pulled it faster past the men over their heads. In truth, it is the noise of the wind which fires generate that sounds like a roar."

I pressed some more, "But if we could see the fake smoke, then could…"

Suddenly I caught Errol's twitch of his head. My eyes glanced over and I saw him frown at me for an instant. Then his face turned neutral again.

I did not understand fully, but said no more. I looked past Karlyle and saw Keven. His eyes were still closed. He had not moved since before the start of the fire, or rather, false fire.

Once again, Eagle screeched overhead. Keven opened his eyes and spurred his horse closer to us.

We waited for him to speak: "I have just flown over Raval. It is taken! I saw gold uniforms and the banners of Duchess Mariom's army. One thousand strong is my estimate of the enemy encamped around the city."

"Can you tell us how much infantry and how much cavalry?" Errol asked.

"It looks to be entirely cavalry. I estimate there are about the same number of horses as there are soldiers."

Captain Banator now called out to his officer, "Trent! You will take six men with you and escort our three friends back along the road about a league. There you will get information from them! If they are reluctant to provide it, you may be…persuasive."

I looked at the three men. Their faces dropped at Banator's words.

Trent saluted and pointed out six men from the troop. The three men were quickly herded on their way. Banator waved the officer back.

He spoke quietly. "Threaten them with foul torture, but only rough them up. Do not break bones or cut flesh. They are low in rank and would not know much of value anyway. Once you are satisfied that they have told you all, send them back to Hirst and send a rider to King Ballistor to inform him what has transpired so far. You will then ride to catch up with the rest of us. Is that clear?'

Officer Trent grinned. "Sir, I can already see the sweat on those men's brows. Soon, there will be tears on their cheeks, and words on their tongues!"

Trent turned his horse and rode after his men.

Banator now spoke again. "Officers! To me!"

Three men broke from the waiting lines of horsemen. They were quickly at our side.

Captain Banator continued. "We must plan our next moves carefully. It is my reasoning that this road barricade is positioned to be supported by the force at Raval. If we attack it as I had planned, then we would surely be facing a larger force from the west."

One of the junior officers now raised his hand to speak. Banator nodded his permission,

"Sir, if we act swiftly enough to surprise the group on the road, they might not have time to send a rider to alert their comrades at Raval."

"Two things wrong with that," Banator spoke calmly. "First; total and swift surprise is almost impossible at this treeless part of the road. They will have time to send a rider off before we could completely cut them off. Second; I cannot take it for granted that a signal system has not been set up ahead of time by our enemy. Even if we did succeed in blocking all runners, I must plan as though they were as smart as we would be. They would use signal arrows, or a timed relay of outriders."

Errol spoke next. "We cannot wipe out the blockaders and then race north to Kint. We would still have an intact army chasing us from Raval. Also, we do not yet know what we would be facing at Kint. Gods prevent us from putting ourselves between our enemies!"

Banator nodded toward Errol. "I agree, we must decide how we are to clear this road and keep it secure. I will listen to any and all suggestions."

One of the officers urged his horse closer. "Captain, could we get help from the city of Javin?"

"I had thought of that and dismissed it. Their garrison must stay where it is. If the invasion forces come west through Rekor Pass, then the regiment at Javin is the only one in place to engage the enemy. No…we are alone in this."

Just as Banator had finished, a yell rose from the front of our troops, "Rider coming in from the east! He is ours and riding fast!"

We looked out and saw one of our riders from the company that left us earlier. He galloped up to the road, reined in and halted in front of Banator, "Sir! We have been spotted three leagues north and to the east of here! Enemy patrols ride from Javin road to Talavor road! The patrols ran from us as we saw each other. We did not give chase. First Officer Latilis bids me to tell you he is proceeding as you have ordered and will wait for your signal to attack. If you have new orders, I am to carry them back at once!"

Banator turned to the rest of us. "Then it is decided for us. Surprise is no longer an option. We will attack as soon as we get in position, then race north and hope we do not run into a force big enough to cripple us!"

As Banator started to give orders to the outrider, Errol held his hand up, "If you please Captain, may I make a suggestion?"

Banator smiled and nodded, "I am glad you have one. Do not keep your thoughts from the rest of us."

Errol began, "Since we now have been seen, we know that riders of our enemy will be spreading the alarm. The only force we know for certain that is close is to our northwest at Raval. They are farther away from the blockade then we are. We do have time to attack as was originally planned. I agree that we should still go ahead with that plan Captain, but with a little change."

Banator nodded, "Go on..."

"By the time we ride north and get everyone in position to attack, the sun will be just above the horizon. First Officer Latilis' company on our right will have to charge directly into the sun. That places him at a great disadvantage. We should have him stay where he is to our east. We can have him scout the east toward Javin road as the rest of us break up the blockade. Our company attacking from the west will have the advantage of the sun at their backs. It will be the defenders who must fight the sun, not us. We can make short work of the attack and then turn east. We know that by then the enemy will be coming for us from the west, and my thinking is that he will be sending troops to intercept us at the river bridge to the north of us. We should assume that the bridge is held in force.

That means we should race east once the checkpoint is taken and meet up with Latilis' company. By that time he would have scouted the area and hopefully have found an opening in the enemy's line in which to thrust north."

Captain Banator considered Errol's words for only a moment. He turned to the outrider who waited for instructions, "Ride and give these orders to Officer Latilis: Tell him not to attack when lightning splits the sky. Upon hearing these new orders, he is to begin scouting to, and past Javin Road for our flight to the north. Our objective tonight is to get to the city of Kint. If it is taken by the enemy already, then we must find a way around it and continue north. We will join him after sun has fallen. He is not to worry about finding us. We will find him. Do you have any questions?"

"None, Captain!" The rider saluted and was gone.

Banator now yelled out. "Men, we have rested far too long here! It is time we march to battle! We have twenty leagues ahead of us to reach the enemy! We will attack and clear the road, but that will not be the end of it for the night. Without rest we will march due east and join Officer Latilis. From there we will attempt to break through enemy lines and find friendly troops. We know as fact that we will be pursued. We do not know what lies ahead of us!

"While we march north on this road, you can eat jerky and drink water. Do not over fill your bellies. It will slow down your sword arm! One league from the blockade we will stop and prepare for the attack. I will give further orders then!"

He then turned to us. "Errol, Ceikay, Keven, and Karlyle, I would have you ride up front with me. Beorn, I wish you to ride behind 2nd Company."

I knew it was not the time to argue my position. I nodded that I understood.

We maneuvered into our new marching order and rode north. We paced the horses at a relaxed gallop. I was not near anyone I could talk to, but no one was talking anyway. The dust kicked up from the horses in front of me was a constant irritation. I had never ridden in formation like this before. With so many galloping ahead, even the crushed seashells that covered Talavor Road did not hold down the cloud of dry, gray dust. Before long, I was covered in a gray coating. I kept my mouth shut and my eyes barely open. I wondered if my fellow riders were as miserable as I. No complaints came to my ears. As we rode, I followed the sun's progress. It seemed that it would drop below the horizon before we were in position to attack.

Then a rider suddenly appeared at my side. With my eyes down I had failed to notice him leave the front and fall back with me. He tapped me with the tip of his sword, "Are you faring well?"

I was annoyed by the interruption, "Of course I am all right. Why did you hit me with your sword?"

"Pardon if I startled you, but Captain Banator has bid me to join you as we attack. My weapon is out as is everyone else's. We prepare to charge! You are to stay with me and follow my lead. He will send orders back after we clear the road."

I strained to see around the hundred or so horses in front of me. I could not find my companions. I could see that the riders ahead indeed had their swords drawn.

Suddenly, a bolt of lightening crashed down to the earth and split the sky ahead of us! Immediately everyone around me yelled out a war cry and kicked their horses into a full run. My horse followed. I hung on to the pommel and gritted my teeth. My escort now rode past and grabbed my reins.

He had to yell to be heard. "You must slow your horse! Third Company has to get around us!"

As we slowed, horses began to race past us on both sides. Soon we were left behind. My escort handed back my reins, "We still ride to follow, we must stay close!"

I nodded and we galloped on. Suddenly I saw the regular formation ahead break up in apparent confusion. Then I realized that we had hit the enemy line! Once again I heard men yelling and screaming. Unlike the battle on the walls at Talon Fortress, the screams and snorts of the horses blended with the human screams. The loud clashes of steel on steel almost drowned out the men and animals. I saw men drop from horses. I saw horses bolt away. I saw horses drop to the ground! Even though I was kept away from the fighting this time, my heart still pounded in my chest!

Then, as suddenly as it started, the action ahead of me stopped. I strained to make out details of what I was looking at. It seemed to me that our men had ridden right over the whole blockade. Our companies were all on the other side of the carnage.

"We just ran over them!" I yelled.

Then from a signal I did not notice, my companion now spurred his horse forward.

"Follow me!" He called.

Moments later I was again with my companions. None were wounded that I could tell. Banator had lost his battle helmet. I also noticed that the sun had disappeared below the horizon. Keven now had his eyes closed.

Banator was giving out orders as he rode up to the rest of us. When he saw me he smiled, "Good to see you unscratched Beorn! We pause only to clear our wounded and dead. Then we ride east."

The others dismounted. I followed their lead. Errol came up to me, "Beorn, when did you take water last?"

I shrugged my shoulders in answer.

"Well take some now." He handed me a canteen.

Keven approached, "Five hundred enemy are coming from the west. If we do not move soon, we will be the hosts at this blockade."

"That sounds not so bad for us," Errol mused, "Is that all we will be facing tonight?"

"Would it be so. Five hundred more are racing down Talavor Road. They will be on us before the moon is high."

Ceikay looked around, "We should let our Captain know about this…"

"Do you want me to call him over?" I offered.

"No." Ceikay said, "He comes now."

Banator spoke as he approached, "Do you have news for me Keven? Are we being pursued?"

Keven repeated what he had told us. Banator wasted no time, "Officers to me!"

A moment later his men surrounded us.

218

"Our time is over for dallying on this road. We must ride now. Second Officer Bennis, you will take a squad of men and carry the wounded back to Javin. Send a rider back to Hirst and report our progress. Then you will organize your men for outrider posts. Keep to the points on the road that I have laid out. I will send back riders as I can."

Officer Bennis saluted and quickly left. Banator again yelled out to his men, "Form up companies. We leave now!"

Karlyle called to Banator, "Oh my Captain, may we have Beorn with us this time?!"

Captain Banator yelled back as he rode to the front of the column, "As long as you do not lose him!"

Keven grinned at me, "Do stay close. This night may become adventurous."

Wounds

Soon we were riding east. The stars had already come out and the moon was just rising over the horizon. Once again we ran the horses at a relaxed gallop. This time Banator rode out front. My companions and I were next. The three companies followed us. Two soldiers rode point about two hundred paces ahead of us. Four each rode to the right and left of our troop. They were about two hundred paces out. I could not see if we had any riders separated in back.

As the moon traveled across the sky, we traveled across the plains. I stopped trying to estimate the passing of the time. Finally, Banator raised his arm and pulled up. The rest of us slowed to a stop behind him. One of the point riders came trotting back. He called out as he came near,

"Captain, one of Officers Latilis' scouts is ahead. He has signaled for us to turn to the left."

Captain Banator nodded, "Return to point. We will follow as you lead us."

The rider saluted, and then turned back to the front. Banator twisted in his saddle to face us. "It would seem that a route north has been found."

I looked behind us once more. So far we had not been threatened by our pursuers. We ran with no torches because of the brightness of the moon. I was hoping that they had lost us and we would be able to stop soon.

...And soon we did. Banator held up his arm and our troop came to a stop. Ahead I could see our outriders with two other riders. They talked briefly.

Suddenly Ceikay grabbed Errol's arm in alarm. "We are betrayed! Banator! Ambush!"

Immediately everyone pulled their swords! At the same instant arrows flew in on us from the darkness!

I looked to the front in time to see our point riders go down, arrows still shooting into them as they fell. Once again the world exploded into chaos. Our horses jumped in panic as the sudden yells and arrows filled the night air. I found my sword in my hand but did not know where to strike. A soldier next to me went down with an arrow in his throat. I saw Banator yell out orders but could not hear him. He waved his arm signaling rally to the left.

An arrow struck under his raised arm and he fell! I spurred my horse to him but I was knocked to the ground by a panicked horse that reared and flipped its rider. Then I saw a wall of gold coming at us. Duchess Mariom's men had found us.

I scrambled to get on my feet. I still had my sword. I turned to the charging horde of gold horsemen.

Suddenly I was grabbed by the collar and pulled upward. I twisted my head around and looked into Errol's eyes. He threw me to the back of his saddle. He yelled at me to wrap my arms around his waist. I managed to do just that while I still held on to my weapon. On horseback I could see that our men were desperately fighting, but losing on all sides. I tried to look for Banator but he was not to be seen. The arrows had stopped their deadly flights. We were now engulfed with the enemy chopping at us from all sides! Keven, Karlyle, and Ceikay were at the front of a large group of our soldiers. Errol fought his way to them. His sword was a blur. The ambushers soon learned to stay at a distance from him. He was chasing them down.

Then Errol yelled at me. I could not hear him at first, and then he grabbed me again with his free hand and almost threw me to Keven. I jumped to hold on to his back as I landed on the rear of the saddle. Keven quickly glanced behind. He now positioned his horse to put me between him and Karlyle.

I then looked for Errol...and saw why he had so quickly discarded me...

On a small rise that no one else dared to fight on, Errol was now facing off with another soldier. It seemed that the confused mass of fighting magically opened for Errol and his new adversary.

And this adversary was huge. His horse was every bit as tall as Errol's and the man looked every bit as large as Errol. He was fully protected in gold metal armor. He had a large crescent shaped sword in his right hand and a heavy round shield in his left. His head was covered in a gold metal battle helmet that exposed only his eyes. I was mesmerized by the way the gold armor shone in the pale moonlight. It was grand and terrifying at the same time.

As Keven and Karlyle fought to hold their position, I could not turn away from the two big men who were about to clash. I could see that the two now locked eyes and were moving their horses toward each other.

Errol wore no armor, no helmet, and carried no shield. His broad sword was held in his left hand. He now pulled a short sword from his belt with his right. Errol's face held a look of serene calm...

Suddenly the other man let out a battle cry and spurred his horse forward. His sword swung high as he came! Errol did not move. The shield was thrust straight at Errol as the large curved sword arched overhead and down from the top and in front of the shield! Errol was ready and pushed back on the shield with his short sword arm, and at the same time swung upward with his great broad sword, knocking his foe's downward sword to the side. While Errol's sword was still deflecting upward, Errol was spurring the back end of his horse to move to the right. As he swung to the right, Errol's short sword arm was twisting under the shield and into the side of the other warrior! It sliced only metal armor and the man was not slowed.

The warrior now wrenched his heavy shield downward and hit

Errol's arm. The short sword flew from Errol's hand as the large curved sword again swung in an arch. The enemy's sword headed straight at Errol's left side as the shield was already flying back upward into Errol's face.

Errol continued spurring his horse to the right. That saved him from the sword to his side. The move gave Errol the space to twist his remaining sword back down to meet the thrust of his opponent. The shield was still headed at Errol's head. His free hand now reached up and grasped the shield's left edge. Instead of trying to stop the shield's momentum toward his face, Errol surprisingly pulled back and up on the shield! His horse still swung to the right and Errol pulled his head back as the shield was now pushed over both fighters' heads. Errol's big sword was pointed to the ground after blocking his opponent's sword. Errol now flipped his wrist and his sword flew from his hand! It arched into the air and spun to the right. The move distracted his foe.

…and that momentary distraction was everything…

Errol's huge sword flew to the right as he let loose the shield. Errol now reached for the flying weapon with the right hand! The instant he grasped the hilt, he rammed the sword past and under the shield that was still too high for defense. Errol had caught the great sword with the tip of the blade pointed downward and facing his opponent! The sword was thrust so fast and hard that it pierced the magnificent gold armor and plunged into the enemy's chest!

The great gold warrior lurched straight up and froze for a moment. Then his dark eyes widened in shock. His sword arm stopped mid-thrust. His mighty weapon faltered and dropped to the ground. The warrior swayed in his saddle for a moment, then fell from his horse. Then to my surprise, he looked up at Errol and nodded slightly. His head fell to the side and was still.

…The time it took for that single fight to begin and end was not much more than a couple of blinks of an eye.

The moment that the big warrior hit the ground, the fighting changed! Our opponents were suddenly breaking off and spurring their horses back into the night. The ones who were brave enough to stay were soon cut down. The momentum was all ours!

In a moment the fighting was stopped. The sounds of battle

gave way to the gasping of men and horses trying desperately to catch their breath.

Errol jumped from his horse and ran to a group of men who were standing close and protecting something. The men parted and I could see their captain lying on the ground. I jumped down with my companions and ran to Banator.

Errol leaned over the fallen figure and touched his shoulder. He spoke softly, "Banator..."

To our great relief and joy, Banator opened his eyes. He squinted as he peered at Errol bending over him. He spoke slowly: "I made a grave error...I am sorry. You must get my men to safety from here." He closed his eyes and did not speak again.

Ceikay kneeled down to him. She closed her eyes and put her hand on his chest. After a moment she spoke, "He will not die this night. His heart is strong and his wound is manageable. The arrow in his side is not a fatal wound, but he needs the care of a healer."

Errol stood up and in a loud voice took command, "Officers...to me!"

All eyes turned to Errol. "I am taking command while your captain is down!"

Errol talked calmly, but swiftly. "Captain Banator did not suffer a mortal wound, but he needs a healer. We must make haste and go to the city of Kint. I want torches lit and run out in a warning perimeter one hundred paces from this spot. Tend to the wounded as you can. Tend to the dead as they lie. We cannot take the time for proper burial or rites. Take their food, water, and weapons. Load them onto pack horses. We will need everything we can carry. As for the enemy wounded..."

I did not hear any more of Errol's orders because right then, Keven grabbed my arm and directed me to assist him. He was preparing two horses for a body sling. I had never seen one before, but I soon saw that it worked fairly well.

Keven took the poles of two guide-ons and tied them to the sides of two horses. Then he rummaged through one of our pack animals and pulled out a canvas tent. He cut the tent into a strip long enough and wide enough for a man to lie on. Keven then went to dead horses and cut the reins from them. We secured the canvas to the poles attached to the horses using the leather reins as ties. Now, a wounded man could be carried between the two horses.

With the help of other soldiers who had watched Keven, we made five more rigs for the wounded. The rest were able to ride.

When the wounded were all secure on the horses I saw that Errol and all the rest of the troops were mounted and already in formation. Errol ordered the wounded to be placed in the middle of the column. I saw that some of the wounded were those of our attackers.

He then spoke in a loud voice, "We have been hurt this night! But we are not defeated! The force that ambushed us was not that large. I do not think that the city of Kint is in enemy hands, else we would have been wiped out by a regiment coming south from there. We will ride north to Kint and take our chances and pray that it will be a haven for us tonight!"

Errol nodded to his companions, "My point riders will be Karlyle and Keven. Ceikay and Beorn, you will ride with Captain Banator. Senior Officers, I will have you assign the men to the perimeter guard!"

Errol now turned to the front of the column and spurred his horse forward. We followed. From what I could see in the moonlight, we left over fifty of our own lying under the stars.

As we rode I looked to Banator lying on the stretcher. Through Keven's talent as a Beast Master, the horses that flanked the stretchers walked in coordinated pace to lessen the jolting of the wounded. Banator was unconscious but his breathing seemed smooth and even. I hoped that Ceikay was right…that he would not die this night. Two of our wounded did die on our way north.

We marched through the rest of the night without encountering the enemy. As night was slowly giving way to the dim light of early morn, we saw towers ahead of us. Keven and Karlyle had brought us directly to Kint.

Errol halted the formation about a league away from the city. Karlyle and Keven continued forward until they were under one of the towers. We could not see nor hear what was said, but the longer they talked under the tower, the more I became convinced that Kint was secure from the enemy, else Karlyle and Keven would have either been attacked or would have raced back to us. But I was confused and wondered at the delay.

From a signal I did not see, the two gave us leave to join them. Errol straightened in his saddle and waved his arm forward. He then spurred his horse and we rode toward the city.

As we approached the towers we saw mounted soldiers riding to meet us. They were wearing the red colors of the Rasher Realm. At the front of their column we saw an officer hold his hand up to order a halt. As his men stopped, he continued to ride forward. Errol rode to meet him.

Keven turned to me and spurred his horse at the same time, "Come with me Beorn! You are the King's Witness!"

I kicked my horse to follow and we quickly caught up to Errol. Karlyle joined us. As our group met the Rasher officer, Errol held his hand up to stop.

The officer spoke first: "I am Captain Orius in command of the Rasher Light Horse Regiment garrisoned at this city of Kint. I represent Royal Administrator Bawlston and speak in his authority. Who is it that requests entrance into his city?"

Errol sat calmly in his saddle as he answered, "My name is Errol. My companions with me are Keven, Karlyle, and Ceikay. We carry the King's personal Seal of Authority, and as such, ask that Administrator Bawlston open his city to us."

Errol twisted in his saddle and pointed at me, "We also escort King Ballistor's Royal Witness, Beorn of Minoline. He is to be present at all official meetings we may have with your Administrator. Our military leader is Captain Banator. He commands the troops waiting behind me. He is wounded; else he would be here now addressing you. We have a number of wounded that require your Healers."

Errol now sat taller as he added, "I do not wish to delay the wounded their help too much longer, Captain. Here is the King's Seal if you need to examine it…"

It was Captain Orius' turn to straighten in his saddle. "That will not be necessary! I can see that you are not my enemy, so I will hinder you no further! Follow me to the Keep."

The officer spun his horse back to the city, and we followed at a good trot to keep up.

The city of Kint is similar to Hirst in layout. In truth, most of the major cities in the realm of Rasher were planned out in the same type of spiral design. Kint is smaller than Hirst, and is mostly a trading hub for its surrounding land's main product, potatoes. The city is surrounded by small farms that mostly grow this one crop.

As we rode through town and toward the castle, I noticed ahead that Captain Orius called to several of his riders, each one galloped off at speed as he finished with them. What their orders were, I could not hear.

I also noticed that the city was empty. I saw no one on the streets, nor any lights in the houses and shops. No smoke rose from any roof or chimney chase.

Sooner than I had expected, we left the narrow streets and rode onto the wide grounds surrounding the castle, or I should say, Keep.

The castle at Kint is really what is called a 'Shell Keep.' It is simply a circular stone wall with a thickness of about twelve feet, and about twelve spans high. The original purpose was for storage of supplies and protection against local marauders. It has one entrance gate for wagons. This double gate also has what is called a wicket built into it, a single door to allow individual persons to pass through. Back when Banstron Pass was being widened by King Timonor, this shell keep was built to house supplies for the quarrymen. The Keep was never intended to house a full contingent of military troops. Farmers eventually settled in the surrounding flatlands. A village grew around the Keep. The village evolved into a town, which grew into the city of Kint. The Duke of Rasher Realm appointed a Regional Governor to oversee the northern part of the Realm. The Governor was to be seated in Kint. Therefore, the Keep was enlarged with an adjoining court which housed the Governor and his family.

As we rode into the clearing, I saw the gates of the Keep open. Pages and groomsmen ran out to our wounded. Captain Orius halted and jumped off his horse. He approached Errol and the two spoke for several moments. The rest of us dismounted, waiting for orders. Finally, Orius left and headed for the gates.

Errol got off his horse and came over to us, "Governor Bawlston is waiting for us in the tower. We are to report to him at once. Captain Orius is tending to our wounded. Governor Bawlston's personal Healer will attend Banator in the Governor's private chambers. Our horses will be fed and brushed down by the groomsmen. The good Captain has already instructed the mess cooks to prepare meals for us. He also said that if we need any of our weapons repaired or sharpened, his blacksmiths are already at their forges. The Captain also apologizes for the lack of adequate sleeping barracks. Fresh straw has been laid out along the inner walls of the Keep for our bedding."

"Impressive." I mused out loud.

"At first glance..." Errol uttered as we followed him into the Keep.

I wondered at his words.

Soon we were in the presence of Governor Bawlston.

Twelve guards stood around the top chamber of the tower where we found Bawlston. As we walked into the room, I saw the governor facing us.

Immediately Bawlston backed away. His posture told us that we were to stay at a distance from him. The first words out of his mouth were not greetings or an offer of welcome: "Did you bring them with you?"

We glanced at each other but kept silent. I decided quickly that I did not like the man. I wondered if my companions felt the same. I also wondered at the small buzzing sound over our heads.

Finally, Keven spoke up: "Did we bring who with us?"

Again Bawlston spoke, "Well, I can expect to be attacked, now that you have led the enemy to my doors!"

Errol answered coldly, "You can expect to be attacked Governor. Our nation is in peril, and the enemy is roaming your countryside as we speak. We are not the ones who brought them to you."

Bawlston did not seem to hear Errol's words. "I am told that you are from King Ballistor. Are you what is left of our armies to the south? Do you run to Kint for protection?"

Errol now stepped toward the small man. Bawlston stepped back again and pointed as he spoke, "No one gave you permission to approach me! How do I know you are not assassins sent to kill the Governor of Duke Rasher's Northern Region? Guards!"

Before the guards could respond, a voice behind me yelled out, "Guards, stand as you are!"

I turned my head to see Captain Orius stride past me and over to Bawlston. "Governor, I present five representatives of our King. They carry with them the Royal Seal of Authority. They bring news of war throughout Tavegnor."

"They bring me news? They bring me danger! That is what they bring me!"

Ceikay stepped up to Errol and whispered, not too quietly, "Do we have time for this?"

Errol shook his head and now threw the Royal Seal onto the big oak table in front of Bawlston.

"We bring you the King's orders!" Errol's voice now grew loud and intimidating. "Tavegnor is now in a state of war with known and unknown adversaries! Regional Political Appointees are hereby relieved of governing authority. Regional Military Commanders are now ordered to take command of all forces, military and civilian! No objections will be considered or tolerated! Governor Bawlston, you are hereby ordered to give over all authority and duties to your Senior Military Officer."

Errol turned to face the captain. "Captain Orius, you are now the King's authority for the Northern Rasher Realm. King Ballistor has directed me to reveal his orders to you. Will you clear the room of all non-military persons before we begin our counsel?"

Captain Orius turned to face Errol. "I understand the King's orders. I also understand that Duke Rasher is the Military Commander of my realm. The proper procedure for change of authority is for the King to give the order through my Duke. King Ballistor is to follow Parliamentary protocol even in times of war."

Now Bawlston stepped forward a half step, "What do you

mean? I do not understand what is going on here!" He pointed a finger at Errol, "If you have orders, you talk to me and not my subordinates!"

Errol ignored the outburst and looked straight at Captain Orius, "Duke Rasher is dead. And if you know Parliamentary protocol, then you know that our King does have the authority..."

"Dead?!" Bawlston practically screamed, "What do you mean dead? How can you be sure?"

Errol continued to ignore the Governor. "Captain Orius, are you ready to take command, or should I call in your next Senior Officer?"

Captain Orius looked back at Errol for a moment, and then turned to one of the guards and spoke calmly: "Escort Governor Bawlston to his residence. Secure his comfort and tend to his needs. Do not let him into his private Chambers. Captain Banator is there and is being looked after by our Healers. If Bawlston wishes to leave the city, see that he takes only his personal properties and not any supplies or troops that may weaken the defense of the city."

The guard immediately motioned to two other soldiers. The three of them went directly to Bawlston and stood in front of him. The lead guard now addressed Bawlston, "Sir, you will come with us now."

Bawlston sneered at the guard, and then spoke to Orius, "Captain Orius, You cannot do this. I am the Governor. I am the leader of Kint. I am the Commander of the Northern Rasher Realm! I order you to put these people under guard!"

Captain Orius answered quietly, "Guards, if he does not want to leave with you voluntarily, then pick him up and carry him out."

Immediately the guards grabbed the stuttering governor by the arms and directed him out.

Captain Orius now addressed Errol, "What are your orders?"

Errol walked up to the Captain. "I will ask again Captain, before we proceed any further: are you capable enough to take charge, or should we relieve you of command also?"

To my surprise, Captain Orius did not show evidence of insult or anger. "If our King orders this as you say, then he will have a good officer in place. Now, what are your orders?"

Errol looked back at the rest of us. "Beorn will make clear to you the events of the war as we know them. But before he begins, call your officers in for a war briefing. They should hear what has been done, and know what must be done from this point onward."

As Errol talked, there began a soft ringing noise overhead. It was louder than the buzzing earlier. I looked up to try to find its source.

Errol continued to give orders. "Ceikay and Keven, would you see to the wounded prisoners? If they can tell us anything..."

Keven finished for him, "...if they can tell us anything, then they will."

Ceikay turned to me, "You seem stressed, Beorn. Do not worry; we will not harm them any more than they already are."

For the first time she was wrong about me; I was not thinking of interrogation of any prisoners. I was wondering at the annoying noise overhead...

Errol now addressed Karlyle, "Would you please see to Captain Banator's condition. We need to know when he will be able to join us again."

Karlyle nodded his head and said something I did not quite hear because the ringing overhead was now getting louder.

Karlyle then silently left the room. Ceikay and Keven were already gone. I had not even noticed that they had left. I wanted them to ask me what the distrubance was...

Then one of the guards rushed out of the room. I wondered at his orders....

The ringing now frightened me. I looked up to search the beams above me.

Suddenly, Errol startled me by grabbing my shoulders. He was yelling at me! "Hold! Beorn!"

I was spun around! I looked into his face, which was now about two hands away from mine. His eyes showed for the first time fear...yes...it looked like fear. I then looked past him and saw the big oak ridge beam of the tower roof. I wondered at how the roof above me was now down behind Errol. Then cold touched my back. My hands felt behind me and grabbed the cold stones of the floor. I was on my back! I was lying on the floor looking up into Errol's face

I saw him turn his head and open his mouth in a yell. No sound came to my ears. Then I saw my own eyelids slowly lower and shut out the light.

...I was stretched out over a large boulder on top of a large, flat-topped mountain. I was not restrained by ropes or chains, but I still could not move my arms or legs. I was on my back staring at the bright stars of a moonless night. Groups of stars blacked out and then reappeared. The patterns of blackout seemed to circle in the sky in various twists and turns. I had no understanding of what made the stars act so strangely...

Then the screeches started! Terrifying screams of unearthly creatures that seared the soul! Suddenly I knew what was above me. My eyes searched above me. I saw them. Dozens of scaly black dragons of the nether world. They were circling the sky, blocking out the stars as they flew, and glaring down at me!

Their wings were those of bats, fully ten spans across. Their long necks were snake-like with a diamond shaped head the size of a fully grown man. Their tails were twice the length of their neck. The tips of their tails were in the shape of an arrowhead. Their legs were those of giant vultures, with curved claws as long as a man's arm.

These dragons were completely and utterly black. I wondered at how I could see them so clearly against the dark night.

Four dragons now swooped from the sky down toward me. Their claws outstretched as if to cleave a rabbit from the grass. As they came closer, they closed in on themselves. They then turned on each other in attack. I realized that they were fighting over me! Their screams were more terrifying as they fought. The wind of their wings buffeted me violently. The sound of the flapping wings was every bit as terrifying as the screeches.

I screamed in panic at the fury above me!

One of the dragons now broke away from the others and came at me. His claws pointed again at my chest. Nothing stopped him this time! I felt the stab and tear! My flesh was ripped away as blood sprayed up and over me. I looked down and did not see my ribcage. I saw a big hole where my chest used to be; the spine of my back exposed and sliced in two.

...I closed my eyes to die...

I was unsuccessful. I heard another scream and felt one narrow slice on my neck. I felt the cold wind at the base of my tongue.

My arms now moved to my throat. I could move my arms. I yelled out in surprise, but heard only gurgling. Then I knew I must get off that rock. I tried to turn myself over to crawl away...

Then utter silence and blackness closed over me...I knew no more.

When I opened my eyes again I saw baby dragons sitting next to me. The sky was still moonless and star filled. No black shapes circled overhead...but the baby dragons were next to me. They were quiet. They did not look at me or seem to even notice me at all. They squatted on the rock around me preening themselves and cooing softly. The sound was...was pleasant.

I then looked down at my body...my spine was still exposed...I had been torn apart.

I lay on that rock for an eternity. During the day, flies would come by the thousands and settle into my horrendous cavity. All day long I heard their buzz and felt their tickling. When the night came, the flies left and the baby dragons came back and preened and cooed. They still ignored me.

Something took hold of my hand....I opened my eyes to see the baby dragons spring into the air and disappear.

A tiny star to my left began to brighten. I stared at it as it grew. Then I heard the sound. The sound of my name? Yes, it was my name! The star was calling me! The star grew and grew…then I saw details in the star.

Suddenly my hand was raised and a sharp pain stabbed through it! The star disappeared as I yelled out! Another pain now struck my forehead! I began to struggle to get away from the stabs!

My right hand came up and reached for the left. It was grabbed and held. I closed my eyes and wrenched my head up to strike out at anything. Now the night air was filled with my yelling and the yelling of my name.

…My eyes opened…

…and I was looking at Ceikay.

Her eyes were swollen red and her forehead was bathed in sweat. She stared into my eyes and called my name over and over.

I stopped my struggling and fell back in shock. The back of my head hit soft pillow.

Ceikay was holding my hands in a tight grip. When she felt me stop struggling, she lowered my hands to my chest…my whole and intact chest! She stopped calling my name.

For several moments neither of us moved.

Then she spoke sternly, "Breathe, breathe."

Suddenly my chest heaved and I engulfed air. I yelled out my exhale and began to shake uncontrollably. Ceikay again held my hands tightly until I calmed down. After a long while I was breathing softly and evenly. Neither of us had said another word. Finally, Ceikay smiled and spoke softly, "Welcome back."

I opened my mouth and was surprised at my hoarseness, "I am hungry. I am craving water."

A large bladder bag of cool water and several trays of assorted food were brought to me. I found that after a few sips of water and three bites of bread, my stomach had had enough. I tried to rise from my bed. I fell back exhausted.

Ceikay sat by my bed and watched me in silence. I asked her for help. She shook her head in refusal, "You do not need to be getting yourself up. Flirting with hell's terrors is nothing to brush off so lightly. Now, instead of trying to put your feet on the ground, maybe you should start asking all those questions that are in your head."

I frowned at her words.

Ceikay laughed suddenly and loudly. "Even if I could not sense your curiosity I know you well already. You should already know me well enough by now to not have to ask your question!"

Reluctantly I nodded. She did know me well. I did have questions.

I started with the obvious one, "What happened to me?"

"You were the victim of a poisonous needle-dart; the same type that the monks used to kill the Dukes in Hirst."

"How did I..."

"Shsh, I will be able to explain faster if you do not interrupt me. A needle did strike you, but when, and by whom, we do not know. You had no visible wounds on your body when you fell to the floor in the Keep. It was lucky for you that Errol is so fast. Out of the corner of his eye he saw you begin to wobble and fall. In an instant he was behind you. He had just enough time to grab your shoulders before your head cracked into the stone floor. He laid you down softly as your eyes rolled back and you lost consciousness. We heard his yell two floors down. By the time we ran back up, he had your leather vest and tunic off. He was picking at your linen under-garments searching for a wound. Then fortunately Errol saw the needle before he touched it. The needle was pinned into the bottom of your woolen shirt. Your linen inner shirt was between you and the needle.

"As I said, how it got there we do not know, but the needle itself never made direct contact with your skin, so that surely saved your life.

"We have discovered that these needles are made up of sugars and unknown poisons. When one of these needles enters the tissue of a human, or animal, the sugar begins to dissolve, releasing the poison into the body. In your case, the needle became trapped in your clothing before it could reach your skin. Your trouble came when your body sweat began to permeate your clothing. Once the sweat came in contact with that needle, the needle began to dissolve and the syrup-like poison then soaked through the linen of you inner shirt. Now the poison came in contact with your skin. Your skin slowly allowed the intruder to ooze in…until finally…you collapsed. You would be dead if the full amount of the poison had entered your body, but only a minute amount soaked through the shirt."

I lay there thinking about what she was saying. I said nothing, but nodded for her to continue.

There was a brief pause, so I took the opportunity to ask another question, "Where are the others?"

Ceikay grinned and pointed her finger at me, "The war cannot wait on you. Errol, Keven, and Karlyle went north to Talavor two days ago. Banator is still recovering from his wound. In truth, he is in the room next to us right now. His Healers say that he will be able to return to battle by new moon."

Now my questions began to come in greater numbers, "How long must I stay here in bed?"

"The Healers say 'til past new moon. I say two days, knowing your spirit."

"Where is Captain Orius? Did Errol replace him?"

Ceikay looked at me sideways, "Why do you ask that?"

"I ask because to me, Captain Orius was very proficient the night we arrived here. We still are in Kint, are we not?"

Ceikay laughed and nodded.

I continued, "From what I saw, Captain Orius gave orders for our wounded, our horses, our sleeping areas, and our food. All this he set in motion before we even entered the gates of the Keep. Then he stood up to that coward Bawlston when Errol flexed his 'diplomatic' muscles. Seeing all that, I wonder why Errol talked to the Captain the way he did."

"What way did Errol talk to Captain Orius?" asked Ceikay.

I looked at Ceikay in surprise, "You did not think Errol was trying to talk Captain Orius down from command? Twice Errol suggested that Captain Orius step aside and let a Junior Officer take command. Am I wrong in what I remember?"

"No, there is certainly nothing wrong with your memory. Just something wrong with your understanding."

I kept silent, waiting for her to explain.

"You see Beorn, you correctly saw the efficiency of Captain Orius. Everything he did for us and our men was swift and militarily proper. What you did not see, is what Errol was so livid about."

"You are right. I do not understand."

"Think about the whole crisis, the war in Tavegnor. King Ballistor is in the south and must rush to fight an invader coming from the east. The west has been put in jeopardy by the traitorous Duchess Mariom. The treacherous Duke Hastid has gone to horse with his military in the north. Where is he, and where is word of our forces to the north? We have been blind to information even though our King sent outriders north before the assassinations at Hirst!"

She took a breath and continued, "Why have we not heard from anyone? It is because our roads were blocked very early, very cleverly, and very efficiently by our enemies. This surprise war was planned from the start to quarter the country of Tavegnor.

Now, consider the location of the city of Kint, or more importantly, the garrison at Kint. Once the war began, we know that an advance force from the Mariom Cavalry sliced through the north/south roads and effectively cut off travel and information. You remember the state of Kint when we approached several nights ago, the populous had fled, and the Governor was holed up in the Keep, protected by his garrison. It was on Bawlston's orders that the garrison, commanded by Captain Orius, stay in Kint. Bawlston was too much of a coward to allow the garrison to do its duty."

Ceikay paused to take a deep breath, "First; no protection was given to the civilians as they fled the city. Second; no troops were sent out to find and engage the enemy. Third; no troops were sent out to patrol and clear roads of blockades in order for outriders to race back and forth with vital information and orders. Fourth; if patrols were sent out around Kint, maybe, just maybe, Captain Banator and his companies would not have been ambushed. As a result, numbers of our men are dead."

After another big intake of air, Ceikay continued, "The

cowardly Governor was within his rights to keep the garrison in Kint, because a formal declaration of war had not been announced to him as yet. Captain Orius performed his duty as an officer under civilian command.

"To Errol's anger, what Captain Orius did *not* do is use his intelligence and discretion to override the Governor. Any good, well-trained officer should understand the dynamics of strategics and take the initiative when a Civilian Commander is so obviously inept."

Ceikay ended not unkindly. "So do you now understand? Because of Captain Orius' inaction, many have died needlessly. Pray it will not happen, but Tavegnor might still fall because of the delay in clearing the blockaded roads."

I opened my mouth to speak but my thoughts became broken and the room began to spin.

Ceikay must have seen my expression, or maybe sensed my disorientation, because she leaned over and placed her hand on my forehead. I tried to sit up, but she gently pushed me back down onto the pillow.

"This poison is tricky, Beorn. You think it is over in a hurry, but it may bite you still from time to time. Our Healers suspect that it is a derivative of the Starrow root from Jakor Island. The victim sometimes feels hale and healthy, but a moment later is flat on the ground in a swoon. You must stop asking your questions for now and try to sleep. You will fully recover in a couple of days, and then we shall meet up with the others."

My eyes closed and I heard Ceikay no more. Sleep did come. The dreams and the dragons did not.

When I awoke later I could see through the arrow slit window that the sun was awake also. Ceikay was not at my bedside. I was alone in the room. A tray of fresh bread and vegetables was laid out on the table to my right. No meat was to be seen. I was glad for that. A tankard was on the table to my left. I reached for it and discovered water. It tasted delicious. This time I drank more than before. But I still could not eat what I wanted. The food looked inviting, but my stomach refused to accept it.

I laid my head back and fell asleep again. This time I did

dream. I dreamed of baby dragons and their cooing...

When I awoke, the sun had gone down. Candles were lit in the room, and Ceikay was sitting next to the bed.

"How long have I been asleep?" I asked.

"This is the second day, first night. You seem to be in peace when you are asleep. Your dreams are not what they were at first."

"I did not tell you about my dreams when I first fell. Are you not curious to know?"

Ceikay shrugged, "By your yells and contortions, I knew them to be horrendous. I did not press when you first awoke. Certain dreams, or nightmares need to be kept unspoken for a day or two; just to lessen the reality of the terror for the dreamer. I guessed that you would tell me when you were ready."

Ceikay listened as I related my torturous nightmares. She nodded...she shook her head...she rolled her eyes...she did not laugh.

I ended by saying, "Even though I knew that dragons do not exist, they were real for me at the time."

"Dragons do exist." Ceikay stated flatly.

I nodded my head in polite answer.

Ceikay did not grin or smile. "I am serious. Dragons do exist, Beorn."

Turning my head to look directly at her, I said, "I suppose you have seen them then. And are they all black with a tail end the shape of an arrowhead?"

"I have not seen them, but Karlyle and Keven have. In certainty, they have touched one."

"Do not make tales at my expense Ceikay, they do not exist."

"Some day, maybe, Karlyle and Keven will take you to them if you wish."

"Where are these dragons then?"

"Not in Tavegnor. They reside on Claw Island to the South West. They stay away from man and his world."

"How did Karlyle and..."

Ceikay held up her hand. "No more questions now. I will be leaving Kint soon and plan to take you with me. Dragons can be left for another day. This day knows war, do not forget."

I pressed no further. She continued, "I plan to leave Kint by first light the day after this morn. You must stay here one more day to recover, and then we will go. We will join the others. You are the Royal Witness, and as such, your duties are to the King still."

I still was not sure whether or not I believed her about the dragons, but vowed to someday find out.

"I am ready to go now if you need me to," I offered.

"Try to get out of bed." Ceikay ordered.

After several moments on my feet I had had enough and meekly crawled back into bed and under the woolen blankets.

"One more day then..." I muttered quietly.

Ceikay nodded knowingly, but not teasingly, "Well that is more than I expected. You will surely be ready next morn. Now, do you have more questions for me?"

"If you have time to sit with me, then I have questions."

"Begin the asking then, old Bard." She smiled and sat back in her chair.

I promptly began, "That gold armored warrior that Errol fought in the ambush; who was he?"

Ceikay appeared surprised by the question. "I assumed you knew. Do you remember the name 'Borcke'?"

I immediately answered. "On the field of Talon, Captain Piercon mentioned him. Field Commander Borcke is the Military Commander of all of Duchess Mariom's forces. Captain Piercon would not tell us where the Commander was in Tavegnor."

Ceikay nodded at my answer, "Correct. We found him. He was the golden knight that Errol fought."

My thoughts went back to the moonlit battle. The golden knight on the horse had looked invincible.

I spoke to myself out loud rather than to Ceikay, "I feared for Errol."

Ceikay answered me anyway, "I will tell you that Borcke had never been defeated in joust or battle before that night."

"Then he is dead. That must have powerful consequences for Mariom's forces."

"It has.' "Mariom's forces have retreated west out of the Rasher realm. Captain Orius has taken his men and part of

Banator's companies and now holds the North/South roads for us. Outriders are now racing back and forth with much-needed information."

"Then it goes well for us?" I asked.

"It goes better, not well. Tavegnor is still in peril. We are still threatened by Mariom's forces. Commander Borcke led an army of ten thousand. Most of them are still surrounding the city of Halster to the west. Five thousand of Duke Jaramas' forces are besieged in that city. So far we have not been able to get word in or out. We are unable to send forces to relieve the city because we are still threatened on all sides. Even though Commander Borcke is dead, his troops are still dangerous. He led some of the best-trained and disciplined warriors in all of Tavegnor. There is fear that some of them will break from the siege of Halster and attempt to retake the North/South roads."

"What word on the mountain passes?"

"So far our patrols have seen nothing coming through from Rameda or Banstron pass. Duke Whorton's forces are holding the enemy to the south and east of the Tellis mountain range.""What word of King Ballis..."

Ceikay held up a warning finger to me and I stopped my next question.

"Listen to me, Beorn. Let us come to an agreement. You will not ask any more questions for now. I will give you a complete and accurate report of the war with no interruptions. If, when I am finished, you still have a question, then you may ask. Will you to agree on this?"

I held up my hands in mock surrender to her pointed finger.

"Good, now as for the King; he has joined Steward Rastus' troops at Orth Pass. A bloody standoff is taking place there. There is an old hillfort from a long-ago war that our forces have occupied. Wooden palisades have been hastily built to bolster the defense. Our forces are behind those walls secure for the time being. The enemy so far has not brought siege machines into the pass. They most likely thought that they would race right on through the pass and into Orth and beyond. Siege machines were thought not necessary because of the surprise and speed of the

241

attack.

"From reports of outriders, we know that a force of the invaders landed at Bourne and headed north toward Dannon. Dannon had only a small garrison and was quickly taken. The enemy should have continued north, but for some reason has stayed in the city. In truth, reports tell that a large number has turned south again, possibly to reinforce the attackers in Orth Pass. That is why we have not seen anything in Rameda Pass. As for Banstron Pass, it is still clear. Duke Hastid's forces have attacked further north, into Ballistor Realm."

I sat in my bed and nodded slowly. Ceikay continued, "As for Duke Castus from the south, we have heard nothing. The sea battles still rage. Fleet Commodore Disellis has reported that he is facing two armadas of single-masted, square sails. These types of ships are used by most nations in the Southern Continent. The flags they fly are not familiar to him, so we still do not know who has invaded Tavegnor soil.

"He does confirm that his vessels have safely escorted Duke Castus back to his realm. But the Commodore was forced to withdraw from the port of Esturin before Duke Castus could gather his forces to war. A fleet of the enemy bore down on our ships and drove them off in a fierce battle. Commodore Disellis is forced to try to break the enemy's blockade along Doran's Channel before he can return to retrieve Duke Castus and his armies.

"The Commodore does report some good news though. His vessels have prevented a large landing at Osloman. Severe winds apparently slowed one enemy fleet that was heading to invade from the South. Our fleet intercepted them and turned them back. Commodore Disellis chased them west into the Braccos Sea. The enemy sailed right into a large sea squall and disappeared. Let us pray that the enemy vessels came to harm.

"Talon Fortress still holds. Captain Piercon still besieges it. The Doas Estuary has not been penetrated by the enemy fleets. Hirst is still secure from attack.

"In the Northern Realm of Ballistor, we are now beginning to see what has happened. A force headed by Duke Hastid's son surprised Spar Fortress in the far north. The attack was very similar to Mariom's attempt at Talon. Unlike Talon, Hastid's forces succeeded in total surprise and Spar fell. Hastid's forces were immediately joined by an estimated twenty thousand foreign invaders and preceeded south, taking the city of Darron. King Ballistor's daughter Hellista raced north with a force of ten thousand to attempt to stop them. The two garrisons at Minoline and Heston are tied up with a large force of Duchess Mariom's troops at the base of Delshar Mountain."

Ceikay paused, and then asked, "Do you remember Commander Velstor?"

"Of course. He is King Ballistor's Commander of the Royal Personal Guard."

Ceikay smiled broadly. "Ah, you made a mistake in your memory old Bard. He is the Commander of the King's Personal Guard...it is not called 'Royal' Personal Guard!"

I waited patiently and quietly...

"All right, I will go on," She sighed. "Commander Velstor did not make it north. As I am sure you recall, King Ballistor originally ordered Velstor to head north from Hirst. The King soon sent a change of orders for the Commander to turn east into Rameda pass. There was fear that a force would soon come through there. The Commander's new order was to slow the enemy as he was able. As I told you earlier, no enemy has come through as of yet. Velstor last sent an outrider to report that he was going further into and beyond the pass to seek information on the enemy's strength and movements. His reports of that area are what I reported to you earlier."

Cekay paused and took a deep breath, "Now, do you have questions?"

"Whatever happened to the two wizards Karlyle recruited in Halenester?"

Ceikay suddenly laughed out loud, "Beorn, I know you will ask questions, but it surprises me what you do ask! Those two wizards went to Orth Pass with King Ballistor. They help in the defense."

I pressed on, "What of Captain Bocxer of the Jaramas Realm? He was ordered to march west with a company of men to find Duchess Mariom."

This time Ceikay did not answer. She frowned and lowered her head in obvious thought. Finally, she did respond: "To tell truth, I do not know. We have not heard reports of him since King Ballistor sent him west from Hirst."

"What of our horses from Talon Fortress? Did they ever make it through?"

This time Ceikay jumped up. "Stop! Please! I beg you to let me be! No more questions! You jump in so many directions! My mind is dissolving as I sit!"

I sat in bed waiting for her answer.

Finally Ceikay laughed and spoke, "This last question I will answer, then I leave you to rest! Our horses have indeed arrived. Errol, Keven, and Karlyle already ride theirs. Ours are in the stables awaiting our journey. Now, will you allow me respite so that I may attend to duties elsewhere?"

Nodding my head, I now realized how weary I was. I laid my head down and did not say goodbye to her. I fell asleep suddenly and completely.

No dreams came this time.

The smell of hot fresh bread broke my sleep. My eyes opened to search for the source of the smell. On the table to my right was a tray with a large loaf of dark pumpkin bread. I sat up and happily helped myself to several chunks. This time I ate much more than before. I then grabbed the tankard next to the bread. I tasted rich red ale! Presently my appetite was satisfied. I sat up on the side of the bed. My feet touched the floor and I was soon walking around the room. My legs held firm and my breath stayed with me.

My clothing was draped over the back of a wooden chair by the hearth. I donned my linens and leather outer clothes. Everything had been cleaned and my boots had been polished. Once dressed, I left my room for the first time since I had taken ill. The doorway exited directly into the courtyard. The sun was near the top of the Keep wall to the west. It was at the end of the day! I had thought it morning.

Looking around I saw a number of people hurrying about.

Some were soldiers, some were pages and stable hands, and some were chambermaids. Some nodded to me as they passed, some ignored me. Looking to my right, I saw an open door. Inside I could make out a figure sitting upright in a chair. It was Banator.

I quickly turned and walked into the room. No candles were lit. Banator was still, and the room was quiet.

I held up my hand in happy greeting and was about to speak when a hand touched my shoulder. I turned around to see Ceikay standing just to the side of the threshold. She quickly held her finger to her mouth to keep me silent. She motioned me back outside.

Once back in the quadrangle I raised my eyebrows in an obvious question, prompting Ceikay to speak.

She began in a low voice, "Our dear friend Banator is not faring well. I needed to warn you before you attempted to speak to him."

"Is his wound that bad?" I asked.

"The physical wound from the ambush is healing properly and timely. It is his mind that is sorely injured."

"I do not understand…"

"Banator has convinced himself that the death of Hensha is his fault, and that the men under his command died because of his incompetence. He has turned on himself and refuses to heal."

"He should not think that. None of that is true. Did you tell him that?"

Ceikay touched my arm to quiet me, "We have tried for three days now to talk to him. He does not listen. He does not *want* to listen."

"What does he say when you try to talk to him?"

"He has stopped talking altogether." Ceikay brushed a strand of hair from her face, "In fact, he has stopped eating. He has even stopped moving. Banator just sits in that chair and stares straight ahead."

Suddenly, an unsought memory thrust itself into my thoughts! I grabbed Ceikay's arm. The movement startled both of us.

I asked in earnest, "Ceikay, the night of the ambush, when Banator was struck, and Errol killed Borcke. Did anyone search

245

the body and weapons of Commander Borcke?"

"What do you mean?" Ceikay asked.

"When the rest of us were tending to the wounded, did someone gather personal items and weapons from the dead? Specifically, were Borcke's weapons taken?"

"Yes Beorn, weapons were taken. If I remember, Borcke's body was stripped of his weapons, but we did not take his armor or any personal items."

"Where are those weapons?"

"What does this have to do with Banator? Do you th...?"

Impatiently I asked her again, "Where are the weapons that were taken off of Borcke? Can you tell me or not?"

Ceikay wondered at my aggression as she stared at me, "Why do you ask this when we were talking of our friend Banator?"

I lowered my voice and leaned closer to Ceikay. "Please trust me. This has everything to do with Banator. Where are those weapons?"

She looked at me for a moment. Finally she spoke, "In the armory we may find them. It is common practice to gather fallen weapons in battle and store them in the armory for later use. But I remember Borcke's sword, it was jewel-encrusted. A rich prize like that may have been taken by someone already."

"I am not looking for his sword, please take me to the armory."

Ceikay finally led me to the Master-at-Arms. He let us in without question or delay.

The huge dungeon-like room was bigger than any other room in the Keep. Along the walls were racks of assorted weapons.

In the middle of the room, four large oaken tables stood. Strewn on top were a myriad of weapons. The Master-at-Arms had pointed out that these were the weapons our men had brought in from the ambush.

I now searched through the disorganized arsenal. At first, Ceikay stood and watched me quietly. Then she spoke up, "Beorn, you are a loner, and as such, you are in the habit of doing things by yourself. You should ask your friends to help you, or at least explain what you are doing."

I realized what she was saying and I stopped. I walked back

over to her, "Ceikay, I am looking for a dagger. It is about a foot long with a very thin blade. The sheath is of a dark snake skin with silver streaks through it. The hilt of the dagger is of dull pewter. The design on the hilt is a simple spiral groove that circles three times around. There is one jewel embedded into the side, a red ruby. Please help me find it if is here."

Ceikay looked into my eyes and studied me, then nodded her head, "Beorn, I know this dagger you describe. I will help you. If it is here, we will find it."

The sun was down and the moon was up and looking through the narrow window when Ceikay held up the dagger. Her stilled silence caught my attention.

I rushed over to her and grabbed the dagger. I smiled and leaned over and kissed her forehead, "Thankyou! Now let us go see Banator!"

Moments later we were in his room. The room was dark when we entered. Banator still sat as I had seen him earlier. His posture and expression had not changed. Ceikay began to light candles.

I walked over in front of Banator. Ceikay began to motion me to keep silent. I held my hand up to silence her.

When I approached him I leaned down and put my face close to his. Our noses were one hand apart. I spoke to him, "Hail and greetings Banator. This is your friend Beorn. I have come to visit."

He stared through me and did not move.

"Banator, this is Beorn. I have come to talk with you. Will you not speak with me?"

Captain Banator continued to sit motionless.

I spoke again, "Listen to me, friend. I have news for you. I need you to talk with me."

Still he did not move.

My tone hardened, "Listen, Banator. I tire of your silence. Will you not talk with me?"

He did not respond so I spoke more harshly. "I understand, Captain Banator, that you think you are responsible for many deaths. You have decided that Hensha is dead because of your incompetence. You have decided that the men under your command are dead for the same reason. Well, they are not dead because of you. They are dead because of the war, and you are not responsible for the war."

Banator continued to stare through me.

I pressed on, "Banator, you are one of the best warriors the King has. We need you, but you have made this war too personal. So be it, my friend. Let it be it personal, but still do what is ordered by our King."

I now held the dagger up to Banator's face. "Look at this Banator. Do you recognize it? Does this dagger stir your memories? It should. You know this dagger, do you not?"

Ceikay started to get up but I waved her down.

I spoke again to Banator. "Take a good look at this dagger; you know whose it was. It was Hensha's. She wore it strapped to her left hip, under her cape. Not too many people would know that she wore this, except you, Banator."

I lowered the dagger and leaned closer to his face. I spoke very softly now, "I remember seeing this on her at the cottage. I also remember seeing it on the man who killed her."

I saw that Ceikay was standing now, but she kept silent.

"Banator..." I again spoke quietly, "I know who killed your beloved Hensha. If you want to know, then you will stop this self-pity and rejoin Tavegnor's war. That is the only way I will tell you who killed her. Think on what I say, friend, for I leave in the morn to do my duty."

I straightened, turned, and walked out of the room.

Ceikay quickly followed, "Why did you do that? Do you know what he will do? How do you know that he will respond?"

"Ceikay," I stopped and looked at her calmly, "You may think of me as a harmless Bard who has done nothing but sing for his room and fare all his life. But I am more than twice your age and have seen more than my share of troubled souls. I will never say that I have all the solutions, but I know that Banator needed a shock. He will come after me for the answer."

Ceikay was quiet for a moment, and then smiled briefly, "You should put more effort into your life."

Not sure what she meant, I shrugged my shoulders and walked back to my room. Ceikay did not follow. To be honest, I failed to notice where she went from there. I was in my bed and hoped to be asleep in moments.

The hard press of coldness on my forehead opened my eyes. I looked up to see Banator. He was leaning over my bed and staring hard at me. He then pulled his hand into my line of sight. The cold sensation left my forehead as his hand came up. In his hand was Hensha's dagger.

Banator spoke simply, "We need to talk, you and I."

I lay there wondering if I should be frightened. I then decided that it did not matter if I was frightened or not, it would have made no difference to Banator.

He spoke again, "Beorn, you wished to tell me of this knife. Please do so."

Banator did not back away to give me room to rise. It was clear that he would listen from that close position.

I spoke quietly, "The dagger was in the possession of Commander Borcke, the one whom Errol killed the night we were ambushed. I saw the…"

"Hold, Beorn, I have not been told anything since being injured. Start from the beginning of the battle."

I guessed that Banator had indeed been told everything, only he had refused to listen. But I did not try to contradict him. I only did as he bid. I began from the beginning. I recalled everything I witnessed from the point of first alarm from Ceikay, except I left out the details of my poisoning and the subsequent nightmares.

During the entire time of my telling, Banator never relaxed his position. His face was kept close to mine. Only when I declared that there was no more to be reported did Banator's head rise up. He still sat on my bed. For several moments he did not speak. Finally he spoke, not necessarily to me, but out loud to himself:

"So, that explains how Hensha was taken. Commander Borcke was well known as the top military officer in the Mariom Realm. He was probably leaving his Duchess in Hirst to travel north to meet his armies for the surprise attacks once war started. He met

Hensha on the road. She recognized him as a friend. She had no reason to suspect him…"

Banator's words trailed off and stopped. I lay in my bed waiting for his next actions. Suddenly he turned to the open door and walked swiftly to it. At the threshold Banator turned back to me, nodded briefly, and then left.

I rose and stepped to the door to see that Banator was now standing with a group of officers. They were dressed and armed for patrol. I could not hear their words, but I could clearly see that Captain Banator was giving orders.

Then from the stables, horses were brought to the men. The stable boys handed the reins over and the officers mounted. Captain Banator waved his hand toward the Keep entrance. In moments the horsemen, with their Captain leading them, disappeared through the open gates.

"You succeeded, sir."

I turned to see Ceikay standing next to me. She was also dressed for riding.

"You have nothing to say?" She asked, looking toward the gates.

Not knowing what to say, I simply shrugged my shoulders.

"Well, if you have no questions, then dress for travel. We leave for the North at first light. The kitchen has food waiting for us, but only if you hurry."

The March North

The ride to the capital city of Ballistor Realm was short and uneventful. The distance from Kint to Talavor is a day's ride. We left Kint just after sunrise and reached Talavor just before sunset.

Ceikay and I were escorted by a full company of cavalry. The roads were secure and open, thanks to Captain Orius. Ceikay told me that Captain Orius was patrolling to the north of Kint, and Captain Banator was clearing the roads south and west into Jaramas Realm.

We did not speak much on the way. Only once did I feel like asking questions. I started with Banator. "Ceikay, did Banator talk with you before he left?"

She smiled as she answered, "Yes, we talked before he left Kint. In truth, we talked before he woke you up this morn."

I glanced over at her, but said nothing.

"You are surprised?" She asked.

"You knew that Banator would come into my room, then."

"Beorn, you were in no danger. Banator would never harm you."

"What makes you sure that I was in no danger?"

Ceikay laughed, "Do you forget my talent? I knew Banator's emotions. If I had sensed the smallest threat, I would have not allowed him to get near you."

"Why did he threaten me then?"

Ceikay shrugged as she answered, "He sometimes enjoys the dramatic..."

I shook my head and said nothing more.

We rode on a bit further before I decided to ask another question, "Will we meet the others in Talavor?"

"Do you mean Errol, Keven, and Karlyle?"

"Yes. Are they waiting for us?"

"No, they are not waiting for us, but they may be there when we arrive. I do not know what plans are being made and what plans are being changed."

Once again we rode in silence, stopping twice to rest our horses. The midday meal consisted of venison jerky and biscuits. I studied our escort as we rode. The men were also quiet. Their mouths were shut but their eyes were not. They scanned the road on all sides. The outriders were about two hundred paces to our sides. Ceikay and I rode at the front of the company with an officer named Heldor. Company Commander Heldor spoke only when we addressed him, and we did not address him too often.

As the shadows became longer than the objects they mirrored, we heard a loud screech overhead. I looked up to where Ceikay was pointing. A large eagle was circling us. It then dived straight down toward us. Faster than I could react, the huge bird was already past us and swooping back into the sky. Then I felt the rush of the wind that followed its trail.

Ceikay laughed and waved at the retreating bird. I then realized that it was Eagle, and guessed that Keven's eyes were traveling with him.

The horsemen behind us saw that our reactions were not of alarm, so they continued to ride quietly and alertly.

Company Commander Heldor now spoke for the first time without being prompted. "That bird of prey a friend of yours?"

Ceikay glanced over at him, "Yes....yes they are."

Heldor's expression told me that he was puzzled by her answer.

252

But he did not ask for an explanation.

Shortly after, we began to see points on the horizon ahead of us. As we traveled further, the points grew into towers. We were nearing the great city of Talavor. I had been in this city a number of times before, so I was not anticipating any surprises. The towers were of similar shape and size as those in the cities of Hirst and Brentsad. Ballistor's capital city was built on a rise in the southern portion of the great Minoline Plains. The King's castle was at the center of the city. The main difference from the other two cities was the roads within the towers. Talavor's roads were designed in the shape of a wagon wheel. "'Spokes'" ran from the castle out to the towers. At descending intervals, roads circled the castle. Although Talavor was not any larger than Hirst, the roads were wider, giving an allusion of increase to the city's size.

What did surprise me was the detour we now took before we passed under the towers. Commander Heldor waved at us to follow him to the right, off the road. As I reined my horse to obey, I shot a questioning look at Ceikay. She then pointed to the tower nearest us. I now could see two signal flags waving in an ordered pattern.

Ceikay explained, "The tower is directing us to circle around the city and proceed north. Apparently we are to report directly to a field camp."

I nodded my understanding and kept quiet.

Soon we were past Talavor and once again on the road north. This road was the continuation of Talavor Road we had started on from Hirst. The sun was just falling below the horizon when we spotted the camp. It was the largest single military camp I had ever seen. I saw several thousand tents and hundreds of guide-ons showing company colors; all different.

A squad of twenty horsemen now rode from the camp toward us. As they neared, I recognized the front two riders, Karlyle and Keven.

Keven was the first to speak as we met. "Well met, family and friends! It is good that you join us! This war is about to get exciting and I would dread it if you were not here with us to enjoy it!"

253

Keven bowed in his saddle to Ceikay. "How is our friend back there?"

Ceikay now nodded toward me. "Our friend back there was cured by our friend right here."

Keven smiled at me, "Are you a healer as well as a Bard?"

Karlyle cut in before I could answer. "We can talk well enough when we settle into our tent. As for now, let us finish this journey into camp."

It was then I noticed that Commander Heldor had not waited on us. His troops were riding past us.

We had entered the huge camp and stopped at a large tent at the center. The guide-ons at the entrance told me that it was the tent of the Field Commander. As we dismounted, the tent flap opened and out came Errol. He ran up to Ceikay and pulled her from her horse even before she had a chance to dismount. He swung her around and kissed her forehead. Ceikay went to slap him but he lightly brushed her hand to the side with apparently little effort. She then tried to kick him in the shin, but the thick leather leg armor stopped any damage.

Finally she cried out. "Put me down!"

Errol laughed, he then tossed her into the air. Ceikay flew up and back about five paces but still managed to land on her feet. As my eyes followed Ceikay's arch, I failed to see Errol come at me. Suddenly I felt iron clamps surround my arms and chest. My breath was forced out of my lungs as he squeezed!

"Ah, Beorn, it is good that you have survived your little sugar dart! Now Keven and Karlyle can continue to tease you!"

He quickly released me as I coughed and gasped for a breath.

At once, the tent flap opened again and out walked a fully armored soldier. As my head was turned to one side and facing down, I heard a female voice speak out,

"Would someone get this man some water? I do not want a death in front of my tent!"

I straightened up and turned to the newcomer. She was dressed in the royal uniform of the family Ballistor. She had the insignia of Field Commander. She was tall for a woman, about my height, with long auburn hair that was braided into a ponytail that reached down to the small of her back. Her eyes were green, and she seemed to be about halfway between Errol and me in age.

I knew immediately who I was looking at. I had seen her portrait in the Royal Library. It was the Daughter of King Ballistor, Lady Hellista.

Errol came over to me and softly slapped my back. "M'Lady, may I introduce to you the Royal Witness to King Ballistor; Beorn of Minoline."

Lady Hellista stood at the entrance of her tent and studied me silently. I managed to stop my coughing and bowed formally to her. She nodded slightly in return.

She then turned to address Errol, "Now that Ceikay is finally here, we can begin our march to Stannis. We have lost too much time on injuries. I will not be delayed any further. Make sure you and your three companions are ready to leave camp by the first turn of the hourglass."

Hellista turned to re-enter the tent.

"Pardon M'Lady..." Errol spoke quietly but firmly, "you said three companions."

She turned back to face Errol. "I assume that you are referring to the Witness. He stays in Talavor."

Errol took a step toward the tent as Lady Hellista took a step through the flap. "That is not possible, M'Lady."

Hellista stopped and turned again. This time to face Errol squarely, "I do not have time for your arguments, Errol. The Witness stays here. We do not need him, and he would just be in our way."

I glanced over at the other three. Keven was grinning. Karlyle was busy picking at his right thumb, and Ceikay was shaking her head in obvious frustration.

Errol paused a moment and then spoke: "You are absolutely right Lady Hellista; you do not have time for this argument. We can discuss this later. In the meantime, I will assist Witness Beorn in getting ready for our trip."

There was a moment or two of silence. I stood frozen, waiting for Hellista' response to Errol's defiance. She stood with her mouth slightly open, staring at him.

255

Finally she spoke quietly, "Very well, you lout. The Bard will be your responsibility."

Hellista turned to me, and to my surprise, addressed me by name: "Beorn, I have heard good words about you, but I do not believe that this is the time to put a Witness to Parliament in harm's path. You should be behind fortress walls until such time as formal gatherings can once again be safely planned. If Errol so dares to defy me in this, then I trust that he has good and great reason for doing so."

Errol answered back, "My reason is your father's orders, M'Lady."

Smiling as she shook her head, Hellista turned and disappeared into the tent.

Soon I was tying my bedroll and kit onto the back of another horse. This one was fresh and ready for the march north. I was handed a small basket of dried fruits and smoked meats for a meal. We were leaving the camp as I finished the last of the food.

I asked no questions at this time, but I kept my eyes and ears open as the camp made ready to disembark.

I learned quite a lot...

Lady Hellista was leading a force of two thousand heavy cavalry and three thousand light horse north to the city of Stannis. Fighting was fierce just to the north and east of the city. The forces of Tavegnor were so far preventing the overrun of Stannis, but were hard pressed to hold their ground.

It had been confirmed that forces from Duke Hastid had attacked from the north. His armies were pressing hard from Rogan Pass. Along with Hastid's forces were at least twenty thousand foreign warriors.

Two factors combined to slow the invaders' march south into Stannis: First, the invaders were mostly afoot and lugging heavy supply wagons and siege engines. Second, the northern Rangers of the Wolven Forest were felling and setting clever ambushes in the roads south.

Hellista planned to reach Stannis in just over two days of forced march. We would eat our meals in saddle and rest for sleep only well after the setting of the sun.

We fell into line behind Hellista's Personal Guard. Hellista rode at the front of the column with an officer named Gwellen. I was told that he was the Military Commander under Hellista. I did not have an opportunity to get a look at him since two full companies separated us.

It is possible to sleep while atop a traveling horse. I experienced it before first light of that first morning. It was surprisingly easy, considering I accomplished it without realizing that I had. My first awareness of my sleep-riding was Errol at my side, nudging me with his finger.

"Bard…" Errol nudged twice again, "Beorn, You are scaring the horses…Beorn…"

Finally, my mind and body responded. My eyes opened and my head turned to the sound of the voice.

There was Errol grinning.

"What did you say?" I asked.

"You are scaring the horses, my friend."

Seeing that grin now woke me up fully and understanding came with his words. I looked at Errol guardedly.

"Your 'sleeping' may soon panic the horses."

Before I could growl an answer, he spurred his horse and rode forward.

Keven maneuvered his horse next to mine. "Do not worry; we are still too far from the enemy for you to give us away to them."

He too rode swiftly from my side.

I did not share their obvious humor. I wanted to return to sleep.

It was then that I noticed that the sun was again showing itself. The day was beginning and the ride was continuing. I made the effort to stay awake…a great effort. We did not stop until mid-morn. The horses needed rest. A rider rode back along the lines and yelled out that the march would restart at high sun. I rolled from my horse. I led him to the side of the road the rich green grass. Someone took my hand and gently pried the reins from them. I turned to see Errol at my side.

"Come with me," he said, "I will tend to your horse. You will lay down on your bedroll and no one will bother you."

He must have seen a look of doubt on my face so he added, "Do not worry. I promise that no one will disturb you. Now get your bedroll."

Soon I was lying on the grass. If I snored, I did not care.

Errol woke me at noonday. I was soon on my horse and we were once again on our way to Stannis. The short sleep revived me more than I had expected. I felt like talking to someone. Keven rode just ahead.

As I came along side him, he turned and smiled, "Greetings and good health! You are looking much better!"

"I feel better, thanks be to Errol. I have a question, if you would answer it for me."

"Ask."

"Thank you. The night of the Ball, in Hirst; I am told that you knew that there was danger even before Errol and Ceikay. Is that true?"

"Is that your question?"

"Yes."

Then Keven grinned as he glanced to me, "Then my answer is yes."

I rode next to him waiting for more.

Keven turned to me, "Oh, you want more than an answer. You want an explanation."

Sighing heavily, I nodded.

"Since you asked then, I will explain. Both Ceikay and Errol have the ability, or talent, to detect imminent danger. So do I. Ceikay can 'sense' the explosion of mental waves the instant a human mind triggers action. Errol can 'see' minute and almost invisible physical changes on the human body the moment the mind triggers action, and even before. They both know the instant violence is launched.

Remember, my talent is communication and communion with animals, not humans. But there is one common factor that humans and animals share that my senses are keen to. That factor is smell. Humans smell just like animals."

Keven paused to let me absorb that statement.

He then continued, "Let me ask you this, have you ever heard the expression that dogs can 'sense fear'?"

I nodded and answered, "Yes, it is a known fact that if you show fear to a threatening dog, he will attack you."

"You are correct only as far as you just said. There is more to a dog, or any other vicious animal, deciding to attack. An animal will not attack only if he senses fear; he will also attack if you show weakness."

"I do not understand."

"Let me explain," he sighed. "Fear is not weakness. A heroic warrior for instance can be fearful before going into battle. In truth, if you ask Errol, he will tell you that fear is a good thing before the battle. Only a fool would deny fear in mortal conflict!"

"So, what is the weakness then?" I asked.

"The weakness is the running."

"Go ahead," I urged.

"Let us return to the snarling dog, or in your case, three dogs. That night at Boar's Hind Inn, You were in an uncomfortable situation with three huge mastiffs that had you cornered. Do you remember?"

I said nothing.

Keven laughed, knowing well that I did. "You were cornered, you were frightened. The dogs knew it. They knew your fear because they could smell it! But they did not attack. No, they had you pinned to a wall. They would have attacked you for two reasons only: one, if their masters had ordered it, and two, if you had turned around and attempted to run upstairs. Now the first example we do not have to explain further, but the second; were you to run, that would have shown the dogs weakness. Then those dogs would have known that you would not put up a fight.

"That is why, if you ever get cornered by a dog again, you stare them down and growl. Even though they may smell fear, they will think you are still willing, and able, to defend yourself."

My nod encouraged him to continue. "Humans put off different smells from different emotions, just as all the other animals in the kingdom do. This is something that as of now cannot be controlled or eliminated. And believe it or not, all other strong emotions elicit odors, including and especially hate.

"Hate is what I smelled as soon as those so-called monks entered the Ballroom that night. They reeked of it!

"The difference between me and the other two is important to understand. Ceikay only sensed the explosion of violence an instant before it happened. Errol saw the telltale signs. I, on the other hand, smelled hate the moment the monks entered the room. I could not though, know if an attack was planned or even eminent.

"So the three of us, Ceikay, Errol, and me, knew something was amiss but could not know the extent of the monks' plans. So, that night it was I who first alerted our comrades to possible danger by using signals, but I had to wait for their cues to act if and once violence exploded. Do you see now?"

"How did your nose become so acute?" I asked.

"You mean, how did my sense of smell become so acute, do you not?"

"Yes, yes I guess I do."

"Years and years of smelling sweat."

I tried not to...but I just burst out laughing. I asked no more questions for a while.

As we rode I looked around to get a bearing on all of my companions. It was then that I noticed that Karlyle was not in sight. I realized also that I had not seen him since the night before. Ceikay was close to me now so I nudged my horse close.

"Where is Karlyle?" I asked.

Ceikay looked at me, "I thought you knew. He is two companies behind us. Two of his wizard friends have joined us and the three of them are working on...spells."

Errol rode up to the both of us. "What Ceikay is trying to say is, the three of them are working on ways to combine their mental thoughts and therefore triple the power of their Menta-Physical manipulations."

"I am tired, Errol," Ceikay yawned, "too tired for big words."

We rode on until dusk. No one said much. Sometimes Errol would ride ahead. I assumed it was to converse with Hellista. Whenever he would return to our group, he would not offer information. The rest of us did not ask. Ceikay seemed to recover as we traveled. Her expression was no longer of weariness, but of contentment. She looked to be very calm. My weariness grew with the shadows. The brief rest that Errol had given me was all but forgotten.

When the sun was gone from the sky, a cry was heard that brought me joy: "Halt! We will set camp here for the night!"

Our orderly parade broke to both sides and off the road. I followed Keven who was closest to me. Once off the road, we dismounted. My back failed to straighten all the way. I was convinced that I was permanently crippled at this point and accepted my fate with a simple shake of my head. Once again a hand took my reins. Once again, it was Errol.

He smiled as I looked up into his face. "Just how old are you Bard?"

"Too young to feel this old," I muttered.

Ceikay now came up. "Before you put your head down for the night Beorn, you must eat something. Karlyle has joined us and will have a warm meal for us in a few moments. Try to stay awake long enough for that. You need a good meal working in your body tonight, because tomorrow will be more of the same."

Neither the food nor the thought of tomorrow appealed to me, but I knew that she was right. Food in my stomach now would serve me well.

I then saw Karlyle bending over a large pile of sticks and small logs. He stared at the pile for a moment and it burst into a bright, beautiful dancing fire. I was immediately drawn to it. Forgetting my horse and bedroll, I went and sat down before the fire and closed my eyes. The heat rolling into my face was soothing. The world around me faded.

My trance was interrupted by Keven calling my name. My eyes opened to see a plate of warm food waving in front of my face. I took the plate and smiled my thanks.

As I ate, I began to notice the camp around us. The sky was completely dark with a waning moon just beginning to rise from the ground. All around me fires now illuminated the men and horses of our camp. Some men were eating, some were already laying down on bedrolls asleep. I noticed now that almost no one spoke. The camp was noisy from activity, but not from conversation.

Across from me sat Karlyle and two people I did not know. They were both covered in full-length gray capes that revealed nothing of weapons or armor underneath. I surmised that these two must be the two wizards that Karlyle spent the day with. All three were sitting down and I could see that Karlyle was doing most of the talking. As I watched him with his friends, I realized that that was the most I had ever seen Karlyle talk before.

Errol stepped into the firelight. "Hellista will be calling us to meeting tomorrow early. Everyone must get sleep as they can as soon as they can."

Ceikay frowned as she responded, "Yes, 'father', I was planning to stay up until dawn to celebrate our day's march!"

I barely noticed Ceikay's jest, for I was already heading to my bedroll. Sleep came to me almost immediately.

A hand on my shoulder woke me up. I saw Keven grinning down at me.

"Is it time already?" I asked, fearing the answer.

"It is time for Hellista's meeting. Errol and Ceikay are already on their way. We must hurry."

"Hellista does not want me at her meeting."

"You do not know the King's daughter. You are to be at her meeting."

"She did not want me along for this trip..."

Keven bent lower toward my face. "She has changed her mind. You are to attend...now."

My rest was not to continue. I nodded in surrender.

Keven then backed away to allow me room to rise. My backside screamed in protest as I forced myself to fully stand upright. Keven handed me a steaming tankard of charrol-bean tea. The aroma began to clear the fog from my head.

"You can drink that at the meeting. Hellista will not mind."

The meeting was about one hundred paces away. By the time Keven and I arrived, I had already downed half of the hot, delicious tea.

Keven led me over to Errol and Ceikay. Everyone was sitting

on the ground, surrounding a waning fire. There were about forty officers of varying rank and uniform colors. The five remaining loyal realms were all represented. Errol was talking with a captain from the Jaramas Realm. Ceikay sat with her eyes closed. But it did not appear to me that she was relaxing. Her face showed concentration. I assumed that she was studying the gathering.

A movement away from our group drew everyone's eyes. Hellista walked toward us leading a saddled horse. A page ran up and Hellista handed him the reins. The page and horse disappeared behind a large tent.

"I apologize to everyone for being late to a meeting of my own calling. I have been with my outriders sending off orders and messages. Our time is short so we will not waste it with debate or questions of any sort."

No one spoke or attempted to. We waited for Hellista to continue: "I have not changed plans. We will strike camp at sunrise and push to a position north of Stannis. According to my latest outrider's report, Stannis has not yet been besieged. The enemy is being slowed through Wolven Forest by Rangers. Time is beginning to favor us, but numbers are not.

"From what I have been told, an army of twenty-five thousand is marching south on us. So far, I have fewer than twelve thousand in place to face them. We are another six thousand in this camp, increasing our strength to about seventeen thousand.

"The enemies' forces are mainly foot soldiers, twenty thousand strong. We know that Hastid has at least five thousand light and heavy cavalry. Our forces are all cavalry. As you know, that has advantages and disadvantages. Once we meet the enemy on the field, we will coordinate attack to minimize our disadvantages. I will talk with each of my senior officers one by one as we march today. Input will be required from all of you as to the best tactics to be taken."

Hellista's eyes swept the circle. She continued, "Another factor we must face and consider: The Hastid forces that have so far engaged us all carry the banner of Duke Hastid's son Kalzoral. We have not seen or felt the attack from Duke Hastid's personal forces. He was seen leaving the city of Brentsad days before the attack at Hirst. Where he is now is a dangerous unknown to us."

With a sigh she concluded, "There is no more for me to say or share with you at this time. Return to your companies and make ready for travel. We will be mounted and stepping forward shortly."

Hellista now turned to our group. "Ceikay, I will have you ride with me this morn. The rest of you know your positions. That is all."

Ceikay stood, nodded and then left the gathering.

Hellista turned and went to the large tent behind her. She threw open the flap and disappeared. The rest of us quickly jumped up as she left. The officers scattered to their own camps.

Keven tapped my shoulder. "Let us ready for travel Beorn. The sun waits not for us!"

"Where is Karlyle?" I asked.

"Ah, you noticed that he did not attend Hellista's meeting."

"Yes, and I do not see his two wizard friends."

Errol stepped next to me. "Let us make our way back and prepare for travel."

Both Errol and Keven kept quiet until we returned to our own fire ring. Rather than ask the question now, I decided to wait until I had gathered my bedroll and saddled my horse.

We had just mounted our horses and started to get into marching order on the road when the gray morning sky brightened with the first rays of the new sun. Not a moment later the sound of a horn gave signal to march.

As our horses settled into a column, Keven rode up next to me.

"You wanted to know where Karlyle and his friends were, did you not?"

I nodded, "If you would tell me, I would like to hear."

Keven pointed to the west, into the great Minoline Plains. "The three wizards had ideas to try, so they went off into the plains to work on them in privacy. Karlyle said that he would return to us later this day."

I was sure that my next question would surprise Keven, "Hellista said this morn that the enemy was mostly on foot, and that led to advantages and disadvantages. Why is that so?"

I quickly added, "What I want to know mainly is, what are the disadvantages that cavalry face against foot soldiers? I always thought that cavalry would overrun foot soldiers."

Keven sighed before answering, "It is reported that this enemy to the north is marching with pikemen and halberds at the front and sides. Do you know the tactical reasoning for that?"

"No."

"You see, pikemen carry sharpened poles that are about sixteen feet in length. These foot soldiers march in shoulder-to-shoulder formation at the front of blocks, or squares of infantry. They are designed to stop the full charge of mounted attackers: cavalry. These long pikes would be pointed outward to spear charging horse and riders. The rear of the pike would be jammed into the ground with the pointed end angled up and aimed at the horses' chests. The thrust of the charge would impale horse and rider. This weapon works well against Light Cavalry charges, where the horse and rider are not lance equipped, nor heavily armored.

"Another front line defense is halberd soldiers. These are footmen who carry a weapon that is almost as long as pikes. This weapon has a sharp pointed metal thrusting blade at the end, similar to pikes. But the difference is in the axe blade that is beside the thrusting blade. This weapon can chop. The halberd is therefore, a weapon designed for heavy cavalry. As you know, our riders are mostly equipped with lances for charging and breaking the lines of regular infantry. Both rider and horse are armor protected. The halberd axe is designed to chop at our lances, to break them. The halberd spear is designed to stab through the armor of the horse and rider."

Keven stopped talking and looked over at me, "Do you understand so far?"

"So far yes, but we have archers on horseback, why do we not just fire arrows into their front ranks and decimate them from a distance?"

Keven grinned, "That is good reasoning, except that they also have Shieldsmen right behind the pikemen and halberds. So when an attack does come from the sky, the front lines stop and the Shieldsmen rush to the fore and hold their shields overhead; thus protecting the front lines."

I tried to think of a way to counter. Keven must have guessed my thoughts because he now leaned over to me. "Maybe you should take your turn with Hellista today. She is thinking the same thoughts as you: how to break their lines."

Looking at Keven, I saw that he was not grinning.

He spoke again, "Later if you wish, I will continue your military education. I will explain more of what we are up against. Right now, I notice Ceikay returning to us from the front of our parade. Let us see what she has to say...."

As she neared, Errol came in from the left of the column. I had not noticed that he was away from our side. He spoke first, "Does Hellista want me up with her?"

"No..." Ceikay paused until she had reached our side and turned her horse to the front. "Beorn is requested to join her."

Errol and Keven shot looks of surprise at me.

"What?"

"You heard me correctly. Hellista would like you to join her in conversation."

"What does she want to talk to me about? I have nothing to say. I would not know what to say..."

Errol slapped me lightly on the back. "Just answer her questions. She will be the one asking this time, not you."

I looked to Keven. He only grinned back.

Ceikay spoke, "The longer you stay with us back here, the shorter her temper will be up there."

"Very well. Do I just ride up until I see her?"

"Ride up until you reach her side." Keven quipped.

Frowning to no one in particular, I spurred my horse forward. I galloped past two companies and soon saw a lone rider about thirty paces from the front banners. It was Hellista. At that very moment she turned in her saddle and spotted me. With a wave of her arm, I was summoned. I increased my horse's gait and was soon at her side.

"Good morn to you, good sir. Thank you for joining me so promptly. That is a good habit to foster if you are to be the Royal Witness to the King."

I could not be sure of her tone. I responded simply, "Good morn m'Lady. How can I be of service to you?"

To my great surprise and discomfort, Hellista sudenly broke out in great laughter! Not knowing what I had said, or what I should do, I waited for her in silence.

She then turned to me and grinned. "You have just cost me one copper Kopa Beorn!"

I remained silent.

"Please forgive my rudeness. I do not laugh at you! I laugh because I have an excuse to. In dire times, a good laugh is oft times salvation."

My look encouraged her to continue. "You see Beorn, Ceikay and I had just made a little wager before she left me to summon you. She had told me about you and your amazing talent. She tells me that you are the best Memory Master that she has ever encountered. Better than any Witness in any of the other realms."

"Thank you, M'Lady."

"Do not thank me Beorn. It was Ceikay who said it. Since I do not yet know you, I do not yet judge you."

She smiled and continued, "But that does not explain the bet, does it? Well, Ceikay also tells me that you have an amazing talent for asking questions. So the wager was: that no matter what was said or asked, you would ask a question of me the first time you opened your mouth. And you did!"

I did not know if I should be flattered or offended, so I responded as to the bet. "Surely m'Lady, you should not be required to pay on that bet. I merely asked how I could be of service to you. That is the correct, formal phrase that should be used when one is summoned to a Princess."

Hellista smiled as she shook her head. "No...no, it is much more fun this way. I know it will please Ceikay to the ends of the earth to win a Kopa from me...since she has lost the last three bets between us!"

Now my mind was once again filling with questions, but I was uncomfortable with the asking.

Hellista now offered another subject. "My reason for wanting you to stay behind in Talavor was simple and sound. My father, the King, has appointed you as his Royal Witness. It is not customary for Witnesses to go into battle. They are assigned to the 'niceties' of Parliament."

I still kept quiet. She continued, "As you know, Errol stood for you. Rather, he 'stood up to me' for you. It may seem to an outsider that Errol was forward or impudent with me when we discussed you."

I nodded and she continued, "He was according to royal protocol, but your companions are the only ones who can talk to me so. I know that they would never do harm, or allow anyone to harm me or my father. I value their service, and more importantly, I value their friendship. So, if Errol wants you to come north with us, and tells me so...well, here you are Beorn! I love him that much! As for his siblings, I love and value them just as much."

"Who are Errol's siblings?"

Hellista suddenly pulled on her reins. Her horse obeyed and stopped in the road. I immediately did the same. She looked at me with a puzzled look. I quickly looked back and saw that the whole procession also came to a halt!

After a few moments of Hellista staring into my eyes, she spoke, "You really do not know. Are you telling me that up to this moment, you did not know?"

Shaken and embarrassed, I answered for her, "Errol, Keven, Karlyle, and Ceikay are siblings...brothers and sister..."

Hellista held her horse still. "Beorn, you must have known! They did not tell you? You did not ask?"

I shook my head dumbly, "I guess the thought did not come to my mind."

"Beorn, you are a marvel! "Come..." She spurred her horse forward. "There is much you and I will need to talk about when time allows. As for now, I will not tell your companions details of our conversation."

Hellista then grinned broadly, "Except that Ceikay owes me a copper Kopa!"

We rode for a while longer. I will not give details in this tale of what we talked about, but I will say that she did the asking. The asking was about me and my past. I found that I really liked this

Princess. She was, as they say in the farmer's fields, 'Common as dirt.'

Our ride was interrupted by the cry of one of the point riders to the front of us. An outrider was approaching. With a quick dismissal, I was free to return to my companions. I did not share any details with them, although they pressed me hard.

Soon our caravan stopped for a quick resting of the horses. We ate hard biscuits and jerky. Finally, Ceikay broke a long silence: "Beorn, something is on your mind that troubles you. Should we know what passed between you and Hellista?"

I answered with an accusation, "You did not tell me you were siblings."

For a long moment, silence was my answer.

The others looked at each other, then back to me.

Suddenly, Ceikay laughed and shook her head, "You have just found this out?"

"You never bothered to tell me."

Errol grinned but said nothing. Keven rolled his eyes and remained silent also.

Ceikay answered me, "you never bothered to ask."

Her words stung, but I pressed on. "But you never refer to each other in that way."

Now Errol spoke, "In what way Beorne of Minoline."

"Brother and sister. That way!"

Keven broke his silence, "Well, I know for certain that I do at times, my friend. Is it possible that you just do not hear it?"

"I remember everything I hear."

"Ah, but you do not always listen then. Could it be that you choose not to hear?"

"What do you mean by that?"

"It is obvious that close relationships put you off Beorn."

"I do not..."

It was a relief that Karlyle now rejoined us. He was alone.

Keven was the first to greet him: "Hail, brother of mine! What have you done with your two friends?"

Karlyle answered as he led his horse. "There are strange energies in the skies just to the west of us. My friends are investigating. It may be nothing, but we must not assume so. If there is trouble they will signal me. If it is nothing, they will still signal me. Now, what news if any can you share with me?"

Ceikay answered, "The only news of importance is that Beorn had an unusually long ride with Hellista, and has come back to us with strange strained emotions. He will not talk to us about it."

I could tell that Ceikay was teasing, but I also knew that they all guessed that I was keeping quiet about something.

Once again, the horn sounded and we resumed our march. As we rode through the day I saw a number of officers riding past us in both directions. I knew that Hellista was not wasting traveling time.

Soon Ceikay edged her horse closer. "What do you think of Lady Hellista?"

"I would think that you would bring up our unfinished conversation."

Ceiky answered promply, "It is finished as far as I and my siblings are concerned. Do you wish to continue or answer my question?"

I smiled and shook my head. "Hellista showed that she is not hampered by her royal responsibilities in being a commoner."

"I am not sure what you mean by that, except that you found yourself liking her, am I correct?"

"Oh yes. Hellista made me very comfortable. I admit, at first meeting, I thought she wore her crown very tightly. But she truly is likable."

"You are that much surprised by her?"

I only shrugged in answer.

Seeing that I was not going to offer an explanation, Ceikay smiled, "I will press you no further, my friend."

She then separated from my side and I rode once again with my silent thoughts.

Nothing more of interest happened until our last stop and camp for the night.

That night my companions and I were summoned to Hellistas' fire circle. When we arrived, her Senior Officers were there already. Hellista was standing outside of her tent talking with an outrider. It looked as though he had ridden hard and had not yet had time to rest. Hellista was obviously in earnest in questioning him. I could not hear words from where I was standing, but I could tell that the messenger carried important news. From what part of Tavegnor, I did not know.

Then I saw Hellista hold out her hand. The outrider gave her a rolled scroll. From what I could see, it had the King's Seal stamped on it. The messenger now bowed and left Hellista and the fire circle.

We all waited silently while Hellista opened the scroll. She read to the bottom and stopped, then read from the beginning again. She rolled the scroll up and put it under her arm and looked out at the fire.

Finally she spoke, "You all know Royal Interrogator Davaas. He has succeeded in persuading our Duchess Mariom and her officers to reveal their secrets."

Silence urged her to continue: "It is now known why Tavegnor has been attacked: Duchess Mariom's great-grandfather."

Hellista paused only for an instant before continuing, "I am sure you are all familiar with the banishment forty years ago of Duke Marria the 17th of the Western Realm. He tried to forcibly dethrone the then King Hastid the 3rd of Tavegnor. Duke Marria's forces were defeated at the headwaters of Minoline Lake. Duke Marria was exiled to the Southern Continent. He swore that the rest of his family was innocent of involvement; therefore, they were permitted to stay in Tavegnor. They were even allowed remain in control of their ancestral realm.

"King Hastid felt that leniency would serve better than punishment. So only the rebellious Duke and his close advisors and followers were sent from our shores.

"As we now know, the rest of the family was not so innocent. To our regret, leniency only permitted the remaining family to plot a finish to what was started. Unknown to any of us, Duke Marria settled into southern country called Ramilliad and began making plans for invasion. It took years to persuade the Rulers of Ramilliad that Tavegnor could and should be conquered.

"Duke Marria's plans went so far as to marry the

granddaughter of the foreign king, thereby cementing influence with the Royal family. It took a generation to mold plans into a realistic and viable invasion.

"Those plans were finally set in motion through the vicious treachery of the monks at Hirst.

"Old Duke Marria did not live to see his dreams of conquest awaken to reality. His soul left this earth ten summers past. The offspring he fathered in the south now rule Ramilliad...and also now invade Tavegnor."

This time when Hellista paused, everyone began to talk in urgent tones to each other. She let the officers have their way for a moment or two longer.

"I will say only a few more words, and then we will retire for the night. We know now that Tavegnor was betrayed within and without by the long-ago scheming of Duke Marria and his family in Tavegnor. Our enemy is known to us. His goals are also!

"As for us, there is no change of plans. Marching is still for the morning sun. Before the next sunset, I believe that we will have contact with the enemy. We will have marched hard, but we still must fight harder to protect and defend our land!

"There will be no meeting in the morn, except for the King's emissaries, Errol and his four companions..."

Hellista turned to where we were standing. "We leave when the sun shows itself again. Errol, if you and your companions will come to my tent at first light, I will speak to you."

Errol nodded his acceptance of the order.

Hellista then addressed the others, "You are dismissed. After tonight, we may not know sleep again for a while. See that your men understand that."

I walked back to our camp next to Karlyle. As I opened my mouth to speak he held up his hand to me, "Please Beorn, if you are to be asking questions, I beg that you wait until we ride tomorrow. I promise you that I will be at your service then. I believe that I speak for the others also. Tonight is to be left for sleeping."

Karlyle was right about the need to sleep. I understood and accepted the wizard's suggestion for silence and slumber.

Dreams once again stayed away, but unlike the other mornings, I did not have to be awakened by one of the others. Sleep left me long before first light. I lay by the smoldering logs of the fire and recalled what I knew of the recent history of Tavegnor and its intrigue.

What I struggled with was the action of Duke Hastid to the northeast. Why did he betray Tavegnor? I resolved to keep Karlyle to his word. He would be kept busy answering my questions...

I tired of laying and wondering, so I got up, walked about camp and wondered. Sentries nodded greeting to me as I passed. A few other soldiers could not sleep; I silently waved or nodded as I passed by them also. Eventually, I found that I had made a circle and now stepped back into my own fire camp. My companions were awake and busy preparing for the day's march.

"You all were not concerned with my absence I see."

Keven answered simply, "Ceikay told us you were near."

Once our horses were saddled and packed, we reported to Hellista's tent. She was standing outside giving orders to another outrider. The outrider then bowed his head to Hellista and turned to a waiting horse. In a moment he was riding south from our camp.

"Good and new morn, my friends. Please enter my tent for hot charrol-tea and biscuits."

We followed Hellista in and sat on cushions set around a blanket laden with steaming goblets of tea and warm biscuits. As with King Ballistor, I was uncomfortable sitting informally with royalty.

Errol was the first to speak: "What special chore do you have for us this day my Princess?"

Hellista laughed as she sat to join us. "Are my thoughts so easy to read that not only Ceikay can read them?"

Errol grinned, "Your thoughts I did not read, but it is easy to surmise that we are here for something more than breaking of the fast."

"Could it be that I only ask you to my tent to plan the tactics on our upcoming battles my, smug friend?"

273

Errol shook his head as he answered, "You have capable officers and military advisors for that, M'Lady. You do not need us for tactical maneuvers for pitched battle. King Ballistor uses us for…special quests."

"Maybe, Errol, I asked you here to discuss the treacherous reasons for the invasion of our land…"

Errol grinned back. "We all know that discussions of that sort are not meant for the present. The morning after this war is over is the time for scrutiny of events and motives. This day needs plans, not talk. So, what are your plans for us this day?"

Hellista sat facing Errol for a moment before speaking. Then she reached over and slapped his broad shoulder,

"If you continue to contradict and argue with me, I will ask my father to have you permanently assigned as my servant!"

Errol smiled and bowed his head toward her, "You honor me m'Lady…"

Hellista slapped him again, "And you tease me, you scoundrel!" She then lost her smile and looked at the rest of us in turn.

She spoke of her plans. "My plans for you, including Beorn, are simple. They are also dangerous, but the danger is in the unknown. I pray that your quest will be short and free of injury. My plan for you is to find Duke Hastid."

I looked around at the other four. They showed no sign of tension or surprise. They sat still and waited for Hellista to continue.

"You must find him and his regiments. We cannot undertake an effective counter-attack if we do not know where our entire enemy is. You will not engage the enemy in your search. You must find Hastid and report back to me and my officers as soon as possible. Do you understand?"

"Do you have to ask us that? Your father does that to us…" Ceikay asked dryly.

Hellista smiled. "I meant no slurs to your intelligence. Please forgive me, I ask that out of habit."

Ceikay smiled and held her hand up indicating that Hellista need not explain further.

274

"As for Duke Hastid…" Keven asked, "we are to conclude that your outriders have been unsuccessful so far?"

"My outriders have not returned from the northwest."

"So we are to be your outriders then," Errol stated flatly.

"Yes, I ask this because you are the only ones who can succeed in finding Hastid and returning to me with his location, strength, and movements. Will you do this for me?"

"Do you have to ask us that…?" Ceikay asked again, grinning.

Keven spoke once more: "I have one request of you, Lady Hellista."

"I will grant you anything, Keven, if you stop calling me 'Lady' Hellista."

"Yes, m'Lady, my request concerns Eagle. He is on a quest for me as we speak. I have sent him north to locate a friend of mine. My friend may be able to help us if I can communicate with him. Eagle is to return to me today, sometime past noon. He knows I travel in this large mass of humans. He is too far away for me to communicate any changes. I ask you to look for him in the sky. When he appears overhead he will be looking for me. Since I will be separated from your regiments, he will need to be told of my location. By late evening I am sure that we will be just to the east of Stannis and turning toward Rogan Pass. Have one of your pages tie red and green scarves onto a guide-on and point it in our direction. Eagle will see and know that sign. He will fly in the direction the guide-on is pointed. His keen eyes will do the rest."

Hellista nodded to Keven that his request would be honored.

She then stood up. "I always enjoy the company of my dear friends, but war forces me to send them into danger and away from me. I am sad for myself and afraid for all of you. You must promise me that I will not hear news of your deaths!"

Hellista hugged even me as we left her tent. She whispered into my ear before separating, "My dear friends like you and watch over you. I ask you to watch over them for me."

I only nodded once and smiled. I then turned and left the tent.

Soon, we had passed the point riders and rode northeast toward Rogan Pass. The sun washed us with golden rays.

Rachilow Tell

We rode single file, so I did not have a chance to ask my many questions. Keven rode to the front, Ceikay second, Karlyle third, me after him, and Errol at the rear.

The day was clear of clouds. Before us in the distance stood Bolger Mountain. It is one of the largest mountains in the great Tellis range. Errol had said that we would be just to the northwest foot of Bolger as the sun set. We would then travel to the edge of Wolven Forest and camp for the night.

I had traveled through Rogan Pass several times before, so I knew the surrounding land. It was beautiful country we would be entering.

We left Talavor Road and crossed Tangier Road. Tangier Road is the one that actually enters Stannis City. We stayed to the east of the road and hugged the foothills for the purpose of staying out of sight and away from unwanted meetings. Keven watched for unusual animal activities, while Ceikay scanned the area for human presence. Karlyle watched the sky for signs from his wizard friends.

Errol stayed to the rear and watched all of us. I found that I had time to think. I recalled Tavegnor's recent history. The defection of Duke Hastid was troubling my thoughts. Why had he turned on Tavegnor and joined with Duchess Mariom and the country of Ramilliad?

As we rode, and as I thought back, I began to answer my own questions.

The King who banished Duke Marria was King Hastid the Third. King Hastid the Third was the current Duke's grandfather. The current Duke is Hastid the Fifth. This current Duke Hastid wants the Kingdom of Tavegnor back from the current King, King Ballistor of the Northern Realm.

The more I thought back, the more I realized how obvious it all was. I remembered the history: five years after Duke Marria's defeat and exile, the Parliament of Tavegnor voted out King Hastid the Third and put a new king on the throne. The new king was from the Northern Realm of Ballistor. This king ruled until his death some years ago. In his place Parliament raised his son, the current King Ballistor...Hellista's father.

I rode on, alternating between congratulating myself on reasoning the treason of Duke Hastid, and condemning myself for not being a better student of Tavegnor history. A bard who was not as lazy as I, would have known more details of Tavegnor's political history and intrigue. I resolved to travel straight to the Royal Library after this war and learn what I should already know.

Another matter that had me disturbed was my complete failure in asking my four companions their histories. I felt troubled that I did not care enough to get to know them better. If I had cared, then surely I would have asked enough questions to have found out that they were siblings.

Suddenly, Ceikay reared her horse around and rode back at a gallop. She came up fast and spun her horse in front of mine, forcing me to stop.

"Errol!" She called, "I must ride with Beorn for a few leagues!"

He yelled back, "As you will, sister of mine!"

Ceikay maneuvered her horse next to mine, "What thoughts are making you so troubled?"

"What do you mean?" I asked, delaying any probing talk.

"Do not forget who you are talking to Beorn. I have been riding ahead, feeling your thoughts for several leagues."

Still not wanting to talk, I offered another delay. "This war and the death it brings Tavegnor, it saddens…"

"Hold, Bard! Do not insult me further! I come back to you to help you and you dodge my help. It is not wise to turn away your friends!"

I remained silent.

Ceikay spoke again, "I have come close. The word 'friend' stung you. Why is that?"

I forced myself to remain calm. After all, I did not wish to discuss this matter with someone half my age. "Ceikay, I am better now. I was just being foolish. Thank you for your concern. It has helped."

She looked at me and frowned. "You still lie to me. You have put up a very good shell to block me out. But I can tell that you mean no ill toward me, so I will take no insult. I will ride with you a bit further in silence…friend."

I knew that Ceikay threw out that last word in a gesture of sincere good will. I smiled at her as we rode on.

As our shadows stretched further east along the ground, Mount Bolger stretched higher out of the ground before us. Its granite-faced western wall rose steeply from the plains while the opposite side sloped lazily into the smaller mountains to the east.

We headed toward the steep granite side. Our plan was to stay close to the mountain as far east of Tangier Road as possible. We knew that the city of Stannis was due west of us, but we could not see it. That was good, since the meeting of friends or foe meant delay.

The evening shadows were now pushing the last of the sun's rays up the granite sides of the mountain. Ceikay, who was still riding at my side, pulled her horse to a stop. I quickly did the same. Keven was riding back to us. He briefly stopped to exchange a few words with Karlyle.

I saw Karlyle pull his long katana sword from his back and ride ahead. Keven then continued back to us as Errol rode up.

"There are signs of a running fight." Keven began his report before his horse was halted. "I estimate there were about forty or so horses at a run crossing the path ahead. The tracks show the direction to be from the west headed east toward the pass. There are several weapons and riders' gear strewn along the ground."

"How long ago?" Errol asked.

"Sometime this day. No other animal tracks have disturbed the crossing. There is something else: I have told Karlyle that I saw strange scorch marks on two trees next to where the horses ran. He rode ahead to investigate the burns."

Errol frowned as he nodded, "Let us join him then."

Soon we came up to scattered trees. In the dimming light of the day I could see no signs of tracks. My companions did not seem to have the same problem. They stopped and got off their horses. Ceikay turned her head to the east and closed her eyes. I knew that she was trying to 'find' anyone who still might be close. Errol and Keven walked to and fro studying the ground. Every once in a while one of them would pick up an object at their feet. I looked around for Karlyle. I saw him at a distance away. He was examining a grouping of trees to the east of the path. The bark seemed to have been burned in streaks. Some low branches were also black charred or burned completely off.

Ceikay opened her eyes and spoke: "No one is near; no one alive anyway. Keven, where is Eagle? He could help search before the light is completely gone."

Keven looked to the sky. "I do not know where he is, or what the delay might be. He should have located us by now."

Karlyle rode back to us. "The burns look to be the work of warlocks. From the direction of the strike marks on the trees, it is plain that the fireballs were traveling in the same direction as the hoof tracks of the running horses."

"Which tells us that the warlocks were the chasers." Errol paused, and then added: "Can you tell how many?"

"Three...possibly more. Most likely more."

Errol nodded and mounted his horse. He sat and looked to the east.

The silence gave me an opportunity for a question to Karlyle, "How do you know the number of warlocks?"

He answered without hesitation, "The tracks on the ground tell us that the horses were in a full run. They ran past the trees that I examined. That means that the riders were at the trees for only that brief moment that they passed at a run. At that spot I counted six distinct burns on the trees from the fire hits. The riders had raced past the trees and immediately bolted to the left. The chasing warlocks were throwing into the turn to anticipate their change of direction, hence, the trees being hit so often.

"Now, since the men being chased were at a full run, so were the chasers. Keep that in mind as I explain how fire throwers work. As you know, 'Magic' is only the mental manipulation of the mental thoughts on the physical world around you. A warlock adept at fire throwing can only produce one fireball at a time. The burst of energy is so great to generate, that no one, to my knowledge, can as yet mentally 'throw' more than one. The action can be compared to the throwing of a heavy stone or a heavy ball.

"So if a single warlock were on horseback…at a full run…throwing fireballs at the backs of fleeing horsemen, it would not be possible to hit one tree six or more times in glancing blows from the same direction."

He continued over my silence, "Imagine, for example, you on horseback riding at full gallop. You have six stones in hand. You now take one stone at a time and throw them at a specific tree ahead of you. You will obviously see that the tree's position is changing with every throw. If you are good enough to hit the tree each time, you will discover that the strike marks of the stones have different angles of impact."

Karlyle paused and looked over at me.

I nodded as if I understood. He continued, "Now let us take a look at the trees ahead. As you can see, all the strike marks on this one specific tree are headed from left to right, relative to the running hoof tracks. That tells me that they all were thrown from the same spot and direction some distance behind us. One warlock on a running horse could not have been responsible for all the strikes. I am reading three or more fire throwers in the chase. I am guessing that they each had an opportunity to 'throw' a fireball as they cleared the turn in the path behind us. The path of the fleeing riders took them right past this stricken tree and toward the cover of the forest just ahead. As I said earlier, the warlocks were leading their throws into the turn. Each attacker could see that they had one or two more shots before their prey reached the cover of the woods. I estimate that at the most, one warlock would have made two strikes on this tree before riding past. Therefore...at least three raced by."

Eager to sound like I understood everything, I asked, "Earlier you said more than three is more likely. Why?"

"At least three hit the tree. How many more missed the tree altogether, only a guess can be made."

Errol broke in on our 'discussion.' "We will ride into the forest and find a clearing for tonight's camp. Once again, first daylight must find us already back in our saddles."

Keven led the way and quickly found a clearing. In truth, it seemed that he knew exactly which direction to head.

Once again, it seemed that Ceikay could indeed read my actual thoughts, "With his talent, Keven can find us the loveliest and most secure clearings in any forest."

Soon, camp was set, food was eaten, and the crows nestled in the branches above us. I slept fitfully

First light had us riding further into the pass. We kept just inside and under the forest canopy. Keven kept his eyes to the sky. I could see concern in the Ranger's eyes as he scanned upward. Eagle had not yet returned to us.

Then Keven held his hand up to stop our progress. I saw a red fox in our path. He stood facing Keven, and Keven sat on his horse facing the fox. For a moment no one moved. Then I saw Keven nod, and the fox turned and ran into the forest.

Keven then turned back to the rest of us. "Up ahead are dead men and horses."

Immediately Ceikay spurred her horse forward.

Errol and Karlyle both drew their swords. I followed their lead.

By this time I had more confidence in my own weapons. Each night Errol had worked with me and had given a few tips in the handling of a sword. Instead of trepidation, I felt anticipation for action.

Suddenly, and to my great surprise, Ceikay spun in her saddle and looked directly at me. Her eyes were hard,

"The moment you lose your fear…is the moment you become a danger to us."

I glanced at Errol. He confirmed what Ceikay was saying. "It would seem, Beorn, that Ceikay senses that you are beginning to feel the reckless excitement for battle. I can see by your twitches and the redness in your cheeks that she is right. Do not snuggle so close to the god of war…else he becomes your lover in death."

Those words stung me back to humbleness. "I am sorry. It was only…I do fear…"

Karlyle joined in, "It is easy to be seduced if you let…"

"They are found!" Keven yelled back to us from the edge of the forest.

Grateful for Keven's diversion, I followed my companions. We soon rode out of the woods. In front of us were strewn about a score of mangled bodies of horses and men. I was not surprised by the bodies, but by the sight of the vertical granite wall that faced us as we cleared the trees. I had forgotten about Bolger Mountain. We were still at its foot. I looked up and marveled at the height of the sheer wall. It rose straight up from the valley floor. I had no way of estimating the height.

I then became aware of the lack of noise around me. My eyes traveled back to the ground around me. Along with the ghastly sight was the ghastly smell of death several days old. My earlier thoughts of the thrill of battle were completely forgotten.

Then my talent once again took over. As I looked at some of the faces of the dead men, I remembered seeing each of them before! They were the faces of the 'Man Hunters' that passed us on our way to Brentsad! Some were not recognizable because of disfigurement, but the clothes confirmed that every one of them was of the same Guild.

"These are the man chasers we saw on the way to Brentsad," I said to no one in particular.

No one answered. I saw that they were all busy seeking

answers and clues as to what happened. Everyone else had dismounted. I stayed atop my horse and studied from a distance. As I looked at the scene I began to notice the lack of arrows or crossbow darts in any of the bodies. I did see scorch marks and burn holes on clothing and flesh. It was clear that these victims were killed by fireballs.

Keven began to mutter aloud as he studied the ground. "They all rode ahead at the edge of the forest. At some point up ahead, they turned back to this spot. Here they were met by the warlocks and cut down. Some escaped into the forest. There are tracks of three horses bounding through the trees over here. How far they traveled is at this point a guess. They may have gotten away, or they may be found as the rest..."

Errol interupted, "Their killers did not stay to strip the bodies of weapons or food. Money is still in a number of purses and pouches. The bodies were not hacked or mutilated."

It was Karlyle's turn: "These warlocks used only enough energy to kill. They were very efficient and did not waste their energies on arrant shots. Each thrown fireball hit a target. I see no wide hits on trees, rocks, or ground. Whoever did this was very adept once they had their victims trapped."

Ceikay's words stopped everyone, "There is someone alive up ahead!"

Before I saw it happen, Keven had a crossbow in his hands aimed to where Ceikay was pointing. Ceikay's short bow was drawn with an arrow notched for firing. Errol and Karlyle were both on their horses rushing to Ceikay's side, their swords at the ready once more! I stayed to the back of Keven, my sword drawn also, but without the boldness of before.

"One?" Errol asked.

"One..." Ceikay answered, "in great pain, does not have intent to attack us...he is unaware of our presence."

Errol nodded to Karlyle, and both rode ahead and around a bend in the steep mountain wall to our right. After a long spell of silence, a whistle came to us from up ahead.

"Let us go," Keven said as he mounted his horse, his crossbow still at the ready. Ceikay put her weapon away and mounted her horse. We rode to the sound of the whistle. As we turned the bend we saw what forced the now dead horsemen to turn back. A wall of tumbled and broken boulders stretched from the vertical wall of the mountain to the edge of the forest. No rider could have ridden through or over these huge boulders. The forest at this point was no escape because of the brambles and thick undergrowth. The only direction away from this blockade was back.

Errol and Karlyle's horses were at the edge of the broken barrier. I saw Karlyle standing atop a boulder. He waved to us to join him. Soon we were standing over a deep depression between three wagon-sized rocks. In the depression I saw Errol bending over a dark broken log. As my eyes quickly adjusted, I realized that the 'log' was a man!

"Ceikay, come down here!" Errol ordered.

Without hesitation, she jumped and landed to the other side of the prostrate man. She began to examine his body, looking for wounds. I saw that his eyes were closed. Whether he was asleep or dead I could not tell. Then I remembered that Ceikay had announced that she sensed someone alive.

Karlyle stood atop the rocks and looked up. I could see that he was studying the sheer wall above us. Keven scanned the forest to our left. I looked back into the rocky depression and listened.

Ceikay studied for a few moments longer, then turned to Errol, "He will not live long. His back is broken. He is weak, and more importantly…he wants to die."

"You can sense that now?" Errol asked.

"No, he whispered to me as I bent over him." Ceikay continued softly, "He asked me to release him to death's halls."

Errol shook his head, "We must try to help him live, not die."

It was Ceikay's turn to shake her head. "We are not healers. He is too far removed from life now. Death has his hand on him and is closing his fingers around him. I can only try to…"

Just then the broken man jerked his head upward and cried out, "You must finish what the warlocks started! Let my heart feel your blade…please…send me to my brothers!"

His hand came up and gripped Errol's wrist. Errol let him hold on. Ceikay placed her hands on the man's forehead. She closed her eyes and gritted her teeth. I saw the man's eyes open and look to her. They were hard at first, and then I could see that they softened as she continued to hold his head. I was not sure, but I thought I saw his lips tighten into a thin smile. Whether or not it was relief I saw in his eyes, it was brief. His eyes closed and his grip loosened and fell from Errol. The lips fell open and slack. I knew that death had taken him.

Karlyle was the first to speak: "We must not stay longer. We are vulnerable under this wall."

Keven was next. "The birds are gone. Something threatens them. Karlyle is right. We must leave this place quickly."

Errol looked over to Ceikay. "Do you sense anyone else?"

"No. If someone is above us waiting to loose boulders on our heads, they are out of my range. But I agree with Karlyle and Keven."

"You will get no protest from me." Errol said as he grabbed Ceikay by the waist. In a moment he had thrown her up out of the hole they were in. She landed on her feet next to me. To my surprise, he now picked up the dead man and lifted him to Karlyle. Karlyle grabbed the body and hoisted it from the hole and laid it on the rocks. Errol then bounded out also.

"We will place this man with his companions and be on our way."

Soon after, we were headed away from the sheer side of Bolger Mountain. Keven led our party. His eyes scanned the sky as well as the scattered forest. Although he had not mentioned it since this morn, I knew he was concerned about Eagle.

...once again Ceikay must have known what I was thinking...

"Where is Eagle?" Ceikay called to Keven.

"I wish I could answer," He replied back, "he should have found me by now. My other worry is the behavior of the animals around us."

"Why is that?" I asked.

"They are hiding from us. Even with my talent, they do not respond. They are too frightened of men right now. That could only mean one thing, man is spilling blood close by. It is not behind at the wall where we just came from. It is ahead of us."

"How do you know that?" I again asked.

"The animals are running toward and around us. They are fleeing danger. I am sure that we will find our Duke Hastid before us, and death will be there also."

Before I could ask another question, Errol rode up from behind.

"We are being followed. Riders entering the forest not more than a league behind us. Keven, we need Eagle…"

"Eagle has not come to us."

Errol frowned and shook his head. "Then I need you and Karlyle to circle back to the left. I will take Ceikay and Beorn to Rachilow Tell and await your return. Find out who and how many. Try to determine of they are tracking us, or merely heading in the same direction on a separate quest. Send signals if you find yourself in trouble."

Keven smiled. "If trouble finds us…we shall turn it around on itself."

Karlyle shook his head at Keven's jest. "We will not do anything foolish, Errol."

Errol smiled back but said nothing. In a moment, Keven and Karlyle were disappearing through the trees.

Errol turned to me. "Beorn, stay close to us. If we break into a run, do not hesitate to spur your horse to follow. We may not have time to explain things to you as we go."

I nodded and followed. Errol rode lead, I came next, and Ceikay rode just behind me. Soon we re-entered the thick part of the forest. Errol found a path and our pace did not slow. It was obvious that he knew the location of the Tell. None spoke as we rode. I noticed that the woods were quiet except for our passing. The animals were scarce. No birds could be seen.

Then Ceikay whistled three times in quick succession. Errol turned his head back but did not slow his pace. Ceikay pointed to the right and held up a fist and pumped it three times. I could see that she was signaling information to Errol, but I did not know what. Errol spurred his horse into a full run! I did the same.

We raced forward at an alarming speed through the trees. The branches went past my head at a blur. My horse was still fresh and not yet panting. I was the one panting. I leveled my breathing as best I could.

Suddenly sunlight exploded over me. We had broken from the trees into a large clearing. Errol veered off the path to the left. My horse followed without waiting for me to lead rein. Ceikay was still close behind. I looked past Errol and now could see a large mound directly in front of us. We rode on.

The clearing was a vast circular field of wild grass in the middle of the forest. I estimated that it was at least a league wide in all directions. The mound we were racing to was off center and to the edge of the trees. As we neared it, I could see that it was about two hundred paces wide and about ten spans at its highest point. At the high point were the ruins of a small castle. That was our destination: Rachilow Tell.

Errol led us up the slope and through the broken walls of the castle. I could not tell where the original gates used to be. The Keep was a broken shell that had half of its stone walls lying on the ground around itself. Green moss colored the stones. The top of the Keep was half overgrown with shrubs.

Once inside the castle walls, we jumped off our horses and quickly led them into the Keep. We found the remains of connecting stables. The roof had long ago vanished, but the walls were in no danger of collapse. By this time my horse was panting, but Errol said to leave the saddles on. As Errol and I settled the horses, Ceikay ran to the outer walls. She raised her head just enough to clear her eyes. She scanned the forest around us.

With the horses tethered, Errol and I joined Ceikay. I kept silent, scanning the distance.

Errol spoke to Ceikay, "What can you tell us?"

Ceikay answered as her eyes stayed on the trees. "Before we ran, I sensed a large force coming from the east. Hundreds, all mentally prepared for battle. They are alert and tense. They were heading toward us when I first sensed them. Whether they know we are here, I cannot tell. We did outrun them and they are out of my range, but I am reasonably sure that they will close in on us shortly."

"Did you sense anyone we know?" Errol asked.

"There were too many of them to try to sort out any familiar thought patterns, and obviously we did not stay around long enough for me to even try."

Errol touched my arm. "Beorn, find a way to the top of the Keep. I want you to be our eyes at the top. If you see anything we might be interested in, whistle three short blasts."

"I cannot do that."

Errol and Ceikay turned to face me.

Errol spoke, "You cannot do what, climb to the top of the Keep?"

I shook my head, "Whistle. I am unable to whistle."

Errol stood a moment and thought, then pointed to the ground, "Pick up some stones. If you need to signal us, throw them our way."

"But try not to hit us." Ceikay grinned.

There was no difficulty with finding a handful of stones. The rubble around us provided countless numbers of them. A broken set of stone stairs still clung to the side of an upright wall. I was soon at the top of the ruins of the Keep, crouching on the remnants of the parapet walk.

I quickly set myself to watching the forest edge. I was about twenty spans higher than the flat clearing. The nearest trees were to the west of the Tell. They looked to be about fifty paces from the outer walls. If anyone chose to attack from that direction, we would not have very much time to mount our horses and flee. Then the thought occurred to me that I would not have time to get to my horse if we were rushed!

I then realized that Errol had no intention of running further. I mused that he had sent me to the top of the Keep for my protection. Looking around at my position, it was obvious that this was the most defendable part of the Tell! If I kept my head low, the walls would protect me from arrows from the ground, and the broken steps would allow only one attacker to rush at me at a time!

I sighed and looked down at my companions.

Ceikay stayed at her position while Errol examined the ruins.

As I leaned on the Keep wall scanning the perimeter, I thought of this mound of dirt we were on. It was not really a dirt mound, but in fact, a 'Tell', a series of castles, or citadels built over each other as each, in their time, collapsed. Legend tells that one of the earliest fortresses in Tavegnor was built on this spot. It is thought that this was a good place to defend the pass. Over the years, this fortress was besieged and battered by various invaders. Each time it was destroyed, a new castle would be built over the old one…and each time, the new one was broken by siege. Finally, someone decided that this spot was indeed not a good spot to defend, so they built a religious citadel atop the heap. That edifice lasted barely one hundred years until it came down. Now, it stays in ruins.

Some years past a merchant by the name of Rachilow had gotten information of buried jewels on the grounds. After exhausting his modest wealth in his search and neglect of his trade, the hapless Rachilow cursed the Tell as well as himself. It is said he died penniless in a brothel on the south continent.

Movement brought my thoughts back to the present. At the very far end of the clearing, something caught my eye. It was hard to understand what was happening. A league in distance was too much for my eyes. But I could tell that there was movement in numbers under the trees at the clearing's edge. I picked a stone and tossed it down to Ceikay. I meant to drop it just to the left of her. It missed her by one pace to the right.

She looked up at me. I held up my fist and pumped it three times in the direction of the movements. She understood and nodded. She then whistled softly to signal Errol. He came quickly up from the stable area. I could see that Ceikay was telling him of my sighting. They both climbed up to join me.

Neither said a word as they reached my position. They both looked out at the far trees.

Errol spoke, "I see cavalry with the banners of the Hastid Realm. They are entering the clearing from the north east. They are moving slowly…cautiously. Ceikay, can you 'sense' them from here?"

"No, too far away."

I whispered, "It looks as though we found our Duke Hastid."

Errol grinned back to me. "If not him, then only part of his troops. I do not see his personal guide-on."

Ceikay spoke again, "It seems that they are dismounting. They are resting from trek."

"Would that we had Eagle here..." Errol mused.

My eyes were now drawn to the center of the mass of men and horses. I thought I could see a separation, a group of riders. They were coming this way, heading toward the mound! I nudged Errol and pointed. He studied the group as it got larger. The riders were indeed coming this way. Their speed was slow. It seemed to me that they were in no hurry to get here. Then about halfway between us and their comrades, these riders stopped. They seemed to hesitate a few moments, then turned their horses around. They were soon on their way back the way they came.

Ceikay smiled slightly. "Their nerve gave way to caution..."

"What do we do now?"

Errol did not answer me right away. For the first time I thought I could see doubt on his face. I kept silent, not pressing.

Finally, he did turn to me. "That is a good question. My answer is that the only thing we can do now is ponder our next moves. So we think, and wait."

Ceikay suddenly slapped Errol's arm with the back of her hand. As she did so, she ran to another section of the Keep wall. She bent low and peered over a broken rock. Errol and I both followed her. She motioned with her hand to keep low.

Then she whispered, "To the west, just inside the tree line. More men...scores...alert...ready and eager to fight..."

Errol peered over the wall and whispered back, "Which direction are they traveling?"

"They are coming to a stop at the inside of the woods. I do not know where they are intending to go."

"It seems that we are being hemmed in on all sides." Errol continued, "I should not have sent Keven and Karlyle off. It might prove uncomfortable for us if we are attacked now."

At those quiet words, I began to get nervous...

"Here they come, Ceikay announced calmly.

We looked over the wall. At the tree line stood dozens of horsed soldiers. They were looking at the ruins. They wore the Hastid colors. They were only fifty paces from the Tell.

Errol turned to me, "If fighting starts, you must stay behind me. The only way they can get to us is by the broken steps. I will be near the top of the steps greeting them as they get here."

He then turned to Ceikay. "Ceikay, once you loose all of your arrows, your task is to protect Beorn. Together we will hold them off as long as we can."

Errol drew his huge sword. I could not help but step back. The look in his eyes told me everything: the Sword Master was ready.

Ceikay took her bow from her back and drew an arrow. She did not notch it though. She remained crouched, peering over the wall. I drew my sword and looked down the steps. They were broken, but now seemed wide enough to allow three to charge abreast at one time...

"They have decided." Ceikay whispered, "They are coming."

I peered over and saw about a hundred horsemen coming toward the Tell. They were not in a hurry.

"Why do they not charge?" I whispered to Ceikay.

"Because they do not know that we are here. Possibly their plan is to occupy this Tell as high ground, or only to rest for a spell. They are suspicious, but not enough to be frightened away by 'ghosts' in the dark."

"They will find us, of course, I pressed.

"Of that we can be sure," Ceikay muttered.

Soon the riders were at the base of the mound. They hesitated only a moment, then spurred their horses to the top. We could not see them from our crouched position, but could now hear them. It did not take them long to discover our horses. A yell rose up and men shouted to each other. We heard the sound of swords being drawn from their sheaths. Running feet told us that the Keep was now surrounded. Errol now sat on a broken block at the edge of the parapet. His sword was lying across his knees. Ceikay stood behind him with her bow and notched arrow. I stood behind her with my back to the wall.

Suddenly, a soldier ran through the broken gates of the Keep and into its center. He looked around, searching for the owners of the horses. In his left hand was a double-headed short axe. He looked around until his eyes came to the steps. His eyes then climbed up and saw us. He froze for a moment. None of us moved.

The soldier then yelled back over his shoulder, "Here! I have found them! Come to me!"

Still, Errol did not move from his sitting position. Ceikay pointed her bow and arrow at our discoverer...

In a moment, the floor of the Keep was filled with armed men. I felt relief that none of the soldiers held weapons of missiles. Ceikay had the only bow that I could see.

Still, Errol had not moved. He only looked down at the men. I spent the moments counting. There were twenty-six heavily armed men below us, and of course, more outside the Keep.

Then someone broke through the crowd below us. He was an officer by the mark of his insignia. He looked around the Keep and then raised his head to us.

"Who are you and what is your business here?" He demanded.

I looked to Errol. He still did not move.

"Are you deaf or stupid?" After no answer from us the officer raised his voice, "You would be wise to answer me now!"

Now Errol did answer, remaining seated. "We are emissaries of good King Ballistor of the country of Tavegnor. We are on the King's mission to find Duke Hastid and determine his intentions. I see by your uniform, Captain, that you are a soldier of Duke Hastid's Realm. Perhaps you can assist us in locating your liege lord, or tell us yourself of his plans."

The officer looked around at his men, and then returned his gaze to Errol. This time with a sneer on his face, "The great Duke Hastid is a dead man, and if you are indeed emissaries of the King, then you are also dead.!"...Men! Kill the...!"

Ceikay'sarrow flew instantly through the Captain's throat, silencing any more orders. Errol stood up and faced the top of the steps. Men at the bottom charged! The first two stopped well away from Errol's sword and the others behind crashed into them. One yelled out, "Bring a barrier to charge with!"

An arrow silenced him also.

But the message was understood, no one was going to be able to face the big man at the top of the steps without a shield. I now saw two men pick up a part of the broken gate of the Keep. A path was made as the two men charged up the steps toward Errol. They were pushing the huge oak planks ahead of them. They meant to push Errol back from the steps so that the others could rush him for the kill.

Errol stood waiting. Ceikay's arrows were killing each time they flew from her bow. I took a step forward...

Then with a speed and force that stunned everyone, Errol threw himself at the rising attackers. The gate actually splintered in two! The two hapless men fell back and onto the men behind them. Instantly, two arrows entered the chests of the hapless bearers. Before the bodies could be thrown aside, Errol was pushing everyone down the steps, his sword held in front as a barrier.

I saw Ceikay draw her last arrow. She aimed at an officer just outside the Keep entry. He was waving his arm to bring more soldiers on. A moment later he was dead. She then drew her short sword and waited.

Errol now was the center of everything. He had backed up to the top of the stairs again. Men tried to step up and duel him. They all died. I stood watching as Errol's sword became a constant blur. He parried and thrust with apparent ease. No one came close to striking him. No one could hope to! He had the high ground. I could only stand and watch along with Ceikay...

Suddenly the stone floor I was standing on rushed up and pushed my knees into my chest! My eyes were instantly blinded by a wall of dirt! A great roar of sound and gush of wind threw me high from my sanctuary behind Errol. I found myself flailing in midair, spinning feet over head. As I flew through the air I noticed my hands...I thought it very strange that I had lost my sword again.

The next thing I realized was the impact of me falling into the men on the floor of the Keep. My body slammed onto a crowd and bounced into a side wall. I fell to the ground knowing that I was dead. My eyes closed as screaming filled my ears and debris pelted my body. Terror urged me into action. I opened my eyes and saw a battle axe lying on the ground, brushing my nose.

I grabbed it, then jumped up to face my attackers. There was dust and confusion everywhere. Men were fleeing the Keep. I looked up. Errol was not to be seen. Above me Ceikay was lying on the edge of the parapet at the top. She was not moving. I raced back toward the stairs. Half of the steps and parapet were gone. They had vanished out of existence. I saw Ceikay on the other side of the breach. The gap was two spans across. I could not hope to jump it. I yelled to her. She did not move.

Suddenly the noise of battle started up again. I looked for Errol. He was not on the parapet, nor on the floor of the Keep. Yelling turned me around to face the stairwell. Hastid's soldiers had recovered from great confusion and were now re-entering the Keep. Two raced up to me. I swung my weapon; somehow I cut the first attacker. The second attacker was shoved off the steps by the first one falling into him. More men followed. I desperately kept on swinging.

The roar of battle was now outside the Keep. I yelled for Errol. I knew no one could hear my voice in this nightmare, but I kept yelling anyway as I fought. Then bright streaks of light split the sky around the Keep. The bolts of lightning were followed by the booming explosion of thunder! As I fought for my life and that of Ceikay, I wondered at the sudden appearance of mid-day storms.

Then my heart leapt in my chest. Errol came charging through the Keep entrance! He pushed his way in as soldier after soldier went down before him. He was coming my way! I found new strength and began to swing with control at my attackers. They began to retreat down the steps. I yelled in triumph at the approaching Errol!

The battle then turned on us.

Errol was knocked from behind by a horse and rider. The mounted soldier crashed his horse into Errol's back and sent him flying forward. Errol lost balance and fell to the ground. Instantly men jumped on him. I yelled and jumped from the stairs. As soon as I left the stairs two soldiers raced up. They were going after Ceikay! I slashed at two men on top of Errol, then turned back around and bounded up the steps. I saw that one of the soldiers at the top was about to throw a knife at the unconscious Ceikay. I raised my axe as I raced up. I threw the weapon at his back. The blade did not hit him, but the heavy handle did! That was enough to push the attacker over the edge of the broken parapet. He fell before the knife left his hand.

The second man turned to face me. I crashed into him as his knife sliced my arm. I did not stop my charge. We followed the first man to the bottom. The first man's body broke our fall. My hands were on the second man's head as we fell. I shoved it into the stone floor until I heard the crack of bone. Jumping to my feet, I turned and grabbed a short sword. I looked for Errol. I yelled at seeing him back on his feet and still fighting. He was covered in blood...from himself or his enemies I could not tell.

I knew that I had to get back to the steps to protect Ceikay. As I ran toward them a tall soldier stepped into the Keep. I froze...I knew him...Elexele! He had a sword in each hand. Each blade was covered in blood. His eyes had death in them. I yelled at Errol! He did not hear me. Elexele looked around the Keep. His eyes spied Errol desperately fighting with his back to the wall. Errol had only a dagger in one hand and a broken shaft of a spear in the other.

Elexele took a step toward Errol! I could see that Errol was not aware of the advancing Elexele. I forgot about the steps and jumped at Elexele. I did not surprise him. He stepped sideways and easily knocked me to the ground with an elbow as I sailed past him.

I then heard him yell to a soldier who was following him in.

Elexele pointed down to me as I looked up from my back, "Hold him!

I tried to grab Elexele's foot. He easily stepped away and continued toward Errol. I tried to get up but two soldiers now pinned me to the ground. I yelled once more as Elexele raised his weapons.

...They came down on the backs of Errol's attackers! One by one Elexele cut down the soldiers surrounding Errol. As the last attacker fell before Errol, Elexele quickly stepped back and held up his now empty hands.

I saw Errol standing before him, ready to fight if attacked. The noise of battle had suddenly stopped. No one moved. I lay still under two heavy men, too shocked and spent to resist anymore.

Errol and Elexele stood facing each other, neither one moving or saying a word. Then two more came into the Keep. Keven and Karlyle rushed past Elexele to Errol. They both grabbed a big arm to support their brother.

Karlyle looked around: "Where is Ceikay?"

I once again found my voice as I yelled out, "Ceikay! She is on the parapet! She is down!"

Before the words were completely out of my mouth, Elexele was bounding up the steps. He hesitated for only a moment at the breach. I could see that he leaped to the top of the outer wall and over to Ceikay. Elexele knelt down and gently touched her neck, then scanned her body for wounds. A moment later he called down,

"She is breathing. I do not see a mortal wound! Captain Modela, get my Healer!"

Karlyle and Keven were only a step behind Elexele. They soon were relieved enough to notice their surroundings.

Keven looked down to my direction. "Elexele, can you release your men from atop our friend?"

Elexele looked down to the two men pinning me down and waved a hand to the side. They both jumped up and away from me. I did not get up. Instead, I rolled onto my back and stared up into the sky. My breathing slowly calmed back to normal. I did not have the energy to think, let alone ask any questions. I simply let the rest of the world disappear around me.

Eventually I felt my arm being lifted. I tried to get up. A firm push on my chest kept me on the ground.

I saw Karlyle looking down at me. "Lie still, we are tending to a wound. It is not serious, but needs closing. We do not want you to give too much blood to the Tell."

As I lay back, I began to listen to the sounds around me. I was surprised that I could not hear the groans of the wounded. I did hear the metal clangs of weapons being gathered. Voices also were not heard. Men were walking all around the Keep, but no one talked. I think I drifted into slumber for a while.

Finally, the person who was wrapping my arm spoke. I was

startled by a female voice: "There, your arm will not fester if you keep this poultice on. You can get to your feet if you so desire."

I looked over to see a woman kneeling next to me. She wore the traditional long gown of a Healer, with the House of Hastid colors. She smiled and got to her feet. She held out her hand to assist me up. I shook my head and closed my eyes.

"Can I just lay here and sleep for a while?" I asked.

Karlyle's sharp voice rolled over me in answer, "This is not the time for rest! You are needed."

One of my eyes opened slowly. "What can I possibly do for you? Can you not see? I am too tired to open my other eye."

Karlyle ignored my attempt at humor as he leaned over me. "Time does not allow for your leisure, Bard. You are required at council as the King's Witness."

Those words brought me back to awareness and banished the thought of sleep. I groaned and sat up. Once again the Healer held out her hand. This time I took it. I was quickly on my feet. Karlyle took firm hold of my arm. The Healer turned from us and went to examine a soldier lying next to the steps. From this distance, it looked as though he was beyond the help of the Healer.

"How is Ceikay?" I asked.

Karlyle pointed to the stables as we passed. "Ceikay is in there being tended to by Healers. She will be all right soon, but her headache may linger for a while. She began to awaken as they were carrying her down the Keep steps. She was concerned about you and Errol, so it appears that serious injury has not occurred if she is already asking of her companions and the battle."

"Is Errol all right? He was down on the ground and being attacked on all sides!"

Karlyle smiled as he answered this time, "It will take more than a mere score of men to take down Errol. Yes, he has escaped any wounds, from swords at any rate."

"What do you mean by that?" I asked, "...wounds from swords...do you say that he is wounded?"

"Errol suffered cuts and scratches from being thrown from the top of the Keep when the explosion went off."

"What do you mean by...explosion?"

Karlyle shook his head at the question. "I will tell you of that later…"

Karlyle prodded me to walk with him as he changed the subject. "Elexele will relate events of war in the north. You will listen and later repeat the telling to King Ballistor."

"Did Elexele turn against his Duke?"

"As, you Beorn, I have yet to hear his full explanation. Where Elexele is headed, and what his plans are, he will tell us very shortly. What I do know is that Elexele is not a traitor to Tavegnor."

We now approached a group of soldiers surrounding a large camp fire. "We are here. Let us join our friends and await Elexele. He will return shortly."

We entered the light of the fire. Errol and Keven were on the far side of the circle. Twelve more men, all wearing Hastid Officer's insignia, were either standing or sitting. All were cleaning and sharpening various weapons. All were still clad in full fighting mail and padding. Karlyle and I stepped over to our companions. They both smiled broadly at our arrival.

"Come! Join us, fellow warrior!" Errol stood up and slammed a big hand on my shoulder in greeting. Immediately I fell to the ground in pain! Errol had come down directly on my fresh wound.

Keven was seated and I fell just in front of him. He leaned over and peered into my grimacing face. "I think you just killed the King's Royal Witness, Errol. By the look on his face, I think these are his last moments."

I looked up at Errol, who stood frozen over me. There was a look of shock on his face.

Karlyle added, "If he really did that poorly in battle, Errol, there are better ways to discipline a man…"

Errol did not smile at his brother's jest. He bent down and looked at me closely, "Beorn, I am truly sorry. I had forgotten your wound. I did not mean to…"

I held up my hand to stop his apology. "Do not fret over me Errol. You did me a favor. I wanted to lie down…and so here I am."

Keven shook his head in mock seriousness, "You let Errol off the hook too easily. You have the right to strike him back if you wish."

"I fear that if I struck him, the only thing that will be hurting will be my hand. Just allow me to sit up and settle on the broken wall and I will be content."

Keven reached out and grabbed my good arm. "Come, friend, I will help you sit clear of your attacker."

Errol sat on a boulder mumbling words I could not hear. Keven grinned silently. Karlyle remained standing. I saw that he was looking off into the distance with one eyebrow raised...a look on his face like the first night at the Boar's Hind Inn...frowning with one eyebrow arched high. Errol saw Karlyle's alert manner also.

"What are you searching for?" Errol asked.

Karlyle continued scanning the night horizon as he answered, "Warlocks or Wizards are close by. More than one out there in the trees. I cannot tell exactly where or what the intent is. Ceikay should be here to help me..."

I looked from Karlyle to Errol and to Keven. They seemed to know what he was talking about.

Keven answered my unspoken question: "Karlyle is sensing strong thoughts from other Wizards close by. Unlike Ceikay, he cannot sense intent or emotion. He can only sense that someone trained in 'magic' is using mental probes to manipulate the physical surroundings. It could be either Wizards or Warlocks."

Karlyle spoke, "I should make a trek into the woods. There are persons out there that we must flush out."

Keven grinned slightly. "I will come with you so you will not feel lonely."

Karlyle did not argue. He drew his sword and jumped over the low, broken wall. Keven was on his feet instantly with two short swords in hand. Errol stood but did not move to join them. He called out to them before they left,

"Do not be too brave out there. If there is a threat, give signal and we shall come to you."

Keven and Karlyle quickly disappeared into the night. I started to question Errol on the wisdom of letting those two go alone, but at that moment a soldier walked up to me and handed me a two-headed battle-axe.

I looked up at him as he spoke. "Here is your weapon sir, it is cleaned and sharpened for next battle. You put a couple of good nicks in the blade...a couple of good kills if you take my meaning."

"Thank you," I responded without taking the weapon, "but that is not my axe. I carry a sword and daggers."

The soldier seemed not to take offense. Instead, he grinned big, "You sure used it like it was a favorite of yours."

Errol reached over and took the axe. "You should accept this, Beorn. Karlyle may be able to reduce the size so that you may carry it better." He then handed it to me. I nodded thanks to the soldier and he bowed and walked away.

Errol studied me for a moment, and then asked, "Your face holds a dark look, what troubles you?"

I answered, staring at the axe, "I am a Bard, which is what I want to be when this is over; not a warrior. I mean no insult to that soldier, but I feel no joy or glory in taking this from him."

Errol sat silent for a few moments longer, then answered me, "It is good that you feel this way. The day one begins to like the killing is the day the soul is lost."

I quickly changed our discussion. "Where is Elexele? Am I to hear his report?"

Errol grinned at my sudden change of topic. "Elexele is with the encampment on the other side of the clearing. He is conferring with his officers and will return to us as he finishes."

"Do we march tonight, or do we get a chance to sleep?"

"That has yet to be decided. Remember our King's orders, we are to find Duke Hastid and determine his plans."

Once again I changed the direction of my questioning. "I asked Karlyle earlier but he did not answer. He used the word 'explosion' to describe the walls flying apart on the Keep. What does he mean by explosion?"

Errol opened his mouth to speak, but shut it and just looked at me; finally he spoke. "How do you change from one discussion to another so easily?

"A curse, I guess. Do you know?"

"Do I know what?" Errol started to sound a bit exasperated.

"The 'explosion' that nearly killed us on top of the Keep: what was the cause?"

"Do you by chance or talent remember the smell of the air right after the explosion?"

I thought for a moment about the battle and the Keep. Finally I answered, "I am afraid, Errol, that I did not take notice of the smell of the air. What does the smell have to do with the cause?"

"Well Beorn, there was a smell. A smell I remember from a visit to an alchemist on the Southern Continent last year. He was working on developing a powder that would violently destroy objects, or 'explode' as he described it, when exposed to fire or spark. He showed me a sample of what he had made. It was of the color black, and had the texture of coarse sand. He carefully prepared a small amount with a mortar and pestle. He then dropped a tiny glowing ember from the fireplace. Immediately, a loud bang and bright flash erupted from the mortar. This alchemist would not reveal the ingredients, but boasted that his compound would change mankind's future. I fear that this compound or something similar was used to destroy the Keep."

"And almost killed us," I added.

Errol nodded, and then said to me, "By the look on your face I know you have more questions. Have at me."

I grinned and asked, "How did Keven, Karlyle, and Elexele happen to get to the Tell at the same time…just in time?"

"Keven has told me some; I will share what I know. When we separated earlier today, Karlyle and Keven circled back and quickly found the men following us. Using their talents, Keven and Karlyle evaded the point riders of the advancing troops. They waited for the main column to pass. The column turned out to be soldiers of the Hastid Realm. Leading the column was none other than Duke Hastid's trusted Senior Officer, our new friend and rescuer Elexele.

"Before Elexele or any of his men could react, Keven and Karlyle appeared at each flank of Elexele. With a crossbow primed and aimed at Elexele's heart, and a Katana sword at his throat, he had no choice but to honor our companions' request to stop.

"After a brief council, Elexele was able to convince Karlyle and Keven that no harm was intended toward our party. Point of fact, Elexele had not been aware of us being in the area. His troops were following renegade soldiers of Hastid's Realm. In truth, those soldiers that Elexele was tracking were the ones we ran from on the way to the Tell. You see, when the…"

At that moment, a guard standing watch yelled out, "Commander Elexele returns!"

Almost every man around the campfire jumped up to attention as a horse and rider bounded over the broken wall. I instinctively stood with them. Errol remained seated.

The rider was indeed Elexele. He looked impressive on his big war horse. In an instant he jumped to the ground. A page grabbed the reins of the horse and led it away. Elexele looked around and motioned for every one to sit.

At that point, Errol stood up. He walked over to Elexele. The two men faced off and eyed each other for a moment without speaking.

Errol broke the silence and spoke loud enough for everyone to hear, "Once again I give my thanks to you for saving our lives. My companions and I are in your dept."

He then bowed formally at the waist.

Elexele followed protocol and bowed in return as he replied, "If you feel that you are in my dept, and then I will not argue. But by the carnage I saw around the Keep, you did more than your share in aiding my cause. I am truly glad that we are on the same side."

Both men smiled and clasped forearms in mutual respect and alliance. Everyone else, including me gave a cheer to them both.

Elexele then turned and addressed me. "I see that the Royal Witness is also a fighter…a rare combination. I salute you."

To my regret and embarrassment, I did not respond with any words. I only nodded my head once. Elexele smiled and turned to a junior officer,

"I see no food or wine at this fire; summon the cooks to bring fare for our council."

The officer saluted and ran off.

Elexele now addressed the rest of us. "We will not ride tonight. Rest is what is needed, for horses as well as men. We will depart for the pass after sunrise tomorrow. For this meeting, we must share news of the south and the north. After everyone has been informed, then we will make further plans and adjustments before we gain our rest. 'Ere we begin, all Commanders are to send runners to your men to stand down for the night. Watches will be organized as war footing dictates."

At that, the officers summoned aides who were standing back from the fire ring. Shortly, every troop commander had sent messages. Errol and I had sat down and awaited Elexele's next move. He did not waste time,

"Errol, you represent our King Ballistor; I submit to you to bid that Beorn speak first on news from the south. After that, I will stand and deliver news of the north and the Hastid Realm."

Errol nodded, "As you direct, Elexele."

Errol motioned to me to stand. The formality of the two men moved me to stand tall and erect.

"Where would you like that I begin?" I asked Elexele.

"Start at the point of leaving Brentsad with the belongings of Ambassador Shelaylan."

I wanted to be as precise but brief as I could, but the moon had traveled the span of three hands outstretched before I had finished. No one interrupted or asked questions while I spoke. After I had completed my telling and sat down, men around the campfire talked in low but earnest tones with each other.

Errol nodded to me, signaling a report well given. Elexele stood and stared at me for a long stretch, making me a bit uncomfortable.

Finally he spoke: "Thank you for your report, Royal Witness. You have not yet eaten or taken drink. Sit and break your fast as I speak. My report will be brief, containing only the major events as I understand them.

He then turned and scanned the whole fire ring. "But I must ask first, where are the Wizard and Ranger?"

"Searching for answers and unwanted guests in the night." Errol answered simply.

Elexele nodded and did not press further. He turned to face the fire and began. "Tavegnor has been betrayed from within. It is obvious now that this has been long planned and well organized. I first should relate recent family politics in our realm, or I should say family discord.

"Duke Hastid and his son Rendulus are estranged. Rendulus was obsessed with the fact that until recently, the Hastid name bore the title 'King of Tavegnor.' It did not matter to Rendulus that the Parliament voted Ballistor King. Rendulus felt that his father should be King, and that he himself should be the next once his father passes to the nether world.

"Duke Hastid honors Parliamentary Procedure so does not desire to take back the Crown by force. Duke Hastid felt that if he should ever attempt the Crown, then that attempt would be through Parliamentary vote…accepted legal, peaceful means.

"His son was not that patient. He argued with his father to take the throne from Ballistor by force of arms. The Duke steadfastly refused to even consider his son's urgings. Their arguments became increasingly hostile.

"The Duke soon was receiving reports of clandestine meetings between his son and unknown individuals not of the Hastid Realm. But try as he might, Duke Hastid could not discover the secrecy. Finally, the Duke confronted his son directly. Rendulus denied any plans or actions to usurp power; he swore allegiance to his father and to Tavegnor.

"Hastid was not convinced, but hesitated to confine his son. Rendulus was popular with the legions that he commanded. His reputation as a military leader as well as a formidable warrior garnered a large and strong loyalty amongst the Hastid military.

"Eventually, Duke Hastid began to receive disturbing stories of intrigue within his own castle at Brentsad. He was told that various powerful persons were planning to invade his realm. One name given was that of King Ballistor himself. It was rumored that King Ballistor was threatened by the power of the Hastid Realm, and that Ballistor was actively working against Hastid. It was also feared that Ballistor spies had infiltrated Hastid's closest Advisors.

"As a consequence of these persistent rumors, Duke Hastid was no longer sure of his allies, and he came to accept that his son was not to be trusted any longer. When Ambassador Shelaylan fell to her death, and evidence was produced showing her treachery, the Duke knew his son was somehow involved. Hastid was not so sure of the King's involvement though."

Elexele cleared his throat and continued, "When Errol and his companions came to Brentsad shortly after Shelaylan's death, Duke Hastid was suspicious of everyone. Even the King's Envoys were considered a threat."

Elexele paused and bowed his head toward Errol.

Errol gave a curt nod in return.

Elexele began again, "I say and avow to the King's Envoys that Duke Hastid is not the traitor in the north. His son Rendulus is. Leading ten thousand troops, Rendulus marched to the Spar Fortress in the North Ballistor Realm. He passed the town of Darron peacefully, sending envoys to the Regents of Darron, reporting that Rendulus' march was only to replace the Hastid regiment stationed at the fortress. Since Tavegnor was still at peace, no one had reason to be alarmed. The troops passed unopposed through..."

The sound of fast-approaching hooves cut off Elexele's report. We turned to see a rider jump off a sweat-drenched and panting horse. The soldier stepped up to Elexele and smartly saluted,

"Commander, our scouts report that Duke Hastid is surrounded in Rogan Pass!"

Elexele nodded as if he already knew that fact. Silence from Elexele and everyone else prompted the messenger to continue. "Duke Hastid was coming south through Rogan Pass attempting to find his son. Opposing forces were waiting in strength just south of the pass. Judging by the colors and markings of their standards, these forces are from the southern continent. They had set a strong series of palisades in a line to block the Duke's forces. Duke Hastid is leading only light cavalry units for speed. He does not have heavy infantry or equipment to attack and dismantle the entrenched palisades. Those slower regiments were ordered to follow at speed, but they have not met up with the Duke and may not get to him at all."

"Why might they not get to the Duke?" Elexele asked sharply.

Without pause the messenger continued, "Rendulus' men have circled around from the north with his heavy cavalry and now hold position behind Duke Hastid's forces in the pass. Our outriders have not been in contact with the foot regiments to the north. Duke Hastid is effectively and securely cut off in both directions."

Elexele pressed, "Is he being attacked, or is he being only confined?"

"Sir, he is not being attacked at the moment, but my outriders from the Barron area report a force is marching to the southern entrance and should reach it tomorrow at sunset. This army is made up of southern invaders and Hastid troops under Rendulus' command. They are mainly heavy infantry supported by archers, numbering four thousand strong."

One of Elexele's officers spoke out, "Once they have made the pass, Duke Hastid will be in grave peril."

Errol stepped up to the messenger. "Are there any reports of Ballistor forces from the north west?"

The outrider looked to Elexele before answering. Elexele nodded his head.

The messenger turned back to Errol. "Sir, no Ballistor forces are close by. Last reports have them besieging Spar Fortress and the enemies at Barron."

"What is your name?" Elexele asked the rider.

"Sir, my name is Braccus from the Hastid village of Tinus on the coast."

"Do you have more to report?"

"No sir, I have given what I know."

"Thank you Braccus go then and rest. My men will tend to your horse. Tomorrow before sunrise you will be awakened and handed new reports. You will ride south and find King Ballistor. Everything he needs to know will be in those reports. You will also tell him what you have shared with us."

The messenger saluted smartly and left the fire ring.

Elexele looked around to his officers. "It is now decided for us. We must ride at speed to the pass to break the collar around our Duke. Get what little sleep that you can, because come the morning sun, we march to Rogan Pass."

With that said, Elexele's men saluted Elexele and turned into the night.

Errol and I were left with Elexele. He sat next to Errol and spoke, "We need your party's strength. I cannot command you. I only ask for your help."

Errol picked up a stick and threw it onto the fire as he answered, "Our King has ordered us to find Duke Hastid and determine his plans. Since you are planning a little reunion with him soon, it would serve our purpose to join you."

Elexele smiled and turned to me. "Are you of the same thought?"

"I only follow Errol's lead."

Elexele's smile now left. "Get what rest you can tonight. Tomorrow will be long and may be deadly."

With those words Elexele left us.

Errol and I looked in on Ceikay before we laid our bedrolls out. She appeared to be sleeping comfortably so we determined to do the same.

Sleep for me came swiftly. Again, it was all too brief.

I awoke with great protest. Once again someone was standing over me, telling my tired and aching body to rise and get on a horse. That person was Ceikay. I jumped up and forgot about my pains. I smiled and she smiled broadly back.

"Well good sir," she said, "If I am not allowed rest on this day, then I will make sure that you suffer with me."

She handed me the reins of my saddled horse. Someone had freshly brushed him. He looked fit, much better than myself. I crawled up into the saddle and followed Ceikay. We rode through busy commotion. Soldiers were quietly rushing to break camp. Most were already on horseback and forming into columns under their specific banners. Up ahead I could barely see Errol in the brightening morn. He was mounted and talking with Elexele. As we approached we were joined by Keven and Karlyle. Neither greeted us. Their faces were set as stone.

Ceikay's smile was grim. "I do not need to feel your thoughts; your faces show enough."

Keven answered, "We will confront more than soldiers before we get to Rogan Pass. Eagle has found me and has reported. Warlocks stand in our path and await our coming. They have killed two of Karlyle's guild."

I looked over at Karlyle who sat in silence. His eyes burned red.

Before I could have a chance at a question, we rode up to Errol and Elexele. Both men turned at our approach.

Without greeting, Keven began his narrative. He told of Eagle flying down out of the darkness and what was reported. "Warlocks have appeared east of Stannis. They ambushed wizards who were on their way north...possibly to find and report to Karlyle. The Warlocks burned the wizards into charred husks. Eagle was swooping low and was almost consumed by flying fire as the Warlocks tried to knock him out of the sky. Eagle had to flee over the horizon before turning back. He again found the Warlocks who did not see him return. Eagle reports that they broke off into two groups; one is now in our path to the pass, and the other is moving in to our left side."

Elexele looked to Karlyle. "Are they from Tavegnor or beyond?

Karlyle promptly answered, "Warlocks are not welcome in Tavegnor. Our guild does not specialize in warfare. Also, if my friends were caught off guard and killed, it was not by someone they would have known."

Elexele spoke again, "It may be that they were surprised and caught off guard because they thought they met with friends..."

Karlyle shook his head. "If your words mean traitors, there are none in the Wizard's Guild. Warlocks have come to our land from the southern continent. That I swear my life on."

"You seem sure of your friends. You could be in error this time Karlyle."

Karlyle turned in his saddle to face Elexele. "I know my

friends and I know my guild. I ask you not to continue those words, sir."

"I meant no offense. It is though, a natural and understandable thought from one who has not had the benefit of knowing your friends."

"Then I pray that you trust my words on it, Elexele."

Elexele answered by bowing formally to Karlyle.

As the talk drifted to tactics, Ceikay offered me a slice of dried jerked venison. I smiled my thanks. She then pointed to my saddle. Tied next to my leg was a large deerskin bag, filled, I surmised, with water. I had not realized until now how hungry and thirsty I was. I took a couple of big gnaws at the meat, and then washed it down with fresh, cool water. As I retied the deerskin bag to my saddle I felt a nudge to my arm.

Keven leaned into me. "Are you ready to embark?" He asked.

"I am ready to go."

"Are you ready to join Karlyle and myself to track the Warlocks?"

The expression on my face showed my confusion.

Karlyle now spoke. "We are planning to meet the Warlocks who are threatening our flank. Errol and Elexele feel that a formal witnessing of the contact with the Warlocks will be needed. You will ride with us, but will not attempt in any way to join in the fighting. Your two obligations are to witness and to live to report to our King. It is vital that Parliament is told that no Wizards of the Guild have turned on Tavegnor. If Keven and I should fall, you will leave us and attempt to rejoin Errol and Ceikay. Your talent and your steed should guide you back to them. You will not put yourself at risk to try to come to our aid."

I opened my mouth to speak but Keven held his hand, "Beorn we have no time for your questions, or objections, is that understood?"

I knew that I should quickly agree, so I simply nodded. I now noticed that Errol, Ceikay, and Elexele had already gone. They were leading the soldiers of Hastid north. I was alone with Karlyle and Keven as the columns passed us. Karlyle looked off into the woods to the west of us and gently spurred his horse to a trot.

Keven and I followed.

We were quickly surrounded by thick vegetation among the trees. The path we followed appeared to be rarely used by travelers. Our mounts slowed to a walk. Words were not spoken. Keven and Karlyle used signals to communicate. Some of their gestures I could understand. Both of my companions were intent on listening and observing for signs of danger. I followed closely behind, feeling helpless as well as worthless.

Every so often Keven and Karlyle would change lead on the path. Keven would constantly swing his head as he rode. His eyes seemed to pierce the foliage surrounding us. His head would cock to the side as he listened for any and all sound that would signal danger. Karlyle stared mostly ahead to the path. I knew he was "feeling" for signs of "magic." We ate in our saddles. We did not rush the horses, but kept up a steady pace until well after midday.

Keven was at the front when he finally pulled his reins in. Karlyle and I halted our horses close behind. Keven swung his head from side to side. He appeared to be inhaling deeply. He then turned to us and motioned to dismount. We stood silently under the heavy forest canopy. I looked back at the narrow path behind us. The forest was uncomfortably quiet and still. I turned to watch for Keven's directions. He had disappeared.

Karlyle was holding the reins of Keven's horse. I knew not to ask of Keven's actions. I stood quietly waiting. The thick underbrush made it impossible to see further than ten paces in any direction. The only sounds that came to me were the soft rustling of the wind-rocked branches overhead and the patient breathing of our horses. It was obvious that we were to wait for a signal or the return of Keven, so I determined to try to relax the nerves that were gnawing at my insides.

After a while I leaned against a gnarled black oak tree and started to think back on the start of my journey with the Four.

It seemed that I had just met them yesterday, then at the next thought I felt that I had been traveling with them for ages. At times, they seemed like strangers to me. Then again, they were my closest friends and companions. Through the years I have met and made more friends than I could number. Over those same years I have traveled from town to village and back again, never attempting to look up the friends that I had left behind.

One friend's name was Eccor. He was one of the jolliest persons to stroll down a lane. It had been at least a dozen spring seasons since I had left Arlingdol. I had promised to come back and see him and all the rest of our gaming companions. We both knew that I would probably not make a great effort to keep my word. Another...

My thoughts were interrupted by a strong urge to look over my left shoulder. It was one of those dreaded urges. The type I am sure everyone has gotten in their lifetime, an urge pushing an unknown fear to the fore...extinguishing all other thoughts. I gritted my teeth to help force the urge to pass me by.

But against my will, my head turned to the left. My eyes met another set of eyes, looking straight at me. The fear that engulfed me was not from the starkness of those cold, yellow eyes, but rather the nearness of them. If I were not frozen I could have taken one step and touched the head that held them.

That head was that of a wolf. It was the biggest wolf that I had ever beheld...and it was focused on me! The eyes were almost to the level of my own. The shoulders of this creature were the height of my ribs, which meant that if this thing wished to leap at me...

I could think of nothing to do. I was stupidly leaning against the tree not even daring to move my eyes to find Karlyle. My throat was suddenly very dry and my armpits were very damp. Then the silence that surrounded my world was broken by a soft whistle that came from behind the wolf. Immediately after, a second soft whistle sounded. This time it came from Karlyle. I now saw the brush behind the wolf's head move. I still did not. Then two hands parted the branches...followed by Keven. He walked up behind the massive wolf and placed a hand on its back haunches. The wolf finally moved. He turned from me to face Keven.

Keven then smiled broadly and said one word to the animal, "Friend."

The wolf turned his head back to me and after a pause, seemed to nod once. Well, nods were a mostly human trait, so I thought. But after knowing Keven and his animals, I have since come to see that we do not differ as much as commonly believed.

Still frozen in place on the tree, I looked from the wolf to Keven.

He grinned broadly back at me then spoke softly, "You can move now, but do not do so with any sign of threat. I do not control this beautiful creature totally."

Still not moving nor speaking, I gazed at Keven with an obvious look of confusion mixed with insult.

He must have understood my thoughts since he quickly held up his hand and spoke again, "I do not mean to say that you would make a threatening move to the wolf. I only wish to have you move slowly at first around him."

Before I could answer, Karlyle stepped close and leaned in to me. "Not even I would dare move in such a way as to agitate this massive beast. Even though he already knows me well, he has yet no love for any human...save one."

Karlyle motioned to Keven as he finished. As if he understood Karlyle's words, the wolf pushed his muzzle into Keven's ribcage, nearly knocking him down. Keven grinned even more broadly.

Suddenly the wolf stepped around Keven and disappeared into the brush.

Keven then stepped up to Karlyle and me and began to speak softly but swiftly, "We do not have much time. Bolarus has brought his packs down from the northwest forests. He has been looking for me since the first invaders struck at Barron. The invaders have killed some of his brothers for food and sport. Bolarus has agreed to aid our cause. He reports good news in that the Rangers of the north are fighting along with his brothers to push back the invaders. The pack Bolarus brings will help do the same for us at the pass. He also marks magic users. The Warlocks we are hunting are a short run to the southwest of here. They also confirm the earlier reports of Warlocks at Rogan Pass. These Warlocks have separated from the group that attacked Karlyle's guild brothers."

"How many left do I face to the southwest?"

Keven turned to answer Karlyle, "We face three, brother."

Karlyle shook his head. "It will not be 'We' who face them. You must take your wolves to the fight at Rogan. I duel the Warlocks alone."

"I disagree," Keven said. "You are too vulnerable alone. We must stay with you."

Karlyle held up his hand. "You must not lengthen the time it takes to get back to Errol and Ceikay. Since none of my Wizard companions are in this region, the wolves are the best ones to engage the other Warlocks waiting in the pass. Also, another reason you cannot deny is that if you two stay here, I cannot fight the Warlocks and still try to shield you from their concentrated attacks. I must concentrate solely on my attacks as well as my defense."

"Are you saying we would be in the way, brother?"

This time Karlyle grinned, "Yes, I am."

This time I spoke up to Karlyle, "We cannot leave you alone to face magic users trained in the art of war. They have already killed Wizards, who were together and not alone, I might add."

To my surprise, Keven answered, "They have not encountered Karlyle. He is the leader of his guild for good reason. He will not be taken by surprise."

Then he addressed Karlyle. "What is your plan? You seem to have given this great thought since this morning."

Karlyle shook his head. "Only now since you have gained us the wolves. Before, you and Beorn would have been more helpful here than with Errol and Elexele's men. Now that we know Warlocks are nearing Rogan Pass.

Keven finished for him, "Bolarus really fights for me and will lead his pack into battle alongside me...and me alone. He will not go forth without me to fight the Warlocks to the northeast. Your point is correct concerning the wolves. Therefore, I must leave you, but only after you agree to have some of Bolarus' brothers at your side."

Karlyle considered Keven's offer, then finally nodded.

"...and I can stay with you also."

They both looked at me. Karlyle answered, "Again, I cannot divide my attention between battle and protecting you."

"Have I not proven that I can fight? I do not expect you, nor ask you to protect me," I countered.

Have you not remembered, Bard, that you are the official Witness for the King? You must survive to report all that you have seen and heard."

I shook my head at Karlyle's words. "Was it not everyone's thoughts this morn before breaking camp that I go with you and witness the battle with the Warlocks?"

Keven now spoke. "I commend you on your courage, but you are more valuable as a Witness than as a fighter, regardless of what you have done for us so far. Since we now know that Warlocks have separated, you may still have the opportunity to meet Warlocks at the pass; there you can witness. Have you forgotten why our King has made you a central figure at this time? You are to report back to the Council of Dukes so that the whole country of Tavegnor can record and learn for future protection and defense. It is not your skill with a sword that is valuable; it is your memory…or have you forgotten?"

Twice he used the word forgotten. I stung at his words. "I will do as I am told."

Keven smiled and slapped me on the back. "I do not say these words to insult you, but war is not about what individuals want. It is about trying to survive by using your skills and resources to best advantage. Your skill will redeem itself after we stop this invasion."

I understood well enough to nod my head in agreement, but I loathed the idea that we had to leave Karlyle behind.

Karlyle turned back toward the path ahead. "Talk is over. We have much to attend to."

As Karlyle stepped out to leave us, Keven grabbed him and spun him around. Keven stuck his finger right in his brother's face as he spoke, "Do not make me come back to search for you."

Karlyle grinned and said nothing, then turned and was gone.

Keven turned back to me. "Are you two ready for Rogan Pass?"

I turned and found that I was standing next to the wolf Bolarus.

To **Rogan Pass**

I quietly stepped away from Bolarus but kept one eye on him as I mounted my horse, which did not seem to be at all concerned about the giant wolf. I looked over to Keven who was now mounted as well. With a slight nod he motioned for us to ride from the path and toward the right. I could not see how we would make any swift progress shifting right to left through the thick underbrush. Finally, we came upon a path leading north. Keven entered the path and I followed. Bolarus was not to be seen. I looked around and behind several times but did not get a glimpse of him. Keven prodded his horse to a trot. I followed his lead. Soon after, we came upon a crossing by another, bigger path. This path was large enough to allow wagons to travel, but only one direction at a time. If another were to come from the other direction, one would have to pull off to the brush to allow the other to pass. Keven now increased the gait to a relaxed gallop.

I noticed for the first time movement that matched our own. What I saw were quick flashes of reds and browns skipping through the brush and trees off to the sides of the road. I was about to call out to Keven when I realized what I was seeing, Bolarus' wolves. They were pacing us through the woods. They seemed to have no difficulty dodging the underbrush. Compared to the noise of the horses' galloping hooves on the path, the wolves made only soft whispering sounds, like the rustling of wind-tossed leaves skipping on the ground. I was amazed that I did not hear even the breaking of small twigs as they ran.

Time ran slowly as we ran swiftly. I thought back on the traveling we had done in the last few days and nights. Every direction from the Boar's Hind Inn was our path. Sometimes it seemed so disordered and spur of the moment. Then again I thought philosophically; what was war except chaotic and reactionary?

I knew that the decisions of my companions made sense as they were made, but I could not feel but torn from one crisis to another. As we rode into the evening, I accepted the obvious: by natural law, or the gods' whims…war was uncontrollable in the hands of men.

Finally I scolded myself for dwelling on things I could not control. I shook my head to clear it…

Then I realized that my horse had stopped. Ahead of me, Keven was on foot looking off to our right. He was standing at a break in the trees on the edge of a rise. Past this rise and below us stretched a bowl-shaped valley. I dismounted and approached the edge.

The vista before me was beautiful and inviting. Rich variations of green dominated the landscape. Low rolling hills were in the distance on all sides. Off to my left I could see a break in the hills as they angled past each other. Flowing from this separation was a narrow riverlet gently meandering toward the hill we were standing on. About a league from us the stream turned south to our right and disappeared through another split in the hills. The sun was just beginning to scrape the topmost branches of the trees behind us, causing the shadows at our feet to reach across the valley to the far side. Already, the blanket of night had covered nearly a league of the valley floor. Soon all of the greens would be replaced by the grays of evening.

I spoke for the first time since the start of our ride, "This is why I journey through my life; to see the various rich hues that our gods have painted o'er the land."

Without turning from the vista, Keven answered with a long sigh, "Very poetic, Bard. Soon this dale will be colored in red."

I turned to him but before I could ask, he answered me, "You see Beorn, this river flows from Rogan Pass. That is where the Duke is entrenched. It is not far. All around us men are preparing to do battle. They are hidden in the woods, waiting for orders from their leaders to strike. The leaders are waiting for more intelligence and more reinforcements, but for all sides their wait is short. I fear that tomorrow all will know sorrow."

"But if we are victorious…"

Keven still faced the valley. "It does not matter who the God of war favors, both sides will feel the embrace of his brother."

"His brother?" I asked.

Keven smiled grimly, "Death."

I said nothing more. The sun swiftly fell below the trees and the shadows swallowed the remaining rays of light. Just before night fell onto us completely, a great gray owl swooped silently down and alit on Keven's outstretched arm. The size of this newcomer amazed and startled me, but the wolves surrounding me did not react. The size of the owl was nearly half the height of Keven, yet Keven seemed to have no trouble holding the huge bird on his arm.

I could see that the two were communicating to each other. The owl's head was bobbing as deep hoots and caws spilled from his beak. Keven listened as he scanned the darkening floor below. Sometimes Keven would utter a short hoot in response. I stared, fascinated by the exchange.

Finally, both nodded their heads and the owl suddenly jumped off the arm and swooped down into the valley and disappeared from sight. Keven then turned to the wolf Bolarus. Both stood silently looking at each other. Shortly after, Bolarus turned toward the trees behind us and was away. His companions followed. Keven and I were now alone on our bluff.

We both stood looking down toward the valley. My thoughts somehow left the realm of war and bloodshed and focused on my companion. I turned to Keven.

"I know a little of your siblings' talents, but as for yourself, how do you know to talk to animals? I mean, how…why did you pick this talent?"

Keven stood silent for several moments, and then took a deep breath before speaking. "Why or how, I do not know exactly. I can better answer 'when.' My father tells me that I began to communicate with the domestic animals at the same time that I began to attempt to verbally communicate with other humans. Animals responded to me before I could talk or walk."

Keven turned to me as my face revealed puzzlement.

"You see, as a baby not able to walk, and still struggling to crawl, I would attempt to make my way to an object on the floor. Somehow, our house dog would sense my desire and fetch the thing for me. This happened time and time again with all varieties of animals around our home.

"I even could understand and translate to the adults the words of my twin brother Karlyle when he spoke the infantile language."

Once again my expression prompted Keven to explain. "You see, all human babies speak a coherent language before learning "adult" words. The cute babble that babies speak is actually an intelligent structuring of sounds that make complete sense if we, as adults were to take it upon ourselves to study and to learn. Babies, believe it or not, make up their own, personal language that makes perfect sense structurally and meaningfully. Left alone from the language restructuring from their parents or guardians, but somehow still protected and provided for growing up, human babies would retain their own personalized language.

"Believe it when I tell you this, this infantile human language is similar to that of all the other animals that share this land with us. What separates us from the so-called lower animals is language. Our capacity for advanced language structure and sophistication has propelled mankind far beyond the other creatures of our world."

Keven paused, looked at me and then shook his head as he spoke again. "When I say we have progressed far beyond the other animals, I do not want you to in any way assume that I mean to include the word 'better'…"

I knew full well Keven's meaning. I did not argue the matter.

After a few more moments I pressed again, "So you were born with your talent and…"

"No, Beorn, I did not say that. I cannot tell if I was born with it, or if I had consciously decided at a very young age to pursue it. It is something that I had, and thought everyone had, as I began my self-awareness and understanding. It was at the age of three that I began to understand that humans and animals were different. I remember a specific moment when I began to realize a divide."

Keven stopped speaking and looked down at the ground.

I felt that he would rather not continue so I prompted, "I fear that you have started a story with me, Keven. You should fear my many questions if you do not complete it."

He shook his head but smiled and spoke again after a pause. "I remember being in the barn with my father. He allowed my older brother Errol to bring me out. My father led a goat from the pen and brought it over to a short table. He then tied the goat to the red-stained table and proceeded to pick up what I now know as a two-headed axe. My father sat on a stool and began to rub a flat stone across the edge. My brother told me that the stone sharpened the edge. I did not pay much heed to my brother because at this time the goat was braying loudly and struggling against the rope. The goat was pleading with my father to not continue. I could see that the goat was frantic and wanted to be away from our barn. My father did not listen to the frightened animal. He only continued to sharpen the axe. The goat began to scream out that she did not want to be touched by the 'life ender.' Being three and my first time in the barn, I did not understand why the goat was so frightened. My father did not listen to the goat and ignored the protests.

"Then I saw my father put down the stone and stand. He reached for the goat who now violently jerked at the restraining rope. My father grabbed the goat's head, pressed it onto the red-stained table, and like lightning, brought the axe down onto the goat's neck…"

After several moments of quiet, Keven spoke again. "Of course I know now that the goat was killed for food. Its milk had dried up so it was time for father to bring its meat to our table. I was three of course, I did not understand what was happening. What was going through my little brain in that barn was the puzzlement of why my father did not listen to the goat's pleas not to be killed. I stood there wondering why my father was so cruel. Then I began to think that maybe, maybe my father was not cruel, but maybe he just could not understand what the goat was saying!"

You see, Beorn, trying to convince myself that my father was not a monster forced me to think that not everyone could understand the animals the way I could. From that day on I began to see and understand the differences."

I wanted to ask more, but did not. We both stood looking into the blackness before us.

It was Keven who broke our silence. "We should try to sleep; tomorrow we surely will be busy."

All the while we had been talking, we had been settling our horses down for the night. They were tethered to a tree and were busy eating some oats that Keven had given them. We had taken off our gear and saddles, and the horses looked as though they were ready for sleep.

We unrolled our blankets and laid them on the rocky ledge. The night air was warm and still, but I felt chilled. I knew that a fire was not for us this night, but I dearly wished for one.

As we sat on our blanket Keven somehow knew my want as he spoke again, "You are tired and you are fearful of what comes with the morning sun. It is natural that your bones feel the cold."

He was right. The cold did come from deep within me and not from the night air...

Despite my exhaustion, questions began to push their way into my thoughts. I opened my mouth to give them voice. "Keven how is it that you and your siblings know so much about battle and killing? You act and talk as if you have been through this all before. In my lifetime this is the first such war on our land, and I am much older than you."

In the dim moonlight I could see Keven's smile come back as he answered, "Yes, this is the first such war on the soil of Tavegnor for many years, but we have not spent all of our young lives on this island as you have. In the name of our King, we have assisted allies in other lands in their time of need."

His smile broadened as he added, "Do you not remember Errol's discomfort on the water some days ago? That was not new to him or to us. We have crossed the great waters....let me recount...as...yes, four times."

He paused briefly, and then added, "When this battle is won, we will most likely be sent again."

I began to ask but Keven held his hand close to my face so that I could see it clearly.

"Are you signaling me to end my questions?" I asked.

"We are being joined by another messenger."

I looked about me but could not see any new arrival. The dark night surrounding us masked Keven's mysterious visitor. I listened but did not hear any noises accept the new, constant creaking of far-off cicadas. The dark form of Keven had not moved. He seemed to be looking up at the shadowy branches of the trees. I waited in silence.

Finally, Keven turned to me. "There are men moving toward us from the north. My friends tell me that these men are strangers to this land. Their dress is strange to them. That tells me that they are part of the invading forces. We will meet with them and try to dissuade them from going any further..."

"How far away?"

Keven pointed to our left and down into a narrow dell. "They are traveling in the blind night. The moon is not enough to expose them. If you can see the small valley I am pointing to, that is their route."

I peered down from our rocks. The dell looked like a dim fold in the blackness.

"I assume we are going to attack them."

"Yes, Beorn, we are going to attack them; but not before close to morn. They are still several leagues distant."

Then he added, "It would be wise if you gained some sleep before then."

My body sagged in agreement, but my thoughts would not let me rest.

"Keven, I fear that sleep is far off for me. My many thoughts prevent it. If you can sleep and wish to, I will stand watch for us."

I could still clearly see Keven's smile as he turned to me. "We are surrounded by our four-legged friends. We are well guarded. You must relax and try to rest. We are in a war, and in its battles an exhausted man is a danger to all but his enemy, whether he be a soldier...or Witness."

He then opened his blanket out onto the flat rock. I did the same and lay down. I thought of the Boar's Hind Inn. Their wooden beds now seemed a far distant luxury. My words a moment ago were wrong; I quickly fell asleep and dreamt that I was lying in one of those beds.

I awoke to Keven's nudge and voice. "Beorn, it is time to fill our stomachs. We will have few, if any, opportunities to eat again as this day lengthens."

The night still surrounded us. I wondered at how long I had slept. The moon was not in the sky. The sun had not yet begun to show itself.

Keven guessed my thoughts. "We have just enough time to eat our jerky and bread before the sun begins to push his rays through the trees. Before the light touches the hills across the valley we will be on our way."

Laid out before me was a broken chunk of bread along with several large slices of dried meat. Keven handed me a gourd shell filled with water. I silently nodded my thanks. As I ate in the dark I suddenly realized how well I could actually see. There was a soft glow of light around our little camp.

I looked about me and found the source. Above and behind me was a large ball of soft light suspended from a branch in a tree. I slowly stood and peered at it. I did not know what it was. It seemed to be solid, but there were hundreds of small dark specks that seemed to move, or crawl around on its surface. It was as large as a man's head. I took a step toward it and suddenly it expanded and immediately disintegrated into countless small bits of light! They hovered for a brief moment and then all swooped away and disappeared into the forest!

Keven grinned as I stood with wide eyes and gaping mouth. "Those are glow flies. I have been working on that for a long while now, and have it almost to the point where the effect might be useful."

My sleep had not refreshed me. I was too tired to ask questions, I sat back down and ate my morning meal.

Shortly after, we set off down a narrow path that looked to take us into the valley below. Keven had released the horses before I had risen. He had said that we would not be able to use them on the narrow path ahead of us. Also, the fight we soon would be in would not be a place where a horse would benefit us.

Keven silently led the way. As we traveled I took notice of the brightening sky and the dimming of the shadows in the trees around us. After we had walked about a league the path split into a fork. The right trail continued down into the valley. The left turned back up toward a rocky ridge that seemed to run parallel along the small dale that our enemy was said to be coming from. We took the left trail.

Suddenly Keven stopped and held up his arm. A large black raven swooped down from above and alit on Keven's wrist. Once again I could see that the two were communicating. I stood and waited. Just as suddenly as the raven appeared, he stretched his wings and flew off into the trees.

Keven turned back to me, "We have word of Karlyle. He is on his way to us. You must return to the ledge we slept on this last night. He is being taken there by some of Bolarus' brothers."

"Is he all right?" I asked.

"I am told that he has suffered much, but he is walking without aid."

"What of the Warlocks?"

Keven gave a small smile as he answered, "They were not as fortunate as my brother."

"What of the Warlocks that we are looking for?"

Keven knew my question's meaning. "My friends tell me that there are only men ahead of us on this path. You will not witness Warlocks in this meeting."

Keven's words greatly lifted my spirits both at Karlye's

condition and my not having to encounter Warlocks. But I now became nervous thinking that I was expected to give aid to any major wounds.

I let my concerns be known. "Keven, if Karlyle needs care, I have little experience with wounds."

"I said that Karlyle is in no mortal danger and has no major wounds. You will mainly watch over him as he sleeps to regain his strength. When he awakens, he will need food."

"What about you and the men in the dale?"

"Please do not be insulted when I say this. You would not be the difference between losing and winning this battle. As a Witness, how much detail would you like to remember when wolves begin to rip men's throats and bowels out? When this is over, even those left standing will be covered in blood and flesh not of their own."

I began to speak but he held up his hand, "You will be of better use with Karlyle. He must be able to sleep as soon as he gets to the ledge. He will want to be in the battle if he sees one in the making. If you are there when he arrives, you can convince him that we do not need him in the dale. Get him to stay where he is until he regains useful strength again. We will need him to be ready for the push into the pass."

I could not argue with Keven.

Keven nodded and turned quickly down the path.

I found myself alone for the first time in days. I realized that no wolf stayed with me. Quickly my feet began their return to the last night's rest. My strides were quick and my neck was quicker as I kept looking left and right back over my shoulder. I knew that the wolves were on our side, but I could not remove the thought of a rogue wolf jumping and tearing at the back of my neck.

I was sorely tired but willed my muscles to work harder. My thoughts turned from the wolves to the meeting with Karlyle. Would he want to answer a few of my questions before he succumbs to sleep?

Eventually I was standing back on the ledge where we had slept the night before. No one was in sight. I thought of the horses we had released earlier. I wished that they had stayed at the clearing. I looked into the woods for a short distance, but the horses were gone. I sat down on the ledge and waited for Karlyle.

Sleep overtook me.

Some time later I awoke in a panic. My first thought was surprise that I had been sleeping. I knew right away where I was and why I was here on the ledge overlooking the valley. A sudden noise had wakened me, what it was I did not know. The air was still and quiet around me as I stood up. Looking onto the valley gave me no clues. My eyes scanned back and forth, I was looking for signs of battle. No flags or standards were to be seen below. I turned to the left down the path searching for any sign of Keven returning. No sights or sounds came from that direction.

Not finding answers below, I turned from the ledge. As I stepped toward the tree line my eyes caught sight of a prone body lying at the foot of a large oak. My body froze in mid-step as my eyes darted back and forth frantically peering into the forest beyond. Why I searched and what I was looking for was not clear, but fear does not need logic or reason. It was only after scanning the woods that I looked back at the figure and it was only then that I realized that it must be Karlyle.

Still I did not move. I studied the prone figure trying to find a familiar sign that would mark him. All that was visible were two dirty boots sticking out from under a dark grey blanket or long cape. The cape looked to be fire scorched. The head was covered by the cape as were the arms. I realized that peering from a distance was not answering my doubts.

I stepped over to the figure. Kneeling down close I could now see that the body under the cloak was breathing. The depth and rhythm were deep and easy. With the relaxed breathing, the lack of visible blood stains, and the natural positioning of the limbs, I guessed that this person was not injured. The size of the boots and hidden body were obviously of a grown man. The boots were not those worn by Karlyle since I first saw him enter the Boar's Hind Inn many days ago. I had not seen him wear any different sets of boots since. The cloak was not his either. Still, the size of the body and the sound and rhythm of the breathing convinced me that

325

I had met once again with the Wizard Karlyle.

Making no attempt to wake him I turned and walked again to the edge of the valley. There was still no sign of human activity. The sun and shadows told me that it was well past noon meal. I felt no wish to eat. My throat did want water though, so I drank deeply from my skin bag.

I then returned to the spot I was before and sat down. This time I knew that I would not sleep. I puzzled at why I had slept earlier. It was still morn when I sat down. My thoughts soon went to puzzling over the way time and events seem to get thrown around in my head. Since this invasion started in Tavegnor my companions and I have been rushing from place and crisis without good rest. Plans and directions had been changed and changed again...

With little energy and no desire to move, I sat and watched the shadows of the trees crawl toward me. Soon they had climbed over my legs and I marveled on how the shadows quicken as they grow longer. Out of the corner of my eyesight I could see something was different. I quickly turned to look at the far oak and the sleeping figure. The figure was now sitting up with his back to the tree. His head was resting down on his chest, but it was clearly Karlyle. I jumped up but stood motionless, not knowing if I should approach.

After a long pause Karlyle lifted his head and spoke, "It is a fair meeting, friend. Do you have water that I may drink?"

In a moment I was at his side. He drank long and deeply. Finally he put up his hand to push the bag away.

As he drank I had studied his condition. There were streaks of dried blood on his skin and clothing. Some parts of his dirt-covered clothing were torn and burnt. I saw no wounds that would claim the blood as his own. As I took the water bag away I pulled the cloak off the rest of his lap and legs. The leggings were not the ones he had worn when I saw him last.

I was about to begin asking questions of his encounter with the Warlocks when Karlyle spoke again: "Where is Keven, and have you heard from the others?"

"Keven is with his wolves in the north valley. They have gone to meet with a number of invaders coming down a narrow dale. He was meaning to stop them before they go any further. As for your other siblings, we have not seen them."

Unbidden, Karlyle then answered several of my unasked questions. "I was led here by two of his wolves. They guided me to this opening and pulled me down onto the ground. I knew that they were trying to get me to stay here. I did not argue. When I lay down by this oak they must have felt that they were released from protecting me. They both quickly ran past you and down onto the path. I wondered if battle had been joined yet. I was too tired to try to follow. I put my head down to the rock and thought no more."

At Karlyle's words I marveled at how I did not awaken at their arrival. I felt shamed that I was not alert to aid Karlyle if he had indeed been wounded. I had heard said in times past about soldiering, "you can tell a good soldier by the way he stands his watch."

Putting those thoughts away I offered jerky to Karlyle. He shook his head in answer and stood up. He stretched his limbs and clenched his fists several times. Finally he spoke, "It is time you lead me to Keven, he may want our help if he is not already finished in the dale."

Karlyle looked and spoke as if he would brook no objections. Besides, I wanted to try again to be useful. Without a word I turned and began walking back down the path and into the valley. I had questions still, the Warlocks, the clothing, and more. Those would have to wait.

As we walked down the path I could clearly see that Karlyle was still tired and worn. His breathing became labored as if he were running; his feet stumbled over low rocks or over nothing at all. I tried to stop and let him rest several times, but he impatiently waved me on to continue.

Soon we were at the fork and I turned left toward the dale. Suddenly my way was blocked by two snarling wolves. They stood shoulder to shoulder on the path before me, their lips pressed back and teeth bared. A low growl escaped from one of them. I stood stock still when Karlyle suddenly collided into my back, pushing me forward toward the big animals. I stumbled two steps before I could catch balance again. The wolves both growled and stepped toward me!

In an instant I was being flung back off my feet and passing Karlyle. My eyes never left the wolves and as I was in the air I saw what was happening. Karlyle's arm was rushing past my neck and I could see that he had grabbed me from my back and was hurling me behind him and away from the wolves. He now stood between me and the two snarling beasts. Karlyle held his arm out to them and growled!

"You know me!" He yelled, "You know what I can do with my hands! You will not harm me or my friend!"

The two wolves stopped advancing. Their teeth though were still bared. It now seemed that everything became quiet and still. No man and no beast moved for several moments. Then, a whistle came from the path behind the wolves. Instantly they stepped back and to the side. Keven walked up between them toward us. He was covered from head top to boots in red and dirt. He did not smile in greeting. He stopped in front of Karlyle who had put his arm down by this time.

"I see that the Warlocks have given you quite a challenge," Keven said as he studied Karlyle's appearance.

"I see that you and your wolves have also been busy," Karlyle calmly replied.

Then they both stepped forward and embraced in grateful relief. I stayed sitting on the ground, not wanting to gain the attention of any wolves that might be surrounding us.

Keven and Karlyle broke off their greeting and Keven spoke, "The men behind me will not be meeting their comrades in the battle to come. The failing light of day says that we should find and set camp for the night."

Karlyle looked back over his shoulder. "I do not think it wise to travel deeper into the valley tonight. Do you know of a secure camp besides the ledge behind us?"

Keven shook his head as he answered, "The ledge is probably the only place we can consider for tonight. We should return there."

Finally I found words for my mouth. "Return to the ledge? Can there not be any other place closer? What about Errol and Ceikay? Should we not try to return to them tonight?"

Keven smiled. "It is good to see you too, Beorn. If you wish to search the woods around for a suitable camp…"

Karlyle smiled also and added, "We will gladly await your discoveries of a suitable place to lay our heads. We will be on the ledge awaiting your signal."

I stood up and looked around me. The light was fading as the darkness was swallowing the trees.

I again mentioned Errol and Ceikay. "If the others are in battle we should endeavor to join them."

Karlyle answered, "I tell you now that fighting has not started below us. When battle begins in the valley we will surely hear it. As for fighting tonight, my woodland friends are not giving me any signs of imminent conflict."

I shook my head and shrugged my shoulders in resignation, "We should make it back before total nightfall…"

Karlyle and Keven grinned as they walked past me. We were to spend the night again on the rocky ledge overlooking the valley.

Before we returned to the ledge, Keven led us off the trail about fifty paces through an opening in the trees. Before us ran a little stream that disappeared down through the brush toward the valley floor. No words were spoken nor needed as the three of us cleansed ourselves of dirt, soot and blood. I was amazed and grateful at how I felt after.

The rest of the trek up the path and to the ledge was short and uneventful. Once at the clearing I had an urge to ask questions of both of my companions. Karlyle's fight with the Warlocks, and Keven's battle alongside the wolves needed revealing.

The urge to sleep was stronger though. I ate nothing as I lay on my blanket.

I was not surprised when a hand shook me awake. My eyes opened to the sight of Karlyle peering into my face. He did not have to speak. I nodded and sat up. Only the first paling of the night sky told me that the sun was beginning to rise. Keven was not to be seen. I did not question where he was. I reasoned that he was already communicating with one of his animal scouts in the area.

Karlyle left me as I sat up. He went to the lip of the ledge and with his back to me spoke, "We leave as soon as Keven returns. Get your fill of food and water, for we will take little rest along the way."

Again nodding my head and saying nothing I quickly did as I was told. I rolled up my bedding and stood quietly.

Karlyle's bedding was already stowed and I assumed that he had already eaten. He stood looking out over the valley.

Finally he spoke again, "Beorn, you are not saying much."

I walked over to stand next to him before I answered, "I have questions enough. Do you have time to sit for a day and answer them for me?"

Karlyle laughed and slapped me on the shoulder. "Bard, you have a point on me there. I promise I will make the time for your questions when this battle is finished. In truth, I am sure King Ballistor will require that I reveal all details to you sooner rather than later. What I can say for..."

Karlyle's words were cut short by the appearance of Keven on the path below. He did not speak but motioned with his arm for us to join him. Karlyle and I quickly grabbed our packs and slung them over our shoulders. Karlyle motioned for me to go ahead. As I stepped from the ledge onto the path, Keven turned and began walking at a brisk pace down toward the valley. I heard the footfalls of Karlyle behind. I felt a strange excitement flow through me, even though I knew that we would soon be trying to kill other men as they were doing their best to kill us.

We said nothing as the sun chased away the darkness. We said nothing as the sun's rays began to pierce the branches of the trees and shoot past us to light up the valley floor. We said nothing as the sun climbed above the treetops looking down at us. We said nothing and kept walking.

We had long since passed the fork of the day before, and we still did not stop. My steps stayed in pace with Keven ahead of me, but my lungs were hurting. I felt glad at least that we were going downhill instead of up, but soon the path leveled and I knew that we were now at the floor of the valley.

Still we did not stop. I began to look back at Karlyle to see if he was laboring as I was. He looked to be breathing through his nose. He was looking from side to side and sometimes up as he walked. His eyebrow was arched. I knew that he was scanning for danger or signs of it. Karlyle did not appear to be the worse for the trek so far.

Keven showed no signs of slowing. He also scanned ahead and to the sides as he walked. I let the two do their work as I only concentrated on keeping pace.

Suddenly, to my surprise and great relief Keven stopped. I stood and waited.

Keven motioned for us to stay quiet as he stepped off the path and into the trees to our right. Karlyle quietly came up to me and took my bedroll from my shoulders. I began to speak but he quickly held up his finger to my face and then pressed the finger back to his lips. My mouth snapped shut.

It was then that I realized how quiet the forest was around us. Karlyle scanned the sky with his eyes. He cocked his head to the side as if he were listening for the slightest noise. He closed his eyes and turned slowly around until his face was toward me again. He then opened his eyes and looked at me.

"Beorn..." he whispered, "...when Keven returns he may want us to quicken our pace. That is why I take your pack from your shoulders. You must at all costs keep up with us."

Feeling the hair on my neck begin to rise, I managed a quiet question, "Is someone going to find us?"

Karlyle sighed as he answered simply, "I am afraid we have already been discovered."

Suddenly Keven appeared from the trees and stepped up to us. The look on his face confirmed Karlyle's words.

Keven spoke, "We have men on our left and to the rear of us. We are being tracked. Our presence is known. The animals are fleeing the woods around us. The wolves have not joined us as planned. Something or someone has my wolves occupied. I am not able to stop the flight of any animal long enough to gather further information. I can only surmise one cause…"

Keven then looked at Karlyle.

Karlyle nodded at the prompt and answered. "Warlocks are tracking us. I have felt something for the last league but was not sure until now. I feel their probes piercing the forest. Right now they have only a general idea of our location, but there are more than one, so they will soon be able to get a focus on us."

Keven nodded and pointed at the path ahead of us, "The animals are leaving ahead of us. I fear that the enemy to our left has angle on us and will soon be on the path before we can pass them. We must go into the woods and travel as speed will allow. I am trying to gather such allies that will not flinch from the Warlocks. Let us pray that we get help along the way."

It was my turn to speak, "But your wolves have disappeared…"

Keven quickly answered, "They are not really my wolves; they are their own masters. I do not order them. They choose their allies and their battles. If they feel that they have had their revenge in the dale, then Bolarus will take them away from any more human battles."

Then Keven grinned and added, "Besides, there are others who are not afraid of Warlocks. I will do my best to persuade them to join us."

Keven turned and stepped from the path into the forest. Karlyle and I followed.

The pace quickened and I was glad that Karlyle had taken my pack. I determined not to fall behind. Fear now gave me the energy to keep pace.

It was not long before Karlyle yelled over me to Keven, "It is not necessary to remain quiet any longer! It is now that we quicken our pace! We are known and are being actively chased! I sense at least three Warlocks!"

At these words, Keven's strides lengthened. We matched his speed. Now the branches were going by us too fast to completely brush out of the way. I tried to fend them off with my hands and arms as we now ran, but I was beginning to get a little bloodied by the little jabs and sticks. I did not feel any pain, but was surprised that I was irritated at being swatted by branches as was rushed by.

We made no attempt to remain quiet now. As we ran on I wondered at our distance from Errol and Ceikay.

Suddenly I saw an object spring from the trees ahead and to the left of Keven! The thing leapt from the woods and flew into the way in front of us almost crashing into Keven, who had to leap to the side to avoid being knocked down! The first things I recognized were the wide panicked eyes and flared nostrils of a stag deer. The creature stood on the path before us and stared for only a moment at us. Since our path was blocked, we stood and stared back. Then suddenly the animal lurched to the right and leapt back into the woods.

Keven turned to us. "That was a Man Hunter's arrow in its flank! I fear that they are in league with the Warlocks to cut us off! They are driving the animals before them hoping to slow us down!"

Without another word he was running and we were following. As we ran I found myself focusing on the sound of the desperate gasp of my breath and of the branches as we pushed past. I wondered at how long I would be able to flee.

My thoughts were interrupted by Karlyle as he yelled out, "They are gaining ground on us! We must hurry more!"

I did not have energy to spare but I yelled out, "How do they gain? How can they be so much faster?!"

To my dismay, Karlyle answered as he ran, "I do not know!"

Keven then yelled back as he ran, "Man hunters train their horses for forest chases! They have leather armor over their heads and necks and around their flanks! The horses are the best at charging through trees and thickets to get to their prey! The Man Hunters simply put their heads down and let their horse crash through the woods!"

My lungs were screaming for relief. We ran and I did not care about branches swiping at my face and arms. I only knew that I had to stay close to Keven's back. I quickly looked back at Karlyle. He nodded ahead as if to encourage me to continue forward..

Suddenly my feet and legs left the ground as something heavy hit my shoulders and back! I heard Karlyle yell out but did not understand the words. As I was in the air my ears were taking in the sound and roar of ocean waves crashing into rocks in a typhoon. My face hit the ground as the weight that hit me drove me into the dirt. I found myself on the ground and wondered why.

My thoughts were of utter confusion and chaos. Then I realized that the object that had thrown me down was Karlyle! He quickly rolled off me and stood with his arms outstretched facing behind us. Then I heard another wave approach us. I looked through Karlyle's legs and saw a huge round shimmering orange-yellow ball racing toward us through the trees. Karlyle stood facing it and then suddenly dipped his arms to the side and then brought them up again. As his arms came up, so did the earth before him. The mass of dirt and rocks before us came in direct path of the approaching ball of flame. I saw the wall of dirt fly up and then swallow up the fiery orb!

I heard another wave come at us as I saw another fireball appear from the trees. This time Karlyle threw his left arm to his side and a tree before us snapped to the left and into the path of the fireball. The fireball struck the tree and disintegrated into uncountable sparks and blinding flashes.

"Get on your feet!"

I jumped at Karyle's words and spun around to run. I saw Keven was standing over three bodies and firing arrows from his bow. I froze as I stood looking at the three fallen men. I knew that they were three of the same group of Man hunters that I had seen before. I then heard the death scream of a man in the direction of the woods in which Keven was launching his arrows.

I turned back to Karlyle just as his arms pushed forward. I did not see any movement of any object around us, but the screams that came back to my ears told me that Karlyle had made contact with the attackers behind us.

Keven then yelled out, "Run! They will not stay off for long!"

Once again my legs followed Keven's orders as he disappeared into the woods. I thanked the gods that my body was thinking faster than my head.

As we ran I looked back and to the left. I now saw black

shadows about twenty paces off. I knew that they were Man hunters on horseback. Keven veered to the right and I followed. As we turned I caught sight of Karlyle. He threw his arm toward the riders and suddenly I heard a horse scream out and a large crash of a branch breaking as if from a large collision.

I then heard a loud swoosh of air past my ear and then saw an arrow appear in the tree before me as I ran past.

A horse shadow now leapt in front of Keven suddenly blocking his way! The rider had his arm raised and was ready to swing a large axe down. Without missing stride, Keven ran and sprang up and into the rider. I saw a blade in each of Keven's hands as he was in the air. The axe was the last thing that hit the ground. Keven straddled the dead man as the horse reared away in panic.

Keven yelled out, "We make our stand here! I will not run further!"

Before the words were out of his mouth an arrow flew toward his head! Keven threw up his left hand and knocked the missile to the side with a dagger! At the same time, the right hand was loosing the other dagger at the riders. The left hand dropped the dagger that had deflected the arrow and now reached for the sword in the sheath. In an instant the leading rider tumbled backwards from his horse to the ground. Keven planted his feet wide and raised his sword with both hands.

The rest continued toward us. I stood with my feet planted wide and my sword held to the front, waiting for their attack. There was another roar of wind and crashing of branches to my left. I knew that Karlyle was fending off the Warlocks, but my eyes stayed on the rushing horsemen.

Keven now suddenly jumped in front of me and yelled, "Stay behind me! If they get past me, then you will fight!"

The riders yelled as they charged. They were only about six lengths of their horses from us. Their swords held overhead and ready to strike us down.

Suddenly I saw two shapes leap past Keven and onto the oncoming Man Hunters! As they leapt up they gave out the roar of the great forest tigers.

I had never seen one before this day, and the size of their

bodies and sheer power left me awestruck and frozen. The riders and their horses soon separated. The riders were cast off their mounts and onto the ground. One swipe of the tigers' claws insured that our attackers were dead as they fell. The terrified horses turned and fled back through the trees.

Then a great explosion brought my head around to where Karlyle was. He was not to be seen. I ran back and as I did so the trees in front of me exploded into the air with the sounds of hell's fury! I was thrown off my feet onto my back. My eyes were blinded by dirt and rocks.

I feared that I had finally been killed...

But the scraping of rocks along my back as I slid on the ground convinced me that I still must fight. I ignored the pain, rolled left and quickly jumped to my feet. Once again, I noticed that I did not have my sword. I swung my head around, looking for my weapon as screams of men and tigers swept past my ears. I saw the sword by a now broken tree and ran to pick it up.

As I grabbed it I swung around to help Karlyle. I was alone! The woods around me were now frighteningly still and quiet.

I stood panting...legs planted wide...sword held high and in front...my vision spun as my head desperately swung side to side.

Suddenly a voice spun me around: "Beorn! It is over for now; do not attack me!"

I turned and peered into the trees and my eyes caught movement. I pointed my sword in its direction. My eyes then focused on the figure coming toward me and I recognized the newcomer. Ceikay was followed by several men who were dressed in the same manner as Keven was when I first saw him in the Boar's Hind Inn. I guessed that these men were Rangers also.

Then my mind refocused on Ceikay. I wondered how she came to be here with us.

I was not surprised when she answered my unspoken question, "Well met Royal Witness, I am here because I knew you were in need of assistance."

Confused and not knowing what was going on around me, I shook my head and failed to open my mouth.

Ceikay smiled, stepped close and offered me a bladder of

water. My sword dropped to the ground as I quickly grabbed the bag and raised it to my lips. I had not realized how parched with thirst I had become! I think I would have burst my stomach if Ceikay had not pulled the water from me.

"Do not behave like a horse in the desert! You must ration your recovery. We need you to continue your trek, not to become bloated and sick."

I shook my head, still confused. I needed to rest, not continue our trek.

I then realized that Ceikay was no longer talking to me, she was several paces away and conversing with her brothers. I had not seen them come back. I saw that Ceikay was sharing the water bottle with them. There were, I counted, eleven Rangers surrounding our group. Walking up to Ceikay and her brothers, I saw that an argument was taking place. Suddenly Karlyle jumped back as Ceikay's foot snapped out toward Karlyle's leg, just missing her target. No one laughed or smiled this time.

I heard Keven first. "You cannot go after him alone. You do not know if he will lead you to more of his companions."

Karlyle shook his head, "There are no more. He is the last Warlock; I feel it and am certain of it."

Ceikay spoke to her brother, "You have to refresh your energies, if you go after him now, you go at great risk."

"He is just as worn as I. He is also disheartened and scared. I am the hunter now."

"You are the hunter, but you hunt a wounded adversary."

Karlyle nodded at Keven's words but said nothing.

To my surprise Ceikay turned to me. "What do you say in this matter? You know how tired you are, Karlyle is feeling the same burden. Tell him to stay with us."

To my surprise I quickly answered, "He should go after the Warlock. If he is as Keven compares; a wounded animal...then in truth, the animal should be taken down as soon as possible before he is able to meet anyone else."

Karlyle cocked his eyebrow at me as the other two shook their heads.

Finally Karlyle spoke, "It is settled. The Warlock is running as we debate. I will rejoin you soon."

Keven grabbed Karlyle's arm as he turned to leave, "The price of us letting you go is to allow Rangers to accompany you."

Karlyle smiled and quickly nodded. "Agreed, brother. How many will you send with me?"

Keven turned to a Ranger standing off at a distance. "Eldorn, do you have men to spare to Karlyle to hunt a wayward Warlock?"

Eldorn nodded and gestured to four Rangers, "Belan, Gurdon, Siras, and Thera will keep an eye on our friend Karlyle. They will guarantee that Karlyle does not miss the grand party in the Pass."

Moments later Karlyle and the four Rangers were gone.

Keven turned to Ceikay. "So, what brought you out here into these dangerous woods?"

"I knew you would need my help. You always do…"

Keven smiled and shook his head. "Errol will not be happy with you I am guessing."

Ceikay laughed and put her finger to her mouth, "He does not know I have left to find you. He left me in the safe hands of Elexele and his troops."

"I guessed right then; you are on your own."

"I am not alone. Do you not see your fellow Rangers all around us? They made sure I would safely find you."

Then Ceikay changed her tone. "We should not stand any longer. Battle is overdue and we must get back to our allies."

She turned to me, "You must feel you can continue, since you sent Karlyle off…"

"If you are to make me feel responsible…"

Ceikay cut my words off, "Not at all. Karlyle was bound to go no matter what any of us had to say. When he sets his mind, any real discussion is over. I threw the matter to you because I wanted you to be put in a situation where you would be forced to see that fatigue could, and should be overcome."

Then I realized Ceikay's meaning; I had still a march ahead of me before I would be able to rest.

Shaking my head as I sheathed my sword, I answered her, "You lead, I will follow."

Keven then called out to Eldorn, "Old friend, start us out…if you are not lost."

Eldom chuckled as he turned to lead, "Who was it that just found your hind end?

The rest of our trek was uneventful. I did not lag behind the brisk pace that was set. I felt safe and strangely energized as we traveled.

We walked as the sun once again bent below the tree tops. Shadows lengthened into and past us. Finally, the trees ended and we walked out onto a large clearing in the center of the valley. Before the sun's rays were dimmed too much, I saw what looked like a widening of the mountains off to the distance. It seemed to me that the valley was longer and became wider from this point on. To the right I saw two large mountains separated in the middle by an opening. I knew that I was looking at Rogan Pass.

My attention was drawn by movement from the pass and noise. To the right of us, I saw in the dusk the lights from hundreds of campfires. Men and horses moved among drawn tents and posted banners. Seeing the warm glow of the campfires, I knew that I could not go much further. I wanted to be in one of those tents, asleep and undisturbed by man or battle.

Ceikay took my arm and gently pulled me forward, "Do not worry my friend, a tent awaits you. Let us end this day's trials."

I looked at her and smiled weakly. Despite my normally infallible memory, the final steps into camp and to a tent are as a thick fog. I do, though, remember in great detail the softness of the bedding as I fell into it.

Battle at the Pass

The morning was mostly gone before I roused enough to realize where I was. I sat up and knew that my body would ache from yesterday's run. My legs were stiff and slow to obey as I ventured to rise from my bedding. The tent post was near and I was grateful that it was so. I used it as a steadying crutch for several long moments before attempting to leave the tent. I stood listening to the noises outside. Voices could be heard all around me. They were strangely calm and quiet, not what I expected if we were close to battle. After stretching and twisting to loosen my body, my mind was ready to take charge. I ordered my legs to get me to the door.

Upon entering the outside, the day's air met me with a chill. I shuddered in surprise at the change. The sun was hidden behind clouds thick and dark enough to hold rain. The men closest to me nodded greetings but did not offer an exchange of words. Some were talking quietly in groups, and others were silent and seemed to be lost in private thoughts with themselves. All had war garments on and weapons at hand, but I puzzled at the quiet calm around me. I saw no one that I recognized. I felt no interest in moving further, or in asking anyone for information or instructions.

I stood waiting for someone to come to me.

I was not surprised when Ceikay did just that. She walked up to me and smiled, "Good morn to you, Bard. If you are now ready, you can come with me. Food and drink are waiting for you. After you have eaten you can join us in council."

She turned and I followed. Soon a new smell in the air told me that the galley tent was near. Once again I marveled at the sudden arrival of my hunger. With a nod of thanks I accepted the meal that was offered as we stepped into the circle of tables. I sat down and ate everything given.

Ceikay had somehow left me without my noticing. I looked around after putting down my mug of goat's milk. I was alone among several dozen men who were also filling their stomachs.

Once again I was not surprised at Ceikay's arrival, nor her words: "Now that we have filled your stomach, it is time to fill a wash basin for you."

"Are my thoughts that strong to you?" I asked her as I stood.

Ceikay laughed and shook her head. "It is not your strong thoughts; it is your strong odor."

For a brief moment I was offended, and then remembered that truth should never offend a reasonable person. Ceikay led me back to my sleeping tent and motioned me to enter.

"I will be back for you shortly."

I nodded my thanks and entered the tent. I found new clothes folded on the bedding before me. On a small table were a wash bowl and a cake of lavender-scented lard soap.

Not long afterward I stepped from the tent with a clean coat of skin, and new clothing covering me. Ceikay stood across the path and smiled. She looked me up and down and nodded. "Much better for you and the rest of us. Let us start the day."

She led me through the camp past hundreds of fire circles and the men that surrounded them. They all were dressed for battle and all were quiet and surprisingly calm. Again I wondered that we were not in battle already.

My thoughts were suddenly shifted to the large tent where we now stopped. I noticed that the posted banner was the standard of Duke Hastid.

We stood before the tent flaps and waited. For who or what, I did not ask.

"Beorn, you have not stopped having questions, but you have stopped asking them. Why is that?"

I had no answer to Ceikay's question. I just shook my head and simply offered that I may be too tired to ask.

"Your timing is good! We begin our council again. It is good you join us."

I turned to Errol's voice. He was walking toward us and the tent. His large broadsword was strapped over his shoulder. There were no other weapons that I could see. He wore a leather armored vest. His forearms were covered by leather braces. The rest of his arms to his shoulders were bare to the skin. His leggings were tight to the skin and his boots were leather-strapped up to mid-calf. I could see that Errol wanted no extra encumbrances when battle began.

"Thank you, Ceikay, for bringing our wanderer along this morn."

"Our Royal Witness is ready to begin again."

"Then if he is, let us enter and begin."

Once inside the tent I saw faces that were familiar; Elexele and several of his officers. Keven was standing to the far side conversing with five of his companion Rangers. Upon our entrance the random talk stopped and faces turned toward us.

Elexele nodded greetings and then spoke, "We will begin with a report from the Rangers."

With that said, one of the Rangers standing next to Keven stepped forward, "Good morn and well met. My name is Baristol of the Northern Rangers. I have brought two hundred of our guild to assist you in freeing Rogan Pass. My scouts report that Duke Hastid is well entrenched in the Pass, but his forces are outnumbered and outweaponed by his traitorous son and his allies. Rendulus is between us and his father. His troops outnumber us three to one. They are well entrenched and can fend off a charge from us if we were to try. He has built palisades in anticipation of our arrival. We are not strong enough to break his lines. We are at a stand-off at the moment."

One of Elexele's officers held up his hand and spoke: "What is stopping him from attacking us, if he knows we are here?"

Elexele answered for the Ranger. "I may have the answer to that. Rendulus could overrun us if he were to try, but do not forget he is also in the position of having to keep his father bottled in the pass. If Rendulus turned on us, then his backside would be open to attack from Duke Hastid."

Ranger Baristol nodded in agreement.

"In addition," Elexele continued, "I have thought on the possibility of Rendulus making an effort to communicate with his father in order to convince him to join the rebellion and overthrow of King Ballistor. Although there have been no reports of Rendulus attacking the pass, there have been reports of the traitors bringing up siege weapons to break through the Duke's defenses. I reason that there has been enough time to have had them in place several days ago. Rendulus' forces in the north holding in the Duke would have begun their assault and thus Rendulus would be poised, ready, and waiting to breach the south the moment the order was given. Our scouts see no sign of Rendulus' troops standing at the ready to charge. The reality is, they are actually facing south and more prepared to attack us rather than Duke Hastid."

I finally found my voice. "If we are separated from Duke Hastid by Rendulus, we cannot know if the Duke has fallen already, or if he has indeed agreed to join his son."

"Keven stepped forward in answer. "Your concern and doubt is something we all would share, if it were not for my scout."

He paused briefly, then continued, "Eagle has visited me this morn. He has flown over Rendulus and his troops and through the Pass. Duke Hastid's men stand facing north and south with weapons at the ready. They are tense and ready to fight the other men facing them. Eagle sees clearly the anger and fear in the men's eyes as they wait for attack. It is clear that there is no truce between father and son."

Elexele spoke again, "Let us talk to our purpose. This meeting is to discuss our options and decide our actions."

Turning now to Errol, Elexele nodded.

Errol stepped forward at Elexele's urging. "We do not have the luxury of waiting on Rendulus' actions. Because we are smaller in number we must act with speed and determination to convince the gods to favor us. Duke Hastid has not been able to send messengers from the Pass. If he has tried, they have all been intercepted or killed. He has no way of knowing that we are to the south of his son. My thinking is that if Rendulus is trying to sway his father to turn, then it is vital for us that we let Duke Hastid know he is not alone and not to give in."

I asked another question, "Why not have Keven send in one of his bird friends to drop a written message to the Duke?"

"It is a good suggestion. It had already has been tried."

I turned to the Ranger who had answered me: he spoke again, "All birds have been either struck down by arrows, or the messages have been burned."

Keven added, "I have had Eagle drop weighted messages from out of arrow range, but Warlocks have greeted them with fireballs."

I nodded my understanding and stood back.

Errol then continued, "It is my thought that we send in a handful of Rangers to penetrate Rendulus' lines and get to Duke Hastid as soon as possible."

One of Elexele's officers raised his arm and spoke, "How can we get through if Rendulus is waiting for us?"

Errol answered, "Diversion will make surprise our ally. We will pretend to attack the enemies' front lines."

There were mumblings among the officers.

Elexele spoke again, "Let us listen to what Errol proposes. I am asking the rest of you to consider options and offer alternatives. Speak freely; you know I let my men have their say. If a better plan than Errol's can be revealed, then we use that one."

The tent was silent. I could see men's looks of thought and contemplation. No one spoke.

When enough time passed to make clear that there would be no further options offered, Elexele spoke once more, "I favor Errol's plan. This night we will prepare to attack Rendulus' lines. The time for attack will be tomorrow morn before first light. We will

Tavegnor

have a frontal charge with our strongest attempt to the right of his line. We will sustain the attack until well after the sun has risen. Only at my signal will we fall back. This is only a diversion, so we will not attack with our entire force. We will make a lot of noise to keep Rendulus' attention on us. Any questions so far?"

Elexele's officers looked around at each other but remained quiet.

Elexele continued, "This diversion should allow Keven and his Rangers to find an opening to the extreme left of Rendulus's line. They will travel along the edge of the mountainside and make for Duke Hastid. This is a very simple plan and should therefore work.

No more needs to be said here except for you men to prepare your troops for advance in the morn. You are not to speak of this as a diversion. As far as everyone outside of this tent is concerned, the goal of our frontal attack is to break Rendulus' line. Errol, do you have further words?"

Errol shrugged, "None."

Elexele nodded, and then addressed his men: "Make sure our troops get a good rest before morn. They will need it. You are dismissed."

I turned to leave but Ceikay took hold of my arm and pulled me to the side. We waited until Elexele and his officers left the tent. Soon there was only me, Ceikay, Errol, Keven, and the Rangers standing silently.

I waited for further direction, but no one spoke. Presently Elexele re-entered the tent.

He looked at the others first and then turned to me. "Bard, know that Errol will take you along with him as Royal Witness. My Liege may not fully trust your friends after their last meeting with him. As a Royal Witness he should trust your words. To insure that he listens to you, I will give you my letter and personal Seal to present to the Duke. Do you still have nerve for this?"

"I am not concerned with my nerve. It is my legs that worry me."

Keven came up to me and put his arm around my shoulder. "my friend, you have impressed us so far. Do not tire so yet."

345

Elexele opened his mouth to say something but held back. After a moment of silence he simply said, "If we are clear in our plans, then let us go with confidence and the gods' blessings."

Elexele then turned to leave, but before stepping out he said over his shoulder, "Thank you for your efforts."

At Elexele's departure Errol turned to Keven. "Which of the Rangers are coming with us?"

"None other than myself. The rest of the Rangers will be a second diversion that leaves in the morn. If we are successful, our small number will be enough to get to Duke Hastid."

Errol nodded his understanding and agreement. With no other words we left the council tent and separated from the Rangers. Ceikay, Errol and I went to a tent on the east of our encampment. In it were packs and supplies enough for a two-day sojourn.

Errol talked briefly to Ceikay who then left us.

"Beorn, I suggest that you try to rest and get sleep before we go. It will be dusk when we leave, so it gives you time to lie down and sleep a while."

I grinned at Errol and nodded, "I will gladly try."

Soon I was once again dreaming of the Boar's Hind Inn and its luxurious beds.

I awoke to yelling and cursing. I sprang from the tent as I saw men run past me toward the galley circle. I was about to follow their direction when a hand grabbed my shoulder. I turned around to face Keven.

He held his finger to his lips and spoke softly, "It is time we go. Follow me."

I quickly fell in line behind him as he slipped back into the tent. He then went to the other side and bent to lift the far flap. He beckoned me to go through. I quickly did so. He came through and waved for me to follow him. We ran past several empty tents and into a clearing. Past the clearing I saw the edge of the forest. We gained the trees and kept running. Suddenly we reached a clearing and I saw Keven, Ceikay, and Karlye at its edge, standing over our packs.

Karlyle anticipated my question by answering, "My prey will

not be helping our enemies, nor will he be returning to his homeland."

I understood his meaning and said nothing. I reached down for my pack but Errol waved me back as he spoke, "Do not be in such a hurry to run, Beorn, we must be sure that our timing is right."

He then turned to Keven. "Was the fight realistic?"

"You have to ask?"

"Were you seen leaving the tent?"

"Yes"

Errol continued, "Will we be followed?"

"Yes."

Again Errol, "Do you know how many?"

"At least two dozen."

Errol smiled and asked another: "When will they be on us if we do not move?"

Keven now smiled as he answered, "They were caught off guard with our timing. They have to get word to Rendulus first to make sure his men know of our early departure. We should proceed now, but on a pace that prevents our trackers from losing us."

Before reaching for my pack I held my hand up. "Is someone going to make this all clear to me?"

Errol was the one who answered, "Bard, you deserve the truth and shall hear it now. There is a traitor in Elexele's officer core..."

Ceikay interrupted, "It is not clear if he is a traitor or an infiltrator."

Errol grinned and continued, "Ceikay corrects me and rightly so. We have not been able to identify who this person is; we only know that he exists."

"How?" I asked.

Errol continued, "Ceikay felt something back at Rachilow Tell. When Elexele and his men first joined us Ceikay felt unease from their group. She could not identify the source or the reason for it. Since then she has worked on it in her mind and has now sorted some of the problem. Ceikay, would you continue?"

Ceikay nodded at Errol's request. "At every meeting with Elexele's men I have searched deeply and probed each individual for answers. I have concluded there is one who has a talent such as mine. This person has the ability to mask his thoughts and feelings to an extraordinary degree. He also can sense emotions from others. He cannot read thoughts though."

She paused, waiting for my questions.

I obliged, "If he is like you, why did he not sense that you were probing for him? Or did he know?"

Karlyle answered for Ceikay, "No one is better than Ceikay at her talent. She can probe for thoughts and shield herself from detection while she is doing so."

Ceikay smiled and spoke again. "Thank you for your confidence, Karlyle, but if there is someone better than me out there; then this person would be good enough to shield his existence from me."

Errol now spoke. "Please continue telling your story to the Royal Witness."

Ceikay sighed. "I knew from the start that an officer serving Elexele was shielding thoughts of hatred and betrayal, but I could not separate him from the others. This person is extremely good at shielding his thoughts to those around him. He is confident that his talent keeps him from discovery by one such as me. He was partially wrong; I did discover him, but I was unable to identify him from the rest."

"How did you know that Elexele was not the person you were trying to reveal?"

"You ask a very good question. His mind is strong but simple. I do not mean simple in the sense of an imbecile. I mean that he only thinks in honest duty and purpose. There is no deception in his thoughts. I determined that the very first time we met in Duke Hastid's hall"

Keven now spoke with a grin, "Well, not until we came up with our plan and told him about it. Then he lied as well as the rest of us!"

Ceikay seemed to ignore the remark. "When I was sure of my suspicions, I told Errol and we both approached Elexele. He was not easy to convince but we did succeed in having him try our plan. We arranged for the quick meeting in Elexele's tent and told everyone of our plan to get to Duke Hastid by way of Elexele's diversion. We wanted the spy to either reveal himself, or convince him to take action by getting word across the lines to Rendulus."

I began to open my mouth but Ceikay silenced me by answering, "You wonder how the spy was not able to sense that Elexele was lying."

"Yes." I responded.

"You know that I can shield my brothers from outside probes because of our closeness. You know also that we had to deceive you before because I could not fully cover you. I can however shield Elexele because of his uncomplicated thought patterns."

"In plain speaking, Bard, Ceikay is saying that you have a deceptive mind, and therefore too convoluted to protect..."

Ceikay ignored Karlyle as she had ignored Keven, "Our plan in the tent was to spur this person into action. It worked. We had Rangers posted outside the tent. There were two Rangers assigned to every officer. When Elexele dismissed his men they all went directly to their commands to prepare as ordered. All but one...

"One officer went first to the field mess tent. He poured himself some ale from one of the casks and stood leaning against the cask brace. Almost immediately a wrangler came up and poured himself a cup from the same cask. Looking casually at the two one would not have seen any communication. Our Rangers who stood at a distance could see that they did indeed converse. The officer and wrangler spoke while looking away from each other. No one else was around.

"After a short while, the wrangler put down his half-empty mug and departed into the surrounding forest. The officer emptied his mug and departed for his company. One Ranger followed each man. The officer went to his command and began to give orders to prepare for attack. The other Ranger reported back some time later and reported that his man had slipped quietly north to Rendulus' line."

Ceikay now paused so I thought out loud, "So we let a man get across to Rendulus with information of our plans. But I am guessing that you gave him wrong information to take with him..."

Keven smiled and slapped me on the back. "You do have a

deceptive mind, Beorn."

I began to ask what our real plans were but Errol stopped me. "We must depart now. Even I can see we have followers on our trail."

I looked back through the trees and could see that about twenty or so men were heading our way. Errol pushed my pack into my stomach and quietly motioned me to follow Karlyle who was already halfway across the clearing. I did as I was told. Answers would have to come later.

We traveled in a northeasterly direction. It seemed to me that we did not want to hurry too much. We made no attempt at stealth. Even Keven, who led the way, could be heard stepping on crackly leaves and brittle twigs.

The voices of the men following us could be heard from time to time. I heard shouts and commands behind us. I kept turning my head back to try to see how close they were coming. Several times I nearly tripped onto my face doing so.

Finally Ceikay stepped up to me and explained, "So you do not fret and wonder so, I will tell you, we are not in a hurry because the men behind us do not want to catch us. They are yelling so that we may know that they are upon us. They are simply driving us forward into an ambush that we are willingly going to."

With those words Ceikay became silent while my mind strained with more questions.

We began to encounter large rocks and boulders as we trekked through the trees. Then the trees began to be fewer in number. I then realized that we were now on a path and it was rising in front of us. We were starting to enter the foothills before the Pass.

Our pace was swift but relaxed. It was clear that we were not trying to outrun our pursuers. Keven had taken the lead position and easily guided us up into the hills. Even at this pace the sounds of the men behind diminished and eventually stopped.

Errol had been last in our formation and now he called out, "Hold, Keven! I fear that we have lost our pursuers!"

Keven led us to the top of a boulder where we sat down. Karlyle took this time to lie down, and it looked as if he fell immediately to sleep. Again Ceikay knew my thoughts.

"He is catching up from his adventure last night with the Warlock," she said. "He is quite adept at these regenerating naps."

I nodded and wondered that I should try to shut my eyes right then. The unease of being followed dispelled any hope of a short nap.

So I decided to ask questions. "Do we have time for some of my inquiries?"

Errol nodded and replied, "We have time for your questions, but we may not have time for answers. But you may ask."

I did ask, "What are we doing?"

Keven laughed and answered me, "Those four words have a lot of questions in them, my friend."

Ceikay laughed also as she spoke. "That was not a question. That was a demand to reveal plans!"

Errol grinned and spoke not to me but to Keven, "Do we have time enough for this now?"

Keven raised his head to the sky. My eyes followed his gaze. Hundreds of feet above us something circled. My eyes recognized Keven's animal friend. Eagle was silently soaring over us. His wings were outstretched and still. I could see that he had found what is called an updraft of air. Eagle was effortlessly floating in the sky above us.

After a moment Keven lowered his head and answered Errol, "Eagle will let us know when it is time to move."

Errol nodded and turned to me. "Beorn, we are decoys walking into a trap...ambush if you will. We allowed Rendulus to receive word that we were to make an attempt at reaching Duke Hastid. He knows who we are and whom we represent. He knows that a Royal Witness is on his way to convince the Duke to stay loyal to the realm of Tavegnor. He also knows, or I should say that he has been made to believe, that Elexele will attack his lines as a diversion. This diversion is meant to keep Rendulus' attention away from our small group so that we may slip past his pickets."

Errol paused briefly. I sat and said nothing.

Ceikay chuckled, "Beorn's silence is telling you to continue brother."

Errol nodded and continued as bid. "Now, think on what

351

Rendulus has been told. He thinks that we are in earnest to get to the Duke. He also believes that Elexele's charge is only a ruse and is not meant to break his lines. Therefore, the real threat as far as he knows is us. Therefore, he must stop us. Since we have become the threat, he must send enough forces to stop us at all costs. Believing that his line is not going to be pressed by Elexele, Rendulus will send strength toward us."

This time I did have a question. "In Elexele's tent it was told that we would leave in the morn. I was awakened later by a disturbance in camp. I am guessing that it was set up for us to escape, but we wanted it to fail. Am I guessing right?"

"You guess right," Errol answered. "Keven's Rangers had spotted wranglers milling around the traitorous officer's tent. He was seen talking to them briefly. Officers of that rank do not usually use their time to instruct wranglers. These wranglers then moved out of camp and settled near the edge of the trees where it was indicated in the meeting we would head out. We decided to speed our departure in order for Rendulus to worry about our change of plans. He would then panic and send even more of his troops to intercept us."

I had another question. "If we are decoys, then we are not meant to get to Duke Hastid...correct?"

"Correct, and then again...no," Keven confirmed.

Errol began again, "Our purpose is to draw off as many men from Rendulus' front line as possible."

I asked another. "So Elexele's charge is not a feint; it is meant to break Rendulus and succeed to Duke Hastid in the pass."

Keven spoke again. "Not so correct this time."

Confused now, I looked at Errol. He grinned and spoke, "Elexele is going to charge. And as Rendulus was meant to believe, Elexele will fall back soon after without using full force of frontal attack. On seeing Elexele retreat from the battle, Rendulus will relax his men and order them to stand down. Remember, Rendulus is thinking of us as the threat."

Ceikay now spoke as Errol again paused, "Do you remember Hellista, Beorn?"

I looked at Ceikay. "I am sure you know that I do."

Errol spoke again: "Hellista has brought her army to the outskirts of Elexele's camp. They are crouched just inside the western forest of this valley. Rendulus has not discovered her. She has with her a contingent of two thousand heavy cavalry. They will be poised behind Elexele and his men in the charge. When Elexele gives the order for his men to retreat, Hellista will race her horsemen up between the returning men. At this moment, Rendulus will not be expecting a new charge, especially a charge of heavy cavalry. He will instead be standing down his men. Rendulus will be taken completely by surprise. His line should be completely broken and routed."

The mention of Hellista's arrival brought more questions to me. I was about to begin when a screech from above stopped me.

We all looked up to see Eagle spiral down and signal us again.

Keven nodded and stood up. "It is time to move from here."

He led the way as we continued up the slope. Once again it seemed that we were in no hurry to escape our pursuers. As we climbed upward I listened for the sound of battle below. Elexele's charge should be happening soon...

Ceikay answered my unspoken thoughts, "Elexele has not begun yet. He was to wait for our signal."

Ceikay was behind me as we marched through the rocks and thinning trees. Even though she claimed not to be able to read actual thoughts, my thoughts were that she could. I wanted to press her on that claim but decided to have that conversation at a later time. Instead I asked her about our current plans. "Why does he wait for us and what is our signal?"

Ceikay laughed and replied, "You are filled with questions and have to choose so few!"

I turned my head around to address Ceikay as I walked, "Will you answer the ones I choose then?"

Ceikay grinned and nodded her head. "I do not mean to irritate you Beorn, but you are predictable as well as likable. I will answer you as you ask. We must be sure that Rendulus has fully taken the bait. The men following us are but partial proof of that. We cannot yet know if Rendulus is weakening his line by sending a force to meet us ahead and cut us off from attaining the pass. Once

353

we are certain, then we give Elexele signal."

"When do we know and what is the signal?" I pressed.

Karlyle answered for Ceikay, "We will know when we are attacked from the front. The signal, I will give; and that will be a fireball thrown back over the valley toward Elexele's line."

My eyes and words were directed to Karlyle. "I thought only Warlocks knew the art of fireballs."

Ceikay answered for him, "Karlyle is not a Warlock, but he knows the ways of war."

I understood her meaning. I once again marveled at the company I was with. It was good that Tavegnor had these four Talents on her side.

Twice more we stopped to let our stragglers catch up to us. The second stop marked a change in my companion's moods. They now became serious and quiet. Keven kept looking to the sky at Eagle. Eagle had now flown beyond us and toward the pass.

As we waited, Errol broke the silence. "Where are your men Keven?"

"That is a question I cannot answer at the moment."

Errol frowned and spoke again, "I am relying on their assistance when we engage our ambushers."

Keven did not reply and there was silence until Karlyle finally spoke: "I surmise we may be more successful than we realized."

"Why do you say that?" I promptly asked.

Errol answered, "The Rangers may have been delayed by a force that is moving south to enfilade us."

My expression was my question and Errol answered, "Enfilade means attacking from the side. Our plan is to have Rendulus ambush us from the front as we attempt to pierce his line. Rendulus may have a different idea for us. He may be sending a force south in an attempt to turn our side as another group of his men hit our front. This force heading south may have cut off our Rangers who are endeavoring to meet up with us from the east. If Rendulus prompted this maneuver with the reasoning of cutting off support to us, then we have underestimated him. If he is not aware of the Rangers, then he is lucky also. Either way, we may be at a disadvantage…"

I realized that I was now getting more confused and bewildered. The explanations did not answer my questions as I had hoped. The more I had tried to understand, the more my companions bewildered me. The fault was not theirs, it was my inexperience. I decided not to speak further.

Ceikay now held up her hand and waved it across her mouth indicating silence. Her eyes scanned the woods below us. She was obviously sensing someone not too far away.

"Somewhere in the trees below are several men. They are too far away for me to identify friend or foe..."

Keven stood. He put the side of his palm to his mouth and made a strange caa sound, like a raven's. The same sound answered from the direction that Ceikay was pointing. Keven repeated his call one more time. Then movement could be seen from the trees. A Ranger stepped from the shadows and began to run up the hill toward us. We waited silently as he jumped over small boulders and skipped around the few remaining trees.

Soon he was upon us. He clasped Keven's hand and greeted the rest of us with a nod.

Keven spoke first, "What news, Brennol? We expected you sooner. Have Rendulus' forces cut us off?"

The Ranger Brennol shook his head and answered, "We have not been cut off. Why do you ask that?"

The rest of us turned to Errol...who said nothing and turned his head away.

Keven grinned and addressed Brennol, "It was speculated by one of us that Rendulus was clever enough to send a force down to flank us."

Ceikay spoke, "To be fair to that one person, we expected Rangers earlier than this, Brennol. Why the delay?"

The Ranger grinned. "Baristol slipped on a rock and fell...hitting his head and falling unconscious." Since he was the only one who knew your plans, we had to wait until we could revive him."

Keven did not grin, but frowned and shook his head before speaking again, "A Ranger falls off a rock? Baristol of all men..."

Errol spoke tersely, "Time is a factor. Brennol, how many

rangers are below?"

"Twenty of us are waiting just beyond the trees below, waiting for your orders."

Keven ask, "What of Baristol?"

"He will recover back at Elexele's camp. A headache and a little blood loss will be his companion for this day, but no lasting damage will he suffer."

Errol again addressed the Ranger. "I want you to eliminate the men who are following us. We do not want them pestering us when we engage Rendulus' men. I feel that the time will be here soon."

Ranger Brennol looked down the slope. "When do you want us to take them?"

Keven was the one who answered. "As soon as we separate, take your men to find them. Dispatch them as soon as you are able and then rush on to help us. We will be looking for, and counting on your aid."

Brennol nodded and spoke once more. "Where do we find you from here?"

Karlyle spoke for the first time: "Go north; you will hear the cry of battle. Go to the sound and you will find us."

Brennol nodded and turned from us. He raced down the hill and was soon into the trees below.

Errol looked up to the sky. "Where is Eagle, Keven?"

Keven closed his eyes and answered, "He is coming back to us. We should start out. Eagle will find us in short time."

Errol turned his head north and took a deep breath. Silently he began to walk north. The rest of us followed. None said a word now. I could feel that my companions were tense and on guard. It was not long before a screech in the sky brought our eyes up. Keven looked at Eagle and nodded. Keven then waved his arm north. Eagle circled once, screeched, and flew north away from us.

We continued our trek upward and into the pass. After a short while Errol stopped and turned back to us. His eyes met mine and he walked back toward me.

"Beorn," he said, "I want you to stay behind and out of the battle when battle is met. If we fall, you are to make your way south and to the east, back to Elexele's lines. As a Royal Witness you are to do your duty and stay alive to report what you see. You are not to join us in the fighting."

Up until now I had been feeling uneasy and admittedly anxious knowing we were walking into a known trap. Now with Errol's words, I felt chagrined.

I looked first at Errol and then to the others before I spoke.

My words were slow and deliberate. "When battle is joined my sword will be drawn. You have protected me from the beginning. I have listened to you and have obeyed your direction in the name of our King and the land of Tavegnor. I will not listen to your order. I will fight now with you. If you fall, I will fall with you. At this moment I do not care what it means to be a Royal Witness. I only care that I am with friends. This is what war is about on the ground. It is friends protecting friends. This is my choice and my decision. If you have nothing more to say to me, then let us go forward."

Karlyle looked at Errol and grinned. "I suspect that the Bard will pull his sword on you if you do not give in, big man."

Errol did not answer Karlyle. Instead he looked at me for several moments. Finally he bowed slightly and spoke, "I welcome your sword alongside mine this day. May the gods grant us days ahead for both of us to talk of this when war is done."

He then turned to Ceikay. "What do you feel ahead?"

She closed her eyes. "We are close, maybe three hundred paces beyond. They do not know yet that we are near."

Errol now turned to Karlyle, "What do you sense?"

Karlyle looked ahead into the line of trees before us and said, "There are no Warlocks facing us. That does not mean that none can come upon us unexpected."

Errol nodded and turned to Keven.

Keven nodded and answered Errol's unspoken inquiry. "The animals around us are quiet yet guarded. That tells me that the men before us are veterans, not sweating fear. The animals are poised for flight but await a move from the humans on the field."

Errol spoke to all of us. "If these men are able veterans waiting for us, then it tells us that Rendulus has completely taken our bait and has sent some of his best troops to stop us. Even if we fall now, we have succeeded in our mission."

I now spoke. "I should remind all of us that our mission as given to us is to get to Duke Hastid and determine his intentions. This is what Lady Hellista has decreed us to do. I do not consider this diversion to supersede our mandate from our first order."

Keven slapped me on the back as he answered me, "Do not think that Errol is not heading to Duke Hastid. We can have more than one mission as we travel, as long as those missions parallel each other and do not conflict. Watch that you do not get too bold with our Errol, Beorn. You have already tried his patience with your…"

His words were cut off by the screech of Eagle. We turned toward the sound to see the powerful bird of prey swoop down from the sky and rake the top of a thicket of brush. I saw the claws of Eagle as they pointed down at the brush. Just before hitting the ground Eagle twisted his great wings and suddenly arched upward back into the sky. I then saw two men jump up and over the brush as if in panic from Eagle's charging dive.

At that very moment Karlyle's arm snapped up and punched the air toward the two men. In an instant the two changed direction in the air and flew back as if hit by a giant club. I saw them fall to the ground and lie still. I looked back to see that my companions had all drawn their swords and were facing the line of trees ahead. I drew mine as the first charge came flooding toward us.

Remembering my brave words earlier, I found myself taking a half step behind Errol.

As Rendulus' men charged, I planted my feet and stole a quick look at each of my companions. All were standing alert but appeared strangely calm. None said a word as the horde now rushed toward us. Suddenly from the left a rush of air turned my head. I saw an arch of arrows racing from hidden bows. In an instant Karlyle raised an arm to the arrows and they twisted and fell straight to the earth.

Errol stepped forward and swung his sword. He seemed to me to have grown in height. The men coming near began to falter as

358

Errol walked to them. One big man did step up to challenge Errol. The other men stayed a step behind but kept coming.

I then noticed the quiet. As we braced for killing, and as the enemy was marching for us, no one yelled or said a word. I wondered that there should be a yell from our attackers. It was at that moment that the big man facing Errol yelled out a curse and charged full at him!

His sword raised to stab downward, the man ran up and pushed mightily down at Errol's chest. In a blur too fast for my eyes Errol must have struck first...because Errol now stepped aside as the man fell straight to the ground as blood sprayed from his throat!

Errol quickly stepped into the men remaining and began his slaughter. The rest of us followed and swung our swords. As the first sword hit mine I lost sight of my companions. I was now alone among a sea of thrashing arms and swords! I fought just to stay alive. I knew no tactics or strategy. Men came up to me trying to strike me down. I wanted to stay alive so I swung at anything that came close! I do not know how many men I killed, if any, but I do know that I drew blood.

Suddenly there were Rangers all around me. When they came I do not know, but I felt a surge of power and sliced through two men and moved forward. I saw Ceikay with two short swords in hand. Men were falling before her as she moved but I saw that two were slipping up behind her. I had an opening and I ran to her. I came up to the two and struck out. One fell from my sword. I brought my arm up again.

Suddenly I was on the ground and feet were trampling my body. My hand was empty, the sword gone from my grasp. I looked frantically around but my eyes filled with wetness. I wiped them with the back of my hand. It was blood making me blind. I felt no pain and wondered why there was blood. I tried to get to my knees but I was repeatedly kicked and knocked down. The noise was deafening. The smell was a mixture of dirt, sweat, and blood.

I yelled out but could not hear my own voice because of the noise. I swung at legs and tried to grab at anything that moved. Then something pressed hard and held me to the earth. I reached up and felt a large arm at my throat. My only weapons left were my hands and I clawed desperately at the arm. The arm picked me up by my shirt and dragged me along the ground. I felt rocks tear into my back. My legs struck out at my attacker but only met air. Then I felt my back pressed up against something hard. I reached behind to feel a tree.

Then I knew my assailant as he yelled, "Beorn! Calm yourself and wipe your eyes! Your sword is at your feet! When you are ready to fight, do so! But do not become a berserker with me standing so close!"

Errol then shoved something into my hands. I felt that it was a cloth or rag. I reached out to him but he must have already turned away. I frantically wiped my burning eyes. As I blinked to clear them I began to see my surroundings again. Errol was standing about six strides from me. He was faced off with about a dozen men holding swords and axes. About a dozen more surrounded him but they were strewn on the ground. Their fight was over.

I realized that I could hear the men facing Errol. They were not yelling as in pitched battle. They were panting and grasping for air as they stood just out of Errol's range. Looking beyond them I now saw the whole battle come to a stop. To my left stood Ceikay and Karlyle facing a group of men. These men were as tired and desperate as the ones facing Errol. To my right stood a group of Keven's Rangers. They also faced a line of swords.

There were scores of Rendulus's men dead on the hillside. The ones left standing had no officer insignia on their sleeves.

My mind returned to the moment of charge. I remembered seeing six men in the front who were marked with rank. I saw none of those six faces standing. They must have been struck down, and now the remainder has no leaders to urge the fight to continue. The men were not charging, but they also were not retreating. We were surrounded on three sides. It was clear that my companions were not looking to retreat back downhill. Feet were planted firmly where they stood, weapons at the ready for the next charge.

Errol stood with his back to me. His head turned slowly from side to side. I could see that he was calmly observing the men as they tensely glared at him. As the air stilled and the noise left the battlefield I waited.

Without turning Errol spoke softly, "Beorn, your sword is at your feet. You may join us when you are able. Soon, if I may ask of you…"

I regretted my words as I spoke them, "But the fight is over…is it not?!"

Errol replied simply, "It is not."

Ceikay called out to me, "More men will be here very shortly, Beorn. They will not have been sent by Elexele."

My thoughts suddenly jumped to Keven. He was not standing within my line of sight. My eyes quickly scanned the bodies around me. I saw that several Rangers had fallen, but Keven was not among them.

"Where is Keven!?"

Karlyle answered me immediately, "He has probably stepped away to gather reinforcements for us."

Hope filled me as I realized more Rangers were close…

Ceikay called out, "More of Rendulus' men are arriving!"

Alarm touched me as Ceikay revealed that we had more enemy to face! I then realized that we had been talking as if the men surrounding us had not been there to hear us. They now knew that they would soon get help and therefore were fortified with strength and courage.

Then I remembered why we were standing here, we were a diversion. We did not want our battle to be over so soon. Elexele needed us to pull as many of Rendulus' men from him as possible for as long as possible. My companions wanted this fight to go on…

Ceikay now spoke, "We do not, Beorn, but it is necessary."

She claimed not to be able to read exact thoughts, but my thoughts she knew too clearly.

Now I began to see men appear in the line of trees beyond. They were heavily armed. Karlyle pointed to the left of us and yelled that there were bowmen at the ready. My sword was in my hand now, but I still rested against the tree. I sighed deeply as I waited for the charge. The men closest to us took courage with the increase of their numbers. Swords were raised and grins appeared. The men before us readied for another attack.

The newly arrived men now began a steady march toward us. It looked as though they were to meet up with the ones already facing us. I wondered when the arrows would be loosed on us. My companions did not move. Errol looked as though he had not a concern about the next moments. His eyes were calm and his face was neutral. Ceikay and Karlyle were now both grinning. Ceikay shook her head slowly while Karlyle nodded his slightly. The Rangers that I could see were standing at the ready. Their looks were varied, but not one showed any signs of fear. I could not see my face, but I knew what I felt inside. I wanted desperately to be done with this battle and this war...

A yell was heard and then the swoosh of arrows followed. Karlyle was the first to move. He pushed his left arm up as the arrows arched down toward Errol. At the same time our attackers in the rear yelled their war cries and started the charge. The men closest to Errol did not move. They clearly knew the danger they were in...

My eyes darted skyward as the arrows suddenly veered. Instead of arching down onto Errol, they now altered their course and raced down on a different target, the line of men who stood facing Errol! The screams began as the arrows hit flesh. Men held their arms above their heads in a futile attempt to block the deadly rain. The men who were advancing stopped as they saw their companions fall.

In an instant it was once again quiet around me. The archers had stopped with one volley. The arrows were spent and the stricken survivors stood looking in shock at the newly fallen.

Suddenly the sound of horns in the distance filled our ears. Our enemy immediately turned as one to face the sound. The horns were blaring long and loud. They were blowing a rhythm of alarm! The call was repeated over and over. I did not know what it signified but our adversaries seemed to understand. All of them turned from us as if we were no longer a concern. To a man they began to run from us back up the hill and into the line of trees. Moments later my companions and I were standing alone on the hill.

Errol turned his head to Ceikay. "What is happening?"

Ceikay cocked her head to the side and frowned. For a long time she did not speak. The rest of us waited quietly with our weapons still in hand.

Finally she answered, "They have truly left us. There is no one within an arrow's flight in any direction."

Karlyle now spoke, "It looks as if Elexele has succeeded in his ruse."

Errol nodded but did not speak.

I spoke though, "What did he do?"

Ceikay answered, "The horns have summoned our ambushers back to Rendulus. He is in great need of all his men. It seems that Elexele and Hellista have broken, or are close to breaking, Rendulus' line."

"Where is Keven?" I asked.

One of the Rangers now answered, "He is off gathering help."

"What kind of help?"

Errol turned to me with a grin. "We did not have time to discuss the matter a short while ago."

He continued, "We should gather ourselves and make our way to the Duke's palisades."

Karlyle laughed, "Yes, and then we only have to convince them that we are on their side! The last time the Duke met with us, he did not seem to be too friendly!"

Ceikay's next words made me nod in grateful agreement. "We should take a short time to refresh ourselves before we march onward. A little food and drink, along with a good cleaning would aid our progress a great bit."

Her words brought my attention to the smell and stickiness covering my body. I looked myself over and saw streaks of blood and dirt. The sweat mixed in made me desperate to rid myself of the filth. I shivered with the heat.

I wiped my brow and wondered at the blood. I knew that it was not mine…

"You were in the way of a head that got lopped off. The head hit you and the spray of blood from the body followed."

I only nodded at Ceikay's answer. My stomach churned but I willed myself no further reaction.

We followed Ceikay's suggestion but moved up the hill onto an outcropping of rocks. There we had a good view around us. We cleaned ourselves and ate jerky and stone bread. Errol wisely stopped me from drinking too much water.

"We have still a trek to go. Do not overfill yourself. You will feel the mistake later if you do."

The Rangers had left us. I did not see them go. They must be scouting ahead, I reasoned.

Errol stood and pointed to the pass. "We are ready, so let us proceed to an audience with the Duke."

"Let us hope that he will be happy to see us."

Errol answered his sister, "If he is not, then it is our duty to convince him of the happy reunion, or should I say…it is the Royal Witness who must convey our intentions and give report of our journey."

My companions looked at me but did not grin this time. My stomach churned once more.

Ceikay now spoke, "Keven comes."

"Where?" Errol asked.

Ceikay pointed to the east.

At that moment the screech of Eagle filled the sky. We looked up to see Eagle flying toward us. Then we saw movement on the ground. We saw wolves jogging down from the hillside. There must have been five score of them. Keven was jogging in the midst of the pack. He had found his reinforcements!

We waited on the rocks and I marveled at the animals as they neared. I saw none that I recognized, so it must have been a different pack that had concerned me before.

As the wolves closed on us I edged closer to Errol. To my surprise and relief, they came not onto our ledge, but continued their run around and past. In moments they had run to, and disappeared into the line of trees. I guessed that they were intent on catching Rendulus' men.

Soon Keven was on the rock with us. Errol said simply, "Well met."

364

Keven only nodded his greeting, and then asked, "What plan next?"

Ceikay answered, "Duke Hastid."

My question came next. "How do they know to follow the soldiers?"

"Eagle reported to me the retreat, and I simply repeated the information to my wolves."

Another question from me, "Can someone tell me where the Rangers went?"

Errol laughed, "We thought you had changed! You begin again with scattered questions!"

I frowned as the others grinned, "If you wish me to be a Royal Witness, then it is questions I must and will ask, else without answers given, I have no report to give."

Ceikay spoke, "Well said, sir. Truly we do not laugh at you, we smile because it is a good sign to see some of the old Bard."

"We waste time now," Errol said, "we must find the good Duke to determine his intentions and report back to our Lady Hellista."

"But surely Hellista must know by now that the Duke is fighting for Tavegnor…"

Errol grinned as he answered, "Surely she does, but that does not change the fact that we must make contact somehow."

Soon we were in the line of trees heading north toward the pass. We saw no signs of the enemy. Keven was out front with Errol behind him. I was placed after while Ceikay trailed close behind me. Karlyle was behind her at a distance. The trek was steep for a while but leveled off as we entered Rogan Pass proper. The trees began to thin. I began to notice evidence of an encampment to our left and right. Soon Keven stopped ahead. Immediately Errol stopped and motioned to the rest of us. We stood silent as Keven began to walk in a large circle. He made several hand gestures and I saw Errol respond in kind. What they were communicating I could not say.

He bent over several times and seemed to pick objects up and study them. Then he stood straight and looked to the sky. I heard no Eagle screech though. Finally he gestured again and Errol walked toward him. His wave told the rest of us to follow.

As I met with the two leaders I could clearly see that we were in the midst of a soldier's encampment. There were campfire rings with cooking pots around. Beddings were strewn all over. It looked as though it was recently abandoned in a hurry. Red hot coals were still smoldering in some pits. I reasoned that the men of this camp were also called away by the horns.

As the others studied our surroundings, I studied the articles left by the soldiers. There was a piece of wood carving lying on top of a bed roll. The carved shape looked like a bear. By one fire ring a shaving knife and water bowl…the water was still warm. Several tobacco pipes were strewn around…trampled and broken as they were tossed down in the rush to leave. Personal kits were in various stages of discard.

Keven came up to me. "Their haste to leave tells us that Elexele has done well with his charge."

"What do we do now?" I asked.

"We continue into the pass and meet with Duke Hastid."

At that moment Ceikay yelled out from across the camp, "We have guests!"

I looked in the direction of the yell. Out of a line of trees opposite Ceikay stepped a man holding aloft a large parley banner. I had seen such a flag years ago and knew what I was looking at now. The banner was a pale yellow with two black hands apposing each other with palms facing. This was the accepted sign of parley between two combatants.

In an instant Errol was standing next to Ceikay. Keven had left my side and was now walking briskly to the right of the other two. Karlyle was walking to cover the left side. I did not know where to go, so I stood still.

The man paused for several moments, looked around at the camp, then back to Errol and Ceikay. He began walking toward us. He wore the uniform of an officer of the Duke Hastid Realm. As he came closer I could see that he was Centurion rank. Closer still, I now recognized him as one of the officers that faced us so long ago in Duke Hastid's Hall. I also remembered his expression from before. He had looked as though if given the order, he would have unleashed his men to strike us down. I did not like the man.

Knowing who he was, I rushed to Errol. Before the officer could get into earshot I spoke, "He was in the Duke's Hall when we were there. He was toward the back. His looks at us were not friendly…"

Errol did not respond, but Ceikay did. "There were certainly hostile thoughts toward us that day…"

When the officer came within twenty paces of us he stopped and spoke, "You are not of this camp. I wish to know your names and your intentions."

Ceikay made several hand gestures that I did not understand. Errol nodded as he stared at the officer. No answer was offered.

After an uncomfortable pause the man spoke again, "My parley flag gives me the right of answer. Again I ask, who are you and what are your intentions?"

Errol now spoke, in a deadly tone, "Your flag shall not protect you if your men do not show themselves in the next moments."

The officer stepped back at the unexpected threat. His expression told me that Errol's words were taken seriously. He looked back over his shoulder and gestured to the trees. A moment passed, then again more time...

The now worried man yelled out, "First Soldier Goendal! Show your men!"

Out from the trees stepped over two score of soldiers. They were heavily armed with various swords and bows. They stood a pace from the line of trees and lined in formation facing us.

Once movement stopped, the officer faced us again but did not speak. Instead he glared at us.

Errol stared into the officer's eyes. "Any more, Ceikay?"

Ceikay shook her head, "No more in my range."

Next Errol called out to Karlyle, "Anything that might interest you!?"

Karlyle answered simply, "No!"

Errol looked at Keven who answered, "If there where more on the way, Eagle would have warned us!"

Errol turned back to the Hastid officer. "Now, soldier, what was your inquiry?"

The man bristled at the obvious insult. He took a deep breath

367

and spoke, "Once again I offer this parley. Do not threaten me, or I will justifiably order my men to cut you down."

My companions did not move at the threat. I looked at the men facing us. They were on guard to charge if ordered.

Errol's tone was soft but deadly. "When the parley flag is offered, it is customary that the parties show themselves as a gesture of truce also. You kept your men hidden until I requested them shown. Therefore, your flag does not mean a thing to me."

Errol looked past the officer to the waiting men along the trees, then back to the officer.

Errol continued, "I suggest that you do not threaten us again, sir. I also suggest that you think about your questions and ask us in a polite and friendly way. You see, the next words, and the way you phrase them will determine my next course of action."

I could see that the officer was a brave man...who was also intelligent enough to heed Errol's words.

"My apologies; I should have shown my men before, but we have been hard pressed by Rendulus's troops. They have shown themselves not to be trustworthy in previous meetings."

The officer paused and took a breath, then spoke again. "I am Centurion Foust of Duke Hastid's personal staff. I have been sent by my Liege to gather information on this camp's sudden clearing, and also to attempt communication with the Duke's son, Rendulus. I ask you who you are and your alliances."

Errol's tone did not soften to match the Centurion's. "You know who we are. Your memory cannot be as short as that."

Foust answered without hesitation, "You are correct. I do know you. But I stand by parley etiquette in asking your names."

I noticed to my right that Keven's chin dropped to his chest. He sighed and shook his head.

Errol grinned as he answered, "As parley dictates then. I am Errol of the Northern Realm. My companions are Ceikay, Karlyle and Keven. We are emissaries of the King of Tavegnor. We are also on mission from Lady Hellista. She has ordered us to find Duke Hastid and determine his alliance in this invasion. We have with us the Royal Witness to the King. He is Beorn and he demands to speak to your Duke Hastid."

The Centurion briskly nodded and turned to his men. He gestured with his arm. His men visibly relaxed and put weapons away.

He then turned back to Errol, "Thank you sir. Can you tell me what has gone on here and the reason for it?

Errol surprised me by answering, "The Royal Witness can give you report of the field."

He then turned and addressed me, "Beorn, will you give our good Centurion a brief report?"

Errol's request was once again a directive I would not refuse. Although I was taken off-guard I stood forward and nodded.

Before I had a chance to begin Errol spoke again. "Begin at Elexele's last meeting with us, and please be concise and therefore brief. We do not want our meeting with the Duke to be delayed much further."

I knew that Errol's last comment was directed not at me, but at Centurion Foust.

My report was brief but complete. Centurion Foust nodded his head but did not speak.

He turned to Errol, "Your Witness has made it clear what has happened, and in such a telling, that I believe your intentions are as you say. You will have secure escort to Duke Hastid's tent."

Errol turned his head to Ceikay.

She kept hers eyes on Foust as she answered, "He is an honest man. He holds no treachery toward us."

Errol nodded, "Thank you, Centurion Foust, for your escort."

The officer bowed his head and turned from us. He walked back to his men. They were already lining up for escort. They formed two lines which we were expected to walk between.

Keven grinned as he looked at the men awaiting us, "Are we flies amongst spiders?"

Karlyle grinned back and answered, "These spiders may find that we are not flies, but wasps with dangerous stings..."

No one spoke as Errol stepped forward. We followed as he sheathed his sword. I gladly put my weapon away. With our new companions we entered the narrow of Rogan Pass.

Meeting

The walls steepened and closed in around us as we walked. Trees gave way to large outcroppings of rock. The road we were now on was narrow and well used. It has been a favored route for trade but never one for large movements of armies and their supplies. There was room for one wagon in either direction. The walls closed to the edge of the road. I could see now why Rendulus was hesitant to attack his father; the south entrance to Rogan Pass is a good defensive position.

The sounds of footfalls now echoed around and above us. No one spoke. My companions appeared relaxed but I knew that they would not be taken by surprise if ambushed. I looked to the sky and was pleased to see Eagle circling silently overhead. We were surrounded by more than a score of men whom I did not trust, but I was glad for my four companions.

Abruptly the walls gave way and we entered a wide bowl-shaped valley. It widened to about a thousand paces and looked to be a league in length. The walls still ran steep all around but the clearing was flat and clear of trees. Ahead I saw Duke Hastid's camp. Hundreds of tents rose upon the flat ground. As we approached I could now see wooden pikes slanting out of the ground toward us. This line of sharpened trees was the defensive palisade that Hastid's men had hastily thrown up. I noticed to my right and left the stumps of the trees that were hewn. The men must have worked very swiftly when they realized that they were bottled in the pass.

We gained the palisade. There was no opening to the line. Instead several makeshift wooden ladders were lowered down from the two span spikes. Our escort split off and Centurion Foust motioned us to be the first to climb into the camp. Errol nodded for Keven to be first, then Karlyle, then Ceikay, then me. Errol stood facing the line of soldiers as the rest of us went up the ladder and over the top. I jumped down on the inner side into a ring of armed soldiers. They were well armed but had no weapon drawn. Keven, Ceikay and Karlyle stood facing the men. My friends still appeared calm. I was not so sure of myself.

A thump spun me around. Errol had jumped from the top and landed behind me.

He grinned, "Sorry."

The circle around us widened as the rest of our escort climbed into camp. Last to get over was Foust. He walked up to Errol but stopped four paces away.

The Centurion glanced at his men then addressed Errol, "We would have your weapons before you have an audience with our Duke Hastid."

Errol shook his head and answered, "We surrendered our weapons to Duke Hastid once. That should have proven that we mean no harm to him. We are at war now. We will not make ourselves so vulnerable again."

Centurion Foust slowly drew his sword from his sheath. His men now did the same. My hand went to the hilt of my sword but stopped when I saw that my four companions made no move for their weapons.

Foust pointed his sword at Errol. "You are in danger if you do not do as I request sir."

In an instant Errol was standing at the Centurion's side. The officer's sword hand was now wrenched upward with the sword facing the sky. A large dagger was pressed against the startled man's throat as Errol's nose touched his.

My eyes darted to the men closest to us. Their startled looks told me that they had also missed Errol's spring. I looked to my other three companions and they were calmly standing as before. Their weapons were not drawn...but their eyes told all. They were ready to strike.

Not a sound was heard for several moments. Errol's eyes bored into Foust's. Foust's eyes were wide with shock.

Finally Errol spoke.., coldly and softly: "You are a very special man. No one has threatened me as much as you have, and still lives. Now, by the order of King Ballistor of the Kingdom of Tavegnor, you will take me to your Duke."

"BY THE GODS! What is going on here?"

I turned to see Duke Hastid come up behind the ring of menacing soldiers. The line parted as he rushed into our circle. He was armed but did not draw his sword. Ceikay, Karlyle, and Keven turned to face him as he approached. Errol stayed with his back to the Duke...the knife still at the Centurion's throat.

Duke Hastid stood and glared around at us. He then rested his eyes on the knife held at his officer's neck.

He put his hands on his hips as he spoke, "Why do you come into my camp and threaten harm to my Centurion?"

Errol's eyes stayed on Foust's as he answered, "If you thought that my Lord, you would have already drawn your sword."

Again, moments passed with silence.

Hastid kept his eyes on Errol as he finally spoke again, "Everyone, put your weapons away! Sir, I ask you to do the same. You have my assurance that no harm will befall you in this camp."

Without hesitation Errol stepped back and released Foust. The dagger was slipped into its sheath. He turned his back on the still-armed Centurion. He then bowed his head to the Duke in acknowledgement.

Duke Hastid nodded in answer.

The Duke then looked at his officer whose sword was hanging down and not yet sheathed. "Centurion Foust, thank you for your foray into the pass. Get your men back to their posts and then come to my tent for further directives. You may put your sword away now."

The Centurion stiffened and nodded his head in salute. He putaway his weapon and barked out orders to the men surrounding us. They dispersed and left only the Duke and his personal guard.

Duke Hastid now looked at each of us in turn. He shook his head, but I saw no malice or anger.

He then spoke, "Normally I would have bid the Centurion to give report on what he had learned. He is a good soldier but does not seem to know your potential for doing harm to others if pressed. I sent him away to gather his composure and calm down. I assure you he will not begrudge you any ill will later. I ask that you forgive him as well."

Errol answered, "He is alive. That is proof of my forgiveness."

Duke Hastid laughed and shook his head, "Old Ballistor has chosen well with you four..."

His smile left as it had arrived as he continued, "In Foust's stead, will you give me news of the outside?"

Ceikay answered, "The Royal Witness has been brought to you for that very reason."

"Then follow me to my tent if you will. I will have food and drink brought for you."

The food was good, the wine was delicious, and my report was long and detailed. The Duke commanded that I begin at the beginning. His beginning was the first meeting we had with him in his Hall. His questions were such that I was convinced that he was loyal to Tavegnor and to King Ballistor. He was anxious for the capture of his son Rendulus. Centurion Foust had rejoined us as I had begun my report. He stood by his Duke and listened quietly. I saw no anger or resentment on his face.

I came to the end of my narrative and bowed my head slightly to the Duke. He nodded in return. He walked slowly in a tight circle with his head down.

His thoughts began to escape his lips, "I want to ask my traitorous son why...how he could consider overthrowing the legitimate crown of Tavegnor? What were his justifications? Would he allow me to live if I did not side with him...?"

We stood in silence as the Duke thought out loud, not waiting for, nor expecting answers from us.

He then stopped and faced Foust, "Ready enough men to accompany me south to find my son. Keep showing force at the north palisade. I do not want our friends left besieging us to believe that we are now ripe for slaughter."

Centurion Foust saluted and quickly left the tent.

Duke Hastid turned to another officer. "Make an opening one span wide in the south palisades. I will ride with horse today."

The officer saluted and was gone.

The Duke addressed Errol, "Now that you have found me, you must be eager to report back to Hellista. You are bid to join me as far and until you find her. We leave shortly. I will have horses for the five of you."

Duke Hastid turned and left the tent. My companions now sat for the first time. I collapsed onto large pillow cushions, not caring if they were reserved for the Duke's private comfort.

My eyes closed and my head dropped.

Keven nudged me back from the brink, "Sleep must wait, my friend. We are bound to go."

We exited the tent to find five stallions at the ready. I was surprised at the darkness around me. I had forgotten that this day had already been well advanced when we entered Hastid's tent. I looked at our horses. These steeds were well-muscled and broad-shouldered. I saw that they had leather war saddles and were equipped with slings for missile weapons. We mounted the horses and soon we were in line behind the Duke. I saw that he was conversing with several of his officers. Some were mounted and several were on foot. I assumed that the ones afoot were to stay and man the north palisade. Orders were being distributed as one by one, the officers ran past our group.

Then the order to ride came. I turned to Errol, "We should be sleeping."

"We should be at peace." He answered simply.

We soon were at the south palisade. An opening was before us. It was wide enough for two horses abreast to go through. We crossed through and were soon into the narrows of Rogan Pass. The outriders held torches, making the walls eerily lit with phantom shadows.

Suddenly the walls reverberated with the blaring of alarm horns! I could not tell from which direction they were calling. The signal was clear to Duke Hastid though. He was about forty paces ahead of me and I saw his reaction. He turned his head and spurred his horse around at the first sound.

He yelled out to his men as he now rode past me, "The north! The north! They are attacking!"

Soon we were charging back through the south palisade. I could see men running with torches and weapons north through the camp. Once in camp my horse stopped and refused to run further. I saw that my companions had left me behind. I tried to spur my horse forward but he reared and I was thrown off!

The damnable horse ran through the tents and I was left on foot. My sword was swiftly in my hand and I ran with other men toward the north palisade. Soon the mass of running men slowed to a walk. I kept running to find my companions. Before me I saw a line of soldiers stretching beyond my sight to both sides. The night sky cloaked my eyes from distance. The mass of men now before me made me understand why the others had slowed to a walk. There simply was no room for anyone else to move.

What next caught my notice was the fact that there was very little action at the front of the palisade. I saw men yelling and gesturing but no real fighting or missiles in the air. Then I saw Errol standing at the top of a high section of the defensive wall. His siblings were standing to his right as was Duke Hastid. I began to make my way to my companions. Ceikay then turned and looked my way. She soon laid eyes on me. She waved and motioned me on. I pushed my way through the now milling men and onto the parapet. The noise of battle could be heard, but strangely it was not at the wall. A battle was being waged beyond the darkness in the north section of the pass. A battle in which we, it seemed to me, were not involved.

The moon was not to be seen over the walls of the pass, and the darkness kept answers from us. Finally Keven grabbed onto the tip of a sharpened stake.

He looked back at us and spoke, "I am curious enough now. I

shall not be long…"

Errol yelled out as Keven jumped down on the north, unprotected side of the defensive wall. I saw him run toward the dark line of trees and rocks. He soon was gone from our sight.

Errol cursed something I could not make out for the surrounding noise.

Duke Hastid turned to Errol. "Your brother takes undue risks."

Ceikay answered, "He is the leader of the Ranger Guild. If he cannot get answers, then no one else will."

Errol spoke to the Duke, "If we are to stay here for a while, then you might see to it that the breach in the south palisade is closed."

"The order has already been given," the Duke replied.

The battle noise in the dark was constant but distant. Soon, I sat at the base of the planted spikes and dropped my head. I knew that if need be, my friends would wake me for fighting. It was obvious to me that Duke Hastid felt no need to send his men to join in.

My dreams were many and violent. My rest was not restful.

My eyes opened to the first glimpse of morning light. The tops of the walls surrounding us were lit with the rays of the morning sun. The light bounced down to the floor and dimly met my confused gaze. Slowly I remembered where I was and what we were doing,

I stood up, wondering at the quiet around me. I was handed a tankard of hot broadleaf tea. The server smiled at my thanks and went to others along the wall. My eyes searched to find my companions. I saw Errol standing by a fire ring. He was talking with Duke Hastid and several officers of rank. Ceikay and Karlyle were still atop the palisade wall, looking north into the line of trees. I climbed up and joined them. They nodded greetings and continued to study the distance. As the light of the sun made its way down into the valley, I could see that a forest stood almost a league from us to the north. I saw no movement except rising wisps of smoke from dying fire rings. The sound of fighting had ended sometime while I was sleeping. The restful sound of a lazy wind met my ears. The late morning air smelled of clover.

I wondered at the death hidden behind the trees before us.

"What of Keven?" I asked of no one in particular.

"He has not returned," was Ceikay's reply.

At that moment Errol jumped up to join us. He looked out to the trees and held his gaze for a few long moments. He looked to the sky and back to the trees.

Finally he spoke, "It is Duke Hastid's opinion that a force has attacked the enemy to the north."

Karlyle grunted, "Was that not obvious to everyone last night?"

Errol did not respond. Ceikay shook her head and said nothing. I looked out across the flat piece of land in front of the palisade, wondering who was beyond the trees.

Since no one was talkative, I asked a question, "Did any of you sleep?"

Ceikay and Karlyle turned to look at me.

Ceikay was the one who answered: "Your thoughts do jump around, Beorn. Karlyle and I have not been awake much longer than you. Errol is the one who has not rested."

I waited for Errol to speak up, but he was looking into the trees. It was not clear whether or not he had heard my question. My eyes followed his. There was no movement in front of us, nor any sound of men or battle.

Karlyle spoke, "So, leader of ours, what else has the Duke revealed in his wisdom and insight?"

Without turning, Errol answered, "He is holding war council with his officers. I was asked to leave."

Ceikay jumped up. Anger was in her voice. "We do not have reason to stay in his camp any longer. It is time to find Keven!"

Karlyle stood. He did not speak, but the anger in Ceikay's voice also filled his eyes.

My legs had me standing also.

Errol shook his head as he still gazed into the trees. "Duke Hastid is a careful man. He is set in his ways and is as stubborn as he is old. It is not that he does not trust us. It is a lifelong habit of close council with his men."

Ceikay was not mollified by Errol's words, "Hastid is a fool and insults us by his mistrust. We were charged with finding him and we have done that. It is time to make our way back to Lady Hellista and report what we have found."

"You forget Keven," Karlyle said simply.

Ceikay suddenly whirled as Karlyle jumped to the side. He barely escaped the kick aimed at his shin.

Errol spoke again, "We will stay here for now."

Ceikay turned on Errol. "Hastid has not even said a word of gratitude or thanks to us. After the Witness's report he simply dismissed us!"

Once again, Errol did not respond. He only looked into the trees.

Ceikay was about to speak again, but a runner came and called up to us, "My Lord would have advice from you. If you would come with me, he asks that you share his food and drink."

Karlyle grinned at Ceikay.

Her anger though was not lessoned by the runner's words. "Tell your lordship that we are leaving to look for our brother."

Errol stood and turned to the runner below, "Tell your lordship that we would be pleased to take his food and drink, and that we will also be pleased to give him advice in return. We shall be with him shortly. Is the meeting to be in his tent?"

The runner nodded as he answered, "The Duke is in his tent, but he wishes an immediate joining of council. I request that you follow me now."

Ceikay began to speak but Errol silenced her with an upraised hand as he spoke first: "We shall come now then. We do not need to follow you though, the location of the Duke's tent is known to us, so please run ahead and tell your lord that we are on our way."

Errol's words were polite and quiet, but once again, the way he said them made it clear that the runner was compelled to obey and not say a word further. The man nodded and turned from us. He was out of sight and hearing in an instant.

Ceikay glared at Errol, "We are being summoned like commoners and you allow it? We should not be treated so!"

"Do not let pride, or your anger, get in the way of taking the intelligent course."

378

Ceikay's eyes bored into Errol's. She did not speak. I waited for her kick.

Karlyle ended the brief silence. "It is only worry for our brother that fuels Ceikay's anger and frustration. Not her pride."

Errol looked at Karlyle, then to Ceikay. "I too worry about Keven. I know I should have stopped him last night, but I also wanted the answers he went to seek. My judgment left me and now I regret my inaction. So saying, though, our duty is to wait for his return with new information. Only then may we get back to Hellista with a complete report."

Errol's words seemed to soften Ceikay. The anger in her eyes left but her frown stayed.

She looked back into the trees beyond as she spoke, "The error was not that we did not stop him, the error was...we did not go with him."

Errol nodded slightly as he climbed down from the parapet. The rest of us followed.

Duke Hastid was polite but formal. His tent was plain and modest. His table was the same. The food was good, but it was no different from what was given to his men outside. My opinion of the Duke evolved to seeing him as set deeply in tradition but not enough for pomp or show. I began to understand Errol's reaction to the Duke. There was no insult in Duke Hastid. He was simply protective, and surely, because of his son...distrustful.

As I ate more than my share of foot soldier fare, my attention was on the conversation between Errol and Duke Hastid.

It was polite, but curt. The Duke spoke first, "I understand your Ranger is still not returned. May I ask where exactly he ventured to?"

"Into the forest to find answers," Errol answered simply,

"Answers to what questions?"

"The questions that have been in your head since last night."

"If you would humor me, please tell me what questions are in my head."

Errol smiled slightly. "I would not presume to do that, Duke Hastid. It would be overstepping my position."

"Oh but you just did, young man," The Duke snarled.

Ceikay snorted at those words. The Duke glanced at her, and then turned back to Errol. He was silent for a few moments. I could see that the Duke was trying to be very patient.

Finally he spoke, again in a polite tone, "I understand why you do not like me, Errol. That I will forgive, but I still require a straight answer."

Errol answered just as politely, "It is not that I dislike you, sir. It is only the fact that you have given me no reason to like you. As for giving you a straight answer, you already have it."

There was a pause in the tent. The officers surrounding us were visibly tense. Ceikay and Karlyle were both visibly relaxed.

After a few moments, nodding slowly, the Duke responded, "Rightly and fairly answered. The fault is mine."

"I see no fault in anyone." Errol looked around the room, and then continued, "It is as it has been, and time may change our opinions."

"Or may not," was Hastid's reply.

Errol's tone softened. "My brother went to determine who was confronting your besiegers north of us. It is obvious that they have been disrupted. By whom, is the question to be answered."

Duke Hastid nodded, "That is the surety of it, and you are correct. My mind has been occupied with the question. My question to you now is; when does the Ranger Keven return with the answer?"

Errol shook his head. "I will not be able to answer until he walks out from the trees beyond."

Duke Hastid began to pace in thought. His chin was on his chest, his breathing shallow and even. The tent was quiet while he walked in circles.

He began to talk aloud. "My Elexele and possibly the Lady Hellista is engaging my son to the south of me. To the north my jailers that have had me bottled in this pass are now being engaged by an unknown force…"

The Duke then stepped up to Errol. "Tell me Errol of the Northern Realm, personal emissary of our King Balistor. What shall I do?"

Errol bowed his head slightly, "It is not my place to tell you to

380

do anything, Duke Hastid of the North-Eastern Realm."

"Then sir, do not tell me. Advise me."

Errol answered immediately, "Send scouts south and north. Prepare all of your men for horse as soon as possible. It is clear to me that the siege is over. It only depends on news from your scouts in which direction you should attack."

Duke Hastid glanced at his men, then back to Errol. "My Senior Officers advise me to stay here behind the palisades. My force is not large enough to break through those surrounding us."

"One who waits in defense waits for defeat. We know your son Rendulus is now preoccupied with forces to the south of him. The north situation has changed. The opportunity for the offensive is close at hand. Surprise is a good ally if used timely. If we attack the right foe in the right direction, we destroy the siege entirely. The force remaining against us will either face a much reinforced Duke Hastid, or turn and run."

The Duke began to pace once more, and once more, the silence became loud. He then turned to Centurion Foust who had been standing at the flap of the tent since our meeting began.

"Centurion Foust, is the breach in the south wall still there?"

The officer answered promptly, "We closed the breach as ordered last night, Sire…but I have made sure that it can be taken down in a instant."

Duke Hastid stepped over to the Centurion, "I want a similar breach in the north wall. I want scouts sent out to the north and south. I want information as soon as they can find it. I want every man to prepare themselves for quick march. Battle gear only."

The orders given, the Centurion saluted crisply and exited the tent. Duke Hastid turned to the rest of the officers. "You know your duties; prepare your units as I have directed. You are dismissed."

They saluted crisply and were quickly gone.

The Duke turned to the rest of us. "You are welcome to travel with us, no matter the direction we choose. I only ask that you bring me Keven's findings if he returns before my scouts."

With those words Duke Hastid bowed slightly, turned to the tent flap, and passed through to the outside.

I stood looking at the flap for a moment, and then to each of my companions. Karlyle was shaking his head with a slight grin on his lips. Errol had no expression. Ceikay frowned.

Finally Ceikay spoke, "Did he thank anyone? Did I fail to hear his thank you? Did he not say he was thankful for our help and advice? Was I not listening when he said thank you to all of us?"

She then turned to me, "Royal Witness, I ask of you, your memory recalls that the Duke said thank you to us…does it not?"

Finally Errol addressed his sister. "Could you not sense Hastid's true feelings? You tell me what he was thinking of us."

Ceikay paused and became quiet, then answered, "Remember Errol, I cannot read actual thoughts. I can feel emotions. Only through emotions can I determine motives. And through one's motives, I can guess what one's thoughts are. Duke Hastid has no real emotions that I can feel. He is a cold man who keeps reason in charge of passion, and therefore, he is difficult to decipher."

Karlyle spoke up, "It seems that the Duke is a very angry man. That should be obvious."

Ceikay calmly turned to Karlyle and answered, "One does not need to be a Talent such as me to see an emotion so stark as anger when someone does not wish to hide it."

I rushed to ask another question, "Errol, when we were in Hirst, the King gave you his Royal Seal. He said it gives you authority to take command if necessary. Why did you lead Duke Hastid to believe that your authority was limited and you only could advise him?"

Ceikay answered for Errol, "Because my brother chooses not to lead men if another is capable. Duke Hastid is capable…"

I addressed Ceikay, "Yes but Errol has a natural leadership air about him. People cannot help but follow."

"You are right, Beorn, but leadership ability is not the same as leadership desire."

Karlyle joined in. "Errol would rather convince men to lead themselves rather than lead them himself."

"Yes, but I have seen Err…"

My words were stopped by the upturned hand of our subject of talk.

Errol turned and faced the three of us. We waited for his direction. "It is not important or useful to discuss me at this time. It is also not important whether we are thanked or not. It is now important to find Keven. I will tell Duke Hastid of our desire to go into the north woods and so not to expect us in his next foray."

With that said we now left the tent. As Karlyle, myself, and Ceikay headed to the north palisade Errol broke off to locate the Duke.

He paused and then called out to us before disappearing quickly behind a tent, "Oh...and I should thank him for inviting us along with him!"

Ceikay's silent glare told me that had Errol been close, his shin would have been in danger.

We were back atop the north wall for only a few moments before Errol once again joined us. I noticed that he stayed at a distance from his sister. Ceikay seemed to have forgotten his earlier remark.

Karlyle spoke first, "Are we ready to embark?"

Errol nodded in answer.

Ceikay spoke, "The day will be losing its light before long, sooner because of the high walls of the pass."

"What about me?" I asked. "Am I still committed to your company, or will I just be in the way out there?"

They all turned to me. Karlyle arched an eyebrow. Errol was expressionless. Ceikay grinned.

Errol finally answered, "You are with us until the King orders otherwise. Or until you are killed."

Errol's words caught me up and I turned to him with a surprised look.

He grinned silently.

Karlyle now handed me my bedroll and sword. I had forgotten my gear. I noticed that my companions were all armed and ready for travel. Without a word Errol jumped from the wall and onto the flat ground before the tree line. The rest of us followed. We walked calmly but briskly toward the trees. I looked back once and saw dozens of heads peering up from behind the palisade. I saw movement in the middle of the wall. I saw that a section of the defenses were starting to be taken down. The breach ordered by Hastid was begun. No one had tried to stop us. No one had cheered us forward. We were now on our own.

I agreed with Ceikay; the Duke should have thanked us...

Then I thought out loud, "Were we not to wait until Keven returned to give report to the Duke?"

Errol answered as he walked, "The Duke only asked us to give him Keven's report when Keven returned. He said nothing about us having to wait behind walls for his return. Who is to say we will not be able to bring Keven back with us?"

Before I could ask a question Ceikay whistled. Immediately Errol and Karlyle stopped. I almost ran into Karlyle's back.

Ceikay was now standing still and had her eyes closed.

"We will be having visitors soon. If we do not hurry to the trees, we may be seen."

Karlyle spoke as we started again and hurried our pace, "I assume they are too far away for identification."

"Yes." She answered, "But I know that there are many heading toward us...hundreds, and they are everywhere in front of us."

We trotted toward the trees ahead. We were about three hundred paces from the forest edge when Ceikay stopped again.

We stopped with her as she spoke, "I feel extreme anger and excitement before us. I doubt the safety of the trees ahead, since soon they will be engulfed by thousands of men ready and eager for fighting."

As my companions stood looking into the trees, I turned to look at Duke Hastid's defensive wall. I wondered if the newly opened breach could be closed in time. I then realized that we were now far away from the protection of the palisade...that we were now between the approaching army and our refuge.

I looked to Errol. He stood looking calmly ahead. So did his two siblings. Karlyle had an arched eyebrow. Ceikay had her head cocked slightly to the side, as if trying to hear sounds still too low for understanding.

My eyes strained at the tree line. I saw no movement and heard no sounds.

Suddenly movement came from the left of us. I jerked my

head to see a deer jumping from the trees and onto the flat ground on which we were now standing. Then more deer and other game animals began to emerge.

Ceikay said simply, "They will be here shortly."

Errol spoke calmly, "It may be wise of us to make our way back from whence we came."

With his words we all turned our backs to the trees and began to walk. My companions seemed calm to me. My heart was racing faster than my legs were walking. I wondered when we would break into a run.

I looked at the distant and small looking stand of spikes ahead. The palisade wall beckoned me to hurry, but my companions compelled me to stay at their pace. I spoke out to no one in particular, "Would it behoove us to quicken our pace?"

Karlyle answered me, "I like that word...'behoove.' Good choice Beorn."

I glanced at him as we walked along. He grinned at me.

Errol now answered me also, "It would not...'behoove' us to hurry before we are forced to. They are not close enough yet to threaten us with any type of missile weapon. It would behoove us to preserve our energies for a last defense."

Suddenly a screech above brought us short. We looked up to see Eagle soaring from over the tree line and toward us. In a moment Eagle dove upon us and I instinctively ducked in alarm.

When I raised my head I saw that my companions were facing the forest again. I looked there also but saw nothing. My eyes turned to the sky searching for Eagle. I failed to find him. I looked at the still too far away palisade and Duke Hastid's men.

Turning back to the trees I began to draw my sword. I stopped my hand at the hilt when I saw that the others had yet to draw their weapons. Ceikay and Karlyle exchanged quick glances.

Errol stood silently, not moving, but smiling broadly!

Then movement came. All along the whole thousand-pace line of trees before us a dark line suddenly appeared. It seemed to me that it spilled from the trees and onto the grass before them. The long line sort of quivered and then steadied before my eyes. Then as I squinted for a better view, I realized that the shimmering movement was made up of men. I could make out bits of shiny armor and weapons. As the line of men solidified before us it seemed to me strangely quiet. I wondered at the lack of shouts and yells.

I stole a quick look at my companions, they had not moved. I feared that they were contemplating a defensive stand here.

My eyes went back to the dark mass of men. The line before us now completely spanned the two walls of the pass. The line was still. I saw that they were standing at formation just beyond the trees. I could not see how many men were behind the first line, but it did not matter. One line was too much for even my friends standing in this open field.

My companions still did not move or speak. I waited...ill at ease.

Suddenly horns sounded before us. Then I saw movement again. From the trees came something else. At a dozen evenly spaced spots in the line I saw men step forward and to the side, opening a gap. Then from those gaps came more men. They were holding aloft banners. In the middle of all the line one banner stood out that I immediately recognized.

I found myself looking at the Royal Banner of King Ballistor of the Kingdom of Tavegnor!

My eyes darted from the flag to Errol. He stood as before. I saw no surprise on his face. Karlyle raised his eyebrow just a little higher. Ceikay nodded slightly.

She muttered softly to herself, "I knew it..."

I looked back to the banner. Around it I could see more, smaller banners appear. Then I saw more men come further from the trees and onto the flat ground before us. They began to walk toward us.

Ceikay spoke out as the men appeared, "We have found Keven."

Karlyle answered, "It appears that he has found the King."

My thoughts were now jumbled and confused. Desperately I struggled to grasp what was happening before us. Moments before, we were walking into the trees to begin our search for Keven. Then we were suddenly turned around and heading for the safety of Duke Hastid's wall. Then Eagle stopped and turned us back around. Now we were staring at the Royal Banner of King Ballistor. The one we parted from ages ago at the south of Tavegnor.

Now Ceikay was saying we had found Keven. My eyes could not yet identify any of the men coming toward us, but Ceikay confirmed that Keven was one of them.

My throat was suddenly very dry.

Errol brought my thoughts back to focus. "Let us go meet our brother...and, it seems, our King."

Errol stepped forward, and of course we followed. I stayed a pace or two behind, still not sure of what I was seeing.

Ceikay turned her head to me, "Your confusion will be ended soon my friend. We will have many questions answered before this day is over."

As we approached the advancing men, I was soon able to identify Keven. He was leading a group of twelve on horseback. Six looked to be Rangers and the other six wore the uniform and insignia of officers of King Ballistor's personal Guard. Keven's grin was soon evident. He rode up to Errol and dismounted.

To my surprise Errol reached out and grabbed his brother in a big suffocating hug. Keven's feet left the ground as Errol arched his back. Keven let out a mock yell of alarm and Errol released him back to the ground. Karlyle stepped up and did the same. Upon release Ceikay stepped forward, but unlike her two brothers did not immediately reach out. She stood face to face with Keven. She looked down at his shin as if to kick it.

Ceikay frowned in contemplation, and then spoke, "I really should do it for what you did."

"Or you could give me a hug of greeting instead."

Ceikay shook her head...then threw her arms around him. She was the one picked up this time. Then just as quickly, Keven put her feet back to the ground.

After a short pause Keven spoke. "Well, what have you been doing while I was away?"

Ignoring Keven's question, Errol asked his own, "Where is the King?"

"He will be along presently. He is making sure what is left of the enemy is not going to be able to counter-attack."

"What are your instructions then?" Errol asked.

"Our King has instructed me to inform you that he will be along presently."

With that said, we stood around for a while. No one spoke. We just waited…

After a long spell Keven spoke again: "Maybe someone should tell Duke Hastid that the King is here."

"Do not ask me to bring news to him," Ceikay said dryly.

Errol's and Karlyle's inaction made it clear that they were not in a hurry to report to the Duke.

Finally I spoke up, "I could run back and tell him. He should be here to meet the King. The King should not have to wait for him."

Errol turned to me, "Duke Hastid can see the King's colors from his position on the wall. He should already be here with us."

Karlyle then added, "That is a good point you make. So why has Hastid not been able to make his way out to us?"

Errol looked back at the palisade wall. "I assume he has already exited the south palisdes and therefore, is not aware of our King's arrival."

Errol turned back to me, if you would be kind enough to make a return visit to the encampment, a runner can be sent to the Duke. It would relieve me greatly."

I was not sure in his tone whether he was sincere, but I nodded and turned to leave.

At that moment, one of the King's men spoke up. "If you would allow me, I would like to join you sir. I am Centurion Arnor of the First Royal Guard. I can act as the King's personal emissary."

Keven spoke, "It seems I am at dreadful fault and I apologize sincerely. My manners are missing and I neglected to introduce anyone. Let me begin with the honorable Centurion…"

For the next several moments names and introductions were made between us, the Rangers, and the King's men. No one seemed to appear insulted at the breach of protocol.

Finally it was time for Centurion Arnor and me to depart to the wall. It was also time for me to start asking questions.

"How does the King find himself here? When we last had contact, he was rushing south to Orth pass to aid Duke Whorton."

The Centurion glanced at me as we walked, his horse being led behind us. "Your questions lead to a telling too long for me to answer here. I am sure that there will be time for answers later. For now, all I will say is that the enemy attacking us from the south suddenly turned from invasion to exodus."

"Are you able at least to tell me why?"

Once again the Centurion looked my way as he answered, "Talon Fortress and Commodore Disellis."

Before I could ask more our eyes caught sight of horses coming toward us from the breach. It looked to be three horses and two riders. Centurion Arnor and I kept walking. Soon the riders were halting in front of us. The rider in front saluted Arnor as an equal. The rider was Centurion Foust. Foust nodded to me and for the first time that I saw…smiled.

Foust spoke first to me, "We see that it did not take you long to bring reinforcements, sir."

I replied simply, "The reinforcements came to us from the unexpected. If you are looking for answers, I am not the one you need to speak to. Allow me to present Centurion Arnor of the First Personal Guard of the Realm of Ballistor."

Centurion Foust answered, "We have met before on several other occasions." Both men nodded in formal greeting.

Centurion Arnor held out a Royal Seal as he spoke, "As the emissary to the King, I request an audience with Duke Hastid. The King sends greetings and hopes that their meeting will be soon and also that it will be a happy one."

Centurion Foust nodded. He then motioned to the horseman behind him. I saw that the other rider was a young page. He now led the riderless horse forward.

"If you would please mount, Witness, I will escort you both through the wall."

As I reached for the reins, Foust added, "But I must tell you that Duke Hastid has left our camp and gone south already. He left before the King's banner was revealed. I do not know for how long he will be away. If you decide to stay outside and wait with the rest of your companions you may still have the use of my services."

Centurion Arnor bowed slightly as he answered, "With your permission I would like to enter your camp and wait for your Lord. It would give me opportunity to see your situation in order to give our King a thorough report when the time is appropriate."

Centurion Foust bowed and answered, "We thank you for your arrival and aid. Please follow and give me the privilege of escorting you through our defenses."

We followed Foust's direction and were soon riding past the long deadly looking spikes of the palisade wall.

Once inside I noticed few men in camp. The only ones to be seen were those standing atop the north wall.

Seeing my questioning look, Centurion Foust answered, "Duke Hastid has already taken his men south to find his son. The Duke dearly wants Rendulus to answer for his actions."

He then turned to Centurion Arnor. I have food and drink in my tent. You are welcome to refresh yourself before your inspection."

"Thank you for the offer, but I wish to see more of your defenses if I am allowed."

"You are allowed, and I am honored to escort you. Let us review my men at post first, and then I can take you to the south wall "

The two Centurions seemed to forget that I was in their company. They walked off, leaving me to stand alone. The page had taken the horses away. I looked about me and wondered what to do next. I decided to enter Foust's tent. Food and drink would be my companions for now.

The sound of horns drew me back outside. Their call was coming from the north. I knew the message, King Ballistor was being announced.

I rushed to the north wall and made my way to the parapet. I stood with a line of soldiers watching horse and banners marching from the trees in the distance.

Suddenly the rush of feet and yelling to the south turned me around. Below by the tents several soldiers were running to the parapet. As they got closer I could hear words become clearer.

"Dead!"

"He is slain!"

"Elexele!"

The men with me on the wall were now jumping down to meet their fellows. They were calling back and throwing out questions of the others. The noise and confusion in camp was becoming alarming!

Before jumping down from the wall, I turned back to the north. I saw the small figures of my companions turn and face my direction. They stood still for a moment, and then began walking back toward the palisades.

More words turned me around again,

"The Duke is returning!"

"Rendulus is being brought into camp!"

"The battle is over!"

"Dead!"

The words faded as everyone ran toward the south palisade. The arrival of King Ballistor forgotten, the north palisade was soon manned by only one person.

I looked back once more to see that my companions were now jogging back. I could not stay to greet them. I jumped down and left the wall empty of post. I was compelled to join the rush to the south wall.

As I ran, the commotion in camp was increasing all around me. The general rush was to the south. Men were calling out to each other as they ran. More words were coming to my ears.

"By whose hand?!"

"….before Hastid's arrival!"

"Hellista was there!"

"Dead by the sword!"

"By his own hand?!"

My thoughts were to stop someone and press him for answers. My legs kept me going toward the south palisade. Soon I was past the last of the tents and fire rings. The wall before me was lined at the top and at its base with soldiers pressing and pushing each other for position. They were attempting to get good positioning in order to look out onto the field beyond the defensive wall. The breach was still open but was clogged with men.

I stopped short of the wall and made no attempt to press in with the others. One officer stepped up next to me but said nothing. I recognized him as one of Centurion Foust's junior officers.

"What news causes this uproar?" I asked of him.

As he stared at the breach and the crowd in front of us the man answered, "Rendulus is dead and Duke Hastid is bringing his son back to camp."

My thoughts did not keep up with my next words, "The Duke wants to question him though…"

The officer turned to me but did not respond in words.

I quickly added, "I mean; do you know if…the Duke had a chance to question his son?"

The officer answered as he looked back to the breach, "I was riding in Duke Hastid's company when riders came up to us to report of Rendulus' death. The Duke never saw his son alive."

We stood together and looked to the breach. I had many questions, but could not find the right one to ask first.

Without my bidding, the officer began to speak, "Duke Hastid was demanding answers from the scouts who had brought the news. The Duke was fraught with rage at his son's death. I had never heard such a wail of sorrow and anger from one's Lord. I stood with my men watching as the Duke pressed the scouts for answers. The answers I did not hear, as I was ordered by my superior to ride back at great speed to prepare the camp. I saw no more and know no more than what I have told you."

I nodded in acknowledgement and thanks. We stood once more in silence…waiting and staring at the breach.

Noise from behind turned me around. Errol, Keven, Karlyle, and Ceikay were suddenly at my side.

"Tell us." Errol's words were not to be resisted.

Quickly I told them what I knew. The officer was pressed for more answers. He only confirmed my words.

"Where is Centurion Arnor?"

392

Errol's question surprised me. I had not thought of where the Centurion would be.

The question was answered by the junior officer, "Centurions Foust and Arnor have ridden out to meet Duke Hastid."

A thought came suddenly into my mind, "How did you know to turn from the King and come here?"

Ceikay looked at me and said simply, "You called us."

As the others looked at me I cocked my head to one side.

Ceikay quickly answered my unspoken question. "Your mind is known to me and easy to feel, Beorn. I offer no disrespect or insult in saying that. The longer I am with someone, the truer the path.

"When you became aware of the commotion and excitement while standing atop the wall, your thought waves intensified. Those waves then rushed outward from you and met me with force. I could not help but understand that a very serious event was charging you so. When you then disappeared from atop the wall, I told my brothers we needed to return at speed."

Commotion brought our attention to the wall. Men were now gesturing and calling out. The crowd at the breach surged forward out onto the field beyond the palisade.

In a moment Errol was atop the wall. The men around him separated enough to let the rest of us join him. We looked out and saw a procession of horses headed toward us and the camp. Duke Hastid's banner could clearly be seen in the front. Soon I could recognize the riders. The Duke was riding stiffly up front with the two Centurions directly behind. The rest of the company was following in a file of two. Midway into the file was one riderless horse being led by one of Duke Hastid's officers. The officer was bearing the banner of Rendulus, the Duke's son.

As the group came closer we could now see that the riderless horse was pulling a hay cart. We could also see that the cart carried not hay, but what looked to be a cloaked body. We knew that it had to be Rendulus.

The men around us and all along the wall were now still and silent. Everyone knew that the Duke had loved his son dearly, even though the son had been a traitor to his father.

In silence the riders came through the breach. The soldiers on the wall and around the breach silently saluted their Lord as he passed. Duke Hastid acknowledged no one. He rode with his head up and his eyes hard. Without prompting, Hastid's horse took him toward the large command tent. The rest followed.

As the cart came through the breach I saw Rendulus' body laid out straight, covered in a large, green and purple satin shroud. A large sword was lying across the chest of the fallen prince. As I turned my head to look at the trailing riders, my eyes darted back to Rendulus.

I called out, "Elexele!"

The others turned to me in surprise.

"That sword!" I cried out and pointed, "That is Elexele's sword. Why is it on Rendulus?"

"Are you sure?" Keven asked.

Karlyle answered for me. "It is what he does best brother. That is why we invited him along, remember?"

Errol shook his head and then jumped from the wall. He walked toward the cart as it passed. My companions and I followed his lead. Errol reached the leading horse and gently grabbed the hanging reins. The horse stopped at Errol's bidding.

Errol then motioned to me, "Come over and confirm, Bard. It looks like Elexele's sword, but there are many that are similar."

I needed no further inspection but I came close to the cart and looked at Errol. "Elexele's sword has no jewels on its crossguard or pommel."

"Other broadswords have the same lack of refinement as well." Errol countered.

"This is true, but I have seen only one with the name of 'Elexele' engraved on the grip."

Errol stepped closer to the body and the sword. He saw that there were letters on the grip. He smiled grimly.

He then released the reins and stepped back. Ceikay now spoke, "Beorn has confirmed troubling news."

I turned to her. She had her head lowered. Keven and Karlyle shook their heads at the cart as it continued toward the center of camp.

"What does this mean?" I asked.

Errol answered, "It means that the sword that killed Duke Hastid's son belongs to Elexele."

"So Elexele met and defeated Rendulus on the battlefield. Where is Elexele, and why is his sword not with him?"

Errol answered me again, "We have not that information. There are several possibilities I will not speak to just yet."

The suggestion was for me to stop inquiring.

Now the soldiers surrounding us were silently following the death cart. My four companions stayed back at the breach. The four were silent also, but their faces were telling me of great concern. Ceikay then walked through the breach and stood looking toward the narrows of the southern pass.

It seemed we were waiting for something to happen. I wondered at the King's arrival to the north of us. I spoke out loud at the thought. The others only nodded.

Then Ceikay spoke as she pointed toward the narrows, "Elexele is coming. He is alone."

We followed her finger. A rider on horseback was slowly approaching. I recognized Elexele in the distance. He was alone as Ceikay had announced. As he came closer I could see that he had no armor or weapons showing. He had not replaced the sword that now rode with Rendulus. Soon, others on the wall cried out their sighting. Almost immediately a full company of twenty armed soldiers rode from the camp and galloped to Elexele.

Errol suddenly turned and spoke as he walked back through the defensive wall. "We should report to the King."

Karlyle, Keven, and I began to follow. Ceikay shook her head and made no move join Errol.

On seeing Ceikay's refusal, Errol stopped and addressed her. "What is it you feel you should do?"

"I feel that Elexele is going to need someone to stay close."

"That is not our responsibility."

"I believe it is."

"You believe wrongly, Ceikay."

"I believe strongly, Errol."

Errol stood silently eyeing his sister, then sighed and spoke to

Karlyle and Keven. "Would you two stay with her then?" Make sure she does not enter into any foolishness."

He then looked at me. "I would have you accompany me to the King. He will want you to witness."

I nodded and followed him as he left. The other three stood looking out to the approaching Elexele.

Errol slowed enough to allow me to catch up. We walked together in silence. The camp around us was once again alive with action and noise. Men were rushing back and forth on different errands or assignments. We walked north through camp and soon heard the blaring of horns ahead. They were announcing the arrival of the King of Tavegnor. Men began to gather and walk along with us.

Ahead I saw the two Centurions Foust and Arnor. They sat upon their steeds awaiting the royal arrival. Errol and I rounded the last of the tents in time to see King Ballistor enter through the north breach. We were not close enough to hear the exchange of greetings between the King and the Centurions. With a salute and a nod, Centurion Foust turned his horse and started toward us. Centurion Arnor maneuvered his horse to the side to allow his Lord to pass, and then Arnor followed with the rest of the King's company.

Centurion Foust rode past the two of us. As the king approached us he smiled and pulled up his horse. Errol and I both bowed our heads in greeting. King Ballistor stopped in front of us. He looked down and smiled broadly.

King Ballistor addressed us, "Well met, my friend and my Royal Witness. You two will follow me. I would have you in war council with Duke Hastid."

We both bowed as the King spurred his horse to follow the Centurion. The horsemen following pulled up and Centurion Arnor motioned for us to follow directly behind the king.

Soon we were facing the front flap of the personal tent of Duke Hastid. As King Ballistor was dismounting the flap opened and Duke Hastid emerged. He stood tall at the opening. King Ballistor strode up to him.

Duke Hastid bowed but his king waved him to stop.

King Ballistor spoke first. "Please, it is I that will bow to you. I am told that you have been burdened beyond words of comfort in this battle. Your son is dead, though you wished to see him again. Your blood has been taken fr…"

"My blood has betrayed Tavegnor."

King Ballistor showed no signs of affront at Hastid's interruption. The King continued, "This is true, but it is clear to all that he meant not that your blood would be spilled."

"What is done is done," replied the Duke. "My name and my family have been shamed by treason. I give my possessions to the crown and forfeit all my lands back to Tavegnor."

At the Duke's words a murmur arose from the soldiers surrounding us. I saw the officers glance back and forth at each other.

Duke Hastid continued, "I ask for nothing, but I demand one thing before relinquishing my Dukedom."

King Ballistor was about to respond, but Duke Hastid held his hand to continue, "I demand a blood reckoning as my last point of honor. It is my final right."

At these words Errol groaned out loud.

King Ballistor looked hard at the Duke. For moments the two stood rigid and silent.

The King broke the silence. "I feel it is time the two of us talk privately in your tent. That is *my* demand."

Immediately the Duke bowed low and turned. He took hold of the flap and motioned for his king to enter. The two men quickly disappeared and Errol just as quickly turned and headed to the south of camp. We soon met with his siblings. They were standing in the center of a clearing of a circle about forty feet in width. This circle was surrounded by soldiers of Duke Hastid. I saw that along with Errol's brothers and sister stood Elexele.

As we approached the circle an opening was made for us by the soldiers. I could now see the expressions of the four in the middle. Karlyle and Keven wore looks of stoic hardness.

Elexele held a look of calm resignation and peace.

Ceikay was the one that held my attention. Her eyes were red with fire. If I had not known her I would have guessed that she

397

had been crying. Her lips were tight and her nostrils flared. The anger was open for all to see.

Errol once again groaned as he walked up to the four. He looked at each one before fixing his gaze lastly upon Elexele.

Elexele was the one who spoke first. "It is good to see you safe and well, my friend. Your diversion worked better than we could have hoped."

Errol took a deep breath but did not speak.

Elexele then spoke again, "It is simple to relate. Our attack along with Hellista went well. Rendulus was utterly taken by surprise and out-fought. His men soon were running into the west. Rangers and wolves kept them from gaining distance or escape."

Errol's silence told Elexele to continue. "Rendulus, even though a traitor to his father and his country, was not a coward. He rallied his men time and again to battle. He would not choose retreat nor accept defeat. My men tried in vain to subdue him with no or little harm. I had ordered my archers to still their arrows. It was clear that my men could not take him down without killing him.

I came near in the final moments of battle and implored him to come to terms. He was resolved to die by heroic means. I stepped forward with the intent to disarm and grapple him to the ground. I was successful in knocking his sword away from him. It was then he ripped off his armor and tunic to bare his chest."

Elexele paused for reaction from Errol. Errol stood silent.

Elexele continued, "Rendulus then yelled for me to slay him where he stood. His arms were outstretched and his chest was heaving. It was then that I made the terrible blunder. In my self-righteous anger I stepped forward and pointed my sword at his chest. The tip was a hand span from his skin.

Elexele shook his head and sighed. He then spoke again, "I was about to verbally condemn him for his treason, but before words left my lips Rendulus grabbed my blade with both hands. In an instant he had pulled and jumped forward at the same time. My broadsword ripped through his chest."

Again Elexele paused, again silence filled our ears.

He then continued, "Rendulus, son of Hastid, my liege Lord,

sank to his knees. A grin of triumph faced me as he succumbed. His left eye winked at me knowingly. I let go of my sword and Rendulus was dead as he fell to his side onto the bloody dirt."

I stood behind Errol as Elexele told his tale. I began to understand what was happening around me.

Ceikay now spoke, "I will not allow this to happen."

Errol quietly asked, "Have you made this clear to the soldiers surrounding us?"

Karlyle answered for her, "You can believe that she has made it very clear, brother."

Errol looked to Karlyle and then to Keven. "What do you plan to do in this play of hers?"

Both answered together, "She is our sister."

Errol's voice became low and intense. "Make your answers clear to me."

Keven was the one who answered, "You know full well the clarity of our answer Errol. Ceikay is right. If this is to happen, it is wrong by all decent thinking. If she is set to attempt to stop this from going forward, then we will be with her."

Karlyle now spoke, "We ask what you will do, brother."

At that moment commotion behind us stilled Errol's answer.

We turned around to see Duke Hastid and King Ballistor coming toward us. Both men looked grave. The wall of soldiers parted for them. The two Royals stopped five paces from the inner circle. No one spoke. No one moved.

Finally, Duke Hastid broke the silence with his loud words, "My son Rendulus, my one and only heir, the last of the bloodline of the ancient family of the Hastids has been slain!"

Hastid squared his shoulders and looked around. He spoke again, "I feel my age now, with nothing more to hope for. I have given up my realm to the crown of Tavegnor. For my loyal service and sacrifice to Tavegnor, King Ballistor has granted me one final request to salvage family honor!"

Silence waited for him to continue: "I ask for blood revenge on the person responsible for my son's death!"

At those words Ceikay jumped forward and pulled her sword! Immediately three of Duke Hastid's officers lepted in front of their

Lord and King. The ring of Errol's sword resounded in my ears as he stepped to his sister's side.

The circle around us erupted in the motion and noise of a hundred men drawing weapons to fight. I spun my head to see two short swords in Keven's hands. He stood to the left of Elexele. The sound of a hundred wolves suddenly wailed from the walls surrounding us. I looked to his brother. Karlyle had his hands held high in front of him. Flames were dancing at his fingertips. He faced the men to Elexele's right!

I stood behind Ceikay and Errol. My sword was somehow in my hand, pointed between the two.

I was terrified as I stood with my friends. I also knew with certainty that I would fight to the death alongside them.

Once weapons were drawn, stillness came over the circle. The only sound was the foreboding of the wolves' howls bouncing from the rocky walls.

The King and Duke had not moved. Soldiers and officers nervously glanced to the two for orders and direction. None were given...

King Ballistor finally spoke quietly but with barely controlled anger, "You five must remove yourselves from this circle. This is not your place."

Ceikay was not dissuaded, "I disobey you, my king. I will not step aside to allow this."

"You not only disobey me, but you dishonor Duke Hastid."

It was Karlyle who responded, "The dishonor is in killing an honorable man."

"King Ballistor's voice softened slightly as he sighed "It is more than that. It is a matter of sovereign rights...and a father's grief."

Ceikay spoke again, "Sovereign rights for whom, Royalty? And as for the father...the son betrayed him!"

King Ballistor's voice hardened again, "Do not discount Royal Sovereignty, Ceikay. It is the only guarantor of stability and safety of the realm."

"You are wrong sir. The only real guarantor is individual sovereignty. Without that, Royal Sovereignty could not be supported, except by force of arms against the very people it claims to protect!"

King Ballistor sighed deeply at Ceikay's words.

He then addressed Errol, "Errol, we have no time for this. You must convince your sister of the danger of her actions. Yours as well, if you support her."

Errol answered King Ballistor bluntly, "I, like my sister, cannot support this law of blood revenge. I am saddened that you do, my Lord."

King Ballistor lowered his head before answering. It seemed that he was struggling to find words.

I cautiously glanced at the men surrounding us. They had not relaxed since swords were drawn.

When King Ballistor spoke, it was softly. "I am saddened that you think that of me. I do not support Duke Hastid's family law of blood revenge. But I must support his right to exercise it. Even though I am repulsed, I am honor-bound to allow his request. His sacrifices have earned him that much from me."

Ceikay spoke again, "What of Elexele's loyalty and sacrifices? Are they for naught?"

"It is not for me to decide. It is for Elexele's liege lord to choose."

"You are the King of Tavegnor. You have the power. You can force Duke Hastid to stop this."

"You forget in your passion, Ceikay, that I am King of Tavegnor by consensus only. If I trample on the Dukes' rights, they can combine their votes against me in parliament. The power of the king would be weakened, and therefore, our country would be weakened. We cannot risk it at this critical hour."

"Better to be honorable and brief than to be…"

Elexele suddenly stepped forward and put a hand on Ceikay's shoulder. He spoke softly into her ear. I was close but could not hear. She shook her head at his words. He spoke again. While this was happening I looked around me. Weapons were still pointed and arms still holding them tense.

I looked back at Elexele and Ceikay. The look of anger deepened on her face. She shook her head again.

Suddenly Elexele straightened and stepped quickly to the side and past Ceikay. She took a step to intercept him. He thrust a hand out to push her back.

Elexele now stood directly in front of Duke Hastid. No one else had moved.

Elexele breathed deeply as he spoke, "When I became a page to Prince Rendulus I made a solemn vow to protect him and any of his family. I also vowed to uphold any and all laws, customs and wishes of the ancient and honorable family of Hastid."

Silence met his pause. Ceikay angrily shook her head.

Elexele continued, "I have killed my mentor and prince. I did not desire to do so. It was in my power to keep him alive. It was my carelessness that killed him.

Again, silence filled the air. He then continued, "As a man of honor and a loyal officer of the Hastid Realm, I ask...no...plead for your blood vengeance, my Lord. If I did not ask this, I would forever know myself as dishonorable."

Elexele then turned to Ceikay. "For what you attempt this day I thank you and love you for it. But I beg of you also, many men will die here if you insist in this. The shame will be on my shoulders."

Elexele looked at Errol, Keven, Karlyle, then back to Ceikay. "If this continues, you will dishonor my name...since the deaths will be because of me."

For many moments Ceikay did not acknowledge Elexele's words.

Then, slowly she stood back from her defensive stance. She straightened up but did not look at Elexele. She slowly put her sword to its sheath. She paused for only an instant, and then put her weapon away.

Immediately Errol did the same. Keven, Karlyle and I followed suit.

The soldiers surrounding us did not.

Elexele bowed deeply to Ceikay and then turned back to his liege lord. "My Lord, I have taken your son's life. I give you mine."

For the first time since Ceikay started this confrontation, the

Duke moved from his stiff stance. I had noticed that he had not reacted to our aggression. He had simply waited in silence.

Duke Hastid stepped forward toward Elexele. Elexele's sword was in the Duke's right hand. King Ballistor stood silent. His eyes were cast downward.

Duke Hastid stepped to one pace from Elexele.

Ceikay pulled at her waist band and her sword dropped to the ground. She then stepped next to Elexele and faced the Duke. She held her head high and stood silently.

Duke Hastid looked at her and then to Elexele.

Hastid drew a breath and spoke for all to hear. "I, the last of the Hastid line stand before the man who has slain my only son and heir! The sword I now hold is the weapon that killed my son!"

He held up the sword with both of his hands. The tip of the blade pointed to the sky, "This blade that has spilled the blood of the last heir of Hastid is honor bound to spill the blood of his killer! This I do now and without delay!

Duke Hastid then slowly lowered the blade to Elexele's chest.

The point pressed into Elexele's skin. Duke Hastid took a deep breath and squared his shoulders as he looked squarely into the eyes of his loyal officer. Duke Hastid exhaled and took another breath. Suddenly the blade sprung up and the point sliced through the air and stabbed the sky!

"I have avenged my son!" Duke Hastid raised his voice further as he continued, "The blade that has drawn the blood of my son has now drawn the blood of his slayer! I am satisfied. This blood revenge is satisfied!"

Turning to Ceikay he bowed deeply and added softly, "…and I hope you are satisfied, my young lady."

I saw Ceikay blink. Then I noticed that Elexele was still standing. I then saw Elexele lower his head. He was looking at his chest. Ceikay then leaned forward to look at his chest. Errol stepped forward to look at Elexele's chest. King Ballistor took two steps forward and looked at Elexele's chest…

I turned back to Keven and Karlyle. They looked back at me and shrugged their shoulders. I then turned around and stepped forward to look at Elexele's chest. On his chest was a lone drop of blood. It was slowly sagging from a tiny puncture wound made by the tip of the blade.

It was Elexele who spoke first, to his liege lord: "My Lord, I do not understand…"

Duke Hastid answered him, "Understand this, you are out of proper uniform in my presence. You have left the men of your command to the south. I assume that you had ordered them to stay away from my camp so they would not be tempted to help you as your five friends here attempted to do."

Duke Hastid then turned to Centurion Foust. "I want you to have my page ready a proper uniform for this man. First Centurion Elexele is to ride south and bring his men into camp. We have a bit more rebellion to put down."

The Duke spun and looked at Errol. It looked as though he was about to say something but he turned to King Ballistor instead.

The Duke shook his head as he addressed the king, "Your Talents would have exacted a terrible toll on my men. It is good to keep them on our side."

King Ballistor answered simply, "I told you that they would rebel…"

Duke Hastid grinned back briefly; and then his face became serious again. "I take you at your word what you said in my tent. Are your words still offered?"

"You will still have your lands and a vote at the next meeting of Parliament. Does your offer of wine still hold?"

Duke Hastid bowed deeply to his King. "My honor and privilege to escort you to the command tent, but I must excuse myself from your company for this night. I loved my son. I must mourn. I beg that you do not take offense at my absence."

King Ballistor bowed again to his host. "You give no offense, and I take none. I call a war council for tomorrow sunset. Will that give you time to grieve?"

"My grateful thanks to you my Lord. I will order the command tent to be supplied with fresh food and drink."

King Ballistor nodded and turned to Errol. "As for my rebellious envoys…you will be at the war council on the morrow…if you still wish to serve your king."

404

My four companions remained silent.

The King nodded his understanding, "I do not blame you if you wish to leave."

Finally, Errol spoke, "This war is not yet finished, Sire. We will still serve Tavegnor."

"I am grateful that you offer that at least. " The King sighed, "The main battles seem to be won, but spies and stragglers need to be ferreted out. My orders for this night are for you to rest, nothing more than that."

So saying, the two Lords turned from the rest of us to head toward the tents.

King Ballistor paused, and then turned around and spoke to Ceikay: "If you are wondering at the offer I made to the Duke, it was to allow him to keep his Dukedom and all his wealth if he honored my request to spare Elexele. He gave me no clear answer either way as we came to this circle. I knew nothing of his final decision, but I was praying fervently to the gods that reason would rule over passion."

The king paused again, and then asked, "Did you not know…or feel, Duke Hastid's thoughts that he would spare Elexele?"

Before Ceikay could respond, Duke Hastid spoke: "She knew my thoughts. Up to the moment I placed the point of the blade to Elexele's chest I had planned to make full thrust."

"What caused you to change at the last?" Asked the King.

"I do not know. Some inner urging, a thought, a reasoning, mercy…I do not know."

With that answer, the King and Duke left us standing around Elexele.

Karlyle now stepped up to examine the wound. A small line of blood was already drying on the skin.

Karlyle raised an eyebrow as he spoke, "Do you not feel faint? Perhaps we should call a camp nurse to comfort you…"

Suddenly Karlyle yelped and jumped to the side…Ceikay's boot had landed hard!

Suddenly the voice of Centurion Foust called out, "Soldiers of the Realm of Hastid; salute First Centurion Elexele!"

As one, the men surrounding us stiffened and held their swords to their chest, blades pointed upward. Centurion Foust stepped up to Centurion Elexele and held out his arm. Both men briefly clasped forearms.

Foust spoke again, "If you would follow me, Centurion Elexele, your uniform must be prepared."

Then he raised his voice once more. "Soldiers of Hastid, you are dismissed. Those of you who are on post tonight; your duties await!"

Before following Foust, Elexele turned to Ceikay. He said nothing. He took her right hand into his. He brought it to his mouth and kissed the tops of her fingers before gently releasing his grip. He looked at Errol, Karlyle, and Keven. He nodded to each in turn and then spoke to Keven, "Were the wolves really going to attack?"

Keven smiled grimly. "I surely did not ask them to come to our aid, but I think they would not have heeded my order to stay away."

Elexele then turned to Karlyle, "I must ask how you do that fire when we have more time."

Karlyle grinned back, "I am grateful you did not have to see it at work…"

Elexele nodded and then turned to me. "Thank you for your sword Bard…Beorn, Royal Witness to our King."

I bowed my head in embarrassed acknowledgment.

Elexele at last turned to Errol. "It is not only good and wise that I call you friend, but a privilege as well. For my sake, may your sword never face mine in anger."

Soon the Centurions and soldiers were gone from the circle. The four Talents and I were left in silence.

Keven was the one who broke the silence. "So my little sister…this…force, or urging, that made Hastid still his hand. Would you know anything of it?"

Ceikay looked at her brother but stayed silent.

Karlyle answered for her, "Ceikay knows thoughts. She does not control them."

We all looked at Ceikay…she stayed quiet.

Errol then spoke, "May the gods protect us all if she is learning

Tavegnor

to do that…"

Again there was silence…

Finally I spoke, "What shall we do now?"

Errol answered, "Tonight we will set our tents with our King. His camp will be just outside of the north palisade. Once our tents are set, we will slumber like the dead, for this invasion is over."

"Over?" I asked.

"The King told us, Beorn."

My blank look told Errol to continue. "The King is going to wine as we stand here. He has called for war council not for this night, nor for the next morn. He has called it to be later tomorrow. The urgency of rushing to battle is over; therefore, the invasion is over."

"I see, but how…"

Ceikay spoke, "Beorn, my head hurts terribly. Your questions will only make it hurt more. I beg of you to let us go to camp now. Tomorrow's council will surely have the answers you seek."

"But what of a big decisive battle? What happened at Orth Pass? How did the King get up north?" I pressed, "There are more to fight…!"

Errol answered with a patient sigh, "Do not wish for any more battles, there have been enough already. Wars are, by their nature, chaotic and unpredictable. Consider us fortunate that we were not witness to every battle fought. Be assured that only scattered remnants of the enemy are left. For this moment, let us press our pillows 'til morn. Questions and answers should be left for tomorrow. For mercy's sake, let us rest!"

With his words I nodded compliance. We left the circle.

…Of course, I knew the morn would hear my questions…

This Telling Ends

Epilogue

Thus ends the story of my first adventure with the Four Talents. Below is a brief telling of the war council in Rogan Pass. If you wish to review the Official Parliamentary Witness Report of the failed invasion, go to the Royal Library of Records in the central city of Talavor. It is a more detailed accounting of actions and events throughout all of Tavegnor. Of course in that report, I have left out any personal conversations between myself and others.

Present at the war council in Rogan Pass were the King, his daughter Hellista, the Four Talents, Duke Hastid, Centurion Elexele, all the Senior Officers of the camp, and myself.

Here, the full story was told:

No one person or event decided the outcome; the invasion was stopped by the combined forces of Tavegnor. I deem it important to note that two actions are considered among the most critical: First, the invading armies from the southern Realm of Ramilliad decided to withdraw their fleets when the taking of Talon Fortress was quashed; and second, the battle of Orth Pass was another major setback for the invaders. With the invaders driven from our southern lands, King Ballistor was able to rush north up the east coast to meet the remaining large force from Ramilliad. Traitors and invaders alike were crushed in the forest north of Rogan Pass. Thus, King Ballistor was able to enter Rogan Pass to relieve Duke Hastid.

The siege of Talon Fortress was broken when the armies of Duchess Mariom broke camp and returned to the west. Captain Piercon of Mariom's army disavowed his Duchess and swore allegiance to Tavegnor. It was reported that Duchess Mariom was already being transported to Talavor to be held until she stood in front of Parliament to answer for her treachery.

Also during the war council, plans were made and forces were sent throughout Tavegnor to subdue any straggling enemies still under arms.

By Duke Hastid's decree, Elexele was given the station of First Centurion of the Hastid Realm.

As for the Four Talents, they were allowed to return to their northern homes to reunite briefly with family. Then, carrying a flag of truce, they were to embark on a vessel with the destination of the country of Ramilliad.

King Ballistor declared that he wanted diplomacy rather than revenge. The four Talents were to act as the King's emmesaries mend relations with the two countries. As Royal Witness to the King, I was given the responsibility to gather all information and actions from the surviving Dukes and record them officially. Because of several interruptions, this gathering took me through two growing seasons before I was able to present the finished recordings to Parliament and the Royal Library.

The first interruption came almost immediately; I was not a part of the peace making mission at first. Circumstances soon made it necessary for me to join my four friends in Ramilliad. It should be noted that the expedition to Ramilliad was not a simple affair for my four friends. I did travel with them on their second visit south when final peace negotiations needed Witnessing.

I was fortunate to be included in more of the Four Talents' adventures later on. I plan to put their personal telling down on parchment ere long.

As Royal Witness to Our King Ballistor of
the Realm of Tavegnor, I hereby aver that these
words I put to paper this day are true and accurate.

Beorn of Minoline